# CHAOS

Kindle Alexander

**Chaos**

Copyright © Kindle Alexander, 2023

ALL RIGHTS RESERVED

Edited by

Jae Ashley

Pam Ebeler, Undivided Editing

Mildred Jordan, I Love Books Proofreading

Cover art by Reese Dante

Cover content is for illustrative purposes only. Any person depicted in the content is a model.

ISBN print book: 978-1-941450-68-0

# Trademark Achkinowledgement

The author acknowledges the trademarked status and trademark owners of the trademarks mentioned in this work of fiction.

# Note from the Author

Chaos has been fully edited by a team of trained editors but no manuscript is perfect. Please email me with any mistakes you find at kindle@kindlealexander.com.
Creative license was taken with this story. It is a work of fiction.

# Dedication

Kindle, you are forever in our hearts.
Perry, you're missed every day.

# Chapter 1

He eased his heavy work boot from the foot pedal. At the same time, Dev "Devilman" Fox lifted the tip of the tattoo machine off his client's arm and wiped a towel over the newly inked skin. The sound system changed songs and Dev mentally sang the words to "Renegade" as he pushed back in his seat, stretching the tense muscles of his shoulders and neck.

"Crank it," Dev yelled at Millie who was working somewhere in his carved-out piece of office space inside his father's motorcycle shop. The beat by Styx was a personal favorite that he'd spent his entire life listening to.

His old man, his father, better known as Fox, the president and co-founder of the Disciples of Havoc motorcycle club, had made sure his only son got an almost spiritual knowledge of every rage-against-the-establishment song ever recorded. It didn't matter if the sounds came from angry metal or hardcore rap music, if it spoke against the corrupt government and law enforcement systems, Dev could sing every word by heart.

Many prophetic lines from those songs adorned his own inked body.

They were the anthem of his heart. The meaning of his life. Another way to give the institution his double middle fingers. No one governed him and the fuckers should stop trying.

Instant fury shot like an erupting volcano across every fiber of his being at the thought of what that fucking bitch Dallas District Attorney had done to his brothers and their motorcycle club.

Ray-Ray, a full patch member of the Disciples, needed to be voted out of the club, stripped of his colors. He should be forced to give up his cut for exposing the club to the scrutiny and grief of that goddamn cunt. She was the current source of all their bullshit problems. How had not one of the club's old timers remembered that Ray-Ray had tapped that snatch over twenty years ago? He was so damned tired of all the leaks and breaches of trust within the club's members. Fuck 'em all for the constant state of chaos they were having to live in.

And that fucking DA… Her days were numbered.

He'd make sure of that.

Dev shook his head hard, trying to lose the sudden vengeance. If he let his mind have the pleasure of traveling down such a dark road of retribution, he'd lose sight of the client in his chair.

Concentration was key in his line of work and a damn hard thing to find these days.

Between the club problems and the hours' long tattoo he'd started and wasn't connecting with on any level, the tension in his neck had solidified into a solid ache. With a forceful stretch to the left then the right, he tried to ease away the tightness gripping his muscles.

When the song's whistle blew and the tune's beat kicked up a notch, Dev started a controlled head banging motion. His mind wandered as he closed his eyes. The music's cadence soothed the rough edges of his growing irritation with the stench sitting across from him at his workstation.

Stench might not be a bold enough word to describe the guy's aroma. No one achieved that scent by missing a bath or two. That disgusting odor had been nurtured and built upon. Did the guy actually live inside a fucking dumpster? One of those giant steel cans of rotting filth. Filled with days' old decaying food and dirty diapers. The kind of trash that sat outside in the sun all day long during the hottest part of an oppressive Texas summer.

Dev cast a disgusted look at his client's mouth. Fucker's gums hadn't stopped flapping since he'd started the tattoo hours ago. He saw remnants of food still stuck between Stink's teeth.

His fucking breath was God awful offensive just like the rest of the man.

Over the years, Dev had developed the ability to block out the nervous chatter from the clients in his chair. A true gift because people could get a hell of a lot of anxiety while being inked. But this dude brought a whole new level to oversharing. He never shut up.

Dev had even switched from his preferred tattoo pen back to his coil in order to increase the buzz of the machine.

A great idea that, again, worked in every other situation except this one.

Dev's refusal to reply to any comment didn't deter the man.

Beautiful visions of reaching out and popping this guy in the mouth kept filling Dev's mind. As clear an image as if it had actually happened. He imagined his balled fist darting out. A quick, forceful hit, right between those thin cracked lips, knocking Stink's teeth out in one expert jab.

To be fair, Dev had perfected the unexpected yet very effective punch to the face. His go-to move in most situations. No one ever saw it coming. It said more than any of his words ever could.

Dev grinned at the mental image of clocking Stink. How the skin might split open. That briefest flash of confusion as the man absorbed the blow.

Except in his mind, he'd then leap over his stupidly expensive client chair, directly into the guy's lap, and pummel his lights out. He moved cartoonishly fast in beating up Stink, giving one right after another in a volley of fists.

Lost to the mental imagery, Dev nonchalantly lifted his shoulder in an accepting shrug. It wasn't too late to make that shit happen. Then again... He'd hired Millie full-time months ago to clean and sterilize his instruments as well as the entire parlor. She was good with blood. Surely, she wouldn't mind some teeth and flesh thrown in. She had a dark gothic vibe about her.

Maybe that was one of those employee benefits she kept prattling on about. At the very least, it might help break up the monotony of her day.

This time he gave a mental shrug at the direction he'd taken to help justify kicking this guy's ass. He'd do it for Millie if nothing else.

"Lookin' good. You were worth the wait," Stink yelled over the music. He lifted his arm to better see the freshly inked skin.

Such a bullshit amateur design.

Why Stink had waited months for this appointment was beyond Dev. Any beginner tattoo artist could have inked some skank's fake titties on the guy's forearm. The design only highlighted her chest. They were oversized for the body holding them up. The super-defined tits were hard and round. Full of silicone with two fat nipples perfectly centered and appearing to protrude out from his forearm. Stink had requested the 3D effect. He'd come up with some idea to twist his arm to make the breasts bounce. Fucking loser.

Not that Dev was above a titties tattoo, but over the last few years, he'd developed a pretty decent business with his own custom designs. People paid thousands of dollars for one of his original drawings that took months for him to complete. He couldn't remember a time he'd worked from a cell phone image of a real-life stripper's bared breasts.

As Stink moved his arm, testing the bouncing theory, the scent of stale cigarette smoke and something that reminded him of fermented vomit wafted to Dev. His stomach twisted hard.

"I found you on that ink show. You know the one..."

Dev tuned him out again but held back his groan. He regretted ever being a guest judge on *Ink Life*. His schedule had packed up tight for months and months after the show aired. Hell, he might be scheduled out a year by now. It had forced him to follow a fucking routine. He hated the monotony of a damn schedule. It wreaked chaos on his creative side. Nothing ruined a good vibe like a fucking time clock.

Now this douche client had made it to his chair because of that dumbass show.

And just like that, his racing thoughts switched gears again as the connection Dev had tried to make all morning finally materialized. Sudden heated anger again lit a fire inside his soul, causing his gaze to narrow.

*Fucker.* He knew who this loser smelled like. Smoke Dixon—his best friend's dying loser father and full patch member of the Disciples of Havoc.

The man might be on his deathbed and Dev couldn't think of a more deserving person to be there. Dev hated that sorry motherfucker to his core and wished him a long, painful trip to hell where he belonged.

Vengeance toward his client replaced loathing in rapid-fire succession, making his head crazy and his fists curl. In most things, Dev responded with unbridled emotion. He never claimed to be level-headed. He didn't need things like facts to deal out his own brand of justice if he thought it was warranted. His gut was rarely wrong.

This loser may not be Smoke, but he'd pay for that man's sins.

Besides, Dev didn't need to consult his Magic 8 Ball to know this client had left a trail of victims in his wake. The guy absolutely reminded Dev of Smoke, a bully, picking on the young and underprivileged just because he could. Karma was in payback mode today.

First, he'd make these cheap titties into a big fat scrotum. He barely held back his grin. Ten minutes and he'd be done.

Since he had such a gift with the iron, he'd be able to hide the redirection of the tattoo. He'd give it a couple of days, maybe weeks, before anyone recognized the ball sac inked into this guy's titty design.

He leaned in, preparing to make this next ten minutes hurt the most.

Unfortunately, Stink bent over to watch him work. All that bad breath built around them as Stink rattled on about the hardships of waiting months for this appointment.

Yeah, Dev was done. Pissed off threshold reached.

Dev reared back. His small chair rolled several inches away to add to the dramatic flair as he said, "Dude, back the fuck off. You fuckin' stink. Ever heard of a goddamn bath?"

This might have been the first time Dev actually looked his client in the eyes.

*Initial assessment wrong.*

He'd dubbed this guy a poser. Now he recognized the demon stirring behind those soulless eyes.

Not the first time he'd seen pure evil in human form. Hell, he had lived his entire life on the other side of the law, but this guy had sinister intent beneath all those foul smells and dirty, oversized clothes. If auras were a thing, Stink's was dark and dangerous. Void of rehabilitation.

Stink and Smoke merged into one person.

Yeah. Fuck that.

How had he missed so much while tattooing this fucker?

Dev felt more off than ever before. He blamed Tena, his ex-wife. She was making his life and their daughters' lives a living hell. He barely had time to wipe his ass under all her constant emotional bullshit.

That was a thin argument for what he'd missed but one he let hold because the only other person to blame was himself, and he didn't like that one bit.

"Renegade" ended. Dev's fucking mind raced. Nothing new. But it still amazed him how his thoughts could travel so many directions during the mere four minutes of that song.

"Turn it down, Millie," Dev called out.

What he needed was a bump to make his shit right.

Thin lips sneered at Dev in some sort of commiserating grin. "No time, bro. I'm drivin' cross-country to finish a job I carelessly didn't the first time."

Yeah. Dev had gotten the grin wrong too. Damn it. He saw no humor in that wicked expression. Something unseen yet dementedly pleasurable played in his client's head. This was the only time he'd stopped yapping his mouth since he had first arrived at the parlor.

A *'job'* usually equaled some sort of mob-boss speak, describing the end of a person's life.

"I'd ask about what job you had such a hard-on to finish, but then you'd have to speak. Your breath's a shithole, man." Dev reached behind him, grabbing several breath mints from a tray he kept handy. He placed a handful of individually wrapped candies on the small table separating the two of them.

The oil holding Stink's hair back from his face looked natural, not from any over-the-counter manscaping product. His client wore all black, but not well. Biker boots, jeans, a T-shirt, and a heavy black pleather jacket he'd hung over the armrest of the chair. He was boney, with hard edges to his face and body. The kind of skinny that spoke of decades of addiction.

Dev scanned the jacket. They were in fucking Dallas, Texas. Even deep as they were in the fall months, no one ever voluntarily wore more clothes than necessary. Climate change was kicking this part of the world's ass. Hot as the devil's anus most days.

Thanksgiving looked like it would involve a swimming pool party this year.

"Between you and me." Stink popped a breath mint into his mouth and reached for his cell phone in his back pocket. He searched the phone, giving a cocky lift of his brow as he spoke the secret words.

"Keep eatin' those." Dev motioned his head to get Stink to chew more of the mints. One would never be enough.

Stink chomped as he swiped his finger over the screen. "I'm out for fuckin' blood. Don't know how the menace survived our first…interaction, but I ain't gonna leave shit half done this time. I hate this prissy fucker. Ruined my goddamn life."

Dev narrowed his eyes, instantly taking the side of this unknown life-ruiner.

"Who you after?" Dev asked quietly, rolling farther backward on the stool, laying the machine on the bureau behind him. Their session had officially come to an end. All he needed now was as much information as he could gather if he planned to step in and help out.

Dev stood to his full height, peeling off then tossing his disposable gloves into the trash, or close to it, and again stretched his back, shoulders, and neck muscles, trying to appear interested. He reached over to his sound system, pushing the button to mute the music altogether, making sure he heard every word.

When Stink aimed the cell phone's screen his way, the image shocked Dev, but he kept his composure, refusing to show how offensive he found the photo. That said something since Dev had seen a lot of fucked-up shit. The victim, a man, was nude, bound and gagged, bleeding profusely from the slices all over his body. Raised and angry cigarette burns peppered his chest. The gaping leg wound alone spoke of some dark, demented torture shit happening.

"Go on. Take a look. His name's Julian Cullen. You know him?" Hate dripped from Stink's tone.

Dev's brows dropped, his eyes riveted on the man's face. When he didn't take the phone or turn to a new photo, Stink flipped through several more. Whoever this guy Julian was, he'd been tortured by multiple men if these images told the story.

"Should I know him?"

Stink lifted a shoulder in a boney-ass shrug. "He's one of those high and mighty prostitutes. He dated the guy who owns the Dishology restaurant group. They came to Dallas all the time." The dude's breathing increased with his growing agitation. His eyes shifted back and forth as if lost to memories.

"Nope, never heard of the guy." Dev had barely heard of Dishology and didn't know the DFW connection to the company.

"I'm not a goddamn queer. It's him, you know. He makes me want it." Stink's sudden outburst almost made Dev laugh out loud. Seriously, this guy had some fucked-up mental shit going on.

"I like dick," Dev mumbled. Of course, Dev had no idea about the depth of Stink's fascination and didn't care. He'd have let the guy walk out of there with a bad tattoo, but now those pictures alone gave Dev a reason to end him. He had the victim's name and a possible place of employment. All he needed was an end destination to know where Julian lived. Fucker needed to leave his parlor before Dev blew it and finished him off right there.

That bothersome cunt DA had local law enforcement all over him and his club. It'd be damn hard to hide the body locally with all the constant surveillance. His fist clenched tighter at the missed opportunity.

"He ruined my fuckin' life. How he survived makes no damn sense." Stink shook his head and stared at his phone screen. "I left my mark though. He sure can't be as pretty as he once was." The ugly, hate-filled sneer returned, but the man's gaze was lost again to a memory. "Fuckin' perverted fuck. I showed him perverted."

"Where you headed?" Dev asked, going to stand in the doorframe of his private inking room. He crossed his arms over his chest, his hands fisted tightly, and waited for Stink to clue in that their session had ended.

"Coronado, California." Hate and malevolence no longer laced his words. Stink switched gears so fast Dev had to retrace his steps to think about what he may have missed. "I saw you were in one of those one-percenter biker gangs."

"Club," Dev immediately corrected. Then rolled his eyes at himself for engaging this twat.

"I see myself like that. Besides the sheer pleasure it's gonna give me, I could make this kill like an initiation into your gang, but I'd wanna come in as a full patch member." He grabbed his pleather jacket. "I look good in leather. What do you think?"

Fucking loser had ignored his correction in terms. The idea this guy wanted in the club…

Oh hell no.

But apparently he had all the balls in the world sitting in his chair. As if killing someone showed a person's true grit and nature and spoke to their ability to be a full-fledged club member.

Stupid fuck.

The way the local authorities were breathing down his club's back, they certainly didn't need this tweaker out in the world, talking up his plans to join the Disciples of Havoc.

He'd already decided Stink was at the end of his life, but fuck if he didn't want to be able to make that decision again for the first time.

Dev gave a non-committal grunt, left Stink sitting there, and headed toward the cash register in the main room. He had all the information he needed, and Millie had her work cut out for her in disinfecting the bacteria Stink left behind.

"I think we've had enough for today," Dev said with all the annoyance this situation had collected.

"Bullshit. I booked four hours." Stink bristled, but Dev was already behind the front desk, working the iPad service system to charge the total payment due. Since he always required half down at the time the appointment was booked, he had credit card payment information already in the system.

"I'll schedule you two hours when you're headin' back through Dallas," Dev suggested and gave himself a two-hundred-dollar tip for all the shit smells and bad attitude he'd had to deal with today.

"What about wrappin' it? And that green ointment stuff," Stink asked, coming through the doorway, his arm still sticking out.

Dev ignored him as he worked through a plan in his head. The Disciples of Havoc had an extension of the club in San Diego. As the charge finalized in the system, he used the pad to log in to the cameras positioned in the parking lot. He scanned back until he spotted Stink arriving.

Dickweed wanted to become a full patch member and didn't have the decency to roll up on a Disciples business on his sled. Dev resisted the growl of annoyance bubbling up in his chest. He screenshotted the fucker's cage, making sure to capture a clean image of the smoke gray Charger's license plate number.

*Smoke* gray… As if karma were pointing Dev in a certain direction.

"All that cleanup's for pussies. Not real men like you. You'll be fine," Dev said distractedly, turning the cameras in different directions of the vehicle to gather several photos.

"So everything you said on *Ink Life* was bullshit? You spent half your time talkin' about the importance of keepin' the fresh ink clean." His client chuckled as if he were now in on the secret. "Pussies."

Millie's normal personality was damn mellow. She went with the flow on everything…generally. But she came around the desk, giving Dev a severe glance. Her pinched-up features said he'd grown another head, and she didn't like it at all.

She wasn't wrong. Dev was a slob in every part of his life except with his work. In this shop, he'd feel comfortable eating off the floor with all the cleaning and sanitization he required. He never wanted to be the reason for anyone to leave with an infection. Once they left, it was on them but not from him or based on his advice.

"Do I make an appointment?"

"Nah. Just stop by. I'll fit you in." Dev was done with this guy. He went around the reception desk toward the front door of his shop. He pushed it open and decided to go through first, not wanting to be on the tail end of the smell. Stink followed him out. Dev went one way, deeper into the building. Stink went the other direction, toward the rolling warehouse doors of his father's bike shop. He didn't look back, only listened to ensure Stink left the main building without pilfering anything from the shop.

"I don't think you did the right thing," Millie called out as Dev clomped up the staircase to his mother's office. He waved her off. She had to know he didn't do anything willy-nilly in his business.

Now that he'd wiggled in some free time in his day, he had calls to make and lunch to eat before his next client showed.

# Chapter 2

Dev banged his way through the bike shop's office door. His mom, Carly, barely glanced up from her computer screen before saying, "Your hair's too long. I can schedule you an appointment with my stylist."

Like every other time he came through the door, it bounced off the doorstop and shot back at him. He balled a fist as he considered finally having a fistfight with the metal to prove who really controlled things around here.

But his mother's voice acted like a balm to his manic thoughts. The anger he'd been harboring since letting Stink leave eased as quickly as it had built. The racing in his head slowed to a pace lap, about as quiet as they ever got. She always had a way of taming his ass.

He'd never questioned her mysterious abilities. As the long-time wife of the founding member of the Disciples of Havoc motorcycle club, then having Devilman as a son, she should have been walking around in a constant state of high-level anxiety. But she didn't.

At least with him, his mom was generally cool, calm, and collected and as pretty as ever, both inside and out.

She wouldn't agree with his last observation though. Carly Fox had taken to aging like a cat dunked in bath water. She fought it tooth and nail. She'd spent thousands of dollars on fillers, facial treatments, personal trainers, and many tiny nips and tucks. She was forty-five years old going on twenty-four.

She also didn't give a single shit what anyone thought. As badass as she was as a mother, she brought that same attitude to the club's accounting. She meticulously kept track of the books for every business the club owned. Her ability to deal with the mundane chore of invoicing the receivables while managing the payables spoke to her above average intelligence. Nothing ever slipped through the cracks.

While she did all that, she still made time to consistently keep his feet solidly on the ground and moving in a forward motion. He loved her dearly.

"My hair's pissin' me off. I'm sick of it," he grumbled and resisted the urge to run his fingers through the longish pieces on top.

He sent the door flying closed in the same banging manner he'd used to open it.

She squinted as she looked him over, lifting her fingers off the keyboard. He'd gained her full attention. She easily dialed into her unique motherly intuitions, quickly and efficiently assessing whatever current mood held him captive. She actively read him without asking any questions.

"I've been thinkin' about a buzz cut or shavin' it," he added, his mind still very much distracted by the piece of shit he'd just let walk out of the building. His bad feelings had only sunk lower with the hundred steps he'd taken from his shop to this office.

Had he made the right call by letting the loser leave? Surely, someone who smelled as bad as Stink didn't have too many people who would notice if he turned up missing.

Feeling like he'd lost a chance to relieve some of his tension, Dev had to resist the urge to call in a few local favors to track Stink before he got too far down the road. He might be able to show Stink a couple of new techniques as he ended the loser's life in the same way he tortured that Julian guy.

*Damn.* He ducked his head and turned, going to the small desk on the opposite side of the room from his mother before he changed his mind. His fists ached to live the fantasy in real time of knocking that douche's teeth out.

"Gotta make a call."

He'd been having to watch his own back for far too long. The paranoia and worry of what government agencies were currently tailing the club made his decision-making abilities unreliable. What he did know for fact was that those images Stink showed him of the battered and beaten pretty boy bothered the hell out of him.

Stink fucked that guy up. Whoever Julian Cullen was, he needed serious protection. The Disciples were damned good on the defensive regardless of whether or not people like Julian wanted them there.

The ability and desire to defend a community was the biggest difference between being a patched member of a bike club and the dark destruction behind many of the gangs running these streets. In Dev's universe, regardless of what he looked like or how he portrayed himself to the world, he lived and died by a code of ethics. Pretty boys being beat to shit for nothing more than enticing a man? That shit was unethical as hell. Eye for a fucking eye.

Robin Hood had always been Dev's number one superhero. He'd eagerly show Stink what being preyed upon felt like.

That stupid motherfucker bragging like that… That shit turned Dev's stomach. Then trying to negotiate his entrance into the club off an unwarranted death? Like they'd ever have the loser in the first place.

Dev clamped his teeth down on his lip, letting the stinging pain center him. His thoughts may have slowed, but they were still all over the place. Dev plopped down into the empty office chair as if he'd been on his feet all day, working a grueling manual labor shift, and let go of a heavy sigh. The chair squeaked and rolled under the abrupt addition of his weight. It seemed to know its way to put him in the dead center of the desk, in front of the computer screen and keyboard.

He quickly typed his credentials into their proprietary club software. They were far more technically equipped than any other bike club he'd ever been around. Again, his mother's doing.

Dev went through the thirty-five steps of logging into the program—okay, just three, but each came with its own layer of frustration as he tried to get the sequence of numbers and letters entered properly, all from memory. This program was a red herring. It didn't hold a lot of information just in case they had another early morning raid by the police, or the feds, or the local girl scout troop. All were about the same level of concern. Nothing more than annoying gnats flying around a person's head on a muggy fall evening. He hated those goddamn insects.

The contacts loaded on the screen. The size of the database spoke to the empire his father had built. They were twenty-one thousand members strong these days, spanning twelve countries. His old man, a king in the field of bike clubs, generally looked like he'd rolled out of bed after a good night of drinking and whoring. Which technically hit the mark.

No matter how much shit his club brothers gave him about being the crown prince to the Disciples throne, he didn't have the temperament or desire to ever fill his old man's motorcycle boots when the time came to pass the title down. Who in their right mind would ever want to manage this band of misfits while having both local and federal law enforcement doing their best to fuck things up on the daily?

His mother cleared her throat, redirecting Dev's thoughts. He took it as a sign from the gods of karma or whoever spiritually guided him. She was the proper answer to his question of who would be suited to take over. His mom already handled almost all the club business. Every member shielded and protected her in ways she didn't fully appreciate but learned to live with a long time ago. She led this club. His father's contribution to her efforts came through his brute force and bad to the bone reputation.

Dev's sister, Shanna, though, was a little badass in her own right. She'd chosen nursing school. She trail-blazed a path completely devoid of anything club-related or at least Dev liked to pretend that way. They'd have to see.

With a final keystroke, the screen opened to a search bar, drawing Dev from his skittering thoughts. The fucking sprinting in his head, always jumping this way and that, never fucking stopped. He had to force his focus back to Julian Cullen of Coronado, California.

"I see the look of determination on your face. Be mindful. We're in a precarious situation right now..." his mom warned.

He moved his fingers over the keyboard, bringing up the details of their San Diego club. He found the local chapter prez's cell phone number.

"Yup. It's the reason he left the buildin' unharmed," Dev answered and reached inside the desk drawer, using his palm to push against the hidden compartment artfully installed in the desk. No matter how many times they were raided, no one had ever found the secret space. He pulled out one of the two burner phones. A small, loaded pistol and thousands of dollars in cash filled the rest of the hidden drawer.

"Okay." Her tone still questioned his actions. Whatever her disapproval, he gave her room to have it. She was the best mother in the world. He certainly hadn't made it easy on her while growing up. His antics, once he'd hit puberty, had been a bitch for everyone involved.

His brother, Keyes, could attest to most of his misdeeds while growing up. Goddamn Keyes. Fucking Saint. Could barely tell a lie. It was why his buddy kept his mouth shut and fists flying most of the time.

The crazy volley of thoughts in his head made it harder than normal to stay focused. He needed a bump or a fist full of Adderall, preferably the first one. Speed, meth. Always his drug of choice. It made him feel bulletproof.

When was the last time he'd partied all night just to get off? Hell, who knew.

He must be going through something substantial, even life-altering. All the signs were there. Of course he was.

Most likely, he'd finally matured into a full-fledged adult. Gross.

The Disciples clubhouse. He needed to spend more time there. They had every possible drug and drink known to man. Willing women—dirty, eager, up for anything—the club had their fair share of club whores ready to spread themselves for any patched brother. Why had he stopped going there?

Well, another obvious answer smacked him in the face. Women weren't his thing these days.

Could he name the last time he had sex with anything more than his fist?

The date didn't come easy, which meant Dev was really having a life-disrupting moment. He liked to fuck just to fuck. He liked to watch people fuck. He'd always tossed himself in if given a chance. Sex had defined many of his adult years. He loved ass play too. Any ass really. Rubbing against his prostate gave him the best orgasms.

Why wasn't he missing sex more? *Shit.*

Nervous energy had his leg bouncing as he expertly popped the battery into the burner phone. The comforting familiarity of the movement brought his focus back to the here and now. He powered up the cell and pushed in the number displayed on the computer screen, then pressed call.

"Yo. Parker," the leader of the San Diego club answered.

"Devilman." All the introduction he ever needed. "I got somethin' for you."

"Yup." Communication like this was all the entire club needed. No unnecessary words.

"Bama plate comin' to your backyard. Dude's name is Micah Abbott if the intel is to be believed. Tag 'em. Next, Julian Cullen, Coronado. Sounds easy enough to track. He doesn't know what's comin' for him. Watch his six."

"Done." The phone went dead.

Dev used the burner to send the license plate number he'd captured earlier. Then sent a description of the car and the guy. He watched the screen until he saw the "text read" notification from the other end.

He had no doubt in the end result. Dev removed the battery and snapped the phone in two. The tension of the last few minutes dissipated. His stomach rumbled with hunger as he got to his feet.

"Wanna grab a bite?" Dev asked his mom, who sat there staring at him, her work in front of her completely ignored.

"Do I wanna know what just happened?"

"You got it figured out, I'm sure. Want some grub?" he asked, getting a better look at her. She didn't look like she was eating much these days, as thin as she was. "You're awfully skinny."

"I'm on a special diet. I have a procedure tomorrow—" She started to explain but he cut her off with a raised hand.

"Mom. Seriously. You look fuckin' great." All his concern poured out through his harshly barked words, wanting her to finally hear him.

She lifted a hand, stopping him from saying anything more, and she was right. They were having a useless conversation. He'd tried to make her see herself more clearly for years.

"I'm doing a breast lift tomorrow, then I'll be done for a while. Call Keyes. Your father says Keyes went over and saw Smoke. It didn't go well. Smoke's not expected to live through the week. Sounds like Keyes could use a friend." His mom used the perfect diversion.

"Stupid motherfucker," Dev murmured about Smoke. He stood, grabbing the pieces of the burner phone. He'd toss those as he rode out. "I hate that fuckin' cunt bastard. He can't die fast enough for me. Why'd Keyes even go over there?"

"Language, Dev. I'm still your mother."

He rolled his eyes like he always did when she got on to him about his colorful language. He'd talked this way since he was a toddler. Eventually she'd have to get over it.

"Be careful tomorrow." He opened the office door. "If you need a ride, call Millie," he tossed over his shoulder, teasingly. When he hadn't offered himself as her driver, she gave a huff. The joke hit its mark.

He met his father halfway up the stairs leading to the office that he took down two at a time.

"We have a run tonight," Fox said, his voice gruff and stern.

Where his mother searched for her youth, his old man had years of worry written in every sun and wind damaged line of his face. He had fifteen years on his mother. Old man was really beginning to take on a new meaning.

Dev nodded. The stealthy, secret drug runs were an adrenaline rush. Exactly what he needed to help tamp down this excessive energy pulsing through him. Only he, Keyes, and Mack, another club brother, went on these side hustles that his father had brokered years ago. They were designated as the muscle of the operation. A show of force against those who purchased from them.

They were lucrative and low risk. The club acted as the middleman in the transaction. They made loads of money with minimal effort, and that only came in the manner of brute force, making sure shit didn't go sideways.

"Keyes?" Dev asked. The single name was enough of a question as to whether he should say anything to Keyes about tonight.

"Can you?" his old man asked over his shoulder at the top of the stairs.

Dev lifted a confirming hand as he started toward his sled.

The minute the sun hit his face, everything in his world righted. It didn't matter that the oppressive heat hadn't let up for barely a minute this fall. He loved the smells, feels, and sounds of being outside. The gentle breeze was always moving, circulating, finding its way. Much like the thoughts in his head. He and that bitch, Mother Nature, sure had shit in common. Dev palmed his phone to see if Keyes had time for lunch.

=♥=

The soul-filling scenery might just be the best reason Ryan Cashin James, "Cash" for a good while now, had chosen to spend his two-week vacation in Arkansas's river country. Truth be told, it had little to do with this being his parents' most recent forever home.

He hadn't been too keen on the RV his parents had chosen to call home for most of his life. But the clean air and slow pace spoke to something deeper and meaningful inside his hardening heart.

The spiritual awakening that happened every time he jogged these trails caused him to run a little farther than normal and kept each of his steps hitting the pavement in front of him, even as sweat dripped off all parts of his body.

Apparently this region was locked in a late-in-the-season heatwave. They had experienced some of the warmest temperatures ever recorded for the river country. It was damned hot outside.

In his head, he heard his mom's voice scolding him for his use of profanity.

No matter his age or how far underground his life had taken him, she was the voice inside his head, asking him to be the best possible person he could be.

If only life were that easy.

In the real world, the relentless negative forces and roughly etched lines of good versus evil were far harder to navigate than his bohemian missionary parents prepared him for.

The tragic horrors he'd witnessed firsthand had caused him to run, bike, and lift weights to an excessive degree to help keep his head straight and eyes focused forward on the prize of a better life for everyone involved.

He spotted his parents' RV that had seen better days twenty-six years ago when his mother, Marilyn, and his father, Norman, put their life savings—which, if he remembered correctly, was roughly five hundred dollars—into a used travel trailer and began their vine style ministry. The trailer represented their traveling Sunday services as well as their home. To this day, they were still wide-eyed idealists, determined to change the world with the power of love.

If only that were possible.

Cash trudged up the steep hill to his parents' current campground. His father's pulpit and lawn chair pews sat empty between the newish truck he had bought for his parents and their travel trailer.

He guessed he was their church's biggest donor. His heart smiled. For all the years of his youth, they'd taught him love, acceptance, friends, and family were the true joys of life. The smile in his heart grew. His youth, especially once they had given up on public school and taught him at home, was the happiest time of his life. They gave him a wealth of love to support his solid foundation.

Cash slowed as he got to the entry of the camper. His mother's decorative crosses and his father's handmade weaponry sat on a table outside. Their sales helped subsidize the ministry. Or rather…they paid for his parents' meager lifestyle.

He ducked his head to keep from hitting the top of the doorframe and took the few steps up into the trailer while checking the time on his smart watch.

He had three hours before his flight departed.

"Cashin, my sweet boy, you only just got here," his mother said, complaining as she'd done since he'd gotten the news his vacation was cut short, called back into work. Her arms were elbow deep in bread dough, kneading the sticky clump.

As a child, he'd been mesmerized that something so gooey could turn out so delicious. Her fingers stopped moving, her sad face rose toward him in confusion.

"We haven't seen you in two years. Can't your job give us a full week with you? Surely, there's someone in the hospital that can hold them over until you return."

"Mom…" he started, going around the kitchen island that posed as an additional cooking space as well as a dinner table, office desktop, and laundry folding station if the current items on top spoke of its versatility.

Cash hedged, thinking over his words, trying to ignore the guilt that always hung over his head when he lied about his employment.

He stopped about a foot from her, lowered his gaze from her eyes, focusing somewhere around her nose. "It's a new position. I have to prove myself. If they call, I have to go."

"Daddy, help me out here," she said to his father who looked up from the Bible he studied from, peering over the wire rim of his bifocals. He was lost in thought if his expression said anything and didn't look overly willing to engage.

"What, Mama?" he asked. Since it had only been the three of them for all of Cash's life, he knew his mother was on a time clock with her answer. His father had given her about fifteen seconds before he'd revert to his studies, preparing for his next sermon.

"Cashin's work called him back," his mother said, reminding his father.

"You just got here, son," his father said, his gaze moving to him with the same confusion his mother used. "I thought you were staying a couple of weeks."

"I was, but they need me," Cash answered vaguely.

His father nodded as if that made perfect sense and turned back to his wife of thirty-five years. "They need him, Mama." All the explanation needed, and he turned back to the Bible again.

Their church's five or six parishioners really got a well thought out Sunday service until the weed came out. Sometimes that was within the first ten minutes, other times they got as long as thirty minutes of a biblical lecture. Then the service turned to a morning and afternoon of sitting on the porch, eating a potluck lunch and filling their souls with all the wonderfully philosophical thoughts a good high could conjure.

Cash fought a smile. If there was a summation to Cash's life to date, this was the moment. His hipster parents had found God about the time Cash was born. Their brand of acceptance, love, and let-go-let-God had never found a true following no matter how much of their lives were dedicated to their "missionary" work.

This rundown trailer, parked in the rolling landscape of Arkansas, spoke of everything good in his life. They had never landed in the best areas. They'd been robbed more times than Cash could count, but his parents loved everything about their lives.

And he loved them.

He didn't love the bunk bed he'd grown up sleeping in, which was still reserved for when he visited.

Cash shrugged at his mother as if his father had settled everything. He leaned down and kissed her soft cheek. "I'm sorry. I'll be back as soon as I can."

"You say that then years go by. Each time I see you I feel like you've grown another inch taller and that line between your brows is more pronounced. It makes you look mean. Maybe that's why you don't have a boyfriend. You look so scary." She knocked him in the arm with her elbow as tears welled in her eyes.

"How's that?" he asked, teasing her as he smoothed out his face, hoping to ease his brows that always seemed to draw together when he thought about the tightrope of his undercover assignments.

"Better," she said, sniffling.

"And I'm not an inch taller than I was before. I think you're getting shorter," he teased, reaching for the apple in a basket of fresh fruit she had out for him.

He'd topped out at six feet three inches tall and did everything he could to keep his body strong and healthy.

"I'm gonna take a shower. I have a car picking me up in about forty minutes." He took a big bite out of the juicy apple. A sweet treat by his best estimation.

"Car's picking him up? Do you hear that, Mama?" his father asked. His nose was still buried in his reading. "He's made it big if cars are coming to get him."

She nodded, reaching out, carefully taking him into her arms without dousing him in bread flour and dough. She hugged him tight. He returned the hold, letting her goodness fill his heart. She always gave the best hugs.

"Promise me you'll come back soon. I miss my son."

He put his cheek on the top of her head, not agreeing to her promise. He refused to tell her another lie.

# Chapter 3

Dev pulled his Harley Davidson Heritage Cruiser underneath the open pavilion at Fish Trap Lake. He let the pipes rumble for several long seconds, marking his territory for the few people brave enough to bear the heat with a takeout lunch at the lake. A chick sitting quietly in the corner quickly got the hint, gathering her things.

A dude fishing nearby required a couple more revs to gain his attention and get him moving on.

He should probably feel bad for pushing them out. The chick looked like a professional sneaking out to have a quick bite and a moment of solitude. He was doing her a favor. She shouldn't be on this side of town, alone like she was.

The rumble of Keyes's pipes signaled his approach, the grumble increasing as he closed the distance. The woman's sensible high-heeled shoes marched a little faster at the apparent realization more trouble was coming. Dev cut the engine, lowered the kickstand, and got off his sled in one fluid motion. The bike rested at an angle as he pulled the sub sandwiches from his saddlebag. He'd crammed the two sandwiches, chips, and soda cans inside together. The chips didn't feel like they'd fared too well. Keyes was sure to give him shit about it but would no doubt scarf them down anyway.

Back in the day, he and Keyes used to cut class to come hang out at this lake. They'd learned to swim and fish here. After watching some older Boy Scouts earn their badges, they'd also learned to build a fire and cook the fish they caught. Keyes had even called this pavilion home several times throughout his life when his old man had kicked him out of the house as a child. Dev used to sneak out to join him and sleep under the stars. Funny how it had never occurred to him to have Keyes just come stay at his house. He'd always been the one to follow wherever Keyes landed.

They considered themselves rebels, two people born to be wild. Dev raged against anything and everything the world had to offer, while Keyes was in a truly dire situation at home. How had he missed the complexity of his friend's life while joining him in every step he made? As a kid, it all seemed normal for them. But looking back on it... the words *fucked up* rang truer.

Why did a balanced life look so attractive these days yet feel so far out of his reach? Because he'd been goddamn trying to find one and only got a serious case of road rash for all his efforts.

His phone rang as Keyes's sled came into view, turning down the walking trail leading to the pavilion.

He palmed the device, seeing the name he'd given his ex-wife: Raging Cunt. It was as if the universe had heard his question about a normal life and wanted to remind him of the shit he still had to deal with.

In the long list of really bad decisions of his life, she currently held the number one position.

Just thinking about talking to her made his shoulders tense, instantly on guard, as he swiped a thumb across the screen to answer. He brought it to his ear, her tirade already in full swing on the other end of the line without him issuing any greeting. Dev sighed.

"This is the fuckin' suburbs. You're fuckin' Devilman. Get it, *the devil*. What the hell are you thinking putting us out here? There are actual soccer moms who live on this street. I can't do it. I'm not going to do it. Where the fuck is Sunnyvale anyway? I can't fucking get here without getting lost. I thought you were joking, you fucking pussy."

Furrowing his brow, he suppressed the growl threatening to erupt as Keyes edged closer to the pavilion.

He couldn't explain why he'd moved his bitch of an ex-wife, Tena, and their two daughters, Abi and Mae, to Sunnyvale. Hell, he'd bought a house there. A badass house because, per his ex-wife, every person in the house needed two thousand square feet to move around freely on their own.

He'd also put security on them—an emotional, gut driven decision. Not due to any real credible threat. The only reason he could come up with for such a move was that he'd liked watching his girls thrive in an ordinary life during his brief stint at normalcy while living with Holly.

Holly... Dev almost snorted. She'd turned into a psycho bitch herself. He hadn't told Keyes that one yet.

Then again...he'd been involved with both of them. So maybe he was the common denominator?

Nah, he refused to take credit for Tena. True bitch to her core. Always had been. At a particular time in his life, those qualities had been attractive to Dev. Tena was tough, abrasive, and barely wore any clothes. The ones she wore were only because she had to.

She'd made her banging body an open canvas to Dev while he learned his craft. She was possibly a showcase of his very best artwork. She had a colorful inked body that she loved to show off.

But her attributes ended there. Tena drank too much, smoked too much, and had an intense pill problem. She liked the high-dollar shit. She was becoming too fucking expensive, refusing to put a single dime of the money she made into paying bills. As far as he was concerned, she had no redeeming qualities. While she allowed a nanny to care for their girls, she made even that a battle. She had to stop firing the caregivers, because no matter who filled the nanny role, she was at natural odds with them.

"What do you want?" Dev shot out when Tena finally took a breath from her ranting.

"I'm going out. Your stupid nanny's off tonight. I need money and I need you to get your ass over here and take care of your children for once in your stupid life."

Her argument struck a nerve...hard...just as she intended. Yeah, there'd been a time he wasn't a good father, but that was only in the beginning. Shit changed fast by the time Abi started crawling. Now, he spent more nights with his girls than anywhere else. He'd even proudly worn the *Girl Dad* T-shirt they'd given him for Father's Day.

Every dime he made went to her and the girls. No matter how many different ways he explained the club's current financial problems, she just kept spending money.

He dragged a hand over his face. His attempt at resisting the fight didn't work. He took her bait, saying what he felt deep inside his heart. "Goddamn, Tena. I fuckin' hate you."

"I'm not fucking you anymore for free so stop trying," Tena countered. "You need to get the girls from school today and drop me some money on Venmo."

She always took his insults as flirtation. That was the main reason they had ended up in this situation in the first place.

"I can't be there until after eight tonight. You're gonna have to wait."

The way she screamed into the phone pierced his brain, making him jerk the cell from his ear. Keyes watched him, parking many feet away to keep the roar of his pipes from overpowering his conversation.

The only thing Dev said before ending the call was to yell, "I better not get a fuckin' call they weren't picked up from school. Got shit I gotta do to pay for your fuckin' life."

He refused to listen to another word of the litany of hate she had about her life, his life, his career choices, or lack of a substantial income, and ended the call.

Keyes stalked toward him. His buddy's gait mimicked that of a predator. The king of the jungle who was on a casual stroll through his lands. Every muscle worked in a symphony, each prepared to tense after being forced to flex. The questions in his gaze made Dev lower his eyes and silence the ringer, so they weren't interrupted again. She'd stalker call and text him until she got her way. They didn't need her to ruin their lunch.

Dev rolled his tight shoulder muscles, attempting to change his mood. "Fuckin' Tena. Who we fuck at fifteen shouldn't hang over our heads for the rest of our lives."

Keyes, who towered over Dev in both bulk and height, chuckled and reached out a hand, initiating their standard dap-slap greeting.

How Keyes could stay so fundamentally good after living the life he had was beyond Dev. But he respected it and matched his buddy's laugh.

"Maybe because you fucked her without a condom for ten more years. Look at the bright side, you could've had twenty kids with her by now."

"I fucked everybody without a condom. My number of offspring should be much higher," he teased.

"What the fuck, Devilman?" Keyes feigned anger, or maybe not faking it. It was hard to tell with Keyes. His buddy's attention had shifted to the table where their lunch sat. "Chips at the bottom of the fuckin' bag again? How many times do I have to tell you—"

"Apparently, one more." The perfect comic relief to help Dev let go of his annoyance. "Cal says hi and happy belated birthday."

"Mmm," Keyes growled.

Cal personally built the subs they'd shared for years now. He'd also fed Keyes many times when he ran these streets alone. "You ain't payin' for the grub. You're supposed to be grateful, ingrate."

Dev got another grunted, "Mmm."

"My mom said Smoke's at his end and you went over there," Dev said, taking the seat on the other side of the picnic table. Keyes followed suit, but the table didn't fit their big frames as well as it used to.

"He can barely breathe. How hasn't he died?" Keyes muttered. "Those fuckin' prospects he recruited need to go. I'll never vote 'em in."

Dev grabbed the bag of food and dumped the contents between them. Keyes stopped a can of soda from rolling off the edge of the table. He couldn't have agreed more about the Disciples newest prospect pool. There were about fifteen of them who needed to be cut if for nothing more than they had no respect for anything or anybody.

"Agreed. Their days are numbered. We need to bring up the motion next time church is called. Just be done with them all." He lifted his gaze, judging how torn up Keyes might be after seeing his old man. There wasn't any emotion reflected in his friend's face. Only the low rumble of Keyes's stomach, apparently appreciating the sight of the food. "Mom said the tire shop was turnin' a nice profit again." Keyes took over the tire shop a couple of years ago when his old man first fell ill, and it had been steadily improving…until that fucking raid stalled progress.

"Yeah. I've already started quotin' prices on holiday tires. I figure we'll make up the ground we lost durin' the raid. I reupped my advertisin' on those in-store shoppin' carts. They work crazy well. Figure people'll shop for groceries in the stores again durin' the holidays," Keyes said, flipping the edge of the paper to unroll his sandwich. He used too much force, the garnishes continued to roll, making Keyes have to scoop up the sandwich. With it palmed in his hand, he took a huge bite, tearing a large chunk out of the hoagie as he placed a napkin on one thigh.

A napkin. In his lap. Dev raised his eyebrows.

His brother wasn't hiding near as much as he thought he did. Civilized people and his mother at Thanksgiving and Christmas dinner made them put napkins in their laps.

"You got a haircut," Dev mentioned. Repeatedly trimmed hair was not a typical dress-code habit of a Disciples of Havoc biker.

Dev started mentally ticking off all the little changes he'd noticed in Keyes. His normally scraggly beard was now cut and kept neat. He suspected a brush was pushed through it. His long hair wasn't several different lengths now and may have some of those expertly cut layers in to make it look fuller.

Keyes wore a T-shirt and jeans, both looking like they were recently purchased brand new, not from the thrift store they sifted through regularly.

His brother didn't make eye contact or acknowledge his words. Instead, he opened both bags of chips, eyeing each. He picked the bag with the least broken chips, tossing the other on the table with disinterest.

Dev found humor in the action and reached for the bag. At some point, he was going to have to start digging to see what his buddy was hiding. But like he had decided months ago, he let his suspicions be enough since Keyes seemed happier. More than anyone Dev knew, Keyes deserved happiness in whatever form it came. He'd tell Dev more when he needed to know.

"We have a run this evenin'. My old man asked if you were in?" Dev asked, taking a much smaller bite than Keyes.

Keyes swallowed the lump of food in his mouth and opened the can of soda that hadn't made the roll down the table, taking a long drink to help wash the oversized bite down. "'Course. Normal time?"

"He didn't tell me any different," Dev said, his mouth full of food. He talked and chewed at the same time only because Keyes hated that shit. His buddy was super tidy, had an innate sense of cleanliness and manners that he was born with—not that they could figure out what side of the family those had passed down through—and was the gentlest of giants about ninety percent of the time.

That other ten percent rivaled Dev on the crazy meter.

"Who's that?" Keyes tilted his head to take a look behind Dev. Dev glanced over his shoulder too. He hadn't heard the Dallas PD cruiser pulling up to the pavilion. It was always a roll of the dice whether to bristle at a cop or flip them off in a salute, knowing they were on the Disciples payroll.

"Tay Grisby. He's got somethin' to say so I've been avoidin' him the last few days. I don't really want to hear it." Dev took another bite as Keyes swallowed, reached for the napkin to wipe the crumbs off his hands, then beard. He wadded the paper napkin up, tossed it aside, and bowed that big chest, looking like the threat he was.

Dev liked the way Keyes's chest expanded about five inches bigger every time he wanted to look intimidating. At a little over six feet tall, Dev had muscle, but not like his friend. Most people feared his brother when it was Dev that could cause the most destruction in every situation.

Keyes stood to his full height, holding his ground as the officer came under the pavilion's cover. The cop eyed Keyes closely as if judging the threat. Keyes looked mean as hell, which was one reason his old man included Keyes on his secret drug runs.

Dev took another bite, watching the show of force playing out in front of him. He got involved when Grisby's hand shifted to rest on the butt of his pistol attached to his belt. "Calm down. It's too fuckin' hot outside for a cop to be out of their climate-controlled cage. Why're you here?"

"You've been avoiding me," Grisby said and cut his irritated gaze to Dev. "I don't like having to chase you down. It's not part of our deal."

"Quit flirtin' with me," Dev said, taking another bite of his sandwich. "You want a go at this? All you've ever had to do was ask." Dev raised a single brow at the cop.

Keyes just stood there, a stoic sentinel. His fists balled at his sides. Keyes did silence so well. Grisby had been on the Disciples payroll for years. Up until their last invasion, he'd been excellent at keeping the club one step ahead of everything going on behind the scenes that they weren't privy to.

The one thing Grisby had in spades was homophobia. Dev's implication hit its mark. Grisby got his back up. Stupid fucker.

"That shit's not ever funny, Devilman. Where's your old man?" The disgust was clear in his tone.

"Why?" Dev asked. Grisby was the informant, not Dev. If it concerned his old man, his location was the last thing Grisby needed to know.

"Something's going down. There's a change happening. I don't know what and I'm not sure where it's coming from."

Okay, that was cryptic. Dev could play along. "More than what we've been dealin' with?"

"Yeah," Grisby said, looking serious, acting uncomfortable as hell.

Now they played twenty questions.

Dev took a smaller bite of his sandwich, coming up with nothing. The threat could literally be from many different directions.

"What do you know?" he finally asked.

"Tell Fox to get his connections in the feds to sniff around." Grisby hooked his thumbs into the shoulder straps of his bulletproof vest as he eyed Keyes. "Does he have to stand that way?"

"I don't know," Dev said and turned to Keyes. "You have to stand that way?"

Keyes's intimidating gaze stayed leveled on the cop, but he didn't otherwise respond.

"Seems so," Dev answered and reached for the bag of chips. "He's an animal who hates cops. I think that's the best you're gonna get."

Keyes grumbled. Man, he and Keyes had this good cop, bad cop thing down. The joke was so funny in Dev's head that a chuckle burst out of his mouth.

Officer Grisby looked between the two of them. His hand lowered again to the butt of his revolver. "Tell your old man what I said. I don't like having to track you down. You should have answered the phone. Then to have this big oaf trying to intimidate me. It's bullshit and not part of our deal."

Dev glanced at Keyes then met Grisby's gaze. "Don't think he's actually tryin'…yet."

The cop huffed out a breath. "I'm gonna assume this is a show to protect the balance since we're in public, but I don't like it."

"I'll mark that down in the minutes. Get gone, cop."

Grisby pivoted around and left the pavilion, grumbling under his breath. Dev let it go. Keyes tracked every step the cop made all the way to his cruiser.

"Come finish your food," Dev said, letting Grisby's ominous tip go for now. He'd relay the message but had all he could deal with today. Tomorrow he'd worry about the federal concern. Whatever. They were already under federal investigation and that had turned up squat. Let the bastards come. Not the first time, wouldn't be the last.

When the police cruiser pulled away, Keyes finally rolled his shoulders and took his seat again. "Fuckin' cops. What did that even mean?"

"Who knows," Dev replied. "Did I tell you Tena's a fuckin' cunt?"

Keyes chuckled and started back on his sandwich. "I've heard that before."

# Chapter 4

Cash lifted his gaze to the rafters adorning the halls of Methodist Hospital in Dallas, Texas, as he strode in silence to the predetermined meeting location. Well, not in complete silence. His high-dollar loafers gave the slightest clicking noises as he walked down the dull vinyl-covered hallway.

Funny how much money he spent on his wardrobe when he'd been raised with a handful of T-shirts and athletic shorts from thrift stores. Cheap children's clothing had a way of stretching. His smalls became larges and grew with him over the years. According to his dad, those had been his mom's jackpot finds.

*Stop.* No more trips down memory lane. Those were coming too frequently since he'd landed on Dallas soil. He needed to focus. Find his inner A-game. Concentration and observation were critical at this point.

Cash truly walked the line.

How he'd ended up in an oversight department within the Exempt Operations Division of the United States Attorney General's office, going undercover to root out corruption among his fellow federal agents, was a long sordid tale.

All right, it wasn't that long.

About five years ago, the AG's office had approached him with the offer. He'd been a fresh-faced undercover agent within the DEA and had quickly made a name for himself after being assigned a years' old case that he'd managed to close within a few months.

It hadn't been hard. The well-connected, seasoned special agent in the field had financed a very lucrative off-duty lifestyle for himself by being on the take for years.

At the time, Cash wore the values his parents had instilled in him like a cloak of justice. He hadn't thought twice about turning the agent in and closing the case. Right was right. So taking the position with the AGEOs had seemed like the perfect opportunity. He continued working for the DEA and took on secret special assignments for AGEOs as they arose.

And while he'd lost his rose-colored glasses, he'd still closed three additional cases for the AGEOs, all involving rogue agents. He'd gained quite the reputation with his superiors while somehow keeping his "secret undercover identity" under wraps. That was also unheard of in his current line of work.

Only he and three other people in the AG's office had any idea that when he was assigned to a case, he also sought crooked federal law enforcement officers. He'd wondered how he kept that secret so private except that his lack of friendships or other meaningful relationships screamed the answer to that query.

His entire adult life was chock full of undercover assignments and not much else.

Though, he did love working out. Most of his free time involved whatever local gym he could locate or health food store to peruse the shelves for any new finds.

He wasn't lonely though. He liked his life.

Time alone came easy for Cash. He never felt the urge to share with anyone. Life had made sure of that.

In his newest assignment, Cash had learned, for many years and various reasons, different agencies under the umbrella of the DOJ had infiltrated the Disciples of Havoc. Undercover agents were layered deep inside the bike club. Under a cloak of secrecy, Cash was tasked with finding the responsible parties for the theft of missing money from the sales of the club's illegal trafficking operations.

What goods were being trafficked and how the government participated in those sales were not his concern. He wouldn't muddy the water trying to understand the government's current position inside this one-percenter motorcycle club. That part didn't matter. He had his assignment.

From these elite operations, he had learned that good versus evil was really better stated as less evil versus more evil. Cash stood firmly on the side of less evil.

But his focus wasn't coming easy this time. Being in Dallas again was doing a number on his head. His scattered thoughts pulled in distant memories he'd dealt with and filed away many years ago. That messed with the small amount of prep time he'd been given before arriving, namely the three-hour flight from Arkansas to Dallas.

He'd assured his superiors that his history in this city wouldn't be a complication.

Perhaps he'd been wrong.

As he turned the corner, down another long, deserted hall, he thought about his cover as a healthcare administrator. It didn't allow much access to any actual suspects in the thefts. If his past told his story, then this was nothing more than a sloppy and telling decision by an arrogant lead agent used to getting one over on his superiors. Or, as Cash liked to think, the beginning of the end for the operation.

Seemed simple enough.

Not the rocket science smarts his superiors thought he used to identify those on the take.

Add to the mix that the Dallas area law enforcement didn't have a reputation for being on the up and up on any government level, from local to federal. He had to assume everyone working in Dallas was rogue until they proved themselves otherwise.

In the hushed briefing he'd had with the attorney general himself, Cash had learned every member of his new undercover team posed as a healthcare professional in one way or another. Methodist Hospital had a long-standing agreement with the federal government to give a safe harbor to undercover operatives.

The agents were never identified to the hospital.

The agreement still remained an utter secret which was quite remarkable in this day and time. Another point Cash had a hard time believing.

Hiding in plain sight only went so far.

His most consequential question of the day was why have this cream of the crop team, with agents from both the FBI and DEA, working on the sideline, inside a hospital the Disciple brothers never used?

It made no sense unless the hospital somehow aided in the theft. And there was zero evidence to support that claim.

The stress in his shoulders grew. Safety was always an issue, but that outlaw biker gang brought its own set of security issues. He didn't have the privilege of shooting from the hip on this case. He needed facts, not assumptions.

The truths had to present themselves.

This assignment was fluid at best. A constantly moving target. The pieces of the puzzle shifting with no rhyme or reason.

Cash stretched his neck and let the worry building there slide down his tailored-suit-covered arms. He aimed for a passive confidence, aware of all the surveillance tracking his every step through these halls. He didn't allow himself a moment before he turned another corner and spotted the room he was looking for.

The door unlatched on his approach without him having to use his identification badge to enter. He lifted a hand, pushed through the door, and entered an older waiting room that had been turned into the team's temporary conference center.

All heads snapped his direction. Four people sat at a table in the middle of the open space. Two wore scrubs, the others were in the usual attire of the DOJ—*Men in Black* came to mind.

"Special Agent Ryan?" the point person at the head of the table asked, using his undercover name, Cash Ryan. He lowered his laser pointer from an overhead screen.

Cash nodded. "Call me, Cash."

"Take a seat. We haven't been here long. We'll catch you up."

He pulled a chair from the corner, dragging it over to the small table. He sized up the agents. One in particular hit his heart like a sledgehammer. He was so unprepared to see her that he dropped the chair, causing it to scrap loudly against the floor.

All eyes shifted back to him, including hers.

"Excuse me," he murmured and righted the chair. His fixed gaze never left her extraordinary face.

She and her brother were nearly identical. It didn't matter that he'd only seen her once over sixteen years ago. He'd know her anywhere.

"You're Shanna Fox."

She narrowed her gaze as she assessed him, her face becoming fiercely formidable. She didn't say a single word.

Of course he knew Devin Fox's involvement with the Disciples of Havoc. Had even spent a small amount of time soul searching his past and how it would impact his present objectives. He eventually decided he could, if push came to shove, arrest the man he owed his life to.

What he hadn't expected was to see Dev's younger sister at this meeting. Surely the government had fully vetted her before putting her on this team.

*Jesus.* After everything he'd seen so far, how could he be sure?

Why hadn't he had this crucial bit of intelligence before walking into this meeting?

"You two know each other?" one agent asked, nonchalance dripping from his tone, but curiosity blazing in his eyes.

"Not that I know," Shanna replied, instantly on guard.

Cash decided against responding. He didn't trust his voice.

Could Shanna remember him?

The attorney general's office knew of Cash's past. They'd all agreed there was little chance Dev 'Devilman' Fox would remember Cash as a boy from their onetime interaction all those years ago.

Very brief. One day.

"Cash is joining our team from the mothership in DC," the man clearly in charge explained, skirting around the sudden confusion in the room. "I'm Malik." His hand swept to the right. "Joe is an internet specialist and will be your handler. You apparently know Shanna. Emma is her handler."

A fist came across the table from Joe, along with a good-natured grin. He met the fist bump.

"She can regularly bring you to your knees," Joe teased, hooking his head toward Shanna.

Emma groaned and made a dramatic show of rolling her eyes.

"It's never gonna happen between them, but Joe won't give it up," Emma explained and reached a hand over the table in greeting. "I'm Emma and I need to know what's going on here. Is this some new layer to add to the team because our plates are already pretty full?"

Her curious gaze shifted between him and Shanna.

Shanna's brows remained furrowed as she glanced at Malik as if he might have the answers.

"Had any of you read the reports, you'd know Cash lived around here as a young boy. Isn't that correct?"

Cash nodded, intertwining his fingers, locking them in place in his lap. "Lived here might be stretching it. I went to Dallas ISD, where your brother went to school for less than three months."

Shanna looked blankly at him, questioning such a simple explanation. "I'm five years younger than he is. You wouldn't have known me through school…"

The sudden rush of emotion caught Cash off guard. He sat back in the seat, staring into the eyes that looked very much like the Dev he remembered from back then.

He'd had no idea these long buried memories would resurface like they had. It wasn't a time in his life that brought easy memories for him. Images played like a slideshow through his head where he'd been a victim of some of the most hateful bullying he'd ever witnessed since.

His parents had always been wholesome people. Naïve to the troubles of the world. Putting their innocent child inside such a tough as nails elementary school had doomed him.

That was the last public school he'd ever attended.

"I—" He started and stopped, glancing at Malik. "It's all in the report, right?"

Malik nodded, perhaps with the briefest hint of compassion in his eyes. "Catch up on your own time. Ryan comes to us from the federal levels of the DEA. He brings his expertise to help get us more fully on the inside of the Disciples. I was just getting to that point when you arrived."

"Why?" Joe blurted before Malik could move on.

Any attention Cash had garnered was lost to the questions so clearly forming in his counterparts' faces. Malik lifted a hand to silence those incoming questions.

"The stakes have risen. Higher-ups see us as dragging our feet. They want answers. As a whole unit, not only our team, the directive is to infiltrate every part of the club to take greater control of events as if we haven't been trying to do that very thing. Shanna, they want you more on the inside."

She glanced up from where she had been reading in the file, most likely about him. "What exactly are you saying?"

"I think it's clear. They want you to put your nursing degree cover on hold and work within the club."

Shanna's face paled. "They'll never believe I want anything to do with them." She shook her head at the new directive.

"Your job is to make them believe," Malik instructed. Any compassion to what that might mean was lost in his steely command.

Emma sat back in her seat, her gaze on Shanna. "This will put her at great risk with no quick answers. We know what happens to the women who join the club. They have one job and that's to be at the disposal of those nasty men. They'll always think of her in that way even if they can't act on it because Fox deemed her hands-off. We're better off moving forward like planned. Our pace is good. The intel we've gathered so far is phenomenal."

"I don't question my directives. Neither should you. We do what we're told," Malik said. "And I honestly agree with this new direction. They've had us sitting out here with our thumbs up our asses, waiting for intel to cross our paths. It's time to move in closer. Be prepared to act when they call on us. Hopefully it's soon because I refuse to live through another one of these never-ending hot summers."

The shifting pieces kept moving as Cash tried to get a read on each agents' internal motivation.

"If we're ready to continue, Cash Ryan is a healthcare administration consultant from California. He's been hired in a yearlong assignment by Methodist Hospital. We're assigning Cash to Devilman's detail. Shanna, we want you to focus on the women in the club, specifically the ones they call club whores. They have a story to tell, at least one is always present when the club president is around. She has to know something. Cash will be moving into Devilman's new property in South Dallas. Joe will be hidden inside the unit with Cash, acting as your official handler, as I said. He'll monitor everything. Anything you need, he'll work out the details and get it to you. Also he'll relay real time information back and forth from the local office to you, Cash."

Cash nodded. Having Joe on the inside with him was standard practice. He felt bad for Joe. He'd barely see the light of day for the length of the time Cash lived in the apartment, but

Joe had clearly signed on for the job. He had to know what he was getting into.

"Shouldn't I be moving into one of Dev's apartments then?" Shanna asked. "It'll make me appear as if I've had a change in attitude. More accepting of my brother, not so put off by the club's values."

"Good idea. Then you and Joe will be on-site to assist Cash if anything arises. We've secured two of the four apartments in your brother's building through the shell company set up to look like they employ Cash. That leaves one additional unit left vacant. Talk to your brother. Get him to lease that space to you. That's the easiest way to get that done," Malik instructed and moved the laser pointer back to a slide on the screen.

Joe opened his laptop, repositioning it on the table to share with Cash the PowerPoint presentation Malik currently worked from.

The blessed numbness Cash associated with his assignments returned. His mind went clear as he focused on the newest details.

He could do this. Shanna had just surprised him. Nothing more.

# Chapter 5

The unrelenting heat slowly roasted Dev from the outside in. The area needed a fucking cold front to plow through and cool this bitch down. Led Zeppelin jammed on the Bluetooth speakers inside his helmet. Music being the only reason he ever voluntarily wore a dome when he rode. The volume pushed past the recommended capacity as the song thumped through his head and vibrated against the helmet.

Dev navigated the pothole riddled pavement known as Red Bird Lane. The bike bounced and swayed on a road that had seen better days twenty years ago.

He took a left turn, edging by the largest pothole on the street, heading into the Red Bird Lumber Yard. He idled his sled at the secured gated entrance as he took the helmet off, shook out his sweat-dampened hair and stared at the motion-sensing camera angled toward the entrance.

The lock unlatched and the gate crept open.

Dev secured the helmet on the bike and drove through the maze of freshly cut and stacked lumber. Each pile had been intentionally stacked to be taller than the warehouse built in the dead center of the property owned by the Disciples. One

of the most lucrative businesses in their commercial portfolio. With the demand and price of wood increasing by
the day, Red Bird Lumber Yard washed more cash than the
rest of their businesses combined.

His old man had taught him decades ago that operating
on the older, poorer side of town allowed the club to hide
in plain sight. Nobody cared about the less fortunate. The
general public wore blinders. Easier to pretend they didn't
exist than try to do anything to truly help.

The police barely patrolled the area, and when they did,
it happened on a regular timetable. The Disciples set the
patrol schedule. The officers were on the payroll, rewarded
in cash to keep their eyes forward and ears closed.

What couldn't be seen from outside the fence was the actual warehouse building in the center of the property. Also
hidden were the armed security guards ready to act when
necessary. All were members in some way or another of
the Disciples, and all were true-blue Texans with anarchy
in their souls—the ideal candidate for their brotherhood.

His old man banked on their nonconforming natures,
slowly building a small army behind these gates.

He tipped his head at Tank, a long-standing patched
brother and head of security for the property, as he passed
by a larger pile of lumber. Tank's grin split big. His front
two teeth were missing but Dev guessed no one would ever
know. The guy never smiled and barely spoke unless bark-
ing out an order. Tank was known as the groundskeeper
of this property. One of the many father figures who had
helped raise him into the man he was today.

An overhead door cranked open on his approach. He
could hear the sounds of an electric saw cutting through
lumber in the distance.

He pulled into the darkened building. He brought his
Harley to a stop and cut the engine as the big overhead
door closed shut behind him. The air conditioner blasted
cool air into the large, almost empty space, sending a light
chill over Dev as he got off the bike.

Dev ran his fingers through his damp hair, waiting for his
eyesight to adjust to the dimmer interior after such a bright
ride over. High heels clicked on the polished concrete slab.
The sound surprised him. The club whores weren't allowed on

the premises. Even his mother didn't venture in this direction. These were sacred grounds.

The smell of fresh liquor, skunk weed, and strong floral perfume hit at the same time. He knew exactly who approached. Daphne.

"Your daddy told me to come get you," she said and appeared in the slash of sunlight several feet away. At barely eighteen, she was technically legal, but too young to be a part of this world as far as Dev was concerned. But she'd already been inducted into the circle of women, the club whores, who were taken care of by the club...so long as they *took care of* the patched members whenever they wanted.

"You shouldn't be here," Dev drawled, his spine stiffening with irritation. He crossed his arms over his chest, giving his most menacing stare.

She didn't flinch at his tone or his look. The problem was that she'd grown up alongside him. She might even consider herself his little sister in the ultra-dysfunctional, modern biker family sort of way.

What Dev's mother didn't know and a secret he'd had to keep since he was about ten years old was that Daphne's mother, Dixie, was his father's personal property. She'd found her way to the club eighteen years ago, needing a daddy for her baby. She didn't get one of those, but she was pretty enough, and slutty enough—willing to do anything—that she'd caught the club prez's eye.

Very few had gotten the chance to fuck her since. Hell, that wasn't true. She'd fucked every brother for various reasons. A reward for a job well done? Fuck Dixie. Had a bad day? Fuck Dixie. Need a willing third? Fuck Dixie. But it was all at his old man's instruction. Nobody ever touched her without his father's permission.

Daphne sauntered toward him, reaching out to slap his arm as if he'd said the silliest thing on the planet. His brows furrowed at her boldness. She was the only one who ever got away with that shit. Even his real little sister, Shanna, had enough sense to regard him as the devil he was.

"Mom and Fox are downstairs fuckin'. It helps him stay loose before y'all ride out. Come on." She spouted the words like it was the perfectly ordinary occurrence that it was and flipped around on her heels, stumbling slightly in the execution. She took several stabilizing steps to stay upright. Dev shook his head. The girl still hadn't mastered how to properly navigate those ridiculous high heels.

He stood there watching her, his eyelid twitching. He loathed the idea of following her.

His old man was a perverted son of a bitch, an exhibitionist to his core. He had some fucked-up rationale about how others seeing him banging some chick equaled manliness. And he had no compunction about that "other person" being his son. Seeing his dad's old ass screwing fell into the hard *no* category for Dev. He stalled as long as possible, frozen in his spot.

At the concealed door that led downstairs, Daphne paused to glance over her shoulder.

"Come on, Devilman," she sing-songed as if they were in a happy place. "Your old man's finishin' up. He knows you don't like my mom."

Dev grunted, not disabusing her of that notion. He didn't dislike her mom, per se. He didn't actually give two fucks about her at all.

Drawing in a deep breath, he strode forward. And like the little bitch he was destined to be, he finally followed her through the door. He pounded down the steps, two at a time, getting right on Daphne's ass as she pushed through the doorway at the bottom. Dev kept his growl of irritation contained. That door should have been locked for everyone's safety. Jesus, did anyone actually run this club anymore?

What they'd skillfully hidden from prying eyes upstairs worked openly downstairs. A two thousand square foot basement that had been carved out of the white rock below the foundation.

Part of the space housed a vault harder to break into than Fort Knox. Only three people in the world knew the entry code sequence—Dev, his old man, and his mother. The only one who could change the code, if necessary, was his old man.

Long tables ran the length of the rest of the space. Various activities played out on those surfaces. Tonight, it looked like a standard drug mill operation. Trusted, seasoned prospects worked at several tables filled with pills. Others looked to be cutting coke. A couple of large pallets, filled with closed cardboard boxes sat to the side.

What made him hesitate before coming down was happening in a corner. By the grunts and gasps, there were three of them banging away. A partial wall helped hide whatever nakedness he wouldn't be able to scrub from his brain.

"Yo, Devilman. What brings ya here?" Diesel asked, drawing his attention to the brother. Diesel wasn't too many years older than Dev and stood against the wall, brawny arms crossed over his chest, holstered weapons on each hip. He guessed that meant the brother was in some sort of security guard capacity.

Dev lifted his chin in response and watched Diesel's eyes follow Daphne.

"What's in these boxes?" Dev asked Diesel as he sauntered over to the pallets, curious about the contents.

"Don't know," Diesel answered as Dev used his pocketknife to cut through the packaging to reveal several much smaller boxes, each filled with Fentanyl patches.

Dev blew out a breath. There had to be tens of thousands of patches on these pallets. A goddamn motherlode of the shit. His lip quirked in a grin as he grabbed one full box then another. He could taunt his ex with these to get her to toe the line. A great bargaining chip that could make his life bearable, at least where Tena was concerned. He grabbed a third box for good measure.

"Keyes and Mack are waitin' out front," Tank's voice intoned from the overhead speaker. Thank hades. Dev tucked his haul under his arm and started for the door. He'd rather swelter in the heat than spend another second in this room.

"Tell 'em I'm comin'…" his old man called out, his voice haggard. Dixie giggled at the innuendo his father probably hadn't intended. Dev slammed the door shut behind him without a response.

He climbed the twenty steps, mental exhaustion weighing him down. More than anything, he craved some fucking normalcy in his life.

Where the fuck did he find that?

=♥=

Cash extended an arm to reach for a bath towel and still came up short of grabbing one. He was forced to step out of the hotel room's shower, the water cascading off him as he went.

He tossed one towel to the floor to soak up all the water he trailed before taking another and rubbing quick swipes over his body. He attacked his face with a vengeance, digging the terry cloth into his closed eyes as if that alone would block the relentless carousel of memories spinning freely through his head.

What a joke. Lifting weights hadn't helped. The miles he'd run on the treadmill hadn't either. Before that, hours of prepping for the undercover assignment that officially started in the morning hadn't helped.

On the way to his room from the gym, he'd swung by the hotel's bar and had a few drinks. Even that hadn't proved an effective escape from all this emotional overload.

If only it were random thoughts of Dev. He could get past those. He always did. Instead, he carried around this foreign feeling in his chest. For some inexplicable reason, he needed to protect the biker. The strength of the urge made his body hum. He wanted to crawl out of his skin to make it happen.

No amount of talking himself down eased the irrational urge.

He ran the damp towel over the mirror in frustrated swipes to push the condensation away. He left behind streaks on the fogged glass. Enough mirrored bits had been cleared to see the weariness in his eyes. The same sadness he'd carried for years, through multiple surgeries and physical rehabilitation. At least he'd survived. Not only that, he'd thrived. The lessons learned through the long recovery made him both mentally and physically stronger.

Clearly, not as strong as he had once thought. The inner focus that guided his every decision had vanished. This wasn't the first time he'd been triggered back into the past. But this time, refocusing took longer.

He was here to do a job. One he planned to complete. If he found a way to help Dev, he'd do it. If not, well, life had taken them down different paths. Some might call them opposing. But it was the way it was.

Cash brushed his teeth then ran the brush over his hair.

After hours spent reviewing surveillance photos, what he wondered about the most was all of Dev's tattoos.

He had a memory of watching Dev in class as the then-boy drew caricatures on the side of his schoolwork. The evil devils he'd drawn had confused Cash. He had never seen anyone purposely choose to engage with the darker side of life.

The photos of the man today... Cash's body tightened. Those were forever etched in his memory. Dev had turned out gorgeous. Seriously a stunner. Beautifully made and handsome, tempting as sin. He carried himself as a rebel, one who faced life on his terms. Dev's extensive rap sheet spoke of someone unafraid to break the rules. His Child Protective Services records hadn't been easy to read either.

He dressed in a pair of athletic shorts and a T-shirt as he reexamined his gut feelings. The operation's leads, those above Malik, were clearly not running the case well... A quiet rap on the room's door drew his attention. He'd been so lost to his past he'd completely forgotten the gravity of the situation that had brought him to Dallas in the first place.

He took quiet steps toward his weapon on the desk.

The gentle knock came again. A softer knock, maybe a woman. Maybe a ruse. He edged up to the peephole to see Shanna Fox standing alone in front of his door.

"I'm alone," she said quietly as if she knew his thoughts.

*Hmm.* He lowered his pistol, stood behind the door and pulled it open. She came fully inside, glanced back at him, and lifted both hands in the air as the door closed automatically behind her. She grinned.

"I'm sorry, you surprised me..." He stood there, gun in hand, feeling silly for the precautions.

"No, it happens every time someone new learns who I am," she explained. Her voice was softer when she added, "I only came by to say I've been fully updated on your file." Her direct gaze never wavered from his. "I was young when all that went down with you and Dev. Too young to remember the attack itself. I have questions and can't find the answers in Dev's file."

Yeah, he bet she had questions about a time that stayed locked in his head and never escaped his lips. Cash went for his desk, holstering his weapon.

"You were targeted by a gang of intermediate-aged children. Dev took up for you but not before you sustained substantial injuries."

Cash nodded at the sugarcoated explanation. "I wasn't expected to survive."

She nodded. He couldn't tell if she had known his death was the ultimate goal in the street gang attack or not. "Dev jumped into the fight while he sent Keyes to run for help."

Cash nodded again.

"Why were those kids after you with such a vengeance?" She tilted her head as if she could somehow glean the information she wanted directly from him, without him having to speak the words aloud.

Cash now knew the answer, but only after the years' long court proceedings to punish those involved. He still found it hard to say the gang members had targeted him due to his perpetual happiness, his easy acceptance, and the writing on the wall about his sexuality.

The older bullies had set their sights on him from the first day he had enrolled in their school.

"You don't have to answer. Why did Dev jump in to help?"

Cash honestly had no idea. They'd been classmates and nothing more. For Cash, he'd watched Dev flagrantly disregard the rules of the school. The young boy never turned in one scrap of homework but could make straight As on all the tests. That had intrigued Cash. He remembered trying to make friends with Dev, saying *hello* to him at every opportunity but never got a single response in return.

"Don't want to answer that one either?" Shanna let out a frustrated breath, her brow furrowed.

"I don't have an answer. I've been through years of counseling and the required mental health care the job requires. I have a proven track record. I can handle this job." He started to go through the diatribe he'd been scolding himself with all evening.

"You knew me when you first saw me," Shanna said, cutting him off. "I was four when it happened."

Finally, she asked a question he was willing to answer. "You were a teenager when the first conviction came up for parole. I was in Maine at the time, and we live-streamed the proceedings. Dev wasn't there, but you were with your mom. It's how I recognized you so fast."

"Your attack stayed with me for a long time. When I took this position, I looked for you, but they sealed your information," Shanna explained, she looked pained as she spoke. "Now I understand better why."

"It took me quite a while to get back on my feet again. I was homeschooled after that." Cash let go of an unsteady breath and partially shared what he remembered. Something he hadn't done with anyone since the attack. "It turned out to be a targeted gang initiation. They tagged me as a goodie-goodie Christian and gay. An easy target in a rough neighborhood. They planned to end my life that day."

She let go of her own breath and pierced him with her stare. "Then I'll tell you a truth. That day in court, when I was thirteen years old, I decided to go into law enforcement. Where Dev always uses his fists to stand up for the underdog, I wanted more power at my back. It was because of you and him that I'm standing here today."

"How did you get on this case?" he asked. He aimed for a tone somewhere between questioning and encouraging.

Her gaze narrowed on him. She struggled to answer, and he wasn't certain why. She also gave nothing away in her stare. So damned tough.

"You're not the only one holding personal secrets close. All I'm willing to say is that I refuse to become one of *them*." She went for the door, placing her hand on the doorknob. "You're moving into my brother's new rental property tomorrow. Over the last few years, he appears to be putting distance between himself and the club. Keyes seems to be doing the same thing. I'm not sure it's gonna be enough to keep either of them out of the crossfire. But my father and the others? They're in over their heads and deserve what's coming to them."

She had no doubt in her mind what she said was true.

"I won't hesitate to arrest your brother if that's any concern to you, but there is a small part of me that hopes he's an innocent." Cash revealed his one truth, and the world didn't swallow him whole. "If he's disconnected from the club, my hope might be more credible."

She grinned broadly and laughed an almost silent laugh. "My brother's not innocent by any stretch of the imagination, but I'd rather he turn state witness than spend the rest of his life in prison." After a minute of silence, she shook her head, and added, "And I don't see it happening. He's an anarchist to his core...but he does love those little girls, so maybe."

Cash nodded. Very much the impression he got of Dev's file.

"I haven't eaten, and there's a lot to this case. Why don't I order in, and you fill me in?" Cash suggested. Shanna had helped pull his thoughts back to center. For that, he appreciated her. And having one Fox at his back helped ease the burden of being completely alone on this assignment.

Shanna froze in her spot as if assessing him again, but this time it was different. She surprised him by pointing to herself. "Gay. I'm with Emma right now. If that's what's on your mind."

"Gay too," he said, pointing to himself, resisting a laugh. Apparently, she thought he might be looking for a hookup. Definitely the wrong Fox for that one-night stand.

With those cards on the table, her pretty face morphed into something extraordinarily attractive. "Well then. I have connections for dinner. I know the chef at Beto & Son in Trinity Grove. If I can get us some food delivered, you want some?"

"Absolutely," he agreed, having no idea what food category might be covered by a Beto & Son but willing to give it a try.

She visibly relaxed as she reached for her cell phone in her back pocket. "I'll order if that's all right with you. Emma's downstairs. She can grab my laptop from the car and come up. Sound good?"

He nodded, feeling like the facts in the case had shifted again. They'd established a tentative truce and were building a solid rapport. Everything in his gut said Shanna had spoken the truth. If nothing else, he wouldn't have to be alone tonight which was good. He didn't think he could lift another weight to work off any more tension.

# Chapter 6

"You're late," Tena said, flicking her cigarette on the front porch ledge, smashing the butt out as she took the steps down.

"I'm ten minutes early," Dev argued, walking through the freshly cut lawn toward the front door of his Sunnyvale home.

While darkness had fallen, every light on the property was on, lighting his way. That explained their through-the-roof electric bill.

"Who's that?" he asked with a chin-tilt in the direction of the car idling at the curb. The one that had blocked Dev from parking in his usual spot.

"My ride," she said as if that should be obvious and rolled her eyes in such a way to make sure he knew the stupidity of his question.

Her high heels ate up the front walkway in her hurry to get inside the waiting car. Her strut was catwalk worthy, a master in a pair of shoes that lifted her height by at least five inches. She was still short though.

When she turned on her heel, she gave all the attitude in the world while sticking out a hand and clicking her long

"Y'all eat dinner?" he asked, looking inside the house as he grabbed the door from Abi and nodded her inside. He resisted the urge to look over his shoulder as the car pulled away. Mae's body went ramrod straight, and he put her down in the front entry. She grabbed the wings Abi held and the door closed behind them.

"We were waitin' on you," Abi said nonchalantly, not an ounce of emotion in her tone as she twisted the lock on the front door. At least someone in the house listened to him about their safety.

"You know, there was a time you were excited to see me," he said, patting Abi's head as she walked around him toward the kitchen.

Abi had just turned eleven and was a little badass in the making. She loved makeup, jewelry, pop-art, and TikTok. She videoed herself all the time. He was the one blocking her from taking her videos live online, making her resent the hell out of him. He didn't give a single shit. He knew firsthand the kinds of predators who lived online and off. He'd protect her from life's demons as long as he could.

"I don't remember that time." She tossed her long hair over her shoulder, heading toward the kitchen table.

Mae was jumping up and down beside him, extending the wings to Dev with both hands.

"Here, Daddy. Abi didn't want to wear hers so you can."

The wings were green and yellow with lots of glitter. He held back his groan. The things he did for his daughters. He took the offering and moved around her, shrugging out of his cut. He tossed it over the sofa and pushed one arm through the elastic band holding the wings to his back.

He hadn't known when he'd bought the things that they came in different sizes. Unfortunately, he had bought the adult versions.

Mae just liked him so damn much. He'd do anything to make sure that trend continued.

When he put them on, her face went through a range of emotions, from anticipation to excitement to extreme love.

"You look so pretty, Daddy," she finally said, beaming her immense approval. Her arms lifted, and he swept her up as he went through the house. Regardless of what Tena thought about their home, he liked the open floor plan, pretty paint colors on the walls, and the high ceilings encased in rich crown molding. He had a strong sense of pride for what he'd provided for his kids. They were in a better environment and tucked away safe if anything did happen to him or the club.

"What's for dinner?" he asked.

"Mama said you'd fix us dinner," Abi said, working on her homework.

Of course Tena did.

She was such a fucking bitch.

=♥=

Dev stepped out onto the back porch, quietly shutting the screen door behind him. He didn't turn on the light, needing a few minutes of darkened solitude before he spent the next few hours going over the custom designs he had to ink over the next few days.

Why was it so damned hard to get the kids to bed at a decent hour?

Their little bodies needed peaceful rest, and he bet their brains did too. It had to be after nine. Abi was still awake, reading. Who read before bed? But Abi liked her books in that same way that Shanna always had and look how good that turned out for his sister. A nurse. Pretty impressive. He wished the girls had a better relationship with Shanna. They needed a good influence.

At least the nanny had found a way to add structure to the girls' evening rituals.

Homework, dinner, bath, pj's and bed.

Maybe he remembered his mother trying to do those same things when he was little. No one could have wrangled him into bed like he did the girls, and if they had, it was only because he planned to sneak out the minute the lights went out.

Abi was a real influence on Mae. She allowed Mae to share a bedroom because of her fear of the dark. He found his heart regenerated under the love and care his children had for each other.

Dev tucked his fingers into the front pockets of his jeans and listened to the sounds of the night. They had space here on the property, maybe two acres if he remembered correctly. The lawn was nicely manicured, per the requirements of the HOA. The prospects had built a privacy fence around the property line. They stayed hidden. The fence and their utility building office made it easier for them to do their jobs. Eventually, he wanted to build the girls a swimming pool.

It all felt so normal to be there in Sunnyvale. A good, protected life. Why didn't Tena see it that way?

He'd also gotten into the rental property game, but he'd kept that a secret from anyone inside the club for fear his brothers might want to move in. They sucked at paying bills on time, or at all for that matter. Right now, that investment did nothing more than hemorrhage money. All the code requirements for the remodels were a government-issued pain in the ass. He was months into owning the property and hadn't made a dime yet. He had to stop thinking about that. Otherwise, anything good left in his attitude would tank.

His ink business had taken off. He'd signed off on a merchandise line on a whim tonight. Apparently, he had a YouTube Channel that Millie had created and was working on a TikTok with Abi's help. That might have been the only time Abi had ever shown him true respect before. His budding entrepreneur daughter wanted to monetize his appearance on Ink Life.

"She came back for the shoes," Con-man said, stepping out from his hiding spot.

Dev swung his head toward the prospect who startled the shit out of him. His heart pounded under the fear. His fists ready for the fight.

"What the fuck are you wearin'?"

*Shit.* The glitter wings. He'd completely forgotten about them. He clamped his jaw shut hard. If he could shoot laser beams from his eyes, he would have vaporized Con-man in his spot.

"What the fuck do you think I'm wearin'? I'm a goddamn fairy. This can't be the first time you've seen them on me. You're supposed to be lookin' out for my kids."

The prospect looked confused.

There was a moment when the guy opened his mouth then closed it again. He finally lowered his gaze to the concrete. "I don't normally look in the house. I don't wanna see nothin' I shouldn't…"

"You better not be lookin' in my goddamn house," Dev shot out protectively. "Unless you hear somethin' that makes you need to look."

He understood the difficult position he put Con-man in but didn't give a single shit. He had to offset the pussy position these colorful wings put him in. He was an authority figure to the recruits. He had to show strength at all times.

"I..." the prospect started. "You..."

"I. You. Yeah, shut the fuck up," Dev grumbled, as if the guy were as stupid as he could be.

Only then did Dev shrug the wings off and drop them on the patio table. He pulled out a heavy iron patio chair, scraping it along the concrete, and took a seat. He pushed his legs out in front of him, crossing at the ankle. "Has anything out of the ordinary happened?"

When the awkwardness between them continued, Dev let go of a sigh and kicked at the chair closest to Con-man. The only invitation he was going to give. Dev crossed his arms over his chest. Warmth and humidity hung in the air, dampening his forehead.

Finally, Con-man took the chair, remaining on guard if his stiff spine said anything. "Not like you're thinkin'."

"What am I thinkin'?" Dev asked, lifting his gaze from his boots to look at the prospect.

"Your ex keeps puttin' on a show for the guys. Makes everyone uncomfortable. We work hard to be unseen, but she parades around barely wearin' clothes, seekin' out the guys' attention."

Of course Tena would do something like that.

"I thought you didn't look in the house."

Con-man sat up straighter, if that were possible. "She comes outside. Whatever she's on seems to be becomin' a problem. Last night she came out the front door that way."

Tena was a damned hard thing to resist. He'd had a hard time trying to quit her himself. Didn't matter. He didn't care who fucked her or who she fucked, but he had one singular concern. "She's off limits. I don't want any slip ups when the girls are home." Dev covered his eyes with a hand. She made everything harder than it had to be. "I'll talk to her."

"It's a quiet neighborhood." Con-man seemed to have something else on his mind.

"Hmm," he managed. He wasn't going to pull the topic from the man. He pondered the Tena issue. She had to keep her clothes on. What was she thinking? No matter how desensitized the girls were to Tena's nudity, they had to see that other mothers wore their clothes all the time.

"Do you do ink for club members?" Con-man asked.

He sometimes inked for his brothers. They tended to like a lot of ink but didn't require it to be the best quality and certainly didn't want to pay the high prices for his custom work. If the prospects found out, his chair would be full all the time at the lower rate.

"My schedule's pretty full, but what're you wantin' done?"

Con-man finally dropped the guard he'd been hanging on to and eased back in the seat. "I saw this snake that I thought was cool. It started from the thigh and went onto the belly. It's been stuck in my head, but I'd want it to come up my arm and land on my pec. Something mean and fierce."

How the fuck could this guy not realize Dev was responsible for all of Tena's ink? The snake coming from the thigh went between Tena's legs, covered her cunt, and finished on her belly. It had been Dev's first vaginal tattoo. The snakes head resting on her belly had a sexual meaning to them. Dev was the serpent and the location showed where she wanted his load to land when he finished.

How many of these prospects was she fucking?

She strutted around naked all the damn time.

Her perfectly shaped breasts were fully inked as was all the skin between her legs. She was a calling card of inked sexuality. He wasn't kidding about her hooking. Sex was a sport for her. One she should earn a gold medal in.

He felt defeated as fuck.

"Talk to me after the holidays," Dev found himself saying. "I'm goin' inside. It's been a long day."

"I heard Smoke was dyin'. I didn't know him…" Con-man started, sincerity in his voice.

"Then your life is already better than mine," Dev cut him off and rose from the chair. He didn't look back as he made his way inside.

# Chapter 7

Something about this area of South Dallas spoke straight to Dev's heart. He loved riding through these streets, close to the Bishop Arts area, between there and Trinity Grove. The contrast and struggle between the new and old, in both attitude and aesthetics, appealed to him.

New businesses settled in next to the old family homes, built back in the days when this area was considered solidly middle class. Way before Dev was ever born. He respected the tenacity of the holdouts, hanging on to their property while the community progressed around them.

He didn't see the rejuvenation as a takeover but instead as an attempt to bring a lost vibrance back to a special part of Dallas. Dev had spent more nights than he could count, committing both the rundown homes and new modern architecture, including all the different types of people that came along with both, to the pages of his sketchbooks.

He had dozens of drawings depicting his views of the changes. Showing the give and take between the moderately wealthy versus those struggling to hang on to their roots.

Another bonus to the area was that they were on the edge of downtown Dallas. The decorative bridges and towering skyscrapers were a scenic backdrop and only a few miles away. So when a property had come up for sale, he'd jumped at the chance to own in this neighborhood. The first property he'd ever purchased by himself.

He'd bought the large single-family home that had been converted into four smaller apartment units. It had required a considerable amount of work, but he'd tackled the remodel with the stash of cash he had saved and ended up taking one of the units to live in himself.

Dev let the pipes of his Harley rumble as he slowed the bike, taking a corner onto his street. A U-Haul sat parked in front of his house.

He didn't remember the leasing company notifying him of a new tenant.

A U-Haul could mean a lot of things.

His mouth watered in anticipation over the possibility that there was a robbery underway. His always pumping inner adrenaline, kicked up a notch at the opportunity to unleash some pent-up energy.

The idea grew, building merit inside his mind.

Tingles set the nerve endings along his skin to a flutter at the prospect of a fight. He lived to find a robbery in progress, especially if it was to his property.

He'd come in with his guns blazing.

Dev didn't slow his roll. He drove past the U-Haul, its raised sliding cargo door allowed him to see inside. As if popped with a pin, his balloon of anticipation deflated.

Damn.

That wasn't his shit stacked neatly in the trailer.

Surveying the area, he didn't see anyone around as he popped the curb and drove up the center walkway to the front porch. Sure, it was a dick move to park on the front porch, but he didn't give a shit, he owned the fucking building. Besides, he was a dick. Dev grinned at that thought as he angled the bike, riding up the two front porch steps.

He let the bike idle and removed his helmet, pushing at the hair falling forward over his eyes. He decided right then to have his mother schedule that hair appointment she'd nagged him about getting. With a flick of his foot, he engaged the kickstand, but continued to let the bike rumble loudly under the covered awning as he reached in his saddlebag. He produced his cut, sliding it on for nothing more than the intimidation it generally brought. Then grabbed his pistol, tucking it into his back waistband.

He finally cut the engine and lifted a leg over the bike, waiting for someone to acknowledge his presence and clue him in to what the hell was going on at his building. Since the rest of his saddlebag contained all the drugs he'd been able to swipe before yesterday's run, and the cash he'd made for going along on the deal, he unbuckled the custom made bag and draped the heavy load over one shoulder.

Two young, well put together Hispanic men came bounding out the front door, happily trotting down the steps. They didn't pay Dev any attention. Then the man following those two caught Dev's undivided interest. So much so that his racing mind, which had sped up to a million miles per hour in anticipation of a fight, went suddenly blank. His gaze tracked each of the man's steps as he took the front porch steps down and headed toward the truck.

The guy didn't look like he belonged in this neighborhood, but boy was Dev glad for the chance to see him. Tall, tight, and fit. A body sculpted together in one of those fancy gyms, not from any sort of physical labor.

Talk about mouthwatering. Fuck, he'd like a piece of all that goodness. His cock plumped, zeroing in on what it wanted.

He wondered if the pretty young professional could handle all Dev had to give.

With his lip tucked between his teeth, Dev stared at the curve of the pretty boy's ass.

If his face came anywhere close to the hotness of that body... Jeezus.

Dev's cock hardened so fast he almost winced at the pain from being cramped inside his jeans.

He looked down at his dick. What the hell? He'd just been thinking of shooting a robber point blank between the eyes, now he was hard as fucking stone.

Dev forced his gaze off the pretty boy. He needed to get his head—both of them—back in line.

With his eyes averted, the racing in his head revved up. This time, the chaos filled with images of him bending the pretty boy over his Harley, driving hard into that bouncing ass.

He didn't even know this guy.

Maybe the pretty boy was married.

Maybe he worked for the moving van company.

Maybe he owned the company.

Maybe he was from the leasing agency.

Dev gave an internal shake to loosen all the random questions pelting his noggin. Why did it matter?

Dev's feet moved him forward as he glanced back, watching the first two guys jump into the back of the U-Haul.

"What's goin' on?" Dev finally asked from his position at the edge of the front porch steps. His gaze went back to the man. Quiet descended over his thoughts again.

Pretty boy's head jerked toward him. A small intake of breath showed his surprise, as if Dev had gone completely unnoticed.

Weird. In every situation, Dev always owned all the space around him.

Everyone paid attention to him.

"I'm moving in," the pretty boy, with the perfect sweep of chestnut-colored hair, said and took the end of the sofa as the other two navigated it off the truck.

Pretty boy didn't say *we*, he said *I*. Then promptly ignored Dev again.

Dev's eyes narrowed as the pretty boy and one of the other two men moved the sofa toward the building.

With a smirk, he plodded a slow gait inside, cutting off the moving team from entering first. His only excuse for his rude behavior—other than rude being his default choice—was he suddenly realized he didn't appreciate being ignored.

Especially with such a monster hard-on tightening his jeans.

The guys followed behind him, up the staircase. He moved methodically, step by step, reaching for his house key.

He wondered how heavy that sofa really was. But they didn't complain.

"You're my neighbor?" the pretty boy called out in a friendly tone. "I'm Cash Ryan."

Dev looked over his shoulder, continuing to cut them off from crossing the landing to the other apartment on the second floor. This Cash Ryan must be renting the unit directly across from his. Pretty boy held the bulk of the sofa from the rear, still only halfway up the stairs.

For the third time in a matter of minutes, Dev's head cleared.

It startled and confused him to have so much silence in a place that typically rivaled noise levels in Grand Central Station.

He didn't care for confusing. Especially not today.

His damn cock sure didn't seem to mind, though. It had only grown more painful at the sound of the deep, inviting voice.

"I own the buildin'," he finally said, gathering his wits as he opened his apartment door. He still paused before stepping inside, finally letting them by with the couch.

When Cash passed him, he stuck out a hand. "I'll be quiet. Barely know I'm here."

Dev looked the guy up and down before taking his offered hand. The face did hold up to the rest of the physique. A strong, clean-shaven jaw, perfect pouty lips, a straight nose that might have shown hints of a break sometime in his life, big green eyes, and short, chestnut-colored hair. Fuck, he was beautiful in a highlands kind of way.

"Can't say the same for me," Dev answered.

Their eyes met and held. The handshake lasted for what seemed like forever. All the pain and suffering of the last few weeks instantly vanished. His breath slowed and his senses went on high alert.

In that moment, his dick wasn't his guide. He was being filled from the inside out with a sense of peace that was fucking weird.

Cash didn't shy away from Dev's boldness. He let go of his hand and started walking away, the sofa taking all his attention again. Dev watched that ass go. The man wore his clothes so tight he could make out the crease bisecting his ass cheeks.

The sizzle he'd been missing for a while now flared, burning a trail of desire over every fiber of his body.

Oh hell. Dev made himself go fully inside the apartment, still staring at the guy's ass as he slowly closed the door. A pretty boy next door. Maybe the universe did like him after all.

=♥=

The apartment building's back door swung shut behind Cash, plunging him into the pitch-dark interior. If creepiness were a factor in judging how empty the building was at the moment, then he was indeed very alone. However, his handler hid inside Cash's apartment above.

Out of all the scenarios Cash had conjured in his overly active imagination about the sexy Devin Fox, he never imagined how bad a landlord he would be. This building wasn't fit for tenants. Besides the property being in one hell of a bad part of town, there were zero security measures to keep the occupants safe. Anyone could pick the basic lock on both the front and back doors in about five seconds flat.

The fancy new BMW they'd assigned him to help cement his undercover profession as a medical consultant wouldn't last a week without an attempted theft in this neighborhood.

All his intuitive gauges pinged in the red zone. He couldn't muster a single good feeling about any of this, and that was with the constant security surveillance team sent with him by the attorney general's office.

His partner, Special Agent David Durham, had worked with him on his last two assignments. There were three total on David's security team, including David, who was tasked with the responsibility of providing protection for Cash. Right now, they were secretly set up in a rental across the street that offered full sightlines. Yet Cash still felt completely exposed.

He envisioned about ninety different ways this could go very wrong.

No question, someone in the local division was playing games with this case. It could easily be to the detriment of his entire team.

The mismanagement pissed Cash off, and he couldn't wait for his check-in with the AG's office.

This dereliction of duty in securing him a reasonable place to execute his undercover assignment was about the only thing that could take his mind off the sizzle that had ignited deep within him whenever he remembered the way his hand felt inside Dev's for the first time.

The handshake was bold and direct, confident and strong. His dick ached to feel the strength of Dev's palm wrapped around his shaft. Could it be twenty years now since he'd seen Dev? He'd been young, maybe not able to process what he was feeling, but he'd gotten his first ever boner over the bad boy.

Thinking of the foxy Devilman eased Cash's frustration with the job.

Today, when that blue-eyed gaze bore into his, he knew he was willing to cross the lines of appropriate professional behavior to endear himself to the man. Cash envisioned such a handsome man to have the most beautiful cock and heavy sac swinging between his thighs. Dev made being bad look so damn good.

Surprising for a man who had always liked his partners to be on the side of good.

Cash made the turn to the stairwell, but completely misjudged the height of the first step. Even with his long legs that stair tread was still an awkward size step up. He stumbled forward, landing on his knee as he fell all over the staircase, reaching for anything to brace his fall.

He barely caught himself before he face-planted against the hard wood.

Anger, with a good dose of knee pain, had him releasing a string of curse words that could rival any he'd heard in the surveillance footage of the Disciples. He pushed up, gripping the railing tighter, hoping like hell he'd saved the to-go food order he'd been carrying in his other hand.

As he stood, his cell phone vibrated in his front pocket. He fished the phone out to see a text message from Joe.

"*Your phone has a flashlight.*" The word *dumbass* was implied but not stated in the text.

Then the flashlight turned on without him initiating the app. *Huh.*

If Joe had the ability to turn on cell phone apps, why hadn't he done so sooner?

Ignoring the knee pain, Cash bounded the rest of the way up the stairs, two at a time. He'd only made this food run for Joe in the first place. Apparently, the guy ate like crap, making Cash's earlier grocery store visit for him alone.

He'd have to learn these things. That was the toll of being all Joe had to physically look at while hiding undercover inside the apartment for the length of the assignment.

Cash pushed through the front door, again met with complete darkness.

What the hell was up with the lack of lighting?

He let the apartment door slam shut behind after a purposeful shove.

Joe came from the second bedroom that wasn't much bigger than a study, where his surveillance equipment was installed. To the untrained eye, Cash could easily call it a home office. Joe would live, eat, and sleep inside that room while watching everything Cash did, being his direct support staff and right-hand man.

Setting up Joe's eyes and ears had been Cash's afternoon project. He placed recording equipment all over the property. The only space inside the building he hadn't bugged was Dev's unit itself. No one had any real idea what was going on inside there. He needed to get his eyes inside that apartment and plant special undetectable equipment, making sure Dev never knew he was being recorded. Cash's next priority.

"Your fall looked intense, I bet it hurt." Joe said the words as if he cared but his entire focus was on the sack in Cash's hand. "You know it's fajitas, right? It's gonna be all slopped together now."

Joe grabbed the sack and started for the kitchen on the other side of the apartment. Cash's bedroom was just past there. The foyer, living room, and a smallish table and chairs were located in the middle of the apartment.

"Yeah? How did you see that? I couldn't see shit." Out of nothing but pride, he refused to limp as he made his way to his bedroom.

"I tapped into the night camera option you installed today. I could see you pretty well. Good call on adding those features. I was rooting for you to remember the flashlight, but you didn't. Your head's got to be swimming, trying to catch up," Joe rambled as he took the Styrofoam food containers from the bag.

"When are we getting the surveillance equipment for the landlord's place?" Cash asked.

"You have to go downtown tomorrow and pick it up. It's brand-new stuff. They want to train you on the installation," Joe said, popping a piece of the fajita meat in his mouth.

Cash nodded and flipped on the bedroom light before shutting the door behind him. He looked down at his favorite pair of joggers that now had a gaping hole at the knee. Dammit. He loved the way these fit. They were expensive too. The skid and oozing blood meant nothing compared to losing these pants. The government was paying for this. He'd charge another pair as soon as possible.

# Chapter 8

Another same night mandatory church meeting.

What the fuck? Why couldn't these closed-door secret sessions happen at a decent hour of the day? How about a coffee and donuts before the day starts meeting?

He liked donuts. A sugar rush could get the blood flowing pretty good.

Yeah, a good morning church meeting.

Dev fought the yawn wanting to be free. If he dared let it go, a string more would follow, not stopping until he dropped his ass into bed.

A nice warm bed seemed damn enticing.

His old man should have just adjourned the original meeting for this evening—instead of suspending it for a two-hour break—after being told that sorry motherfucker, Smoke, had finally kicked the bucket.

A rickety old bucket that had been on borrowed time for years.

What did kicking a bucket even mean?

What a dumb saying.

Dev had somehow managed to talk himself behind the wheel of Keyes's brand-new fancy pickup truck and was pulling them back into the parking lot of the Disciples clubhouse.

They'd eaten a good meal together at a familiar diner with cream colored plastic plates. Then sat hunched over the table, working on the design for Keyes's massive new back ink.

Dev had kept a careful eye on his buddy. He hadn't spotted a single sign that he wasn't dealing well with the loss of his dick of a dad.

His previous suspicions about Keyes came roaring back.

Being so well-adjusted and balanced during such an awful time had to mean his buddy was hiding something major. Dev wasn't a fool. He'd spent his entire life beside Keyes. His friend would have never picked an expensive truck like this for himself. Keyes could barely spend a dollar unless it was absolutely necessary, meaning Dev had been forced to lay two extra dollars on the table to increase Keyes's one dollar cheap-ass tip to the waitress tonight.

One good thing about Smoke being in Dev's life was that Smoke as a parental figure had taught Dev everything he needed to know about parenting. So long as every situation became WWSD—What would Smoke do?—then Dev methodically did the exact opposite.

Smoke was also Dev's club brother once he'd earned his patch, teaching him it was okay to hate his siblings. That joke cracked him up but only for a second. His brow dropped when he replayed how his father had singled Keyes out to tell him the great news about Smoke. The side of Dev that always stood up in protection of his friend leapt forward. Smoke wasn't the only Disciple to hurt Keyes over the years. The rest of the club had turned their backs to the rampant abuse, making them culpable as far as Dev was concerned.

The shoddy hierarchy between him and his old man was beginning to blur into a haze of *fuck you*. Father, brother, leader of a club Dev was positioned to take over one day. Factor in distrust, abuse, and lack of respect between him and his old man. And that was before his old man had put his hands on Dev tonight, manhandling him as he reared forward to stand with Keyes.

Shit was always so complicated.

None of this was working for Dev like it once had.

He'd be smart to take a page from Keyes's new playbook. Then burn that bitch, use the ashes to create a potion, and spray that shit over his body every single day.

Although, being considered number two in the organization had some benefits. At dinner, he'd fired off a group text message to all of Smoke's newly recruited club prospects, putting them on blast for multiple violations to the Disciples charter. Those losers were on the road out of the club. Dev didn't like Keyes being disrespected and Smoke had poisoned those useless prospects to his son.

The way Keyes smiled when he had showed him the group message he had crafted made Dev promise himself no more bullshit ever again.

"Church meetin's happenin' more frequently?" Keyes asked, sitting in the passenger seat.

"Apparently," Dev said, swinging wide to park the truck in an empty space. "I'm not sure I've been included. I feel like flexin' some muscle to fuck shit up. Find out why." Dev put the truck in park and pushed the button to cut the engine. "But if they were meetin' over Smoke, who gives a fuck. I should have killed that bastard myself. I actually can't believe I didn't."

The heavy rain from earlier in the evening had resulted in a biting cold front pushing through Dallas.

Dev glanced over, drawing Keyes's attention. "You good?"

His buddy took a minute to consider the question. Keyes stared at Dev then looked away, out the front windshield for so long he wasn't sure his friend planned to respond.

"Honest answer. Been excluded for a long time. Don't see that changin' with my old man dead. I've wised up from all this. They forced me to get a taste of the world without the club. It's not that bad out there."

Keyes's unguarded explanation touched something inside Dev.

The heady thoughts had him finally letting go of a jaw-cracking yawn that lasted several long seconds in both size and duration.

It spoke of a tired that was years in the making.

He'd spent ten hours hunched over back-to-back clients today, working nonstop.

Tomorrow was going to be another long day.

"My brain's fuckin' racin' again. It's speedin' up to a thousand thoughts a minute. It makes everything harder for me, but you know I get what you're sayin'. We've been fucked up since birth, and this club's at the root of the problem."

Keyes interrupted him before he could get on a roll. "Be careful self-medicatin'. The shit you do's addictin' as hell. You know I'm always here for you."

"I got you too, bro, but I need a fuckin' bump," Dev said, scrubbing a hand down his face.

"So, you're back on?" Keyes asked. Nothing else mattered to his friend as much as Dev's mental health and possibly downward spiraling addiction. Keyes didn't get it, though. He never had. Methamphetamines sped Keyes up too much. But it was like a nectar from the gods for Dev.

Rampant sex had been his serious addiction, requiring actual restraint to master. And that bitch called him back time and again, pulling him in. Meth? He could put that shit down on a whim and not touch it again. For Dev, meth gave him focus.

"No, not back on yet. I have it sittin' there waitin' though. I gotta get out of my head if it's nothin' more than for a few hours."

And there was his bottom line.

"You need to go to the head doctor," Keyes said, like a broken record. "They have real medicines to slow your shit down. Help you out without destroyin' your fuckin' body, like I keep sayin'."

"*You* need to go to the head doctor," Dev shot back. Keyes was a different kind of fucked-up than Dev but still very screwed in the head.

"No doubt I do," Keyes answered with a bark. An exasperated hiss escaped, showing his buddy's disgust.

Two could play the game of how crazy the other was living their life.

"Wanna talk about the reason for that particular tattoo?"

"Fuck no, I don't," Keyes replied in a bluster, as if that were now the stupidest thing Dev had ever said. "If I wanted to talk about it, I would have said somethin' durin' the last two hours we sat together to set the design."

Exactly the comic relief Dev needed.

He barked out a laugh and leaned his head against the headrest, letting levity have the moment. Based on the firm set of Keyes's jaw and the tic double-timing there, he didn't see the humor but also didn't say anything more.

"I know I gotta figure out my head," Dev finally agreed. "Tena's not doin' too good. She can't handle the burbs but the bigger problem is she doesn't wanna be a mother every day. She needs a better partner."

"Why'd you put 'em all so far out?"

Dev rolled his head against the headrest, turning from Keyes to look out the windshield. "I don't know. I got this feelin' I can't place, but I think the real reason is that I want the girls to have a more normal life."

"Hmm," Keyes said in agreement.

"I go stay out there three or four nights a week. I take 'em to school on my days. I figured halftime could give Tena time to herself. I also got 'em a full-time nanny. Like she teaches them manners and how to eat with all the different forks and spoons. My mom loves her. And the chick wants to be called Nanny. Isn't that some shit?"

"Hmm," Keyes said again, this time softer with more hints of approval.

"The school they go to is cool. Like really normal. Tena's bein' a bitch on purpose. I got an earful this mornin' when I dropped 'em off. Tena picked 'em up from school the day before wearin' one of her slutty tank tops, no bra. They could see everything. She's so fuckin' proud of her body and tits. They wanted to call CPS on us. It wouldn't be good if they did. She's strung out hard. Spendin' too much money on everything." Dev swiveled his head back to Keyes. "It's why I haven't used. Tryin' to be basic for the girls. They don't know Tena's a hooker. Don't think they need to know, right?"

Keyes paused then nodded. "I don't know how to parent, but it sounds like you're doin' all the right shit. At least you're tryin'. What about Holly?"

Dev gave a humorless laugh. He hadn't told Keyes the truth about Holly either. "I think she's more a transition piece. She's a closeted speed freak. Like Tena just in a more normal package. I finally figured out she wanted me for my connections. Got me to bring her all sorts of shit. Just like Tena."

"Do you need your apartment back?" Keyes asked. He'd been staying at Dev's old apartment when Dev started shacking up with Holly, months ago.

That was why he hadn't told Keyes he had broken it off with Holly. Keyes would sleep in this truck before he ever burdened Dev. "Nah, I got another place."

Keyes furrowed his brow. "When did you do that?"

"While back. No big deal. Old house with four apartments. Fixin' 'em up. Rentin' 'em out. Didn't tell the club. Not that it's a secret. I'm not jivin' well here right now." Dev shrugged, nodding toward the clubhouse. Sugarcoated, but hit the high notes.

They both looked in the direction and sound of his old man's pipes, alerting them to his arrival. He was hardcore that way. He rode his Harley everywhere, no matter the weather conditions.

"He's lookin' aged," Keyes said.

"He's knockin' on sixty." Maybe he'd already had that birthday. Who knew for sure. "That's a hundred and seven in normal people years."

"He should get his ass to the doctor too."

Dev chuckled. His old man hadn't been to a real doctor ever in his life. He didn't believe in modern medicine or the for-profit healthcare system. Yet his old man had been mighty proud of Shanna getting into nursing school. He was hard to figure out.

"There's a divide comin' between me and my old man. It's growin' pretty solid. I don't like the way he disrespects my mom. Times are different. That shit doesn't fly the way it used to."

Keyes barked out a harsh, bitter sounding laugh. Dev wasn't sure what it meant except Keyes had never engaged in the whoring ways of the club. To his core, he was gay, and always had been. Came that way. He never even pretended to indulge in the opposite sex just to fit in with everybody else.

"It's messin' with my mom's head. She got her tits done again." Dev saw the repeat plastic surgery sessions as a cry for attention. She spent most of her time alone these days.

"She's still young," Keyes said after a few long seconds of silence. Dev looked over at Keyes, their troubled gazes held. "Fifteen when you were born so forty-four now. Your dad's gonna be sixty. They're in different places."

He and Keyes shared something meaningful in their exchange.

Who knew what.

Fuck his old man.

Dev let go of a breath as a giant raindrop slapped down on the windshield, drawing his wayward thoughts to the storm ramping up again outside. The crack of booming thunder with bolts of lightning streaking across the sky spoke of the fury warring both outside and inside his heart.

"Remember how we always wanted to start a custom bike company?" Dev asked, thinking about all the planning they'd done in their younger days.

"Think about it on the regular. I never wanted to do tires."

"Not sure I ever wanted to do tattoos like this. I used to draw pages and pages of sled designs. I wanted to do custom art to help drive the price of our sales up…" The memories held Dev transfixed. "Now, I'd do custom bikes but make 'em affordable for guys like us."

"Yeah. Let's go." Keyes pulled at the door handle to open the truck's door. "The sooner we hear what they have to say, the sooner we can leave."

"This Sunday for your ink?" Dev asked and reached for his handle.

Keyes nodded and ducked out of the truck. The door slammed before Dev grew a pair and followed. The few minutes of unguarded conversation had him bared raw.

He darted out. Even with a fast jog, the downpour had him soaked and chilled to the bone by the time he pushed past the prospect guarding the front door of the clubhouse.

Dev shoved his shoulders back, standing to his full height, and bowed his chest. He refused to take anymore shit from the old fuckers in this club.

=♥=

Lost in thought, Cash let the screen of his laptop dim while staring off into the silent living room. He scanned the furnishings. If the cozy surroundings spoke to his tastes, he apparently liked earth tones and reds.

He'd never had to purchase his own sofa or kitchen table before. Between assignments, the government put him up in long term suites, waiting for his next gig.

Why did his life suddenly feel lonely?

He wasn't certain except he'd never had an assignment start so slowly before.

When the computer went dark, it took away the only light in the room.

What was the deal with always having the lights turned off?

He reached across the end table for the designer lamp, extending his fingers as far as they would go and still couldn't quite reach the small knob.

Cash lifted from his comfortable position on the sofa to better reach the lamp.

At the same time the light switched on, a large crack of lightning struck so close, the living room momentarily illuminated. A harsh boom of thunder followed, rattling the windows. The sparking of the transformer could be seen through the small slats of the closed blinds. The apartment as well as the entire neighborhood block went dark.

They'd lost their electricity. Complete darkness again.

Seemed symbolic of the case too. So now, he sat in utter silence, alone in the dark, and still no idea how to begin this case.

The sky opened up, the rain pounding against the building. A violent fury of wind and weather just beyond the window.

The chilly damp air from the cold front blew through the building, reminding him why this apartment complex was not ready for tenants.

Thank goodness the heater worked. It warmed enough to stave off the extreme chill but not quite efficient enough to go without the long sleeve sweatshirt and joggers he wore. Well, at least when it had electricity to make the unit operational.

Joe's loud snore trumpeted in regular intervals in the background.

They'd have to work on silencing the snore tomorrow. Joe's quiet as a mouse reason for being there wasn't going to hold with those sounds echoing throughout the unit. Another more concerning point. If that loud clap of thunder hadn't awakened Joe, how much help could he be if things got dicey?

Cash went to the window, standing to the side, watching the wind and rain drown the homes on the street. He had listened closely to all the sounds inside the building, all night long. Dev wasn't home and hadn't been there in over thirty-six hours.

He went for his cell phone still plugged into the charger in the bedroom. It had to be two o'clock in the morning.

He'd waited until Joe had gone to bed to do a quick briefing with the AG's office and had stayed in the messaging program long after he'd given his official statement.

His direct report from the attorney general's office, Lily Collins, now Deputy Assistant Attorney General Collins, had a history as a field agent. Cash had needed someone to talk to about all the transparent and not so transparent signs that were pointing him in every which direction. Deputy Assistant Collins confirmed they had the same experience with the Dallas field office's lackadaisical approach for quite some time. It was their primary reason in installing Cash deeper undercover to sort through all the chaos and misdirection.

He understood his assignment, but how could he learn anything new when placed so far on the outside of the entire case? Being inside Dev's building was proving to be a nonstarter. How did he put himself in front of a man who was never present? At this point, no matter what time Dev got home, he couldn't force any sort of meaningful interaction.

What were his choices? Staging some sort of apartment emergency? How much time would that give him with Dev?

In talking over the possibilities and probabilities of the case, Deputy Assistant Collins had come to the conclusion that the wrong sibling had been tapped to go undercover. No one had ever tried to recruit Devilman. If there were something nefarious happening within the DEA team, bringing Shanna in might have made the Dallas office look effective without truly changing any outcome of whatever plan was playing out.

But could they actually get Dev to break ranks? To turn on his club brothers. As farfetched as the idea seemed, a night alone stewing over the possibilities had the notion taking root in a more concrete way. Except he'd bring Dev in under the AG's umbrella to help investigate the Dallas DEA's involvement.

Having Dev work with him to expose the mismanagement of the local DEA field office might solve this case faster than anyone dared to hope.

That brought him full circle with his initial field report concerns. He'd still have to have some quality time alone with Dev to learn more about the man. To figure out if they could approach him with the idea.

Cash could get a tattoo.

With a snort to himself, he shot down the idea. As much as he liked ink on others, it wasn't his thing, and they were damned permanent.

He grabbed his phone and went to the window along the back wall of his bedroom. As fast as the rain rushed in, it ebbed to a hard sprinkle.

The neighborhood's eerie quiet kicked up a notch.

The faint sounds of a muffler let Cash know that Dev rumbled down the small alley before he ever saw the 69 Mach 1. He stood there as a set of headlights came into view. Dev had a thing for loud, vintage vehicles.

Cash had shut and locked the gate when he'd arrived home this evening. Based on the way Dev used the hood of his car to nudge at the gate, he hadn't expected anything more than the flimsy latch to be set, easily knocked open. The exact reason Cash had initiated the padlock. The car idled in place for several long seconds, as if Dev were in some moment of indecision.

He quickly thought through the options. Dev could ram it and avoid the rain or get out of the car and go through the motions of having to open the locked gate, on and on.

A fifty-fifty chance as to what the biker might do.

The car reversed then stopped, the driver's side door opened. He could feel Dev's frustration when he made it to the gate and saw it was actually locked closed. He had to go back to the car, cut the engine to get his keys.

Dev pushed the gate open then hopped back in the car and started forward again. He pulled to the back of the building and parked at an angle. His hood pointing in the direction of Cash's driver's side door.

Why?

The man fascinated him. What it might be like to be so free to be yourself. Dev wore his confidence well. Cash's grin turned into a full smile when Dev looked back at the gate and flipped it off with both hands.

Dev started for the house with that swagger that spoke directly to Cash's cock. A long gait and slightly bowed legs. The tall, muscular frame was currently wrapped in a leather bomber jacket. His dark blond hair was too long for the current cut, which made it its own sexy style.

He couldn't see Dev's face but knew that left brow stayed permanently lowered. The guy questioned everything, and it showed in his face. Cash tracked every one of Dev's steps until he lost visual and faintly heard the back door close.

The mesmerized snare holding Cash to his spot at the window snapped free. He shook his head of whatever invisible tether seemed to connect his being to Dev's. It made no sense.

He listened carefully to each thudded boot step coming up the staircase.

Cash took long, quiet strides toward his front door. He wished he could say he moved there for surveillance purposes only. His palms rested on the heavy wooden door, his eye going to the small peephole when the board underneath his foot creaked. He bit back his curse and held his breath. He had to remember the loose board was there.

Dev froze and turned toward Cash's apartment, staring at the door.

Those full lips pursed. They were perfectly proportioned. Not too thin, and not too full. The way the tattoos on his neck edged his face and jaw outlined his natural beauty. If the sides of Dev's hair were shaved, he bet the tattoos went past the hairline.

Something secretive inside Cash wanted to believe Dev knew he was there, watching.

Dev turned back to his apartment and went inside without another glance in his direction. The door slammed shut hard, the subtle ricochet vibrating through his fingers where they rested against his own door.

Cash eased away, staring at the dark wood. He crossed his arms over his chest. The only real word bouncing around inside his head was...*shit.*

He pivoted on his heels and started back to the bedroom. He was obviously losing his mind.

# Chapter 9

"Your old man wants to see you," Millie spoke directly against his ear. She had a signature move when he was working on a client, where she came in slow, making sure he knew she was there before leaning down to talk loud enough for his ears only. The controlled breath she used didn't send a shiver spasming down his body. The chick always had his back.

This time, her tone was clear that she didn't like interrupting him while he worked. Especially over anything to do with his old man.

He agreed.

"What's he want?" Dev asked quietly. He never stopped the movement of his pen.

"Not sure. He's not happy, but he never is. He wants to see you in the next fifteen minutes. He stressed the fifteen-minute part."

Dev's jaw set. The raging alpha male inside him had grown way past tired of being dominated.

The reality of the situation pissed Dev off. If his old man didn't get his way, this guy in his chair and the chick in the waiting room were going to hear an angry showdown.

Dev thought out his schedule. It wasn't the worst possible time to take a quick break. The perfectionist inside him was in fine-tuning mode, and he probably needed to call it done for the day on this part of the design. It still took several long moments for him to lift his foot off the pedal and shift gears.

"Millie's gonna take care of the cleanup for me. She'll do a better job anyway. We'll continue after this heals. It's a badass design."

They were in the process of creating a sleeve. One that held personal meaning to the client. The dude nodded his approval.

Millie popped her disposable black nitrile gloves in place and immediately took his seat. "It's an impressive design," she said happily, in her comfort place of proper hygienic care.

"I think it looks real good," his customer agreed.

The simple approval was music to Dev's ears.

"Right," he nodded, tossing his gloves in the trash. "We'll keep goin' after the holidays."

"My daughter's out in the waitin' room. It's her first."

Dev nodded, hiding his concern. There was a time that he'd have remembered such a thing, especially for such a longtime client. He'd have something special to give her as a birthday gift.

"I'm gonna need a few minutes, but Millie will handle gettin' everything ready for her."

He'd stalled long enough. It was time he steeled his spine. He went to wash up, giving himself a mental boost to be ready to deal with his old man.

It didn't come easy.

"We're good on time," Millie called out.

Dev used a smile he used on his own daughters as he greeted the young woman waiting in the front room. He finally remembered her. She'd been there several times with her father. If memory served, she wanted a blooming lily on her hip. Something small and quick to see how she handled being inked.

"You old enough?"

"Today's my birthday. I'm legal." She grinned broadly, and Dev nodded, picking up an innuendo that she probably hadn't meant to throw out. He didn't see her as that kind of girl which made the comment funnier.

"Happy birthday," he said, then nodded his head toward his old man's bike shop. "If you hear some hollerin' out there, ignore it. It's all good."

"When I heard you finishin' up, I took a Xanax and have a playlist." She lifted her phone and waved it for him to see.

Dev gave another nod of understanding and pushed through the doors. He'd heard those same words about a thousand times over the years.

It didn't take long to find his old man hunched over a service bay, working on his Harley—his true love in life. His old man had mechanics there who handled all the service jobs from the bikes they sold, but no one touched his personal sled except his old man and that usually came while he tried to work out a problem.

The Harley got worked on a lot these days.

"What's goin' on?" Dev asked, standing on the other side of the bike.

"There's a fuckin' problem with the clutch." He gave a growl while turning a wrench and never looked up.

Dev had to actively dial back the sudden burst of frustration.

He didn't have time for this. He wasn't a mechanic. He didn't even fix his own sled. Literally every other person who worked under his old man was more qualified than Dev to help out.

"I got shit to do," Dev said and started to pivot around.

He hadn't taken a full step in the direction of his parlor before an object whizzed past his ear, slamming against the far wall of the service bay. The force of the hit made a loud clanking noise against the galvanized metal siding that lined the interior walls. Then again when it hit the polished concrete floor.

The heavy tool came awful damn close. The muscles in his back tightened, his shoulders stiffening in response. His hand fisted on its own. Dev slowly turned to see his father rising to his full height, fire burning in his eyes. A new, larger wrench in his hand.

Yeah. What did his old man have to be pissed about? He hadn't almost gotten hit with a fucking metal wrench.

"Don't disrespect me," his father huffed, chest bowed, his breath labored. "You're a goddamn loose cannon. Either passive to the point of embarrassment or hotheaded like a goddamn viper. You're twenty-eight years old. It's time to grow the fuck up."

Yeah, he'd show this demented old man what grown up looked like.

Dev took two menacing steps forward. He had a hard time justifying not murdering the man who just sent a heavy tool flying at his head. His chest heaved oxygen in and out, wanting to show his father by deed how capable Dev was. He couldn't keep his hands from fisting. The restraint he used to keep from diving over that bike and beating the hell out of the man spoke of nothing more than maturity and control.

"Talk about embarrassment," Dev started, his finger lifting to point at his father—another in the long line of disrespectful actions Dev wasn't allowed to do. "Don't you ever put your hands on me again in front of my brothers or I'll show you a trick, old man." It wasn't the endearment it used to be. "Fuck you."

He seethed with anger.

As he spoke, his father came around the end of the bike as if Dev were nothing more than an annoying gnat. "You've gotta learn to channel your anger. You don't have the god-damn temperament to lead this club and can't fuckin' listen to anyone to learn how. You're impossible to deal with."

"You don't even know impossible or loyalty apparently..."

His father came to within two feet of Dev and stopped, crossing his arms over his chest. "But I do. In the next five years, the Disciples will own Dallas/Fort Worth. We're triplin' our portfolio and you don't know shit about it. You're off runnin' after those kids like you're their damn mama. You're a goddamn embarrassment. Diesel's ridin' second at Smoke's funeral."

The disgust in his father's eyes, coupled with the inner child that had never been able to earn his father's time or respect, let the blow hit its intended mark.

His long-standing protective shields slid into place in rapid-fire succession, like the impenetrable armor they'd become.

His focus narrowed to Smoke and the funeral.

"I don't give a fuck. I was never ridin' for Smoke's funeral. I hated that motherfucker. Worst excuse for a human bein'. You callin' him a friend killed my respect for you." Dev didn't like spitting. It was gross, but he did just that, letting it land between where he and his old man stood. That spit represented his feelings for Smoke and the truce enacted between the bike clubs, all riding in to pay their respects to an absolute motherfucker.

In reality, removing Dev as second was a far-reaching decision. With Dev choosing not to ride, his spot in line should have been left open. Thousands of club bikers would attend this burial. They'd all see Diesel riding in Dev's spot. A symbolic move designed to show what the Disciples future looked like.

The hurt of his father's rejection penetrated. This had to rank as the number one most painful emotional time he could remember ever having at his father's hand. That said a lot. His old man was meaner than a rattlesnake.

He refused to let him see how the betrayal affected him, though.

Fuck it all.

Dev wanted out of this goddamn club after spending his entire life trying to live up to an impossible standard. He was never going to be enough.

"Exactly what I'm talkin' about. There's a tradition we follow. When I was your age—"

"Don't you ever compare me to you," Dev interrupted through clenched teeth, deciding to flex his own muscle. "Smoke destroyed my best friend. Then I had to sit back and watch the club let it happen. Then they added their own brand of disrespect to Keyes. Where's the tradition for him? You can't cherry pick the traditions you follow, or for who. I'm not playin' these fucked-up head games anymore. The trash in this club is gettin' dealt with. You all are gonna treat every brother, includin' myself, with the respect we deserve from this point forward."

His father lunged forward, stopping inches from Dev's chest. Spittle flew from his mouth as he yelled at Dev. "That's another goddam thing. A fuckin' text message to the prospects, puttin' them on notice isn't how you deal with our men."

"So I'm a hotheaded mess who can't keep control of myself or I flout tradition by demandin' better of our prospects, askin' them to be what they agreed to be. I put every fuckin' one of them on notice because *that's* club tradition. If they aren't followin' the charter, they're out. If I'd had my way, they'd all be gone as of last night."

Dev bucked into his old man's chest, ready to take this to blows. His father could eat the pavement for all he cared. He had both size and meanness on his side. His fists tightened in anticipation. If this were anyone else, he'd have already plowed over them. The fact that he wasn't pummeling his father showed how much self-control he had gained over the last few years.

Stupid, sorry, piece of shit motherfucker.

"What's going on out here?" His mother's stern voice rang out, commanding attention.

"Your son's always on the edge of pissed off, ready to throw down without listenin' to anyone. I'm goddamn sick of it. Get your ass back in the office, old woman. This has nothin' to do with you. I'm handlin' it like I should have done a long time ago. You babied him for too long."

Oh, was he handling it? Dev was pretty sure he'd thrown the gauntlet back in his father's face.

"He shouldn't talk to you that way," Dev yelled to his mother just to piss his father off more. He physically eased off his old man and mentally pivoted toward psychological warfare. He knew he crossed a line when he continued to speak to his mother, staring his father straight in the eyes. "Maybe you should go fuck Mack to show him how much his traditions suck. It's within your right as a club whore. He's done with you. Y'all were never legally married. We all know he's fuckin' everything with a skirt any chance he gets." Dev tossed out a hand, waving his old man off as if he were nothing more than a flittering gnat, making light of his father's secretive actions and violent threats. Dev wasn't afraid of shit. "So virile. Real man. Woo. Sorry motherfucker. Die already."

The blows hit their intended mark. His father's face took on a hard, red flush as his head reared back in shock, making it clear he never expected Dev to cross that line.

His mother stumbled and sputtered her words, nothing coming out as clear language, as she scampered down the staircase.

Dev tossed his hands in the air again, this time in disregard when neither of his parents could form an intelligent word. He turned away, heading the few steps back to his shop. Done with this. "You can trust, when this club is mine, old man, your fucked-up chaos is done. I don't fuckin' care who you want where. Diesel. Second? Fuck you very much. Doesn't change the facts. When you're dead, all this is mine. Could you die today, please?"

He didn't even want the club, he just wanted to see exactly how red his old man's face could get. Maybe push Fox into cardiac arrest, thinking about the disappointing Devilman taking over his legacy.

At the door of his parlor, Dev turned back to see his mother barreling down on his furious father. He gave the scene a final blow.

"And to get it straight in your fucked-up head, I've never been second. When I decide to be around, I'm in the back, standin' by my brothers who've been treated like shit by your fucked-up selective tradition. You just ensured, I will become prez and shit's gonna change faster than the dirt can hit your coffin." Dev raised both hands in the air, giving a double bird salute, flipping his old man off.

"You swore to me you'd be discreet," his mother screamed, picking up a tire iron off the ground as she got within feet of his father. Dev lifted his eyebrows, impressed. She was physically fit where his old man had turned decrepit. She had a solid chance.

More shit started flying toward Dev, causing him to have to dodge the projectiles. His father raged about Dev, ignoring the real threat as far as Dev was concerned. "Old lady, this is your fault. You let him act however he wants."

His mother screamed a warrior's yell and started beating on his father. "My children know what you've been doing to me?"

Dev ducked inside the ink parlor, knowing he'd need a moment to regroup before he picked up his tattoo machine again. He worried his young client heard the brutality of this particular fight. He closed the door behind him.

Birthday girl yawned at him and smiled, barely looking up from her phone. Her earbuds were in her ears. She looked content as hell and completely oblivious to the turbulence in the other room.

Shit, he needed a hit off the Xanax she was on. Seemed like powerful stuff.

"Hang tight a little longer," Dev murmured. She just stared at him. He decided on sign language and lifted a finger toward her. She nodded.

He ducked out of his shop again, bypassing the destruction he'd incited a moment ago. At this point, one of the mechanics was pulling his mother off his father. She'd drawn blood based on the scratches to his face.

He let them go at it and went toward the parking lot, fist flying forward, violently fighting the air, wishing he'd landed one on his old man. Sent his loser ass to the ground. Allowed himself to redefine the hierarchy through his fists.

Then he'd decide what place to allow his old man to ride in.

# Chapter 10

This felt closer to right than anything else he'd done since landing on Texas soil.

The federal government's DOJ had extensive and researched procedures and rules in place for a reason. They were designed to keep every person they employed protected and safe.

As an agent, Cash knew the boundaries he needed to keep this case within. If he stepped outside of those rules, documentation and reasoning had to be given as soon as humanly possible. It kept everyone on the same page. When those lines blurred, or got crossed for whatever reason, it was damn hard to get the structure back.

No, the AG's office hadn't been forthright with the intel on the utter chaos inside this case. The reason was clear. His approach needed an unbiased level head in order to assess the ground operation. But at least in this moment, inside the field office of the Dallas DEA, Cash felt closer to normal than he had since the beginning.

He'd become concerned it was going to be him against an entire inept regional office.

Today's meeting gave him access to the six-person team who were in-office personnel, officially assigned to monitor all of the DEA's field activity on the Disciples of Havoc. These were the information keepers. The place where the mounds of intel on the Disciples was professionally structured and held securely, ready for whoever had proper clearance and wanted to dig in. It appeared this team worked like a well-oiled machine, in direct contrast to the undercover operatives out on the street.

Cash sat at an eight-foot table, in a secured, smaller room, filled to capacity with six semi-private cubicles. A young intelligence specialist, Ben Cross, gave a refresher on the surveillance gear to be planted inside Dev's apartment. Training he'd had many times over the years.

This morning, Cash had given himself a deadline: one week to ride the current course of chaos. To learn the ins and outs of this case, and to secretly vet his assigned Dallas DEA street team, before he investigated the reasons why they did what they did. For seven days, he was nothing but a fly on the wall, gathering intel before moving forward.

By adding a cutoff date, it helped him ignore—for now—the lackadaisical boredom he found within the entire team. If something didn't change, in eight days, he planned to reevaluate the strategies and actions of every person hired to handle anything to do with the Disciples.

"You have that old school special agent vibe about you," Ben said, drawing Cash from his tactical planning. His focus zoomed back in on the present.

No matter what he'd conjured in his head, he didn't actually like being on the inside of the Dallas DEA building, even with all the precautions they used to get him there. The Disciples had to have people on the inside. What if he were identified before he ever truly got started? Another egregiously misguided step.

"Sorry. They told me the gear was new. I've been trained on this before. I lost focus. Keep going." Cash motioned away his lost focus with his hand, encouraging Ben to continue.

"No seriously. You look like 007. I've never seen any agent embody him so completely."

Cash narrowed his eyes. Was this guy making fun of him? He looked down at his own body. He'd dressed in his standard undercover attire. Since he'd held this same cover for years, he'd built an extensive wardrobe of expensive formal clothing. He generally preferred his clothes to fit his body. If the clothes made the man, he felt more on his game in a suit and tie.

His weapon had been stowed at the door, but his clothing had been made to accommodate those additions too.

The specialist laughed at whatever he saw on Cash's face. "It was supposed to be a compliment. To be honest, I'm not sure why they're having you plant all this. They know everything about every club member."

"You're not to guide, Cross. He's here to do a job."

Cash's brows lifted as he looked over his shoulder to see a woman, another business casual, appropriately dressed employee in the nearest cubicles. She didn't look up from the monitor on her desk.

"Ignore Ben. He talks too much, but you do look good. Wish more of these guys cared enough to fill in their clothes like you do."

"That's Vernie. She's the lead over our department," Ben explained as if he hadn't just been reprimanded.

Cash nodded, his gaze moving back to Ben, taking in what he might have missed about the man. What he had labeled as a young man might not be as young as he'd originally thought. Approximately five-eight with dark hair, dark eyes, military haircut. He wore khakis and a department-issued polo.

"There's so much information, it's been time consuming to get through it all," Cash added, hoping to keep the two talking. He cut his gaze back over his shoulder. Vernie. She looked tough. Dark hair, dark eyes. A female lead usually meant she was smarter than everyone else and didn't take shit off anyone.

"I've been on the case for three years, and I agree with you. We're information heavy on that biker gang. We need someone to put it all together. We need action," Ben declared and lifted a hand to Vernie when she cut her hard gaze to Ben. "That's all I'm saying."

Cash turned back to Ben and gave a single nod of understanding. He wholeheartedly agreed with the simple summation. "When it comes time for you to do a deep dive into the Dallas District Attorney and the biker member she had an affair with, know I planted that information."

"Jesus, Ben," Vernie said. "Shut your mouth. You're coming on too strong no matter how badly you need a friend."

Ben splayed a hand out in explanation, the camera equipment completely forgotten. "All I'm sayin' is there's only two possible answers. Either something isn't being included in the mountain of intelligence we have or there's nothing to find. Either way, we're pumped you're here. I'm ready to be reassigned to something else. Anything new. I've done a fire job here, but jeez. It's too much. Did you see the part where that big one is dating that assistant district attorney? What's up with the bikers and the district attorney's office? But I'm secretly rooting for 'em. They look pretty happy together."

Cash nodded, taking it all in. He'd touched on the details of Keyes Dixon's double life while waiting for Dev to get home last night. "No one knows about those two?"

"Not that I can see in the data. Pretty bold of the biker. They're all like that, just full of chaos, flipping off the world, all the time. Did you see the assistant district attorney's father is Congressman Pierce, Speaker of the House?"

Cash couldn't hold back his raised brows. No, he hadn't gotten that far. He mashed his lips together to keep the million questions he had from spilling out. The entire case was better than a soap opera.

So what game was Keyes playing? What was his angle?

If the DEA had gained the information, surely the club had it too. Maybe not, though. For all the spouting of allegiance and dedication, the members didn't gather together all that frequently.

Vernie surprised Cash when she came around the table, taking Ben's arm, nodding down at the surveillance gear. "You good with this?"

Cash couldn't suppress his grin and nodded. Ben didn't seem surprised to be manhandled from the table when Vernie lifted his arm, pulling him from the seat. "Come on, mouthy. You're done. This isn't the *All My Children, Havoc Edition*." Vernie glanced back at Cash. "He doesn't get out much."

Ben took it all in good fun, pushing his chair under the table, Vernie still tugging at his arm. "You need a night out, I'm your guy. Know all the slappin' places. It'll be clutch."

"I bet you do," Vernie said suggestively, dragging him away.

"My cubicle's around the corner. I'm B Carson 5 on the internal messaging app," Ben said before Vernie pushed him out of view. His voice could still be heard. "Let me know what you need. I'll make sure you have it."

Whether that was Ben's attempt at flirting, or the guy really did need a friend, Cash wasn't sure, but he'd pocket the invitation. He'd probably need both a friend and information before much more time passed. He quickly checked the batteries and charge on the equipment still on the desk, and gathered it all back inside a plain, unmarked cardboard box.

As the clues fell into place, his gut told him Ben was right, but from the other side. Important parts of intelligence were being excluded. His head swam with the possibility.

How in the heck was Keyes Dixon actively albeit secretly dating such a prominent member of society?

Everything he knew about the so-called brothers of Havoc would find Keyes's activities a complete betrayal. Keyes would lose his life over it, which made the risk that much greater.

Cash couldn't let the thought go. He'd make a trip to Tires, see what he could learn.

Not fifteen minutes later, he took the turn into Tires parking lot. Much like he'd ascertained about this particular area of South Dallas, the revitalization ended about a mile and a half ago.

A thriving retail area was less than two miles from this tire shop but that stretch of land mattered. The tire shop was in a rough part of town yet full of expensive cars and trucks in their lot.

There had to be six or seven men working between the vehicles in various states of tire changes. Cash pulled his sports car into the only available spot. The car's engine turned off, a feature he hadn't disabled, and pushed the door open when a shadow covered him and the entire hood of his car.

As he got to his feet, he was careful to button the jacket of his suit, hiding his underarm holstered weapon. Cash rarely felt intimidated. His own size gave him confidence, but Keyes was slightly bigger in both height and bulk. His strong arm, with an enormous bicep, and big palm held a cell phone. He stared at Cash.

Keyes didn't utter a single word. Only his manicured eyebrow cocked upward after several seconds of silence as Cash stood there, reconciling the young boy he'd once known to the man before him.

Keyes hadn't changed. He'd always been a big guy with long hair.

How hadn't Keyes been more intimidating to him as a child? Probably because he had thought everyone had good on the inside.

His next thought was that the assistant district attorney clearly had a thing for big, bad boys.

He grinned and glanced down at the tires on his car, spouting out the question he'd googled at the last red light. Besides the sofa, he'd also never owned a vehicle. Those had always been issued by the government. "I'm looking for a set of run-flat tires for my car. Do you have any?"

Keyes shifted his attention to his phone screen, his thumb moving over the buttons. "Goddammit." His index finger started pushing at the delete button until he began typing again. "Yeah, I can do four Goodyears for five hundred, or let's say four-fifty a piece. Final offer."

The heavy rumbling of motorcycles thundered in the distance, drawing Keyes's attention. His stare looked fierce as he cut his gaze to the entrance of the parking lot. Cash followed the view to see the club's president turning into the lot, flanked by two men. One was Mack—Cash had seen him in the surveillance footage. He didn't know the other.

Where both he and Keyes tensed, Keyes chest expanded. The muscles in his arm flexed and his brows lowered menacingly. That wasn't Cash's reaction at all. He automatically went loose and reached down to unbutton his suit coat for better access to his weapon.

He had no idea if Fox showing up at Tires was a regular occurrence, but it seemed suspect that he'd stop by at the same time as Cash's arrival.

"I'll be back." The rumble from Keyes's chest turned the words into a growl. Cash might have been impressed, but he had to fist his hands to keep from resting one on the butt of his pistol.

Keyes didn't wait for his response. He only turned to leave, taking long strides to meet Fox where he stopped with the others in the middle of the parking lot.

"Did he finish with you?" a guy asked, taking Keyes's spot in front of Cash. He was shorter with the same style phone in his hand as Keyes used. "Were you interested in run-flat tires?"

Cash had to peel his gaze from the bikers to even understand how this new guy knew what they'd been discussing. The question must have appeared on his face.

The guy lifted the device as if it held the answers.

"Does that always happen?" he asked and hooked a thumb toward the bikers. After a quick glance as if the tire shop's employee had no idea three ominous looking bikers had just rolled up and owned the space.

"More often lately. So the run-flat tires, I can have 'em here this afternoon but the mornin' would be better."

Cash split his attention, watching Keyes cross those brawny arms over his chest. He looked fierce as hell and made the other bikers look small by comparison. He better understood why Keyes might take the risk to date the assistant district attorney. The guy was formidable. Those three bikers didn't stand a chance in a bare-knuckle brawl.

"I think I…" Cash had to look down at his loafers, and kicked at the rocks at his feet, to focus on the tires. "How long's the quote good for?"

Keyes needed to be considered as a possible suspect in any crime being committed within the Disciples. The biker seemed culpable of something if fierceness or attitude spoke of criminality.

"You have twenty-four hours. What's your name? I'll hold the quote."

"Cash Ryan," he said. From his divided attention on the scene playing out in the parking lot, Keyes left the bikers standing there and took long, purposeful strides toward the side of the building. The loud rumble of Fox's bike started, followed by the others. Then a competing sound came from the back of the building, shifting Cash's attention in that direction. Keyes revved his engine, drowning everything else out as he drove from around the side of the building.

Fox and team waited at the entrance of the parking lot. They drove out in formation. Fox first, the new guy second, Mack third and Keyes in the last spot. In all the documentation he'd studied, they were described as a hoodlum gang. Local chaos was their deal. Cash's gut swirled, telling him they were so much more. He nodded to the man in front of him who had already ended their communication, his full concentration on the phone as he started to walk away.

Cash dropped down in the car seat and had to restrain himself from following the four-pack of bikers. In this car, in these clothes, he'd be so out of place he'd be spotted. He narrowed his eyes as he pressed the engine button. He had to get on the inside of that club as soon as possible.

# Chapter 11

The drag in Dev's steps made climbing the stairs to his apartment harder than he ever remembered before. The weight of the shit show of his day rested heavily on his shoulders.

He winced remembering the words he'd chosen during his fight with his father. The pain in his mother's voice would leave a lasting mark over his heart.

The rest of the entire afternoon became layering intervals of screaming, watching his mom cry, and a bike shop and service area torn apart. When he left after his last client, he noticed a couple of new Harleys tipped over in the small showroom.

Dev tried to cocoon himself in the solitude of his workspace. He'd kept the music cranked up to drown out the ruckus outside his door. But dampening that noise did little to help the obsession his father had sown with his hurtful words. The idea of Diesel as his old man's second wouldn't leave his thoughts.

That one blow alone had crushed his heart. For a while now, he recognized that his temperament wasn't right for the lead job. He'd worked hard on himself. Tried to be a better man, more responsible and worthy of something good from the world.

He'd carried his load by himself for years now. Tried to care for the family he'd created. He even took care of Tena, and she was a bitch all of the time.

Yet the second spot was going to Diesel.

No club vote. Just a dictator speaking his decision.

Regardless of what anyone might say, Dev's heart knew he'd never been his old man's first choice. The club charter required Dev be the one to follow in his father's footsteps. The lead position dangled over and taunted him his whole damned life. If he worked hard enough, put the hours in, always put his brothers first, someday he'd be given his rightful place at the top.

Instead, his old man claimed he was an embarrassment.

How had it taken Dev so long to see the truth?

Diesel, Daphne's new guy, was moving up the ranks faster than anyone ever had.

His dad's trashy side piece, Dixie, had to be the catalyst behind Diesel's rise. A strategic maneuver to help keep her and her daughter in a power position within the club once his old man retired.

How long had his mother known about all the other women?

Dev had worn blinders for most of his younger life due to the devotion he had once held for his father. Dev stood up for every bullied person he'd ever known. He'd done it all to prove to his old man that he got it. Authority sucked, only there for the protection of the wealthy. It was up to them to help the mistreated in their community. He understood what standing up for people looked like.

Clearly, his old man mistook Dev's efforts for weakness or rebellion.

He was so fucking tired of fighting everyone...

The apartment door across the landing from Dev's opened. His back stiffened, preparing for an attack against a would-be intruder as he shot a stare that way.

Luckily for him, he saw his new tenant before he acted on the threat.

The guy. Pretty boy.

The one who created silence inside Dev's head.

Thankfully, it happened again because he was fucking tired of the constant chaos slapping him in the face.

The running loop of thoughts quieted as his dick stirred and plumped. The door opened fully. Less than two full breaths later, there he was. Short shorts… Dev assumed they were running shorts, not that he'd ever owned a pair in his life. A tight, torso hugging tank in green that Dev bet matched the guy's eyes. Long tanned muscle-lined legs and sculpted arms that bordered on massive. All that hot body led up to a handsome profile.

His cock grew stiffer the longer he stared.

Those full lips parted, making his cock pulsate.

His dick demanded something hard and fast…

His gaze went to the nice sized bulge in the formfitting shorts.

Fuck. Pretty boy was hung. His mouth watered. Man, he could use some physical distraction.

"Hey," Dev said as casually as he could. His tenant wore the white cordless earbuds that Abi kept begging for.

If Dev assessed it all correctly, a cell phone was strapped on the bicep he couldn't see and he held a lightweight jacket in his grip.

Did the pretty boy plan to go jogging? In this neighborhood? At this time of night?

Alone?

Dev glanced over his shoulder toward the windows lining the front entrance, furrowing his brow. He didn't know the exact time. Maybe it was still early…ish. But it was November, so it was already dark outside.

"Where you headed?" Dev asked as he continued to amble up the last few steps of the staircase. Pretty boy jerked his head Dev's direction as if Dev had startled him.

"A jog around the neighborhood," he finally answered.

The pretty boy tossed the jacket over the railing and went into a full-body stretch, extending his arms forward, fingertips reaching. He executed the perfect lunge, making the definition in the cords and muscles more pronounced.

Shit, his neighbor was built like a beast.

"Not out there you're not," Dev barked. "You'll lose that fancy phone and earbuds at the very least. Those shoes, watch, and clothes at the most. If you see yourself as a fighter, you might lose some teeth along with everything else. Sure would hate to see someone mess up that pretty face," Dev drawled, trying to make the words less of a compliment and more a statement of fact.

The guy looked at him confused. He wasn't sure which of his words caused the look so he clarified.

"Not the best neighborhood for a jog at night." Dev reached the top of the stairs.

His tenant looked over at the window, his brow furrowing. His lips curved into a frown as he stood to his full height.

"I'm on SoCal time."

"Yeah." California time. Figured. Dev drew in a breath. "It's also cold out there." He pointed to the jacket slung over the banister. "That jacket ain't gonna cut it tonight. Maybe tomorrow though. It never stays too cold for long around these parts." Dev pushed his apartment key in the front door deadbolt.

He glanced over his shoulder, giving the pretty boy another more pointed once-over.

Maybe he'd get lucky and the guy would follow him into his apartment, but if he didn't, he wanted currency for the spank bank later. He quickly memorized that body from head to toe, especially the currently flaccid yet well-endowed cock inside those tight-fitting short shorts.

He'd at least hoped to be greeted with some inkling of interest. What a big disappointment.

Dev pushed open the door and left it wide open, strolling inside. He used all the swagger he had as a way of defining his invitation.

He should have hired Millie to clean his house.

He'd just done his best James Dean swagger to entice the guy into a shithole.

Sex with his fist became the only real option for the night.

Dev dumped the shit in his hands on the entry table. Admittedly, it fell to the floor because of the mound of detritus that had already been piled there. Then he beelined for the counter since he could smell the bowls of leftover cereal from his girls' breakfast last weekend. The sink was full. The trash overflowed. Dev shoved the bowls in the refrigerator. The only place in the kitchen that didn't have a lot of food.

"I'm finding I might not have judged the neighborhood properly," the pretty boy said from the doorway. His rich voice sounded cultured, educated. An enticing drawl, the origin unidentifiable. "I'm Cash. Is there a gym in the building? A treadmill somewhere?"

Oh he remembered the pretty boy's name. Up until his father's shit fit today, his mind had gravitated to the image of his new neighbor. The artistic side of Dev's brain cataloged the different parts of Cash's body in technicolor. The curve of his jaw, the sweep of his thick auburn infused chestnut-colored hair, the beefy bicep outlined like a mountain on his upper arm. The way his strong hands might fist and flex into the sheets as Dev rammed him into the mattress.

What the guy had in spades were those fantastic lips. Full and pouty. Lots of promise of wickedness to come. Thankfully, he hadn't overly romanticized all the things a perfect pout like that could do to a man.

Dev rolled his eyes. Of course he had.

If his cock could find its way into that mouth, he planned to fuck the shit out of it.

"Yeah, I remember your name. I'm Dev. They call me Devilman for short. No gym. The landlord's a cheap motherfucker."

"I thought you were the landlord," Cash said, confusion in his tone.

Dev reached for the sides to the trash bag.

"I am," he said and chuckled as he stood to his full height, tying the trash bag as he rose.

He wasn't quite as tall as Cash whose chest expanded with each breath he took.

"You should know, the leasin' company was the one who insisted the tenants be able to put their trash outside their doors and I'd take it out every day at seven. I'm not gonna be very good at that. Fair warnin'."

Those perfect lips spread into a wide, toothy, alluring grin. "Got it. Not the best location, no gym, and no trash service. I knew it sounded too good for such cheap rent."

Dev's brows snapped together into a hard, pronounced V. The trash bag dropped from his hands, landing at his feet. "You mean I could've charged more?"

Cash laughed his answer. The genuine sound drew Dev in, easing any lingering burdens of the day. "You inviting me in or am I to shut the door on my way out?"

"I'm not sure anymore," Dev answered honestly and grabbed a new trash bag from the box still on the counter. "I'll admit I'm a pig when it comes to cleanin' house, but I have a bag of really good smoke and Veracruz Café on speed dial. I'm certain after the day I've had, I'll be shit company, but I'm not opposed to sharin'."

"If I stay, would you try to recruit me into helping you clean the place up?" The question, given with humor, made Dev laugh for the first time that day. He didn't use words like charming or flirting, but if he did, that might be happening. His dick was real proud of his progress.

He needed someone to help him escape for however long he got.

The way Dev's life was going, this wouldn't only be a hookup but something far more complicated. The idea dimmed some of the intense sexual attraction that had been riding his ass since he'd first laid eyes on his sexy new tenant.

"Nope. I'll have someone from my club come clean it up in the mornin'." Dev pushed the empty trash bag into the bin.

"Club meaning motorcycle?" Cash asked, leaning against the doorjamb, seemingly undecided if he planned to stay.

The question about a motorcycle club sounded rather specific, causing Dev to peer up at him more closely. Something familiar came from a dark place in the back of his mind. He couldn't quite make out the memory.

Cash held his direct stare, unabashed.

Still, the word club could reference so many things. What if Dev belonged to a boat club...or a golf club...or a real murders club? This fucker didn't know him. So why the automatic motorcycle question? Just because he rode one. Lots of shitheads rode sleds, didn't make them club brothers.

Cash stepped further inside the room and picked up his cut where it had fallen off the entry table. With quick reflexes, he even executed the perfect move to grab Dev's Galaxy pad as it fell from the vest.

"Doesn't this mean motorcycle club?" Cash asked, lifting the cut. "We had a large one where I lived. They were always in the news."

"Yeah." The memory he tried desperately to recall never coalesced as Cash placed the pad on the entry table where it couldn't fall again. Then he shook out Dev's cut but didn't inspect it. Only carefully draped it over the sofa.

His gaze followed Cash's hands. He liked the care he used with something Dev had worked hard to achieve.

They stared at one another again. He liked the pretty boy being inside his apartment.

Cash didn't say anything more about his club. He also didn't run in fear or look at Dev any differently.

"Want me to show you where to dump the trash?"

"I figured it out today. It's fairly full. Does waste management come to the curb in the back to pick it up? That's where I put my cardboard boxes."

Yep, a city boy if he used words like waste management. Dev grabbed the bag at his feet then another full one from the laundry room and started back through the apartment.

"Yeah, good call." Dev filled the pretty boy in, so he didn't venture out on foot alone again. "The area's changin'. I wouldn't be afraid to be out in the daylight. We live within walkin' distance of a lot of shit, but most people around here drive. It's just sus to be out alone after dark. If you wanted a safer place like that, you needed to go a couple miles east or west. How'd you wind up rentin' from my place?"

"I'm a healthcare consultant. I signed a yearlong contract with Methodist Hospital. They're paying for the stay."

A professional who was high enough on the totem pole to have his living paid for. Huh. From Dev's perspective, that had to mean the rent payments were secure. Seemed a bonus. Dev started down the stairs, luckily, Cash followed, putting on his jacket. "Do I shut the door?"

"Don't lock it," he said over his shoulder. "My sister works at Methodist. She's in school but works in the ER. Shanna Fox."

"I don't know anyone yet," he said, trotting down after him. "I'll look out for her. Want me to take one of those?"

"Nah, I got 'em." Dev took the turn on the bottom step and went down the hall.

"I went out the front doors today, taking the walkway around. I should've tried this way."

Dev pushed through the back door to the driveway that split into four parking spaces. His Harley was parked on the back porch, covered, locked up tight. He'd parked his refurbished vintage Mach 1 in the spot directly in front of the door, also locked up tight. A convertible beamer, 8 Series, sat to the right of his Mach 1. The car next to the BMW was the vehicle he drove around the most, his '67 Camaro. Good engine, beat to hell, but he loved that car.

"Nice car," he said to Cash, giving a chin lift in the direction of the BMW.

"A gift to myself for the contract I landed."

"You a doctor?" Dev asked as Cash lifted the lid to the trash bucket.

Pretty boy wasn't lying. He'd taken up most of the oversized trash bin.

"No, I'm a consultant. On the administration side. You're pretty tatted up. Did I say that correctly?"

A grin split Dev's face at the reference. Since the ink covered a large part of his neck, chest, arms, back, and legs...yeah, he had some tattoos. "Close enough. You don't have any?"

"No. Can't commit," Cash said what Dev heard the most in his industry.

They stared at one another again.

Dev didn't mistake the interest given this time. Straight guys never held another man's stare for this long.

He wasn't sure if it was a good idea to fuck his first tenant. When he phrased it like that, the resounding answer was *no*, but man, he liked those green eyes on him.

"How 'bout that dinner?" Dev asked, letting his gaze travel the length of the pretty boy's big body.

"I could be into eating." Cash grinned. The smile held an easy camaraderie. Dev could use some easiness in his life right now. "Just so happens, I grabbed Pegasus City IPAs today. I could be convinced to share."

"Decent enough," Dev shot back good naturedly and started inside. "Come on back upstairs."

=♥=

Cash trailed behind Dev, taking in the man's entire backside, from booted heels to powerful thighs that filled the well-worn jeans nicely. All that goodness led into one hellacious ass. His mouth watered, and for the briefest of seconds, he imagined exactly what that ass might look like completely bare.

*Dammit.* Cash mentally berated himself. He kept having these repeated lust-filled blips. Every few minutes his brain zoned out for thirty seconds, bowled over by an attraction that physically overwhelmed him.

Instead of getting lost in the self-recrimination, Cash focused on what he'd learned in the last five or so minutes.

First, as he'd hoped, Dev had responded to his over-the-top excuse for making contact. Of course, he'd never go jogging in this neighborhood after dark. Clearly, undercover agents weren't on Dev's radar, which in itself was weird. The Disciples had a reputation for staying two steps ahead of every operation the DEA had initiated. They didn't do that by not being vigilant.

Second, he'd somehow wormed his way into Dev's apartment. Cash had to search for existing surveillance equipment without being noticed. It shouldn't be too big a problem with the hovel Dev lived in.

Third, why did Dev live like such a pig? Cash's natural tidiness begged him to jump in and toss away all the garbage of Dev's cluttered lifestyle. He had to fight himself to keep from cleaning the small apartment.

Fourth, the overwhelming appreciation Cash had for Dev as a little boy had carried over to Dev the man. But thankfully, not to the extent that nostalgia overrode obligation. He'd be careful with Dev. Always remembering the kindness Dev had once shown. But ultimately, he'd do what had to be done.

Fifth, his body's reaction to the man. In previous cases, he hadn't crossed the attraction line before. The line being the way his body had tightened, and his cock went rigid the longer he spent with Dev. Thankfully, he'd grabbed the wind jacket on the way out of his apartment, just in case he was forced to in fact run.

Everything about Dev, the casual way he moved, his deep tan, the sandy blond in his hair that looked sun bleached, maybe naturally darker than it appeared, all spoke to Cash.

The way he filled out his clothes. The strappy bracelets dangling off his wrist. The intriguing display of tattoos peeking from underneath the rolled shirt sleeves of the pearl button, button-up.

The enticing sway of his natural strut.

The way Dev's eyes pierced Cash's soul.

The way his hard cock was outlined in those snug fitting Levi's.

Nervous anticipation tightened his fists as he followed Dev back up the stairs. He could go on and on about Dev's unique style. To prove he could, he thought about the expert tattoo design that framed Dev's jawline, making his perfect facial features more pronounced.

He had lips that looked drawn on by Michelangelo himself. A nose that complimented the shape of his face as if molded and sculpted there with the utmost skill.

The slight almond shape of Dev's eyes framed by long dark lashes. The color blue that wasn't quite slate, but not a baby blue either.

Luckily, they had made it back to Dev's door.

He needed back in the agent game.

He should go rub one off in his own bathroom before he did something reckless, like make a show of doing just that behind Dev's closed doors, for the biker to watch.

Dev's unique blue eyes would watch as he jacked himself off…

The reality of what his body wanted to happen tonight shifted his priorities. They did need reliable surveillance in Dev's apartment, but he also didn't want the recorded evidence to appear for his entire team to see. Revenge porn was a thing. He wouldn't put it past any of these guys to do something like that in the name of fun. There wasn't a professional one in the bunch.

Besides, Ben Cross was right. They had mounds of intel on every club member. That was the reason Cash knew Dev was bisexual. Now was the time for Cash to take action. Get Dev comfortable and relaxed. Encourage him to let his guard down.

What could do that better than sex?

"I'll grab the beer. Anything else we need?" he asked, not making eye contact with Dev as he rounded the banister to head to his apartment.

"Nah, I got everything else," Dev said.

When Cash reached his apartment door, he looked back. Dev's shoulder was parked against the doorframe, all of his attention focused on Cash.

The intensity of the piercing stare almost had Cash's knees buckling. The way Dev's face held a knowing smirk—no that wasn't quite right. It was so much more than a smirk. Dev looked like he knew exactly what was on Cash's mind. As if he'd read his thoughts and agreed with spending the next few hours doing all the extracurricular activities Cash had conjured.

Cash squared his shoulders and returned Dev's direct stare. No need to be shy or coy.

That now familiar Dev-induced sizzle slammed through him like a lightning bolt as he pushed open his apartment door. The sex-filled buzz completely died in a swift death as Joe stood in the doorway of Cash's bedroom, surveillance equipment in hand.

"He's into you," Joe whispered excitedly as Cash shut the door behind him. "Good job. We're in. Want these now or to case the place first?"

If Joe picked up on the chemistry between him and Dev, that meant every other person watching the property had too. He bypassed Joe who followed him inside the bedroom. Obviously there were no boundaries between them.

Cash shut himself in the room's private bathroom and grabbed a condom from the cabinet. Then snagged another along with the single packet of lube he generally carried with him when he traveled. He checked his reflection in the mirror. He had a slight flush on his cheeks. He looked down at his body and groaned. The jacket hadn't covered quite as much as he hoped.

Joe had to have noticed. The parting look on Dev's face meant he'd spotted his arousal too. Nothing to be done about it now. He checked his breath then decided to quickly brush his teeth.

"I think you go over there and play nice, earn his trust," Joe said quietly through the closed door. "Wear the watch. If you need me, press the button. I'll call for backup then come get you."

Cash opened the door, his finger to his lips as the other hand lowered the jacket he still wore.

Joe nodded, and whispered even quieter, "Let this play out. It's the first real break we've had with Dev. He hasn't responded to anyone before you. I feel like if you and I stick together, and be quiet about it, we can get this case taken care of."

Joe wasn't wrong. It was also the first time he'd aligned himself with Cash and not the rest of the DEA agents on this assignment. He'd look closer at Joe's allegiance tomorrow.

He nodded and stepped past Joe, going to the refrigerator. He grabbed the six-pack he'd picked up for just this occasion and left Joe trailing after him.

"I can't lie," Joe said, almost silently. "I'm ready for this case to break."

"Shh," Cash said almost as silently. Then he opened the door and stepped out into the hallway.

He didn't disagree, but he doubted Dev would drop secrets so easily.

# Chapter 12

Dev gave himself credit. The silver platter was a nice touch.

He bet pretty boys were used to things being handed to them on silver platters. And he didn't even mean that in a bad way. Images of meticulously styled hair and the shadows of a trimmed beard played across Dev's mind, knocking every other thought away.

Dev blew out a breath as he relived their first meeting and immediately got lost in the memory of that powerful handshake. Cash's hand had fit snugly, enticingly, mesmerizingly inside his.

The entire scenario splashed across his mind in full color. The way the light streamed in from the front windows highlighted the auburn in Cash's hair, making it near impossible to resist the urge to push his fingers into its softness.

He wondered what else might fit so well inside his hand…

The assorted colors of Cash's hair, deep rich browns, auburns, and golds, set the palette currently sweeping across the canvas in his mind.

He hadn't painted in years. He used to love getting high and painting life as an abstract.

CHAOS

Dev absently worked his fingers over the condoms on the tray, fanning them out. Would it be too crass or presumptuous to lay his cock on top and serve it up to Cash like that?

Eight condoms felt ambitious. A grin split his lips. If he were lucky, he'd use about half. Maybe shoot for five by morning. But he liked the show of strength eight made.

The other items on the tray included an excess of lube, three joints, a good handful of edibles—in case that was Cash's preferred ingestion method—ecstasy tabs, a lighter, and two bottles of water because he wasn't a complete heathen. If nothing else, he had them covered for a really good night.

The platter was on full display on the small breakfast table, exactly where the eyes landed when the door opened. He picked up one of the joints and the lighter and kicked one of Mae's stuffed animals to the corner of the living room with the others. After the last fucked-up forty-eight hours, he needed a solid break, and if he couldn't get one of those, a peaceful moment would do nicely. He brought the joint to his lips and flicked the BIC to light the tip. He'd brought out the good shit. Not just any weed for tonight, he wanted something that lasted and made the moment of release that much more…intense.

He inhaled deep and held it.

The best part of his whole fucking life was access to the best stuff. His drugs were top tier. The high already edged through his system as he let the exhale go.

All he needed now was for a pretty boy with a cock as big as his wrist to be the icing on his cake.

Clearly, karma was happy with him.

Some of his best times came by way of the wealthy who wanted to slum it with a biker. They liked it hard, fast, and dirty. They got off on his coarse language as he made them ride his cock.

His body tightened, exhilaration and anticipation helped him envision Cash's ass slapping against his groin over and again.

Dev took long, focused strides across his apartment into the bedroom, getting his sketch pad and pencils ready. He did his best work after getting off while high.

Some client was going to really appreciate his efforts tonight.

Cash's cock inked on some unsuspecting person's body. They'd never know it was there.

Maybe even on his own body.

The sharp rap of knuckles on the front door had Dev taking another hit as he went that way.

He exhaled as he opened the door, setting the mood right from the beginning.

Pretty boy stood there, fresh and clean like an angel.

Maybe the tattooed cock should have wings.

Like the one Keyes wanted.

"Want?" Dev asked, motioning the blunt toward him while opening the door wider and moving back into the living room. His other hand extended to the platter. "I've got party supplies. Take what you want."

Cash looked at the offering in his hand then over at the tray.

His pause had Dev asking, "Wanna eat first?"

Pretty boy shook his head, lifted a bottle from the pack he held. "I'm not hungry. I'll start here."

As Cash went for the refrigerator, Dev absorbed every detail of the way the man moved. He was fluid, self-assured, yet oddly hesitant... Maybe he'd read the signs wrong. Disappointment crashed over him, immense and immediate. No reason to sugar-coat it. He needed to know.

"Did I read the signs wrong?"

His new tenant put the beers in the refrigerator, and Dev lifted the joint, taking another drag. He took a gummy off the tray and popped it in his mouth.

If he was fucking his fist tonight, at least being high would make it better.

"No," Cash finally murmured and twisted the cap off his beer. With a knock of his foot, the refrigerator door was sent closed. Cash's shoulders squared as he lifted the bottle, taking several deep gulps, his assessing gaze fixed on Dev the entire time.

If he read the vibe correctly, Cash took a moment to decide how far they were going tonight. The answer came with an expert flick of his thumb and index finger. The metal cap launched toward the sink, rattling as it landed, causing Dev to grin.

"A man after my heart. Want me to choose for you?" Dev nodded toward the tray.

"What do you have?" Cash asked after another pause before heading over for a closer look.

"Weed that's guaranteed not to disappoint. It's strong. The edibles are stronger. Ecstasy. I have some better shit if you're interested," Dev explained, staring shamelessly at Cash.

The spiced cologne Cash wore spoke of a complex man. The scent drew Dev closer. Fuck personal space.

"I get drug tested for work," Cash hedged. The hesitation returned. Dev lifted the joint toward Cash's lips. Then moved in even closer, inches from standing chest to chest.

"I have that taken care of too," Dev whispered, his voice husky, full of need. Cash's handsome look, strong jaw, and unguarded stare just did it for him.

Romance wasn't anything Dev had ever had a notion to try. His brand of foreplay was adding a condom. Honestly, what else was there? But something deep inside him really liked what he saw. Someone fresh and polished. Maybe not as untouched by the world as Dev had originally thought Cash was.

Which still left lots of room for the devil inside him to spoil the goodness right out of Cash… Ruin him… Bring him to his knees to embrace the hints of chaos lurking inside the depth of the green stare.

Wasn't that really what he did best?

He held the joint to Cash's lips. Their eyes locked. Something hovering between them.

For Dev, his inner beratement stilled. The rapid-fire thoughts, the destructive energy all calmed.

"Try for tonight only." Dev nodded, Cash did too, and parted his lips to take a hit.

As Cash drew in breath, Dev watched the way his lips gripped the paper. He was the pretty boy next door, his sexy hot tenant and neighbor. The kind of guy Dev watched from afar and never fully understood. The man that drew his attention, fascinated him. Life came easier to the Cash's of the world.

Dev tucked his lip between his teeth and fisted his free hand to keep from reaching out to touch Cash as he pulled the blunt away.

"You know I'm gonna fuck the shit out of you tonight," Dev said.

Cash destroyed the sexy moment by breaking into a coughing fit. Even having to step away and bend over as he coughed uncontrollably.

Not nearly as sexy as Dev gave him credit for.

Dev took Cash's beer to keep it from spilling and brought his hand to Cash's back, patting there. "We can stick with the edibles. They'll be better in the long run."

It still took several long moments for Cash to gather himself enough to stand and even longer for him to come back to their moment.

Dev snuffed the blunt. Maybe they were done with that for now.

Cash reached for the beer and took a couple of tentative drinks. His handsome face blazed red from the coughing fit, whether it be embarrassment at Dev's words or a reaction to the weed. Either way Dev found himself drawn to the blush and the innocence of the moment.

And all the ways he could ravish this good boy.

"My parents would be disappointed in my reaction," Cash finally managed before clearing his throat again.

From the look in Cash's eyes and the way he took a steadying step, Dev figured the effects were already taking hold. Cash was clearly a lightweight with recreational drugs. Dev could take all the shit on the tray and be better for it. He stepped into Cash's personal space again.

"My parents would never believe we stopped at weed."

Cash's facial features relaxed. An easy, inviting grin split his lips. Cash gathered the pieces of his hair that had fallen onto his forehead. Dev stopped him, taking Cash's wrist, before he could flip the tresses back into place.

"Leave it there. You're hot, all fancied up, but I like the disheveled look too. Makes you look less godly. Besides, I'm gonna mess it up a lot fuckin' more."

The grin widened. "You're sure of yourself. I think I should take this slow. I'm already feeling high."

"Oh no." Dev shook his head for good measure. "You're gonna learn everything I do is to the extreme. I'm gonna hit that all night long," Dev said. He reached for the ecstasy and brought the tablet to Cash's lips. "You don't have far to go in the mornin', and I sure need the fuckin' diversion."

For all his big talk, Dev wouldn't have forced the pill down Cash's throat. He did though put it against the seam of Cash's lips and meet that fucking sexy green gaze with challenge in his eyes.

Cash finally opened to let Dev place the tablet inside his mouth.

Oh fuck yeah, Cash closed his lips on his fingertips as he swallowed the pill dry. The motion suckled his thumb and forefinger. A hitch of breath slipped from Dev. Jeez that was a sexy move.

Dev kept his thumb inside Cash's mouth, pushing deeper, the digit melded and molded by the sensual undulations of his tongue. His fingertips grazed the light feel of new stubble on Cash's cheek. He relished the sensation and wanted that cheek to rub against the insides of his thighs. He wasn't tender or gentle as his arm locked around Cash's waist.

All that hardness felt good and right pressed against his body.

"You need to catch up with me now," Cash said after popping free his thumb, and nodded toward the tray.

In a showoff move, he grabbed a few ecstasy tablets and dropped them into his mouth.

Cash lifted a brow at his boldness then brought his beer to Dev's lips to help wash it all down. Dev envisioned them sharing food later, feeding Cash what he wanted him to have.

A possessive hand went to Cash's hip, tugging him forward into the hard grind of Dev's hips. "The universe must be happy with me. Sendin' me pretty boys to live next door."

Cash grinned. "Like the heavens are smiling down on us?"

"But you're gettin' fucked by the Devil tonight."

=♥=

Dev had casually tossed the handful of pills into his mouth as if they were nothing more than Tic Tacs. Cash had a mediocre pull off a joint and one pill and his head was swimming.

How could he manage to focus on his job? The reason he was standing inside this apartment in the first place. The reputation he'd developed as being steady on his feet and focused on the end game at all times was tossed out the window as if none of it had ever mattered. His only concern was the man standing in front of him.

He genuinely liked Dev. His heart had eagerly connected, begging him to take this offering, a onetime experience before the cameras started to roll inside this apartment.

Cash needed tonight to feed his soul. A purely selfish action. The fantasy of the man he'd always dreamed of compared to the one who stood in front of him, unaware he looked at the prospect of decades in prison if he didn't turn on his club.

He and Dev would never have another chance like that again.

The beautiful part of actually inhaling then letting that pill slip down his throat was that the sadness of what was to come didn't continue to bring him down emotionally. Instead, it ramped up the desire fueling this very bad decision.

Besides, he'd trained through these moments.

Stay quiet.

Give nothing away.

Keep it all in.

Enjoy the ride. He tossed in that last part.

*You've wanted him since the minute you first laid eyes on him. Let yourself go. Remember every detail to have in your memory forever.*

From the little boy who was fascinated by the rebel in his class, to the fairytale Cash had conjured in his head through the years of recovery and rehabilitation, every decision he'd ever made brought him right here, right now.

Desire burned Cash from the inside out when Dev's lips captured his, his tongue thrusting forward, deep inside Cash's mouth.

Fireworks exploded behind his eyelids as the haze in his head dissolved. Cash found his purpose. He circled his arms around Dev. He lifted his hand to the back of Dev's head, threading his fingers through the soft strands. Cash took Dev fully into his arms as their tongues met and tangled.

Dev's soft, persistent velvety swipes were in direct contrast with the unyielding steel of his body pushing Cash backward. The intent took a second to comprehend. Dev was driving their moment, ushering him into the bedroom.

His windbreaker was pushed down his arms, forcing his hands off Dev. They felt deprived, working quickly to discard the jacket in order to touch Dev's body again. Their awkward steps became frenzied as they stayed locked in the heated kiss.

Cash's back hit the wall. A crash sounded somewhere in the back of his lust-filled mind. Dev stepped all the way into his body, coming in head to toe. The kiss turned incendiary, scalding. His tank was lifted up his chest, and over his head, forcing a momentary break in the kiss.

He peeked through slitted lids. His mouth sought what it had lost. Dev's strong, sure hand encased Cash's jaw, holding his head back against the wall as he lowered his gaze, looking down the length of Cash's chest.

"The pretty boy's got a fuckin' rockin' body." Dev's other palm caressed a trail over the dusting of fur covering Cash's chest. Tingles and goose bumps sprang forward, covering the upper half of his body at the reverent touch. A labored pant heaved from his lungs, unable to control the heavy rise and fall of his chest under Dev's approval.

Dev's nose and jaw led the way down Cash's neck, kissing and mouthing over his shoulder while his palm and fingers found his left pec. Dev lowered his head, sucking the nipple straight inside his mouth.

Deep desire roared through his body in seconds flat.

Dev lapped and suckled, sending wave after wave of pleasure rippling across his body.

Cash tucked his hips, rutting against the biker's hard cock. The guy was such a tease. Dev released the suction he had on his nipple, but not the tip of his tongue licking and lavishing the hard bead. His hand slid temptingly down between his body, a straight shot inside Cash's shorts. Dev closed his palm possessively around Cash's eager cock, giving him a rough, tip to base stroke.

This moment, with this man, was a game changer.

Cash gripped Dev's ass, holding tightly to each fleshy globe, squeezing and pulling them forward as he ground his cock into Dev's hand.

Dev's handsome face, with that sexy smirk, lifted to Cash's. Dev's gaze searched his face as Cash's hips matched the rhythmic motion Dev tried to create. "I promise I'm gonna fuck you so good."

"Yeah?" he managed to reply. At least in his head, the single uttered word came out with excitement and anticipation of what was to come. The hand in his shorts kept moving.

He took in the needy emotion swirling in Dev's blue depths. What a turn-on. Those blue eyes were so damned expressive.

Cash didn't know how much more he could take without blowing his load right there in his shorts.

"I like the idea of you suckin' my cock," Dev muttered, staring at Cash's lips. He twisted Cash, an unexpected move, sending him spinning around, straight into Dev's bedroom. His shorts were pushed down his thighs, then Dev's body came in behind his, those calloused hands roaming as far as they could reach.

Cash looked around the room. If the apartments were mirror images, this was the smaller of the two rooms. A king-size box spring and mattress lay on the floor in the middle of the room.

They were maybe three feet from the bed when Dev wrapped himself around Cash. His hands became octopus worthy, touching and feeling, caressing over every curve of muscle Cash had. His body hummed under the lust and desire this man provoked within him. His cock strained and pulsed, already leaking from the tip.

Dev's fingers turned reverent, grazing tenderly over the scar on Cash's hip. The investigatory touch ran the long length of the ragged scar. Cash looked down at the battle wound that had long been a part of his life. He couldn't remember a time without it there. But watching Dev's tattooed fingers run the length felt full circle, healing in a way he hadn't known he needed.

Images of a young Dev giving a warrior's battle cry when descending with a vengeance down on the boys hurting him played in the backdrop of his head.

Cash was putty to this man. Always had been. How had he ever pretended differently?

A few more puzzle pieces fell into place. Instinctively, he understood Dev's innocence in this case. Maybe not innocent to the world or anything else for that matter, but Dev held the answers they needed and wasn't part of the problem.

This biker needed to be revered, not condemned.

Cash would find a way to protect Dev like Dev had protected him all those years ago.

"Those are pretty intense scars," Dev murmured against his ear, his hot breath sending shivers over Cash's skin. Dev's fingers traveled up the side of his chest, following the scars until he reached the ones made by his many surgeries. "Not someone skilled with a scalpel until right here. I hope whoever hurt you paid for destroyin' such beautiful skin."

"They did," Cash managed. *Thanks to you.*

"Later, I'm gonna need to know what happened and their names. I feel like my brand of justice is different from yours."

The possession and certainty in Dev's words brought back memories of the boy he remembered.

"I wouldn't be so sure." The words were the most honest he had ever spoken. Cash turned, kicking off his shoes to step out of the shorts. His nude body brushed against the rough edges of Dev's clothes. He needed to remove those after this next kiss.

Cash anchored an arm around Dev's waist, wrenching the biker against his chest, leaving no space between them. He descended, pushing his tongue forward against the seam of Dev's lips as his other hand cupped the back of Dev's head and tilted it just the way he wanted.

Something primal took over as his calves hit the mattress. At least in his head, he was sexy as hell as he wrenched the pearl buttons apart. His actions pushed the shirt down Dev's arms. In reality, he probably wasn't as smooth with the way his hands refused to leave Dev's body.

Cash mapped Dev's strong, muscular chest, shoulders, and arms. He reared back from the kiss, taking time to admire the ink adorning all that tempting flesh. Dev's biceps showed strength achieved by years of labor, not from any gym. He couldn't keep his hands off the biker.

He leaned back, taking in all the beauty in front of him, his hands diving under the snug waistband of Dev's jeans.

"Jesus," Cash muttered, helpless to keep the lustful appreciation in his head. "You're gorgeous. How does anyone stand a chance against you?"

Dev gave a cocky, gratitude-filled grin. "Yeah, back at ya. Make no mistake, pretty boy, I'm gonna fuck you then probably fuck you again. Somewhere in there I want you to fuck the shit out of me, then I'm gonna draw you. You're gonna be here awhile."

Something soothing eased over Cash. He'd gotten past his own scarred body years ago. Dev's eyes were too telling though. He'd always caught a flash of pity in his lovers' gazes, the times he went without a shirt, and that wasn't frequent.

Dev showed none of that.

"I wanna feel what it's like to be inside you…" Had he said that out loud? "I feel good right now."

From the grin across Dev's face, he must too.

"You're about to feel a whole lot better," Dev chuckled, pushing at Cash's chest. He happily fell backward onto the mattress. Dev peeled his jeans down his legs. He lowered one knee to the mattress, coming down between Cash's parted legs. Cash scooted to the center of the bed, widening his thighs in invitation.

Dev lifted one of Cash's legs, mouthing and kissing, scooting closer until he came to the inside of Cash's thigh. The biker nipped at his skin, tiny bites deliciously stinging his flesh. Dev gripped his cock like they'd done this a million times before, squeezing and manhandling him until his toes curled.

Cash lifted his hips into the touch and his eyes rolled to the back of his head. He began to roll into Dev's fist. Dev's thumb swept over the slit in his tip, spreading the moisture escaping his aching cock.

"If I suck you, are you gonna come?" Dev slid his other hand between Cash's crease, his fingers finding his hole. Fuck, the man knew what he was doing. Dev's thumb circled and massaged the rim, relaxing him before the pressure of the digit slipped inside. "You're fuckin' tight. You don't do this much, do you?"

Cash coasted on the feels, clamping his eyes shut. The only thing in the world that mattered was Dev's teasing exploration between his cock and his ass.

Dev never stopped fingering his hole as he crawled up Cash's body and placed a warm palm flat against his cheek. "Look at me."

He opened to see the man of his dreams studying his face. Cash lifted a hand to the back of Dev's head, forcing him down for a blistering, soul-wrenching kiss.

The only feeling that mattered was Dev's cock moving against his as the biker adjusted the hand at his ass to stroke both their cocks in unison. Cash's tongue followed the quick rhythm Dev created. He could kiss this man forever.

Oh yeah, he was absolutely going to come. Instinctively, Dev seemed to know and tore from the hold, staying inches from his face as he said, "Hold out as long as you can. Hear me?"

Dev didn't wait for an answer and pushed back on his heels before letting go of a scorching round of curse words, drawing Cash's attention from the certain orgasm to see Dev rolling away from him.

"I'll be back, goddammit." Dev crawled off the bed, the awful words continuing as he struggled to move with the jeans halfway down his legs.

A deep physical need bound him to Dev.

Devin Fox.

Devilman.

His foxy devil.

The man made him feel something substantial for the first time in a very long time.

His outlaw biker.

He couldn't tear his gaze away from Dev who fought with his boots and jeans. What a spectacular backside. The art was insane, but that ass kept Cash's eyes locked right there.

"Fuckin' condoms. Who's stupid fuckin' idea was that?" Dev hopped on one foot, tearing off his last boot.

Cash had to dodge the flying footwear tossed over Dev's shoulder.

# Chapter 13

The idea that he had actually stopped sex to go get protection, when everything inside of him wanted to be buried balls deep in Cash's tight ass, meant he was either finally growing up, or that he'd finally found someone he wanted to protect from himself.

Neither made any sense, but he rolled with it. Dev had fucked some sketchy ass people and didn't want to pass those possible lingering effects on to Cash.

What the fuck was happening to him?

Father of the year... Protecting someone else against a possible STD... Trying like hell to take care of all his responsibilities... He didn't like it one single bit.

He snatched the condoms and lube off the tray. Look at him, Mr. Responsible.

If he made this good for the pretty boy, maybe he'd have a fuck buddy lined up for the length of the lease. Three hundred sixty-four more days of sex. Hope sprang forth. Such a foreign feeling. Based on Dev's experience, they hadn't even made it past first base. Maybe one of those bases could be a 69 with a vibrator moving in and out of Cash's ass. Regret socked him in the nuts. Why didn't he have his vibrator charged and ready to go at all times?

Dev started back for his bedroom only to pivot and reach for another pill and his cell phone.

The devilish smirk he now wore was more fitting for what he had in mind. He liked the idea of Cash being high. It felt damn good to share the relaxation.

Actually, this next pill was more to calm Cash the fuck down. Keep that release hanging on the edge for as long as he possibly could. Hanging on the edge, not leaping headfirst into the abyss was a metaphor for Dev's entire existence.

The draw to his neighbor had Dev jogging back, almost stumbling as he stepped inside the room. The sight of the beautiful man lying across his dark fleece blanket threatened his composure. He slowed, soaking in the scene.

His emotions were raw tonight. Amped by the unusual connection tying him to Cash. Something deep whispered over his being. Dev caught a flash of where he might have belonged in another life.

A simpler place, filled with love and devotion. A fairytale brought to life. The image was so vivid Dev had to shake his head to clear it out.

"What?" Cash asked, turned on his side, waiting for Dev's return. He lifted onto his elbow. The way his muscles worked, flowing and fluid from head to toe, took Dev's thoughts in a different direction.

"Take this for me," Dev said, dropping the phone, lube, and condoms on the mattress. He pressed his knee between Cash's thighs, forcing him to his back.

Cash rested against the mattress. Dev followed, bringing the pill to Cash's lips, a move he'd made a hundred times over the years during sex. Their gazes locked, something passed between them. Fuck if Dev knew what, but it felt honest and akin to trust. Cash wasn't using him for the high and only opened his mouth because Dev asked him to.

He sat back on his heels, taken aback. The pill coming with him. Cash opened his thighs farther, one knee raised, bringing Dev's attention back to the hypnotically enticing body and impressive cock. Somehow the scar that went from Cash's hip up the side of his body added to the sexiness.

Dev committed this vision to memory. He was going to sketch this moment. Somehow capture the innocent confusion in Cash's direct stare while the rest of his entire body spoke of nothing more than carnal sin. He wouldn't get Cash out of his head until he did.

Cash wrapped his fingers around his own cock, stroking up and down in a mesmerizing rhythm. His free arm went underneath his head, angling to better see. Dev watched as the tip leaked a small bead of pre-come under his inspection.

"I can wait on a refresher." Cash nodded to the pill in his hand. "I want to be present for this. Want me to turn over? Or did you change your mind? I'll go either way."

As if Cash already knew the answer, he started to lift himself off the mattress. Dev stuck out a hand and pushed against Cash's chest. Keeping his back against the bed.

"No, stay like you are," Dev said, "Relax for me."

He replaced the pill with lube, squirting a generous amount on his fingers. The way Cash watched him with hooded eyes, had his dick straining for release. He teased his fingers along his pretty boy's crevice before he pressed them through Cash's ass cheeks.

This time he massaged Cash's opening with purpose.

=♥=

Cash heaved in a breath, taking oxygen into his lungs as quickly as he could without hyperventilating. The visual of that man, mixed with the care and tenderness used in massaging his rim, was almost too much to take.

He couldn't remember a time that his partners had ever done anything as reverent as this. The turn-on factor soared. He stroked himself faster, his grip tightening as he gave himself to one of the most stunning men he'd ever known.

"You fuckin' like it, don't you?" Dev growled, wrapping his fingers over the top of Cash's hand. Dev squeezed, sending tingles skating along Cash's body.

Hell yeah, he liked it. He groaned his approval. Words suddenly evaded his thoughts when Dev added a second and third finger to his ass. Dev's thumb continually massaged his tip, relaxing him.

"Ecstasy makes slummin' it easier, huh?"

The words were off, but he couldn't sort them in his head as Dev positioned Cash's cock and leaned in. Seconds before

Dev's mouth touched his tip, the warmth of Dev's whispered breath hit his pulsing cock.

"Don't come, got it?" Dev lifted his gaze to Cash, who was lost in the visual of the moment. "Hold on until we come together."

"I recover quick," Cash barely managed to hiss when Dev placed a kiss on his slit.

"Hold it, Cash. It makes it better for both of us." Dev tightened his fist, his grip firm and unyielding. In direct contrast to the soft lips guiding his cock inside Dev's mouth.

Oh hell, he couldn't put the feeling into words. Pleasure built quickly in his balls. He closed his eyes. The images of Dev playing behind his lids turned psychedelic. His fingers fisted into the blanket and his entire body tensed as Dev's fingers worked his ass in the same rhythm his mouth sucked his cock.

The sensations were too much. He lifted his hands to Dev's head, sliding his fingers into the soft dark blond strands.

This was already the best night of his entire life. Dev's vise grip grew rougher, more urgent, and damn if that didn't make it better. He let the pleasure build with every thrust of Dev's fingers. Dev's wicked tongue joined the game, circling and teasing the underside of his sensitive tip. If Dev kept this up, he wouldn't be able to do as the biker asked. He would come long before he got to see what else Dev had in store for him.

"I'm not gonna last like this."

Dev's mouth popped off his cock, but the possessive grip grew tighter, the fingers in his ass scissored, stretching him faster, harder, with intent.

"Don't touch yourself until I tell you to," Dev instructed.

Cash managed a nod. He would agree to anything Dev wanted, especially if all these feels continued. He was so in.

Coasting.

Feeling.

Falling.

=♥=

Cash was so goddamn responsive it turned Dev the fuck on, amping up his own pleasure. All the decadence he'd imagined in defiling the pretty boy was about to become a reality. Cash was now laid out in front of him like an offering. He grabbed the condom, tore it open with his teeth, and expertly rolled it down his dick. His gaze skidded from Cash's face to his straining cock, unable to look away, so desperate to bury himself in all that inviting warmth.

Grabbing the lube, he popped the top, squirting it directly on his cock, using his hand to spread the lubricant as thoroughly as possible, not caring in the least about the blanket underneath them.

"Grab your leg, pretty boy," Dev hissed, spreading Cash's ass cheeks, using his fingers to push lube inside Cash as he guided his cock to the opening.

As Dev positioned himself, every one of his senses went on high alert. He hesitated before he pressed in, needing that split second to compose himself. Dev pushed against Cash, slowly breaching the natural resistance.

All the oxygen was forced from his lungs when Cash's hot body opened for him, allowing him to sink into all that tight heat. Motherfucker. Cash felt so fucking good, but the visual truly magnified the sexy. Cash's long hard body quivered. The muscles and cords in his neck and body flexed under the breach.

Cash was a sight to behold, gorgeous, alluring, captivating as hell.

As Dev pushed deeper and rubbed up against the pretty boy's gland, Cash's entire body went completely rigid. Every muscle tightened to perfect definition. His handsome face contorted in pleasure. Dev's mouth opened, yet he hadn't caught his breath.

He could lose himself in the image alone.

Dev angled his hips to sink all the way in, their bodies now joined tightly together as Cash rolled forward, reaching for his other thigh, drawing it to his chest.

Dev hissed as he sank deeper inside. "Fuck, that felt good."

Those gorgeous green eyes locked on his.

Dev had never been at a loss for words. Something snarky and shitty usually stayed on the tip of his tongue, just behind his lips, waiting to be released. Yet right now, he could do nothing more than groan as he slowly withdrew from Cash's channel.

He had only one focus as his hips dipped forward into that perfect body once again. And that was to keep himself from coming. Which was proving almost impossible as Cash's muscles contracted and rippled around him, locking him in place.

Cash's body surrounded Dev perfectly, threatening to be his undoing.

"You're stunning," Cash gasped. The sweetly muttered compliment was something he'd never remembered hearing before.

Shallow words of love had never been his thing until right that moment when whispered by this man.

Instinct finally kicked in. His hips remembered what they were supposed to do. Dev drew back and pushed into all that welcoming heat again. He intentionally hit the pretty boy's gland, and fuck it, if Cash didn't look sexier as he rode the rub.

Dev took advantage of the moment, using smaller, measured thrusts as he reached for his cell phone. Thankfully, the camera was accessed by a two click option on the side bar. While his senses had a molecule of reason left, he pushed record and leaned back. The camera aligned with Cash's body as Dev pushed his hips forward again, capturing Cash's reactions on the screen.

Cash's eyes were closed. He appeared caught between anguish and pleasure. The man really responded to the prostate rub. This time, his eyes rolled to the back of his head, his mouth opened to form a perfect O.

It was too much. With the seconds he had before his body betrayed him, Dev panned the camera across Cash's handsome face, over his hard chest, down the chiseled abs, past the treasure trail, to take in the mouthwatering cock. He settled the frame on where Dev pushed in and out of the beautiful man's body.

He'd never so blatantly captured a sexual encounter before, especially without permission, but he'd have to draw every part of this man. When he got what he needed on the video, he dropped the phone and gathered Cash's cock in his hand. Stroking Cash roughly as he watched the other man's reaction. Cash's hips bucked, helping Dev move in and out of all the tightness.

He lowered himself, settling in between Cash's parted thighs, thrusting with purpose now. For purely selfish reasons, he wanted the man to remember him. His hand slid underneath Cash's shoulder, keeping him in place, and pressed a kiss on Cash's collarbone as the sound of his pistoning hips slapped against Cash's ass.

Cash let go of his thighs, wrapping them around Dev, taking the powerful thrusts, and urging him on by the press of his heels against his ass.

"All night," Cash whispered with a haggard breath.

"All fuckin' night, pretty boy. But come for me now." Dev sank into Cash's heat over and over. Nothing had ever felt as good as this man did in this moment. Dev tightened his grip on Cash's cock and stroked with every driving thrust.

How had sex never been this fucking good?

Dev sealed his mouth over Cash's, swallowing his lover's moans with a passionate kiss. Cash responded to the kiss, opening for him, sliding his tongue along Dev's before sucking it into his mouth. The kiss deepened the desire and became the catalyst driving them to the brink of orgasm in a frenzy of lust, teeth, and tongue.

Cash stiffened, his body becoming rigid as the warmth of his release spread between their bellies.

Dev reached down to run his fingers through the mess, before bringing it to their lips to share.

He slipped his fingers past Cash's lips, his lover's tongue circling around his fingers, lapping at the offering as Dev continued to kiss him. The taste of Cash's essence on his tongue sent a high voltage current straight to his balls. The intensity caught him off guard.

Dev cried out as his release slammed into him. He rode the waves of bliss, surrendering to the pleasure of Cash's body.

Peace in the pandemonium.

Darkness no longer lurked around the edges of the chaos that clouded his life. It had been replaced with a sense of optimism and acceptance.

And that was before Cash's brawny arms circled Dev. That big palm caressed up his neck, keeping Dev tucked against Cash's massive chest.

Dev had an odd sense of vulnerability, but at the same time, he'd never experienced such overwhelming comfort in another man's arms. He was no longer alone, no longer facing the world by himself. It felt as if the rough edges of his life were no longer frayed like well-worn jeans.

And that was the dumbest shit he'd ever thought.

Except it wasn't.

"It's my turn." Cash growled against the top of his hair. Cash's strong arms and legs locked around him as the guy busted an unexpected move by rolling Dev to his back. That thick cock between them was hardening. The show of stamina had Dev grinning. He was about to be fucked into the mattress and he was here for it.

Tonight was shaping up to be an all-nighter.

He might not recover as quickly as Cash, but he had pills for that too.

Bring it on.

# Chapter 14

Apparently, the big oaf on top of him snored.

Not a terrible sound but enough to easily track his labored breaths while sleeping.

Dev grinned, letting the pretty boy's body weight ease his indention into the memory foam of his mattress.

Cash was both a stayer and a cuddler.

Dev had never let himself do either of those two things before.

Even Tena had to roll over to her side of the bed after he fucked her. Generally, she fucked him along with the other person who accompanied her. Her choices in recreational drugs elevated the good time by a few notches. That was the biggest reason she was so damn profitable at hooking.

He didn't feel the need to distance himself tonight though. He grooved on how this man dominated where and how Dev tried to sleep. He had enjoyed himself last night. The perfect amount of hot body, prime cardio, and fantastic orgasms to relax him into oblivion.

The voices in his head had stayed at a distance. They were still gone.

Cash calmed his shit better than any drug.

A little needling thought in the back of his mind tried to ruin his good vibe. Had him wondering if the pretty boy was just as dangerous as the drugs. His gut didn't discount the idea. He let that thought end right there.

He extended his hand, patting the top of the mattress, looking for his phone. He didn't find his cell that direction, so went to the other side, patting the bed, extending his fingers as far as they would go.

It had to be somewhere nearby. After their second time together, Cash drifted to sleep for a quick nap. Dev took that time to begin sketching in fast, efficient strokes, committing his memories to paper. That was when he discovered the extended cut of their sex video. The camera had captured the first two rounds of their time together in the sack.

He'd apparently tossed the phone aside, not realizing it was still recording. The stars and moon aligned when the phone landed against the pillow, in a position to view a large part of their vigorous activities.

The video was hot and detailed. Cash's powerful body and nice-size cock were the stars of the show. Along with that badass scar that spoke to something deeper inside Dev.

Dev's current position in bed had come when Cash removed himself from Dev's ass for their fourth and last time. Cash tied the condom off and tossed it with the others into a makeshift trash bin Dev created. Cash then used those big arms to adjust Dev's body as if he were nothing more than a rag doll. He was placed into the center of the mattress, Cash's hard body plopped down on top of his while bringing the fleece blanket haphazardly over both their forms.

His big guy was out to the world in seconds flat.

Based on the caveman moves, Dev decided to let his body experience all these feels of being so wanted. That was ten minutes ago. Now he needed to breathe and to continue to sketch. His fingertips touched the phone case. He had to extend his reach further to actually grasp enough of the case to pull the phone to him.

He lifted the screen to see it was four in the morning and almost groaned at the two percent battery notification.

Before he could get a moment's sleep, he needed to sketch.

Cash's arms tightened around him as he hoisted the heavy lump up and off his body, gently laying Cash on his side next to Dev.

"I just need a minute," Cash murmured, holding Dev to bring him down on top of him. "We can go again." The sweetly muttered invitation didn't go unnoticed to Dev's heart. No one ever did or said these kinds of things to him.

These days, every single time he had sex, he was met with apprehension. His reputation preceded him even if it came by nothing more than sensing his threat. He was known far and wide as Devilman. Devoid of kindness and good intentions. Either given or received.

Cash didn't treat him that way. At least in this bed, Cash showed him value, respect, and a desire to make sure Dev got off.

Not really the habits of a man who jumped into a one-night stand.

Maybe the drugs brought out a tender side of Cash. He didn't think so. The high should be long gone by now.

"What?" Cash asked, his lids parting enough to look at him then around the room. "Do I go?"

Dev shook his head *no* before giving any conscious thought to his answer. "Sleep. I'm gonna draw you. I gotta remember tonight."

Their gazes locked and held several long seconds before Cash nodded. "Then you'll sleep?"

That right there. Cash had said those same kinds of things all night long, making sure Dev was taken care of in a way he'd never experienced before. Dev nodded this time, the lump in his throat making it too hard to speak. The undeniable chemistry they shared had turned into a deeper connection. The magnetic tugs of a more meaningful relationship.

*Huh.* His heart had forgotten that class levels existed. Pretty boys didn't date guys like him. They fucked them and took off.

Pain sliced across his heart at the thought of Cash thinking less of him. Maybe the ecstasy affected Cash's rational thoughts. He pushed himself off the mattress after that dose of reality.

Cash's tired gaze tracked his movements.

"Like what you see?" he asked without looking back. He tried for a flippant tone as he lifted the sketch pad off the floor while looking around for his pencils.

"Yeah." The husky draw of Cash's voice spoke of desire, sex, and sleep.

Dev tossed the sketch pad on the bed, grabbed the pencils, a joint, the lighter, and another fresh condom off the floor. He was pretty damned sated. So much so, he tossed the joint and lighter onto the nightstand. He'd draw their time together with a clear mind.

He plugged his cell phone into the charger and climbed back into bed. Cash's deep breaths suggested he'd fallen back asleep. Dev scooted to the center of the bed. The dips and curves had made Cash adjust his position until one of his big, possessive arms straddled Dev's thigh. Cash's body followed, circling and molding around him.

It was crazy how much he liked the move. Cash's nose pressed into his hip easing the irritation of moments ago. Soft puffs of breath ghosted across his skin. He stared down at Cash. The good yet foreign feelings resurfaced. The pull to his pretty boy made him lift a finger to move that unruly lock of hair that lay so enticingly against his forehead. It was crazy how much he liked the wild strands.

He'd start drawing Cash there. Capturing the look of Cash surrendering to him that now seemed embedded in his heart. The lock of hair pulled the sexy moment together. Dev had caused the pretty boy to lose his inhibitions.

Maybe.

He didn't even know the man.

All this fantasizing.

Dev's whole life was actively falling apart then in walks Cash, making his entire existence bearable again.

Maybe he wanted more with Cash. Honestly, he suspected Cash might too with how eager and caring he'd been in bed. Pretty boy was a machine with an attractive smile and easy attitude. He could give and receive pleasure like no one Dev had ever known before. It had made Dev up his game.

Dev lifted his free leg, bending the knee, in a much better head space than moments ago. He reached for the pad. He had memories to commit to paper.

=♥=

The sounds of squeaky plumbing pipes gently drew Cash from a peaceful sleep.

He didn't want to wake, fighting to stay asleep until the click of a shower door had his eyes fluttering open. He stared at the white ceiling of his apartment, doing a quick accounting of his body. First, the ache in his ass.

Not just his ass, but his entire body felt like it had gone through hours of intense cardio.

His mouth was dry. So were his eyes.

This felt like the tinges of a hangover.

No, that wasn't right.

He lifted his head to see he was still in Dev's apartment, in Dev's bed. The adjoining bathroom door opened wide, letting the steam out.

From this angle, he caught sight of Dev in the bathroom mirror. Thankfully, the mirror was positioned where he could catch glimpses of both the front and back of Dev's wet, muscular body. Dev stood at the edge of the sink, wiping the towel over the mirror.

Cash grinned to himself. The view was spectacular. Dev may truly be the most handsome man Cash had ever laid eyes on. His body was artfully tattooed with intricate designs that he wanted to map with his tongue. Where the front of him still had room for additional ink, Dev's back, neck to feet, was a colorful maze of detailed tattoos.

Cash's cock hardened at the thought of the man only a few feet away.

The ink drew Cash's now sober curiosity. Were those devil horns covering Dev's sacral dimples?

He wrapped his fingers around his cock and gave himself a base to tip tug. He allowed himself a few more minutes to pretend they were nothing more than two men, attracted to each other, at the end of an extraordinary night.

How he wished that were the case.

His stomach let go of a hard, unexpected growl. He could offer to take Dev to breakfast.

The Dallas DEA and his secret DOJ security presence would follow along in surveillance.

The thought of pancakes with special agents spoiled his appetite.

An explicit urge to protect rushed forward. An urgent and needy force, insisting he safeguard Dev from everything about to dump down on his head.

"I'd take care of that, but my ex is on her way over." Dev's gaze met his in the mirror then slid to the tent of his blanket.

*Shit.* He'd been caught creeping. Cash clamped his fist around his shaft and jackknifed up, whipping the blanket off his body to look for his clothes.

What a bad fucking idea.

The room was frigidly cold. His cock shrank as the chilly air hit his heated skin. He gave a full-body shiver. Dev's chuckle had Cash lifting his eyes back to the mirror. Dev had moved, his naked body showcased in the door's frame, apparently immune to the chilled temperature. Also, clearly an exhibitionist. He'd never known anyone so comfortable in their own skin. Dev rivaled Michelangelo's David in his magnificence and beauty.

Warmth flushed Cash's cheeks as he looked away, trying to locate his clothes.

"I put them on the chair over there. You sleep hot. I shut the vents off in here while I cuddled with my sleeping beauty, listenin' to him snore like a locomotive throughout the night."

His foot missed the hole of his shorts as his gaze skidded to a halt on the sketched pages littering the floor. Something other than Dev now had his full attention.

He managed to get his foot inside his shorts, pulling the thin material up his legs as he went toward the papers on the ground. He picked up one of the pages. The lines were strong, the shading minimal but these were all clearly Cash.

His ass hit the mattress, lifting one after another of the pages Dev had apparently sketched. In them all, Cash was naked. His face, chest, and cock drawn in precise detail. They were all pornographic in nature, but Dev had given Cash a superhero vibe. Even with such obviously speedy strokes, Dev captured the emotion in Cash's eyes or by the set of his jaw. He was drawn strong and masculine.

He had also made his scar look sleek and sexy. His frustrating pieces of hair, the ones he battled with every day, were swiped down across his forehead. They added charm to the sketches.

Dev made him look desirable and worthy. Two attributes he'd never choose to describe himself.

"I…" Cash started and stopped, picking up another, probably the most complete of them all.

Cash was in the throes of release. The pencil stroke showed a partial of Dev's body, his cock buried all the way inside Cash's ass. His dick lay hard and dipping, his face in the contorted expression of blinding lust. His mouth rounded in an O. The line between his brows was defined and pushed together.

Any uncertainty of the connection they shared vanished.

Cash glanced back over his shoulder. Dev leaned against the doorway, his cock jutting out toward Cash, firm and ready.

"You're talented. You make me look handsome."

"I make you look like you." Dev pushed off the wall, coming toward Cash. His hand fisted the base of his cock. He stepped around the few pages remaining on the floor, kicking those aside.

"Open your mouth, pretty boy."

Cash did as he was told then spread his thighs to let Dev in closer. His mouth watered. The bulbous head beckoning him to replace Dev's grip with his own. Cash let the cock push past his lips, his tongue helping to guide Dev inside his mouth.

"You surprised me. I figured high-class guys like you wouldn't like bein' drawn so intimately by someone like me. Relax your jaw, babe," Dev instructed.

Dev pushed to the back of his throat.

The words weren't right. Cash reared back, dislodging the cock. His fist circled around the shaft, keeping it close. "If 'someone like you' means a hot, talented artist that absolutely lives up to the name Devilman in bed, then you figured wrong."

Dev thrust his hips forward again, filling Cash's mouth with one sure push. Dev's palm cupped his cheek. The pad of Dev's thumb swept back and forth over his cheekbone as his hips rolled.

The tender caress had Cash closing his eyes, suctioning his lips, loving the cock sliding in and out of his mouth. One hand gripped the back of Dev's thigh, the other palmed the sac drawing up with Dev's desire.

A fierce pounding on the front door had Cash releasing his hold and opening his mouth as he looked in that direction.

"She can wait," Dev hissed. The hand on his cheek exerted pressure to turn Cash back to his cock. "She's a bitch. You'll make dealin' with her easier if you finish me off."

"Goddamn it, Devilman. I saw you read my text. Open the door. Your shithole needs some fuckin' heat out here. You're too goddamn tight-fisted."

Cash lifted his gaze to Dev and whispered, "She sounds sweet."

Dev must have picked up the hidden meaning in Cash's words—the blowjob was done—because he took a frustrated giant step over the edge of the bed, dragging his fingers through his hair as he started for the door.

"I fuckin' hate you, Tena," Dev yelled as he went. "I'm not givin' you anymore…"

"Daddy, it's me too," a little girl called.

"Me too," another more sedate voice of a child said.

"Shit!" The sound of Dev's feet pounding back toward his bedroom was exactly Cash's exit cue. He didn't want to be here with anyone else there, especially not Dev's family.

Dev hurriedly gathered his jeans off the floor as he yelled, "Why the fuck are the girls here and not in school?"

Cash got in gear, grabbing his shoes, pushing his feet through each one as he started out of the bedroom only to turn back and look for his shirt. He grabbed it and the drawing of Dev buried in his ass. No matter what happened going forward, last night mattered. He had a souvenir to mark the memory.

He matched the ends of the paper together, keeping it from unwanted eyes, and tossed the blanket over the other graphic drawings, hoping to shield them from the girls view. Cash started toward the door. He went through the doorway to see Tena. Of course, he'd seen her picture in Dev's file, but he also knew her from his past. What surprised him were the two girls. Abigail favored the Fox side of the family. The other, the little one, Mae, was a spitting image of Tena when she was younger.

"Well, who do we have here?" Tena asked with all the curiosity in the world. She ushered the girls inside, blocking the doorway and making Cash's escape impossible. He took a step back to make room. Tena, though, stepped right into his personal space, not allowing him to pass without barreling over her to get away.

"Are you Daddy's friend? I don't remember you," Mae asked.

"You don't know everyone Dad knows," the older one replied, completely unfazed at seeing him standing in nothing more than his athletic shorts in the middle of her father's living room.

Those were some pretty well-adjusted kids if this made sense to them.

He continued to hold all of Tena's attention. She couldn't be much taller than five feet but commanded the space around them. The boldness that followed everyone in Dev's life had Tena circling Cash, eyeing him as she went. "You aren't his normal type."

Cash had no idea what to say to that or anything else for that matter. As she treated him like a piece of meat, it enabled him to sidestep her, and start to duck through the front door.

"Hey," Dev called out. Cash turned his head as he crossed over the threshold. Four sets of eyes were on him. Dev grabbed his bicep, walking up on him. "I'm sorry about leavin' you hangin' like that. Can I have a raincheck for later?"

Heat bloomed over his cheeks. He had no idea how to answer.

Dev chuckled in his face then did something that seemed to surprise them both, he leaned in and placed a quick chaste kiss on Cash's lips.

"Daddy kissed a boy," Mae sang with all the love and romance of a Disney movie.

"Come on, Mae. Put your headphones on so Mom and Dad can fight. Then we can go get somethin to eat," Abigail said, taking a seat on the sofa.

"Donuts," Mae said, taking her headphones from her sister.

"I already called Waffle House. You can get the waffles. They're like donuts."

Cash didn't say another word. As much as he wasn't looking forward to explaining this new turn of events to Joe or David watching from across the street, he'd rather face a firing squad than stay another minute inside Dev's home with his family.

The girls clearly had a great relationship with their father, humanizing Dev more than the fantastic night they'd shared.

Cash had to think, regroup, and decide his next course of action.

He hightailed it across the landing while his thoughts swirled, and his gut churned. He pushed through his front door with all the grace of a bull in a China shop.

# Chapter 15

"Why aren't the girls in school?" Dev asked, staring at Cash's retreating ass. The guy looked as good leaving as he did arriving. Cash hustled quickly across the hall, almost in a run. Dev only closed his door when Cash's apartment door shut behind him. As awkward and silent as Cash had become, Dev suspected his neighbor didn't do ex-wives or kids that often.

He noted Cash never looked back.

"Who was that?" Tena asked curiously, her tone thoughtful, edging on nice. Weird for his ex. She was straight-up sideways all the time.

"You wouldn't know him," Dev answered, padding toward the kitchen. He needed a cup of coffee. Staying up all night, gazing in wonderment at his sleeping neighbor had left its mark on his heart and his head. And with an exhausting, long-ass day in front of him.

"No, I think I remember him. Is he that kid that got shanked on the street?" Tena asked, following him into the kitchen. "Dev... Remember, he was the target in a street baptism by that gang in our elementary school. You jumped in and stopped them, because you're literally meaner than everyone else combined on this planet. It was an initiation, right? I don't remember what that gang called themselves. But shit, if that was him, he sure turned out fine from that scrawny kid he used to be."

Dev reached for a K-cup and dropped it in the coffee maker, stopping short of pushing the required buttons to make the coffee. He'd been in so many fights growing up. How the fuck was he supposed to remember them all?

"What the hell are you talkin' about?"

She shook her head and came to the counter, leaning a hip there. "That's all I got. You jumped in and saved him from that gang when we were in elementary. That kid would have had a scar like that guy. He had that same hair color and big lips. But the wound was an inverted L-shape. Everybody thought he was gonna die. Your mom went to court. Don't you remember?"

Dev stared at her, having no idea what she was talking about. Tena had done so many drugs in her everyday life, she could be confusing a movie with reality. Not that it mattered. "He's from southern California and none of your business. What're y'all doin' here so early? I thought they had school today. Next week they're off."

"It's not that early," she said defensively. He watched the curiosity about his overnight guest fade to defiance. She was like a superhero who could change into bitch mode in seconds flat. Dev ignored her and pushed the buttons to start his coffee before looking at the clock on the wall.

His eyes had to have bugged out of his head. "It's close to nine o'clock? I gotta get to work. What're you doin' here? What're they doin' here?"

"The nanny quit last night, and I'm done, Dev. I can't…"

"Why'd she quit?" he asked, anger building at warp speed. The peace Cash had brought into his heart faded just that quickly.

Tena looked at him, executing the head and neck roll she had mastered years ago, then lifted one brow. Her back stiffened ramrod straight. She was tough as fuck. "You need to hear me. I'm outta here. I can't do this. The girls are better off with you."

"What the fuck are you talkin' about? Are you ridin' the cotton pony again? You get crazy…"

Her jaw set, proving his point. Goddamn, why did that affect her every fucking month like this? If there was a pill to keep his dick hard, surely there had to be one to make her less of a bitch when she was on the rag.

"You aren't gettin' it. I met someone and I'm hittin' the road." She gestured toward the front of the building. "He lives in New York and wants me to be with him. It's a better fit for me than living this life here with you."

"That's why they're here. You're leavin' them?" he asked incredulously.

His brain went numb. What the fuck?

"Mama's boyfriend's in the fancy car outside, and we're gonna go to New York to visit her this summer. Maybe spring break if she gets settled in time," Mae explained. His gaze slid to his youngest daughter who wore her headphones, one leg dangling off the sofa. It kicked in time to whatever she was listening to.

Stars sprinkled through his vision, his blood pounded heavily through his veins. Mae's voice didn't hold her normally happy tone. Tears built in her eyes as she stared at him. "I'm gonna miss her, but she's gonna call us. She said you'll get us a cell phone."

Abi's head was slightly bent, but she looked ready to eat fire as her hand came out, wrapping around Mae's arm, pulling her against her side. She tapped the screen of her iPad, drawing Mae's attention there while staring holes through her mother.

He felt Abi's hostility to his soul.

In all the ways he'd thought this might play out, it was never in front of his children, right before the holidays. And in his imagined scenarios, Tena would at least be accessible to them.

"Tena," Dev started, holding back the growl boiling inside his chest. The rage coursing through him needed an outlet as his magical night turned to dust.

"I don't want to hear it. The credit cards are maxed out. I'm tired of you controlling my money. I never wanted this life. You did this." Her hand flew out toward the girls. "You were the one who dreamed of a family and me being your old lady. But you changed it all. I'm made to be on the back of your bike, not cooking dinner in your kitchen. I never wanted this life." She shook her head and started for the front door. "I found someone who wants to take care of me. Give me the life I deserve and I'm going for it. You can't hold me back any longer."

His heart broke as Mae openly cried, jumping off the sofa to run after her when she opened the front door.

"It's gonna be okay, baby." He went after her, wanting nothing more than to offer her comfort.

"Show Daddy your new dog," Tena said as she brought a small cage through the door. "He's the reason the nanny quit. She refused to take care of anything else. She's a fuckin' jealous bitch."

Tena put the cage down at Mae's feet with a small bag of dog food. She reached for Mae, hugging her tightly, a hard, quick grip before letting her go. Tena raised a hand to Abi who continued to give her the death glare.

"She's so much like you," Tena murmured, seemingly with complete peace in this decision. "I refuse to feel bad about this. You're the one who changed everything. Not me."

She left the apartment again. Dev lifted a finger to the girls, asking for a minute. He tried for a small smile when confronted with the pain from his children. Then followed Tena out, shutting the door behind him.

"You're breakin' their hearts," Dev said, following her down the staircase, trying to stay calm. "You're their mother. They need you. I thought if you took off, you'd still stay local so they could see you."

"Fuck you and your guilt trip. You have all these ideas about them going to good schools and living normal lives. Figure it out. That's not who I am." At the front door of the building, she shoved through. The hard wood slapped against the inside wall. She double timed down the concrete walkway in her ridiculously high heels.

He followed her out, taking in the scene before him, stopping dead in his tracks on the front porch. The bitter chill caught him off guard in his pair of jeans and nothing more. A black sedan idled at the curb, puffs of exhaust floating on the air. A chauffeur driven Mercedes. The backseat door popped open. A suit-covered sleeve pushed it all the way as if encouraging Tena inside.

"Don't do this to them. It's cruel, Tena." Dev tried to keep his anger and frustration in check. He started down the steps, trying to figure this out before she left. "I'll do my best to free up more money. Give me some time."

She laughed, a hysterical sound, and shot him the finger as she dropped down into the backseat of the vehicle.

He snapped. The anger he'd held back surged anew so fast he lost sight of his thoughts. His head spun out of control as the realization of what she was doing set in. "You're a goddamn bitch," Dev yelled, taking long strides toward the car, ready to take on the machine and everyone inside.

What kind of person encouraged a woman away from her children? The fucker needed to look Dev in the eyes as he actively destroyed his girls' lives. He'd beat the fuck out of the man.

Blind rage had him fist-fighting the air.

What a stupid, sorry motherfucker.

The car door shut, and Dev took off running as the car peeled away.

He managed a solid right hook into the back rear of the vehicle. He heard aluminum crunch under the strength of his hit.

Dev continued to run down the street after the car until it turned a corner and sped away.

His chest heaved as the entire weight of the world landed on his shoulders. What the fuck?

He waved his arms in the air in frustration. The devil of destruction he tamped down daily emerged from within him. His blood thundered through his veins as his mind went dark. The blinding rage made it hard to even see straight. A growl resonated from deep in his chest until he had no choice but to let it out by way of an ugly, primal scream. He pivoted around, stalking back toward his building, frustrated he hadn't even thought to get the plate number on the car. If he had, that sorry motherfucker would be maimed by the end of the day.

See how well Tena liked taking care of a goddamn invalid.

Didn't matter. That shit was going to happen, guaranteed, he promised himself.

*Fuck.* His palms itched to grab his sled and go after those sorry motherfuckers.

The darkness of the beating he planned clouded every one of his thoughts.

Images of setting that car on fire with that fucker inside filled the devil with joy, raging inside him.

He was a fucking idiot for not getting that car's tag numbers.

Once back in the building, he sent the front door slamming shut behind him. The force rattled the windows on the front of the house. He climbed the stairs, two at a time, pounding out his anger with each slap of his bare feet against the wooden stair treads, remembering the hood rat Tena used to be.

At the front door of his apartment, he took hold of the doorknob then froze. He took a step back to gather himself, taking in long, deep cleansing breaths. The hand on the knob twisted so tightly he should've broken the damn thing. Blood dripped from his hand.

He eased off the hold and wiped his hand against his jeans.

A broken doorknob added another thing for him to have to deal with and he was at his limit.

What the fuck was he going to do?

He opened the door to see both his daughters on the floor with the puppy. Tears pouring out of their eyes.

*Fuck.* His life was too fucking hard.

He went to them, dropping down to one knee. Like normal, Mae launched herself at him, her arms wrapping around his neck. In a rare show of deep sorrow, so did Abigail. They needed love and loyalty and reassurance in a home filled with girl empowerment.

Why was that so fucking hard to find?

His hands brushed down their hair as gently and tenderly as possible.

"We're going to figure this out, okay?" he said. Mae nodded, leaning back. Her big eyes swimming in tears. She didn't look convinced. His arm circled tighter around Abi who wrapped herself against his side.

He went to his ass, drawing them with him. He gave all the time, love, and attention he could.

"Let me change," Cash said quietly seconds after the front door lock clicked in place. He had no idea where Joe was in the apartment, but he was certain his actions last night had caused a shit storm of worry and confusion among his team.

The weight of his selfish actions landed like a ton of bricks on his shoulders.

So much for his legacy of being a "team first above anything else" agent.

"All night?" Joe asked from behind him. His tone showed his annoyance and aggravation. Also, his lack of sleep. The answer to Joe's question seemed obvious so Cash didn't reply as he headed to his room.

"Give me a minute to change clothes," he said, hoping for the time to gather himself and come up with some sort of reasonable explanation for why he did what he did.

"Fuck that, Ryan. I was literally on the verge of pushing the nuke button about every five minutes last night. I didn't know what happened to you in there." Joe followed, steps off his heels. When he tried to shut his bedroom door, Joe's hand shot out, holding it open.

"I was doing my job," Cash said firmly, his brows lowering. He gave his most commanding tone and stare over his shoulder. A reminder of who ran this show. "I'm not here to explain my actions to you."

"We're a team. I'm stuck inside this apartment to have your back. Of course, you have to explain yourself to me. I explain myself to you. You're my partner," Joe said, his hands going to his hips.

Cash saw the anxious exhaustion on Joe's face. Joe may not understand all the reasons he was sent to Dallas, but he wasn't wrong and had shown loyalty. Instant guilt crashed over him and it sucked. His incredible night, teemed with passion and desire, that needed time to process had only been his. Joe suffered for Cash's actions.

"I'll do better," he finally said and gave a nod. The words sounded lame. Cash scrubbed his hand over his face. "I was able to work my way into his life. I feel like he's beginning to trust me. I needed to go with it last night, but I'll do better about checking in as I can in the future."

Cash glanced away from Joe toward the window with its drawn curtain. He honestly didn't fully trust Joe, but he was headed in that direction. Maybe it was time to take the leap. Apparently, Joe had let last night ride without notifying anyone of his long absence. That had to mean Joe didn't know who to trust either.

This whole operation was a shit show. Joe's actions intimated that, at least for him, it was the two of them, doing what it took to find the answers. A strong show of partnership. Cash drew in a cleansing breath. He reached for his cell phone, pulled up a music app, and turned a random playlist on to drown out their conversation to any listening devices that may have been installed.

"Okay. My gut says Dev's not connected to what's going on in the club. No matter what his file says, or his rap sheet indicates, that man over there doesn't fit the same MO as the rest of his club brothers."

"That's what I think too," Joe agreed, his tone and expression instantly changing to contemplative. "But we might be the only two who think that way." Thankfully, Joe easily pivoted the conversation to finding the discoveries needed to help solve this case.

"Okay, then I'll be honest with you, and this goes no further." Cash waited for Joe's confirming nod. "I believe, especially after last night, that I can work my way into Dev's life. Get him to trust me then try to bring him in as an informant. He may not be directly involved, but he's smart and clever. He can find the answers. Shanna's too far on the outside and those outlaw bikers don't value women. At this point, it'll take months for her to gain enough trust to learn anything new. She'll probably never be in a position to actually see the inner workings. This entire case is bullshit. Corruption runs too deep. I'm beginning to understand that everything we know, it's all been gathered to mislead. This operation is fucked."

"Yeah…" Joe started then hesitated, crossing his arms over his chest, his brow furrowed in thought.

"You don't think it's possible?" Cash asked, feeling like he dodged a bullet by having his actions last night go unreported. He went for his closet, dumped the clothes on the floor, and opened a closet drawer. He carefully placed the drawing upside down, underneath his underwear. He'd find a more private place for it as soon as possible.

Cash grabbed a T-shirt and quickly put it on. He'd been so bold in exposing his chest and upper body last night, but in the light of day, the scars embarrassed him and always brought questions and sorrow. He never willingly let anyone see them.

An unexpected warmth coasted over him as he remembered Dev's declaration to go after those who'd caused his injuries.

"I think it's the only feasible answer," Joe finally stated.

That instantly drew Cash back into the impromptu strategy session. "All right, answer this. Why have no agent operatives been able to get in the inner circle of this club after all this time?"

He pushed his feet through a pair of joggers, pulling them up as he left the closet, wanting to see Joe's reaction for himself. He got a blank stare from Joe. Then his jaw clamped shut. He crossed his arms tighter over his chest. His leg bounced nervously.

It was a valid question that had no good answer. The hesitant trust they'd built clicked more solidly into place between him and Joe.

Finally.

"Here's what I believe is happening." Cash headed to the kitchen with the phone in hand, needing coffee, and praying he wasn't messing up by revealing his conclusions. "We have too many government divisions at play here. I suspect multiple government employees, in different levels of leadership, have gone rogue. I believe both the Disciples and the local DEA, probably the ATF and FBI too"—Cash opened his arms wide, trying to show how far reaching the case might actually be—"have helped create a chaotic, corrupt mess."

Joe nodded. "It's the only possible answer. But proving a government agent is on the take…"

Was what Cash did best, but he didn't say those words aloud. He did interrupt Joe from saying more. "Stay with me. On the other side, of course, the club president is involved. Probably his wife too, but they're sneaky as hell. Mack, a founding member, might be involved. He rides with Fox everywhere. Devilman and the giant, Keyes, seem to be used for muscle, and not for much else. They ride on the drug transfers, show force. I wouldn't fuck with either one of those guys. There's a couple of prospects that might be government agents. I can pull their files, but Diesel makes no sense to me. The other one I question is Dixie."

"I wondered about Dixie too," Joe interjected. "She appears to have access to everything."

"Agreed. And with all this intel, we don't know who the drugs are being sold to?"

"Too far above my paygrade. I've never known. That intelligence is locked up tight, but they're rumored to originate from South America. As I say it out loud, that's an easy assumption," Joe answered, but the dawning of missing facts showed on his face. "You're here to make sense of it all, and they put you so far on the outside you can't get in."

Cash nodded.

Joe continued. "I'm going to be very honest with you. Every agent I've been assigned to comes up empty handed. They usually come with some sort of leadership at their back, covering for them. The agents are usually here for six months and then reassigned. It feels like my team's only here for show, not to truly find answers." Joe tilted his head in appraisal. "Then you came along. You're different from the others. Focused. It's why I let last night ride."

"Okay," Cash said, frustrated with only hearing these details now. He was tired of the secrecy. Every day turned out to be a new basic level discovery he should have known about before ever getting started.

Cash let the coffee brew and went back for his runners, a pair of socks, and a heavier jacket. He needed an intense workout and time to think. This ridiculous weather made it hard to even know what to wear.

He'd gotten it wrong in the beginning. This case wasn't moving pieces to a puzzle. This was forcing a circle into a square hole. Nothing fit together in any way.

He sat on the edge of the bed, putting his socks on. "If we're a team, why are you just now telling me about the revolving door of agents?"

"Because I don't know who to trust," Joe explained on an exasperated sigh. The insecurity of his confession had him tucking his fingers into his pants pockets. "You're the first person to be able to attach themselves to someone in the Disciples inner circle. I don't know what you did last night, and I'm not sure I need to know, but you've got a lead that makes sense."

Joe's reply held sincerity.

"What other agencies are working on the inside of the club?"

"Don't know everyone," Joe said. "All the ones you said, for sure. There are conflicting undercover agents. Especially since the Disciples opened recruitment again. The brother who just died added a lot of prospects."

"Then having Dev in the number two position might work? But we keep this conversation on the downlow, right?"

"Right." Joe let out another sigh. "I think the person who decided we follow Devilman is probably involved in whatever deception has been cooked up because that guy," Joe said, and pointed toward Dev's apartment, "is hanging on by a thread and has very little to do with the club anymore. His father seems fine with that. He likes Diesel better." Joe crossed his arms over his chest, his leg bouncing again. The guy was sharp as a tack but full of anxiety. "Dev's got a record a mile long. By their charter, the only way Dev doesn't take over the club is if he's in prison. I honestly don't put it past Fox to set up his own son. He's a motherfucker."

"So, expunging Dev's record might be enough to get him to turn to our side?" Cash asked, pushing his feet into his shoes.

"It's gonna take more than that. He's into those children. He's really attached. He's moved them away from here. I suspect that means he knows something's up," Joe said. "He's known for getting these feelings and acts on pure emotion."

Cash nodded, the angry sounds from the hallway drew both their attention. He rose, going to the peephole at the front door.

"I have the cameras pointed in the foyer. Come see," Joe whispered, passing Cash, heading toward the spare room. Joe took the seat behind the desk, his fingers flying over the keyboard, entering his credentials. The screens lit up. He saw Dev trotting down the stairs after Tena who took purposeful strides out the front door, toward a waiting car. He struggled to hear what was being said.

The car was nice and expensive. The back door opened on Tena's approach.

"Can you see who's inside?"

"Maybe on the replay."

They didn't need the audio to hear Dev yelling after her. Cash stared at the beast taking over Devilman. He was fierce in a way Cash hadn't seen before. He wouldn't want to come up against this Dev. The force of Dev's fist hitting the back of the car made it unsteady as it drove away at full speed. Dev ran after it and maybe could have caught them if he'd kept going.

His gentle lover, the man who had kissed him on the lips this morning, had a beast dwelling inside him. Cash tucked that bit of information away. What did it say about him that a small measure of excitement tingled across his body, sending a tickle straight to his balls?

The slam of the building's front door brought Cash back into the moment. His gaze lifted to the ceiling then to the front of the apartment, wondering how the building held together under such a powerful assault.

What happened since Cash had left Dev's apartment?

Cash stood straight and rolled his shoulders. "Call a meeting ASAP between Shanna and me. We'll meet at the hospital. Video conference you in. I won't put you in a position to lie," Cash said. "But I will ask you to keep everything else between us. I believe Shanna can be trusted too. We've got to figure out why we're really here. What does anyone hope to gain by sending me here?"

Joe nodded at the same moment Dev's apartment door slammed shut too but with much less force.

Cash shook his head. He needed time to think. "I'm going for a quick workout. Call me when you get the time of the meeting." He grabbed his cell phone, wallet, and key fob, and headed out.

# Chapter 16

"Daddy, carry me," Mae said as he reached over to unlatch the seat belt securing her car seat and its precious cargo safely in place within his vintage hotrod. She fussed with the harness, but her small fingers weren't nearly strong enough to release it.

When he moved her hands out of the way and pressed the button to free her, her arms expertly wiggled out of the straps to circle around his neck as if her legs no longer worked enough to get herself out of the car.

His sweet daddy's girl always became needy as hell during adversity. He'd be carrying her everywhere they went until he was able to get life settled for them again.

He looked over to see Abi in the seat next to Mae, having a hard time getting the seat buckle to release. He reached over and pressed his thumb into the latch, the buckle slid easily out. Her silent appreciation came by the brief glance they shared.

Under normal circumstances, Abi would have something snarky to say to Mae about her request to be held. Where Dev was inclined to baby Mae, Abi was just as determined that Mae learn to stand on her own two feet—both figuratively and literally. Not today though. Maybe his stoic older daughter was as raw as Mae and had all she could deal with holding herself together.

A slash of pain ripped across his heart again. His fucking kids brought out so much emotion inside him, his heart couldn't take seeing their pain.

Mae clasped her hands behind his neck, her feet kicking against the back of the front seat. In one fluid motion, he scooped her up. Abi got out then leaned back in to get the dog's crate.

"I think she needs to poop," Mae said as he righted her on his hip. Her tennis shoe covered feet dug into his back and stomach to climb up him enough to look over the top of the car. She still had to crane her neck to keep an eye on Abi and their puppy.

"No. Really?" Abi deadpanned.

"Mae, you're hurtin' me," Dev said, lifting her foot off his stomach. She plopped back into place against his side. The puppy became the center of her attention. When Abi's head was no longer visible, Mae started slapping at Dev to put her down.

She was like a comedy show of swinging thoughts, much like himself he suspected.

He took a look around the parking lot to make sure no vehicles were coming or going before he put her down. She was off like a flash, darting around the hood of his car as Abi came from the other side, puppy in hand, heading for the small patch of grass to the side of the building. Mae ran in a half circle to trail after her sister.

He let go of a sigh he hadn't known he was holding and took his first real breath of the morning.

An untrained puppy thrown into the mix was all he needed right now.

Fucking Tena. Goddamn cunt.

"You have to leave him alone and stay still if you want him to potty." Abi scolded Mae who jumped around like a jack in the box of excitement.

She went ramrod straight, all the squeaking she'd been doing fell silent.

Both girls watched the dog intently.

He wondered if animals had performance anxiety. Dev could never pee with everyone watching like that. He reached for their backpacks, the dog food, and box of donuts he'd grabbed on the way over. He'd also made a run to a convenience store ten minutes away to get the girls, meaning Mae, her favorite fairy juice. He grabbed that sack too.

Dev went the long way around the trunk to shut Abi's door and picked up the crate. Maybe his mother was up for some babysitting duty today. If not, maybe he could throw some extra money at Millie to look after them.

"Come on, girls," Dev said at the entrance of the raised warehouse cargo doors. "Let's go see if Momo's upstairs. I gotta client waitin'."

His father came through the office door, trotting down the steps. Dev actively ignored him.

"On mama duty again?" his old man called out. The words dripped with degrading accusations about Dev's manhood.

"I think about your death every single day, old man," Dev murmured when his father got closer. No need for the girls to hear him wishing his father to drop dead right that minute.

"Fox," Mae said. Her everlasting joy had her leaving the dog and running to her grandfather.

"Nice grandparent name," Dev muttered as his father stopped to take in everything he was seeing. They had all tried to get him to call himself something other than their own last name, but his ego wouldn't allow it.

Of course, his father didn't acknowledge Mae who stopped at his feet, dancing around there. "Mama left to go to New York. We're living with daddy now."

His father laughed out loud as if that were the funniest thing he'd ever heard. Fox slapped Dev on the back, harder than necessary in his humor. "Any day now I'm expectin' a titty to pop out your chest so they can nurse." Fox dropped the crass bomb, uncaring how the girls might perceive his words, and started around Mae who lowered her brow. Whether it was being ignored or Dev being ridiculed that bothered her, he wasn't sure. Maybe both.

"Abigail, you aren't gonna say hello?" his father asked, taking strides toward his bike.

"No." Maybe if his old man truly cared about the answer, he would have gone the few feet to her, but he didn't and kept going for his bike.

"Mama, your kid's rude," Fox called out over his shoulder to Dev.

"Where's Mom?" he asked.

Fox slowed as he got to his bike, as if relishing his next bit of news. "She's got a day at the spa for the shit you started."

He took the handlebars and lifted his leg, tossing it over the bike. It was such a fluid move. Dev remembered a time when he was Mae's age and loved to watch his father mount his bike.

Now it just pissed him off.

"Have an accident," Dev called out, seconds before his old man started the bike. Dev juggled the load he was carrying into one arm to fish the cell phone out of his pocket as he started toward his shop. He heard Mae following and looked over his shoulder to see Abi gathering the dog and speed walking after him.

He searched the contacts, pulling up his mother's, and pushed *call* as he reached for the door leading inside the ink parlor. He tried to manage it open with his foot while holding all the shit he carried.

"Hello," his mom answered.

"Y'all, go to your room and be super quiet for me," he instructed the girls. A big burly guy he'd inked several times before sat in the waiting area. He had that same crappy air his father held and didn't look happy as he raked his eyes over everything Dev had going on.

"Do I hear my girls?" his mom asked.

"Yeah, hang on." He dropped the girls backpacks and the dog carrier on the reception desk. Mae danced at his feet, ready to swipe the donuts then take off, running after Abi toward the second office space that he'd made into a playroom for times like these.

Millie met Mae coming around the corner in a near collision, but Millie kept Mae on her feet before she bounded off again.

"Hi, Millie," Mae beamed as she rushed by with Abi hot on her heels. Seconds later, he heard the television turn on and the door slam shut.

"They have a dog now?" Millie asked. The look on her face said what her words didn't: bad idea.

Dev's entire concentration landed on the purse underneath her arm. "Where are you goin'?"

"To have an early Thanksgiving dinner with my son in Colorado this weekend, remember?"

Motherfucker. Shit just kept going sideways on him.

More shocking to his brain was that this was the weekend before Thanksgiving. The girls had fall break next week, and from now to the end of the year, he'd be slammed busy doing ink. Easily putting in ten-to-twelve-hour days.

"I'm coming back on Monday," Millie continued. "I stopped by this morning to get everything set up for you for this weekend. You're booked solidly today and tomorrow because I had to reschedule appointments to fit Keyes's all-day ink in on Sunday."

"Dev, what's going on?" his mother yelled.

Right, she was on the phone. He lifted it back to his ear and nodded the guy back toward his chair.

"If this is a bad time, I can come back. I don't want you to do a shitty job." His client stood, his tone angry and put out.

"Dude, my shitty job is the best you're ever gonna get," Dev bit out, past tired of all the attitude hitting him this morning. "Get in my goddamn chair. I'll be there in a minute."

"Where's Tena?" his mom asked.

"She took off. Dropped the girls off this mornin'. The nanny quit but I might be able to salvage it. I left her a message already. Are you out all day?"

"I'm in Houston," she said. His last hope of making the day manageable went up in flames. "My plan was to come home in the morning, but I can come tonight."

Shit. In his head, he'd just thrown himself on the ground in a complete toddler fit, kicking his arms and feet and screaming in response to the universe fucking up his life.

Dammit. What he actually did was follow the guy to his workspace.

"I'm sorry to ask you to come home. Hell, Mom, I'm sorry about yesterday…"

"Are the girls with you at the shop?" she asked, not letting him swerve off course.

"Yeah. My bitch ex bought 'em a puppy. They're all in their room. The dog's gonna be a pain in the ass. They can't take him out alone. Millie's headin' to the airport to see her grown ass boy in Colorado this weekend."

Fuck, Millie. He went back to the waiting area where she still had her purse hanging underneath her arm but was putting the girls' things behind the counter. He didn't really mean anything bad about Millie. She deserved to see her son. "Take off. I got it."

Millie looked as doubtful as Dev felt on the inside.

"Let me call Shanna and see where she is," his mom suggested.

"She'll be busy. I'll figure somethin' else out." Dev nodded toward the door, urging Millie out. Based on the clock on the wall, his day was starting twenty minutes behind.

"No, babe. She's taking a break from school. She's feeling burned out. We spoke last night. She wants to help out with the club to earn some extra money."

Dev's heart sank at the news. That was quite literally the worst idea he'd heard today and that spoke volumes after everything he'd been through. "That's terrible. She needs to stay away. If Dad finds out... Did she tell Dad?"

"No, and I agree. She and I are going to talk Sunday. The girls are out of school all next week. They can stay with me. I moved out of the Dallas home yesterday. I need a break from your father. I'm staying in Fort Worth permanently. We'll make it work."

"Mom, I'm sorry," Dev said, defeat weighing heavily on his shoulders.

"No, it needed to happen and looks like perfect timing. I don't want to be around your father any more than I have to. I'll transition from the bike shop to home. Let me call Shanna now."

His options were so limited he finally gave in. He needed the help. "I have a client in the chair. I gotta go. If she can come, send her up here. If not, we'll see you in the mornin'."

Dev ended the call. He knew Millie was hovering somewhere behind him. He spoke out loud without seeking her out. "Mil, go on. I got this. Shanna might come get 'em. Thanks for settin' me up."

He had seconds to get his head in the game. He needed a reminder of the design and wondered what Keyes's schedule looked like today if Shanna couldn't come through. As he took his seat, reaching for the plastic covered pad he kept there, he glanced at his client who looked unimpressed. He knew the guy's type and said the words certain to appease the asshole, "Fuckin' ex-wives. Flexin' their muscle to fuck everything up."

It worked. The client grunted his understanding and eased back in the seat as if that explained everything.

He took a deep centering breath, blowing it out on a sigh, as he pulled the guy's file up.

= ♥ =

"Christ," Cash said and dropped the iPad on the small conference room table where he and Shanna sat. Joe was brought in by video. All sets of eyes were on Cash as he leaned back in his seat, his feet pushed out. His arms crossed tightly to help hold his aching heart inside his chest. "It's hard to say 'poor guy' for a man with such a criminal record, but how can you not feel for Dev?"

Joe nodded his agreement, Shanna was more reluctant. Shanna kept giving Cash a low-key smirk. Based on all the snide looks she'd given since they had first arrived, she had to know what went down between Cash and her brother last night.

A little more than an hour had passed since leaving Dev's apartment, and he found himself feeling vulnerable and raw. Last night had mattered. It meant something substantial. It left an everlasting mark. As if the scar running the length of his side and lower back had suddenly opened, exposing him from the inside out.

These feelings were new and weird, and didn't make sense, and that was okay. What he needed was a few minutes alone to settle down, to better reason through what was happening to him.

In addition to the stated reason for this impromptu meeting at the hospital where they "worked"—understanding what had gone down with Tena this morning—Cash had decided to introduce Shanna into the idea of bringing Dev to their side. He'd also asked for her trust...and secrecy. He didn't tell her or Joe about his position with the AG's office, only playing on the concerns each had expressed privately about the DEA's management of the case.

What he hadn't expected to learn was what he'd just read.

The continual knowledge reveals in this case felt very much like landmines.

"If you can get Dev to the point of listening to you, without killing you, then I believe this information can pull him over to our side," Shanna said, motioning to the heartbreaking intelligence she had accumulated.

Of course, Cash was emotionally romanticizing his time with Dev, but separating the man from the club sounded like such a better option for Dev. The biker could negotiate the terms of his withdrawal. He'd have the power of the United States government at his back. Clearing his criminal record was a drop in the bucket of what he could ask for and get if he agreed to help them.

Dev had to know he was already one foot into a jail cell. The fact that he'd not gone to prison spoke more to a fraudulent legal system than a lack of criminal activity that could be laid at his feet. And how much longer could that possibly last? At some point, some do-gooder judge wasn't going to allow themselves to be bought.

Cash's growing need to protect Dev had so much more merit now.

"Who all knows this information?" Cash asked, nodding down at the darkened pad on the small table.

The question finally had Shanna's gaze turning serious. "I'm not sure. I only pieced it together when Joe pulled Dev's medical records."

Joe nodded proudly. "I buried it after Shanna asked me to, but surely Devilman knows."

Shanna shook her head. "I don't think so. It took Dev a few years to settle into bein' a father, but when he did, he went at it hard. He researched schools and areas for them to live. He put Abi in a private school in Dallas and Mae in a good preschool program. That was before he moved them to Sunnyvale. He's changed everything about himself. He's not the same guy who earned that rap sheet. Tena was decent enough in the beginning, but it's like she and Dev are opposing magnets. One does something, the other goes in the exact opposite direction. She's got a serious pill problem. All the sex. Whatever happened today was probably for the best if she's out of the picture."

Cash not only saw the conflict on Shanna's face but felt the worry and sorrow in her words.

"You've told me why you got into law enforcement, but what made you take a job with the FBI?" Cash asked the question he'd wanted to know since first seeing Shanna. "If it's too personal, forget I asked."

"I applied for the bureau a few years ago. It was an entry level position. It took maybe a year for them to trace me to the Disciples. An FBI agent on the inside of the club put two and two together, the DEA approached me. The way the men of the club treat the women is disgusting. I was conditioned to live that life when I grew up. I absolutely refuse to put myself in the club whore circle."

Cash nodded to the pad. "You believe that's enough to get Dev on our side?"

"He'll be mad," Shanna answered in a complete non-answer.

"When's he not pissed off?" Joe asked on a snort. A valid point.

"That's fair but with whatever happened yesterday, between him and my father and mother, and now with Tena this morning, I feel like it can't be good. We've seen they're all running on a taut string with each other. We also have Keyes to dangle over Dev's head," Shanna reminded them. "If Dev was asked to name his family, he'd say my mom, the girls, and Keyes. He'd die for any of them."

"Those are my thoughts too. He has a soft spot for those four," Joe reinforced Shanna's words. "Otherwise, I'd believe he was in fact the devil on earth. He's so bad."

"So we're talking immunity," Shanna started. "While keeping the idea and offer between us? No one on the outside of our circle will know?"

Cash leaned forward, dropping his elbows on the table, steepling his fingers.

The sitting position caused his ass to give a slight tingle in the best possible way. Since he hadn't showered yet today, he could still smell the exotic scent that was all Dev on his body.

He had to find the name of the man's perfectly suited cologne. Cash gave a mental head shake to get back on track.

The options were to either bring Dev into their circle or allow Dev to be busted with the rest of the club.

Due to Cash's employment and close proximity to Dev, Dev would be considered a rat inside the prison walls.

Everything inside Cash resisted the second option.

His hands hit the table in frustration.

*No.* The case came first. What benefited the operation? As hard as it might be to say, nothing had changed.

He was in fact-finding mode. Nothing more. The job was his first priority.

Whatever part Dev played in this mess would be on him. "If the time comes, and it feels right, I'll approach Dev. If not, then he'll have to suffer the consequences like everyone else."

Shanna's cell phone vibrated on the table. Cash saw her mother's name on the screen. "Answer it."

She lifted a finger to her lips, urging them to silence. "Hey, Mom."

Shanna's gaze lowered to the floor. Her normal serious expression turned severe. "Yeah. I can take them home with me until he gets off or they can stay the night with me. I'm out of school this week. I can help."

Her gaze shifted to Cash. Her eyes lit up, and she nodded at whatever her mother said. "I'll call Dev, or should I just go over there?"

She didn't say goodbye when she ended the call. "Dev's ex-wife dropped the kids off this morning to say she's done. She's moving away. Dev has them at the tattoo parlor. She asked me to go get the girls. Dev's schedule is full all day."

"So that's what happened this morning," Joe said. He snapped his fingers and began typing on his laptop.

Cash couldn't help but feel sorry for the guy, but judging by the reaction in this room, they saw this as the break they needed. Energy surged in the air as Shanna stood, pocketing her phone. "I'll be in touch as soon as I know something more."

She gave a smile to Emma and a quick over the table high five, then left the room.

"That family's seriously no good," Joe murmured, distracted. "Whatever you're doing here needs to happen. I've watched her suffer for too long."

He had his team, and there was no doubt in Joe's words, he just wasn't sure how quickly he could make it happen.

# Chapter 17

Dev entered the security code to the building he shared with his parents, having no idea of the actual time of day. It was dark, so he assumed it was late. His last appointment began around seven o'clock. The fucking day had only grown more tedious and delayed with each passing hour.

The deserted parking lot and ominous cloud cover made it hard to know the hour based on the moon's position. The air was warmish again. The insane shifting weather patterns made it hard to know what the fuck to wear. If everyone wasn't sick by Thanksgiving... And he stopped the thought right there.

If one of the girls got sick on top of everything else, well, he'd be dead in the water.

He'd never be able to catch up.

Like he was ever going to catch up.

What the fuck was he going to do now?

Sell the house in Sunnyvale and send the girls back to their private school.

He could convert the downstairs apartment into a multi-level place for them all to live. He'd still need to hire a caregiver to be there most of the time.

They'd have to be careful being alone in the neighborhood.

It was just the same kind of neighborhood where his old man had found his teenage mother walking down the street alone.

That made his stomach twist. He had seriously loved the idea of Abi and Mae having a safe place to play in Sunnyvale.

Fuck no, he couldn't move the girls back to this area of South Dallas. His club was riding on a line. His old man was too arrogant to see the true threats facing the club. The best way to hurt Dev was through his children…

He'd put Fort Knox level security on them for a reason.

*Stop.*

He recognized his racing thoughts and reached for his cell phone with one hand and dug his fingers into his front pocket with the other. He looked down at the lock screen as he drew his car keys out. Ten o'clock. Of course it was. The phone unlocked with face recognition. He searched for Shanna's number as he pushed the key inside the door's lock. He really liked the way Keyes's new truck had all those lock and unlock features. He probably needed to upgrade his ride if he ever got ahead of all the money flying out of his pockets.

Dev dropped down into the driver's seat, letting out a jaw-cracking yawn. Fatigue descended over him like a blanket of defeat. Images of the sexy Cash, and the night they shared, resurfaced. In retrospect, maybe it hadn't been the best choice to stay up all night, but man, he'd had a really nice time.

He liked the way Cash edged off his worry. Put it at a distance and kept it there. Dev unwound and relaxed with that well put together man. Being buried balls deep in that heart-shaped ass had meant something more to him than it should. It still did.

Whether the pretty boy liked to slum it, or just took advantage of what was offered, sex and emotion melded for Dev. He hadn't known that shit was real.

Maybe the universe was speaking to him.

Cash living in the building meant he could sneak over after the girls went to sleep which would help relieve Dev's stresses of the day. He found he wanted to help the pretty boy relieve his struggles too.

The world didn't feel quite so damned dismal with those thoughts.

He pushed the call option on Shanna's contact information and let his forehead hit the steering wheel, listening to the rings. The phone beeped a series of weird beeps, causing Dev to roll his head to the side, looking at the screen. Shanna, and his girls' faces were there behind the option to switch to a video call. He pushed the button and leaned back in his seat, grinning at how happy they all looked.

"Daddy!" Mae shouted. She sat in front of Shanna but still bobbed her body up and down. Shanna dodged her head to keep from getting smacked in the face. No matter the situation, Mae was always glad to see him. "We have a living room fort and Shanna rented Disney. We're watching movies."

Less than a fraction of a second passed before he experienced staggering relief at not having to be included in a Disney movie marathon.

"I'm on my way," Dev said and pushed the key into the ignition and turned. The engine roared to life. The power of the rumble vibrated his seat. "I'm sorry I'm late."

"Let them stay the night," Shanna said. "Mom's coming home early. She moved her flight up. She'll be here by ten tomorrow morning. She wants to take 'em to get their hair and nails done and go shopping afterward for winter clothes."

He took in Abi who had a rare smile on her face. She looked content and happy. Two things he rarely saw in her.

"We've decided this is a vacation week for them and me. I took some time off. Mom wants to take them to San Antonio for the weekend after Thanksgiving. We've just been making all sorts of plans while you work. We figured you'd be busy for the next few weeks. And somebody needs to pay for all our fun."

Abi nodded at him, her gaze not leaving his face. Mae giggled and nodded too. "I'm making my Christmas present list. You're gonna need all the money."

Dev chuckled, knowing that list was long.

"You good, Abigail?" he asked.

"Yeah. Shanna gave me her *Twilight* books to read. I can read it, right?" she asked.

Dev had no idea what *Twilight* was or why he should even care if she read it.

"I think it's okay if she reads the books. We're gonna read them together. They're really long. If we get to something she shouldn't know about, we'll skip it," Shanna said, interpreting his cluelessness correctly.

He couldn't think of one thing Abi hadn't inadvertently been exposed to with him being her father, and her mother being a high-dollar hooker. He didn't say those things, only nodding to Abi who gave him an all-air fist pump in her excitement.

"I'm leavin' the shop now. I can head that way," Dev said again. Another yawn broke free as he put the gear shift in reverse. "I can get them to mom in the mornin'. My first appointment isn't until nine."

"Daddy, no," Mae said dejectedly, the happiness draining out of her.

He couldn't help but smile at her expressive face. "What? You're always on my side. You like to be with me, remember?"

"We have a pallet-bed made," Mae exclaimed as if that outweighed her time with her father. "We're sitting on it." Mae reached for Shanna's arm to turn the phone. Of course all he got to see were knees, legs, and the puppy asleep on them. "It's Disney, Daddy."

"Okay. But y'all go to sleep. Don't keep Shanna up all night."

For the second time in a matter of a minute, he brought Mae's mood down, causing him to laugh. Of course, they planned to stay up all night. They were his kids.

"Thank you, Shanna. Y'all call me if you need me," he said, chuckling.

"Bye, Daddy." Mae waved.

"Bye, Dad." Abi gave him the peace sign.

Dev mouthed a thank-you to Shanna. She lifted a hand and the call ended.

He drove from the parking lot, wishing like hell he'd gotten his new neighbor's phone number. Was it too soon to request Cash be naked and waiting in his bed when he got home?

His gaze lifted to the rearview mirror, watching a car leave its parking space on the street. He'd had a couple weeks of reprieve from being followed. What the fuck ever. Apparently, they hadn't gotten the memo that Diesel was the new number two.

With his jaw set, he slammed his fist down on the dashboard.

Fuck the Disciples. At this point, they were nothing but a pain in his ass.

=♥=

Cash sat in the front seat of his BMW, staring at Gerick Moreland, the current US Attorney General, who had taken his call personally. Having the head of the Department of Justice as his point of contact made Cash nervous and spoke to the gravity of the investigation.

The AG sat alongside his trusted deputy assistant, Collins. They were already thirty minutes into the briefing, fifteen minutes longer than any other time he'd reported in. Cash had disclosed much of the truth of his last twenty-four hours in bullet-point fashion. Based on the blank stares he'd received, he couldn't judge their reactions. But he hadn't been fired, so there was that.

Regardless of how Cash had manipulated his thoughts, made himself believe by getting on Dev's good side he'd have better access to the club, Dev was a decidedly unwanted distraction. It didn't matter. He'd spent hours today convincing himself the true threat lay beyond the man known as Devilman.

A laughable summation. The biker's chosen name had *evil* spelled inside it.

But the facts remained the same. By building a relationship with Dev, Cash could get closer to the club and its members. If he planned his strategies correctly, those biker informants, the law enforcement officers, and special agents being paid under the table by the bike club may reveal themselves.

The plan was solid. Other undercover agents performed in exactly the same manner every day, all across the country. This was nothing new even if it was new to him.

Cash kept his facial expressions neutral and waited.

His innate sense of honesty required he speak the truth, but his gut needed a reasonable mind's clarity before he did something stupid. Like blow this entire operation wide open on nothing more than his deep desire to have Dev be the hero and not a casualty of the potential war bearing down on top of this unsuspecting club.

The AG's face hardened. "Are you sure Devin Fox is the best mole for this job? He seems volatile at best."

Collins shook her head at the AG. She agreed with Cash.

If they could land Dev as an informant, the case would solve itself. Dev had access to everyone and everything. "It's hard to believe this much ineptness can happen in one case. Someone's keeping us at a distance. Allow me the tools to find the person or people responsible. That's why you assigned me. I have a hundred percent closure rate. Devin can find our answers."

He'd given his oath of loyalty and allegiance to the United States government. But what if Dev was the mastermind behind the clusterfuck of this case. He was smart enough to be the root of the problems, no matter how he portrayed himself to the world.

No…Cash didn't think so.

How were Cash's lines already so blurred where Dev was concerned?

His ass answered his question, still feeling the use from their love making.

Love making. He hadn't let himself think the words *love* until a couple of hours ago as he built this report, wanting to do everything in his power to shield Dev from any future fallout.

Since then, every remembered touch was exactly what it felt like in real time: a caress, a gentle guidance, a reverence to the other.

*Focus.*
*Jesus, Cash. Focus.*
*Not.*
*The.*
*Time.*
*Close this argument. Bring it home. Get the approvals.*

"Devin Fox is my way into the club. There's no better in. He should've been used in this way from the beginning. The Disciples charter states clearly that he's taking over the entire nationwide club when his father steps down. We have intel on every club member. There isn't another leader in the band of misfits. Certainly no one capable of washing cash and churning large amounts of illegal drugs through the streets. The only two patched members who have any sort of reasonable thought processes are Devin Fox and Keyes Dixon. I do question Dixon's motives more and more the further I dig through his file. The idea that he has a secret relationship with the Speaker of the House's son. What does that even look like?"

Cash paused, letting the influential connection sink in.

Politically, if this case involved Speaker Pierce, the AG had better have all his facts clearly supported or his career was over.

Was there anything more than the ridiculousness of someone like Keyes Dixon paired with the wealthy, rebel child, Alec Pierce? Maybe dropping the breadcrumbs might buy time to pull this all together, to know better what he faced.

"I also have a small team forming. My handler, Joe, and Shanna Fox. They've all privately expressed their concerns with how the case is progressing. I'm testing their trustworthiness now, but I believe I can draw them in under the AG's special team's umbrella. We'll see, but to the rest of the Dallas DEA, it'll only look like I managed my way into becoming Dev's boyfriend."

"You're walking a thin line," Collins said.

"Nothing new there," he replied truthfully.

The astute stare of the AG held Cash's full attention. The man was so damned hard to read.

The silence extended.

He had learned a long time ago to hold his tongue. Whoever spoke first lost the negotiations, especially when dealing with anyone in the government.

Seconds lapped into a minute.

The minute became two. Cash didn't budge.

"I can see where you're gaining Devilman's trust. He's reckless…" the AG started. Cash nodded. "The largest motorcycle club in the country is moving billions of dollars of illegal drugs through our streets. You must be certain before you act. We can't get this wrong." The AG's eyes lifted to Cash, again assessing him as if that wasn't perfectly clear.

Cash nodded. He'd been sent in blind, knowing very little of the magnitude of what was going on. Perhaps the AG was saying more than he wanted, but Cash needed to know what he was up against.

"Too many hands are pilfering through the profits. It's utter chaos. We have no leads outside of this club and very few leads inside. All our leads have come from you. Where's the money going? Do we know the full scope of the illegal activity they're pushing? Where's it coming from?"

The AG gave a rare moment of emotion, frustratingly throwing his hands in the air. Cash nodded, feeling reasonably sure he'd sold his most current tactical advancement strategy.

"I've never seen anything like this before. How did we lose such control?"

"I understand, but nothing changes for me," Cash said. "My goal's to provide you with the intelligence you need, which I believe I can do if we get Devin on our side. Otherwise, there's no reason for you to keep me here. I would suggest an operative assigned internally at the Dallas DEA's office. Outside of the club members I've stated, these bikers don't have the…wherewithal to steal on such a large level."

"He has a point," Collins said.

The AG nodded. "Do what you need to with Devin Fox. Be mindful. He doesn't strike me as someone who will easily become compliant."

Cash nodded and agreed. The pit in his stomach eased.

"Off the record, if anything you find points to Speaker Pierce or his son, I want to know before anything's done. Day or night. Got it?" the AG said.

Both he and Collins nodded their understanding.

Headlights dashed across Cash's dark windshield. Dev was home.

"I'll touch base when I know more."

Cash ended the call as Dev's vintage ride came to the gate. He swore he heard a string of foul language before Dev exited the car to unlock the padlock keeping it closed.

Of course he left the gate open as he parked in his normal space. Dev looked over at him through the side window. Dev cut the engine, the rumble so loud, the silence took a second to absorb the fading noise. The driver's side door opened, Dev's head popped over the top of the car, waiting for Cash to open his door and get out of his vehicle.

A lie formed inside his head before his hand reached the handle.

"There a problem?" Dev asked.

"Not really. I need to switch my cell service. I have bad reception in my place."

Both of Dev's brows lowered. "Is that in any way my fault?"

Cash stood to his full height and grinned, shaking his head. "Not unless you want to pay for a new cell phone service. I'll happily send you that bill."

Dev rolled his eyes and dropped back down into the car, removing the key from the ignition. His hand hit the lock on the inside door, pushing it down before the door slammed shut. "You got any grub upstairs. I'm just realizin' I didn't eat today."

"You're only realizing that right now?" Cash met him at the front of both their vehicles. Together, they walked the length of the patio toward the back door.

"Not as astonishin' as you just made it sound. I'm not a big eater. Usually grab a burger or two on the way home," Dev explained and reached for the back door of the building, ushering Cash through first.

The words stopped Cash in the middle of the doorframe, his hand going to his heart. "I love food. I love to plan my food, watch videos on how to cook food properly then try to make those recipes myself. It physically hurts me that you don't think about food."

Dev's stance relaxed. He had that undeniably sexy swagger as he watched him closely. Dev grinned happily. The strain he wore on his face evaporated, leaving behind a youthful, handsome, playful man in its place.

A full toothy grin was Cash's reward. Dev reached for Cash's arm, gripping him in such a way that he remained in place as Dev took a step into him. "You know what I thought about all day?"

"Well, clearly not food."

Dev's eyes lowered to Cash's lips. "That quick peck I gave you when you left my place."

He had expected something vulgar about their time together last night, not a reminder of that sweet, unexpected gesture. Cash's cock loved the tenderness of the words. His ass clenched with anticipated pleasure. Dev's eyes glazed over as he stared at Cash's mouth. "You got great lips."

Cash lowered his voice to a whisper and leaned into Dev so not to be heard by all the surveillance equipment around them. "I was thinking more about the moment I rimmed you. You seemed really into it; I definitely was into it."

Cash finished the sentence by flicking his tongue around the shell of Dev's ear.

Dev stepped completely into him. His chest met Cash's chest. "Why're you whispering?" Dev asked in a seductive, husky whisper of his own.

"Where are your children?" Cash replied without missing a beat.

"With their aunt for the night," Dev answered.

Cash took a small step back. Then a larger one. Dev followed, staying in his personal space until the back door slammed shut behind him. The biker's face lifted an inch or two to place a long, heart-filled, semi-chaste kiss on Cash's lips. "Maybe these kisses work like Mae's fairy magic dust. My joy ended when you left this mornin'. Now it's returnin'. Maybe that kiss will ignite somethin' new."

Cash let those words bounce around in his head. They were sweet and easily spoken. Dev had a way with words, mainly due to the way he spoke his mind all the time. Cash concentrated on the child reference, pretending not to know. "Mae is…? Hopefully not a magic fairy you spend time with regularly."

That broke the sizzling connection of their moment, something his heart needed to have happen. His focus had to remain on navigating all the potential landmines forming around them.

Dev's laughter had his body easing off Cash's. A breath he hadn't known he held released as Dev went down the hallway toward the stairs.

"Mae's my five-year-old daughter. I have two girls. You saw them both. Abigail is eleven now, I think. Yeah, eleven. She acts like she's thirty-five." He rounded the newel post and looked back at Cash who followed. "You had to have heard the exchange with my bitch ex-wife. She took off today with no warnin'. She's a cunt. Brought a fuckin' few weeks' old puppy with her." Dev trudged up the stairs, his footsteps heavier with each word spoken. "How about that dinner? Got anything leftover?"

"I have half a wrap left over. No protein…"

"Like lettuce," Dev asked and stopped in the middle of the staircase, looking down at him. "Did you just offer me lettuce?"

"And Beyond Chicken, I believe." Cash couldn't hold in the amusement at Dev's horrified expression.

"My happy place today came with the idea you were next door to fuck as we saw fit, and maybe I could bum some food off you occasionally. You're ruinin' my happy place." Dev spun around with aggravation in his tone and movements. "Goddamn fuckin' no meat eatin'..."

Dev stopped again a few more steps up. This time giving him an accusatory look.

"You ate my meat. Swallowed some animal protein if I remember correctly."

Cash barked out a laugh. He knew the others listening had too. Dev's words were too unexpected not to be funny.

"So, you're saying I should go get the wrap for you?"

"Fuck no," Dev said at his front door. "I'll fare better with my two-day old pizza."

"The one on your stove?"

"Yeah." He must have given his own horrified look because Dev pushed open his front door with a laugh. "We could order new."

"If you're inviting me in, I could pick this place up while you order whatever you want and go take a shower," Cash said, closing the front door behind him.

"You like to clean?" Dev asked, once again abruptly stopping a few feet away as if that were the most exciting news he'd ever heard.

"I guess."

"Well, hell. We're a match made in heaven." Dev pivoted around, coming back to Cash. He took a whiff of his shirt sleeve as he came. "I showered this mornin'."

"You smell the way hospitals do..." Cash said and extended a hand to Dev's chest, keeping him at a distance. He needed to at least pretend to look for previously planted surveillance equipment inside the apartment.

"Bossy," Dev growled, his blue eyes sparkling as he took Cash's palm and brought it to his lips. "I'll shower if you come with me. I want you to use force when you fuck me. Big guy like you could spank my ass. Put me in my place." The words were crass and vivid. Cash's look caused Dev to bark out a laugh. "You have that line between your brows. You look fierce right now to be such a pretty boy. When it draws together and makes that crease..." Dev tucked a lip between his teeth. Something unsaid passed over his expression. "I was watchin' that happen as you came."

"What do you mean watching?"

Dev stepped into him, grinding his hips forward. "You fed me a handful of pills. Makes me see things in Technicolor."

"I what?" Cash asked, not letting Dev turn the tables on him.

Dev responded with a loud boom of laughter, wrapping an arm around Cash's waist, drawing him flush against his body. Everything Dev did turned Cash on.

# Chapter 18

Dev wrenched the tight-fitting athletic shirt over Cash's head. Before Cash could get his arms out of the shirt, Dev clamped his mouth tightly over Cash's, drawing him toward the main bedroom's bathroom. It was bigger, better suited for the shower Cash had mentioned. They'd both fit inside the shower's stall.

The kiss deepened. Damn, he couldn't seem to get enough of this guy. Cash's palms came to Dev's cheeks, angling him to drive his tongue forward. Dev wasn't the only one who had a desperate edge to his movements. Cash gave as good as he got.

Dev locked an arm around Cash's waist, shoving his hand down the waistband of Cash's fitted joggers. The pants left so little to the imagination. He'd watched in fascination as Cash's big cock grew to half-mast. Now, with one slow stroke, it grew hard as steel in Dev's hand.

Cash tore his mouth free from the kiss. His gaze penetrated Dev's. His sexy lips opened into that intriguing O Dev had loved from last night. On the second stroke, Cash's eyes screwed tightly closed. Fuck, he wished he had his camera.

"Feels good?" Dev asked.

"It's immediate with you. I'm right there," Cash managed to say, seconds before his mouth captured Dev's, his tongue driving deep on the very first thrust.

Cash's hips tucked into Dev's hand as he pushed the pants and his underwear down Cash's thighs to free his cock. Cash toed off his shoes and slid his hands under Dev's T-shirt, caressing a path up and over his head. The move was perfectly executed. Cash lifted his lips, the shirt yanked over his head. Cash's strong palm clamped around his neck like a vise, drawing him back into the kiss.

What a fucking turn-on. Dev gripped both of Cash's ass cheeks, his fingers digging into the fleshy globes. He tore his mouth free, exposing the long line of his neck, encouraging Cash to continue the hot kiss there. Cash didn't disappoint. He latched on to the skin, suckling, mouthing and biting. One hand tried to reach inside his tight jeans, the other fought the complicated buckle of the belt Dev had worn that day, trying to free Dev of his jeans.

"Fuck, you're fuckin' hot. Draw blood. Mark me. Give me somethin' to remember you by," Dev panted as he reached down to help with the belt buckle. When Cash sank his teeth into his skin, Dev's throbbing cock demanded release. The goddamn appendage wanted in on that action. His hips bucked on their own accord, driving into Cash's hand lowering his jeans to massage the outline of his cock.

It was too much. With a strong push against Cash's chest, he shoved the man back several feet. He needed distance if he was going to last another minute. His other hand pointed to the shower several feet away. "Go there."

He took several steps backward, watching Cash with a critical but desperate eye. He worked the complicated buckle free. He'd chosen it today because the belt had a cool vibe. Something unique and different from a regular belt buckle, and the goddamn thing was going straight in the trash once he got it free. He would never make that mistake again.

"Stop lookin' at me like I'm dinner. I'm fuckin' you in the shower."

Cash's steps turned as predatory as his hungry glare. He stalked toward Dev, causing Dev to turn and jog awkwardly as he threw the belt toward the trash can and began removing his boots and jeans as he went.

"Run all you want. You can't escape me. When I catch you, I'm fucking you first." Cash's growl hinted at wicked promises to come.

An instant grin split Dev's lips, liking that idea more than he probably should.

"I thought about you today," Cash said in that same sexy tone.

Dev let the jeans fall down his legs as he reached for the bathroom light.

"Yeah?" Dev managed, toeing at the heel of his steel-toed boots, trying to get them off. His steps turned awkward as he reached for the faucet, turning on the overhead showerhead. The water pushed through like a rain shower. Cash's hands circled around his waist, that big body flush against his back. The thick hard cock nestled in the crack of his ass. Cash massaged his palms up the sides of his body, leaving a trail of fire everywhere they touched.

Every part of Dev wanted Cash to shove him into the shower and have his way with him. But there was no way these boots were coming off without being unlaced.

What had he been thinking when he dressed this morning?

Certainly not that this fine man would be waiting for him to get home, talking about things like thinking of him during his day.

Cash's lips landed in the crook between his neck and shoulders, sucking with intention. His hand cupped Dev's pec, teasing fingertips skimmed his tight nipple, circling until he gave a decadent pinch.

"Jesus Christ." His cock wept, wanting those fingers to pinch down there.

Dev bent and lifted a foot to untie the laces of his boots, needing to speed this along. "Lube and condoms in the cabinet. Upper corner."

Cash had no choice but to ease off him, causing Dev to lose his balance and land on his ass on the toilet seat. He never stopped removing the most annoying boots to ever be taken off.

His gaze lifted to Cash. His fingers stumbled as he took a long hard look at the handsome, nude man in front of him. Every part of Cash was strong and defined, sculpted by the gods themselves. He wasn't sure he'd ever seen so much beauty before.

Cash grabbed the lube then condoms and turned back, smiling when he noticed Dev was staring at him. For some unexplained reason, Dev felt Cash looking at him with the same reverence he gave Cash.

It made no sense at all.

"You're beautiful," Cash murmured and lowered to one knee to help him out of his boots.

"I was thinkin' the same thing about you," Dev admitted, letting Cash take his heel and begin to edge the tight hold off his foot. It popped free, sending Cash reaching for the floor to stay upright.

He placed that boot to the side and reached for the other one.

"Why don't I have a shower like this in my apartment?" Cash asked, unlacing the hooks. "Better question, why were you in the other bathroom's shower if you have this one?"

"Honest answer?"

"Always."

"I couldn't stand the idea of bein' thirty-five feet away from you," Dev answered. "I planned to take you to breakfast when you woke up. There's a place I love down the street that I've been eatin' at since I was a kid. I figured you might like it." He had zero to lose by dumping it all out. His life was a straight-up shitshow. If Cash bolted tonight and never came back, at least Dev made an attempt to keep him around. Cash's brows lifted, his eyes followed, and Dev reached out to mess with Cash's styled hair. The one section fell forward onto his forehead. "Don't worry. You don't have to say anything. It'll be short lived. I'm completely clinically crazy. I can't hang on to a thought more than a second. Maybe as long as my next orgasm."

He could tell Cash didn't know if he was kidding or not.

When no other words were said, he was afraid he'd made the night awkward. "I'm just fuckin' with you...."

"No, I get it. I keep thinking about last night too. I don't normally connect with people like I do with you," Cash said. "Your drawings speak to me. I felt it all again when I sifted through them this morning. You're very talented." The boot popped free. That one was tossed carelessly over his shoulder, those strong hands moved his jeans and underwear over his feet, taking the socks with them. "Clinically crazy though?"

Dev grinned. He hadn't been to a doctor's office since he was nine years old. They might have suggested psychological testing, but his mother had his back, insisting it was them not him. Whatever that meant.

He'd turned into his own therapist. Fist-fighting the world and the calming effects of weed were his choices for self-medication. "I might've been exaggeratin' a tad."

Cash's strong fingers circled around his cock as he bent forward, swallowing him whole. Any steam Dev lost came back with a roar, his cock growing hard as a rock inside Cash's mouth. The guy had no gag reflex or a need to build up. Dev hit the back of his throat. Cash reared back, then took all of him back inside that wickedly skilled mouth. He gave two or three good swallows as his hand came back to Dev's nipple, fingers caressing and rolling the sensitive bead. Dev's hands tangled in Cash's hair, an attempt at controlling his movements.

"You fuckin' do it for me, man," Dev hissed. "I won't last. Not tonight. In the shower."

He heaved in a breath, his fingers trailed along Cash's jaw, feeling the hint of the stubble forming there. He had to force his hand away, reaching inside the shower. The warmth was perfect. Cash bobbed his head up and down, swallowing around Dev each and every time. Cash cupped his balls, giving the perfect amount of pressure. Caressing and teasing, driving Dev wild. His eyes closed as he gripped Cash's shoulders, gently pushing at the hunk of a man who made him feel so damned good.

"You recover fast enough." Cash pulled off his cock, only to bury his face in Dev's crotch. His hand continued the up and down motion on his shaft. "You smell good."

Dev ran his hand through Cash's hair. What a sexy move. He lifted his heavy lids to watch, memorizing the way Cash looked bent over him, on his knees, worshiping his cock and balls. Dev tightened his fingers in Cash's hair, tugging his head back. "Worship my ass like you do my cock?"

Cash's grin spread, and he nodded. In that fluid way he had, he pushed back on his heels, standing, bringing Dev up with him.

Cash moved closer, his nose ghosting over Dev's collarbone and shoulder, breathing him in. His handsome face, with that stray piece of hair on his forehead, came eye to eye with him.

Cash grinned at Dev, his big palms brushing back his hair as he spoke. "No matter what else happens between us, you need to know, you really do it for me too."

"Yeah?"

Cash descended, missing his opening lips altogether. His nose coasting along Dev's jaw.

"Yeah. In a big way. I like to date. I don't do casual, yet here I am. Now get your ass in the shower so I can show you what I'm made of."

He wanted to say "*yes, sir,*" but that went against every fiber of his being, so he kept the words inside. He guided Cash under the spray and touched the switch, shooting water from all the heads, enjoying his one splurge in the building.

"Make me forget today?"

"If you can stand afterward, I didn't do my job." Cash took his mouth with a forceful kiss.

The trials of his day faded as Cash's wet body pinned him to the wall.

=♥=

This crossed every single professional line no matter how he tried to spin it.

Instead of dwelling on what he shouldn't do, he did what Dev asked him to do. He gripped Dev's ass cheeks roughly, squeezing and molding the flesh until his fingers dug into the crevice, searching for his hole. Dev wrenched away from the kiss, his head falling back, knocking against the wall.

"Don't open me." Dev panted.

He chuckled at Dev's command, placing the condoms on the small shelf carved into the wall. With a flip of the thumb, he opened the bottle of lube and slicked his fingers. Cash pushed two fingers inside Dev, easily breaching the rim, finding his lover's prostate. He pressed there, massaging and doing the exact opposite of what Dev asked.

Cash slid his other hand up Dev's defined stomach, his thumb teasing its way to his nipple. He pressed his lips against Dev's wet skin. Cash licked over one nipple, his finger and thumb grasping and squeezing the other. He worked Dev's ass, targeting the spongy bundle, the spot that had Dev's hips grinding back and forth into the touch.

Dev reached the hand on his chest and moved it to his neck. "Squeeze and bite at the same time," Dev panted.

He understood the assignment and had no intention of failing. He sucked the disc of Dev's nipple into his mouth, gently sinking his teeth into the soft skin while he tightened his hand around Dev's neck, squeezing. Cash worked three fingers into Dev's ass. His lover bucked against him, moaning his approval.

He teased Dev's hard nipple, then let it pop from his mouth seconds before goose bumps sprang along Dev's body. He tightened his fingers around Dev's neck and sped up the rhythm he used to work Dev's ass, watching his lover's sexy reaction.

Dev started pushing back and forth against his hand. The biker wanted it rough. The moans and groans resonating from deep inside his chest encouraged Cash on.

He liked the idea of dominating this man. It couldn't happen that often. He stood over Dev who leaned against the back wall, arching his body. The grin Cash gave darkened when Dev opened his eyes. He saw a pleading there. A man lost, searching for a way out. The hand holding Dev's neck tightened, his fingers digging into the skin only loosening this time after several long seconds.

Dev's breath rushed in and out of his lungs.

Cash's body slid against Dev's, his nipples hard as stone. The warm water beating down on them, mixed with the steel behind Dev's skin, sent shivers racing in every direction.

"Fuck me," Dev hissed and tried to turn around.

"I'll fuck you when I'm ready," Cash said, having no idea where those words had even come from. He gripped both their cocks in one hand. Dev set the pace, pushing in and out of his fist, over and again, until Cash dropped to his knee and took two good swallows of Dev's cock. Salty pre-come slid over his tongue from the very first taste. Dev was ready. As much as he enjoyed teasing Dev's ass with his fingers, his mouth needed in on the action. Still balancing on one knee, he used the hand on Dev's hip to twist him around.

"Bend," Cash commanded, using his hold to position Dev where he wanted. "Stay just like this."

"Fuck," Dev moaned as Cash's fingers spread his ass cheeks. The biker's forehead hit the shower wall with a thud as Cash teased Dev's hole with his tongue. Man, he loved rimming

Dev. He moved a hand to Dev's hip, keeping him locked in place as he devoured the man's ass.

"Fuck yeah." Dev growled.

Electricity built in the base of his spine, growing in intensity with every sexy moan and gasp from Dev. "You're killin' me. Keep goin'."

Cash reached between Dev's parted thighs and grabbed his cock, stroking.

"Fuckin' christ," Dev panted. He licked and nipped, pushing his tongue inside. Dev's hands came back, holding his ass open for Cash. They were so in sync. Doing this together. "Oh yeah, fuck me, big boy." Water rained down from the showerheads and steam swirled around them, adding to the erotic setting. He prayed he'd remember this moment for the rest of his life.

"I wanna come with you inside me." Dev's impatient tone broke the spell he'd been under.

Cash was so there too.

He licked the water beading on Dev's skin as he stood. Cash pressed himself against Dev's heated body, reaching for the lube again. Dev tried to turn around but staring this man in the eyes would be too much right now.

"Stop playin' with me," Dev growled, the sound rumbling in the enclosed space.

"I thought that's what you wanted me to do." He squeezed lube on his fingers, pushed them into Dev's ass, then squirted a stream into Dev's crease. With the lube tossed back on the shelf, he gripped Dev's shoulder. Then lined his cock with Dev's ass. He rocked his hips forward.

Dev pushed his ass backward, taking every inch of Cash in one thrust. Cash's entire body flexed and tensed at the sensation. Breath no longer mattered. The only thing that did was the understanding that Dev's body was made for him. He withdrew almost completely out of Dev before driving forward again.

"Just like that," Dev said. His head landed on Cash's shoulder as he rocked his hips back and forth, trying to set his own pace. "Harder…"

Dev clasped Cash's hand and brought it to Dev's neck again. He squeezed their fingers, cutting off his own breath for a few seconds. Dev's body reacted to the constriction. His chest arched forward, driving his ass back against Cash. Dev slid his arms around Cash's neck, his fingers tangling in his wet hair. He rode Cash's cock, rolling his hips in perfect time with the rhythm Cash created.

The sound of their bodies coming together, flesh slapping against flesh, was music to his ears.

He wasn't able to do anything more than what Dev wanted him to do. He locked an arm around Dev's waist, holding him tight, keeping him in this position as he pounded into his ass. He bent his knees, driving upward, taking Dev to the tips of his toes.

"Yes... Goddamn, yes," Dev cried. Cash did it again and again.

He canted his hips, ramming into Dev's ass, while he squeezed Dev's neck, choking his lover as requested. He loved the intensity, the sounds, the feel of Dev's body quivering around his.

Losing himself to his own pleasure, he feared another wicked request from Dev would tip him over the edge.

He searched deep inside himself for something, anything that could keep them together, just like this, forever. Nothing had ever felt as good as being inside Dev.

Fire flared hot in his soul.

"I can't... Come," Dev mumbled. Cash instinctively tightened his hand on Dev's neck.

The groan of appreciation tumbled forward as Cash reached for Dev's cock. Dev's body tensed and his ass contracted so hard around Cash. He lost it. He came on the very next forward thrust. If only he could have stopped there, he might have been able to catch his breath. It felt so good. Cash rode his release, thrusting in and out of Dev, over and over, emptying his seed deep inside the hot confines of that constricting ass.

Cash's palm hit the side of the wall. His knees buckled. The arm holding Dev against him gave way, letting Dev slide to his knees. His own head hit the tiled wall as he slumped forward. The water rained down over him for God knew how long as he tried to gather his wits.

He was generally a machine after sex but not now. Dev had taken everything from him. Mind, body, and soul.

# Chapter 19

The terry cloth towel Dev grabbed had to have been used a dozen times by now. He'd given the last clean one to the hulk of the man he'd showered with. He scrubbed the towel through his hair then down his back, lifting his legs as he left the bathroom, drying each one as he went. Drying his cock and ass came last as he rounded the corner to the kitchen.

He was starving, like next level hungry, and wadded the damp towel into a knot before sending it flying toward the laundry room's French doors. His aim had been off to get the doors to open with the wet towel. Sometimes he got lucky. Not tonight though. It hit the middle of one door then slid down in a lump.

The pizza box on the stove was empty. Maybe he'd grabbed the last slice… He couldn't remember.

The cabinet he used as a pantry held all his attention. He opened the two cabinet doors, stepped back, and looked at his selection. He should really have a wider variety of food to choose from.

A can of tomatoes, a can of corn, and a half-eaten jar of peanut butter did their best to entice him.

He reached for the refrigerator door, tugging it open. He caught a whiff of something. Probably from the girls' cereal bowls still sitting on a shelf. He really needed to get better about cleaning up. Dev spotted a loaf of bread that looked pretty new and a jar of grape jelly. He grabbed both of those, absently placing them on the counter. The girls had wanted PB and J and chips. Wait. He had a box of individually packaged chips in the laundry room. He pivoted that direction, using his fingers to comb through the longer strands of his hair, coaxing them off his face and into some sort of order.

Maybe he could entice the pretty boy to stay a few more hours. He could nap, fuck his neighbor, then get a bit more shuteye. Cash could then fuck him into oblivion with some hot good morning sex.

Eat first. Great plan. Damn he was talented at building a great plan of action.

He'd let the pretty boy snack on his ass again. Cash seemed to really like being down there. Dev had watched between his legs as Cash tightly squeezed his leaking cock during his last rim job. He'd bet, with the right amount of encouragement, Cash would come while eating Dev's ass. What a seriously giving partner. Dev's cock plumped just thinking about Cash getting off while licking at his ass.

Better yet, his big ole neighbor had handled him as if he were nothing more than a rag doll. He looked forward to being tossed around by him every day.

Cash quieted his mind better than any drug he'd ever done. Even right now, his head was still silent for the most part.

Content to just be in the moment.

Good, deep sleep looked possible.

Exactly what he needed after such a shitstorm of a day.

He kicked the towel aside, opened the French doors, and reached for the box of chips sitting on the dryer.

Dirty clothes littered the laundry room making him quickly shut the door. He was a pig, living in a pigsty. Cash didn't seem like that kind of guy. If he wanted to convince the man to stay the night, he'd have to do better at hiding his dirty side.

At least the one that left a mess behind.

He chuckled at his joke.

A wicked grin spread while thinking over all the filthy as fuck things he wanted from the strong guy in the other room.

His body vibrated at the possibilities when the sounds coming from the bedroom said Cash was heading his way.

"This bedroom's a weird mix of things," Cash called out.

"Mae's a princess in everything she does. Abi is more goth. She's too much like me. She loves Halloween. They share that room when they're here," Dev answered, dropping the box of chips on the counter. He reached for a spoon from the dishwasher, quickly running it under the spray of water from the sink's faucet just in case it wasn't clean and began to build a peanut butter and jelly sandwich.

"They have this room, and you took the spare?" Cash asked, stepping inside the kitchen. Dev gave him the side eye, taking in the tight-fitting joggers on his otherwise naked body. "I picked up the bathroom."

"You know, I don't normally like clothes on my bed partners, but those joggers leave little to the imagination."

Cash glanced down the length of his body as if that were the first time he'd ever heard such a thing. Impossible based on what greeted Dev down south.

"I don't think so," Cash said, his palm skimming down one side.

"I bet you pair it with one of those size too small T-shirts. You should charge for the show you put on. It's like the openin' scene of every porn I've ever watched."

Cash jerked his head up, looking as if Dev were the strangest guy on the planet. Then he shook his head, almost as if he found no merit in his words. Better. That meant he'd get to see more of the outline of the big cock. It looked good hard, flaccid, and all the ways in between.

"You don't like clothes, I take it." The pointed stare made Dev take a step back and wiggle his hips, sending his cock bouncing around.

"Do you want me in clothes? I can't seem to remove them in any sort of sexy or timely fashion…"

"That's a good point, but we have a problem," Cash said and came within inches of Dev, leaning his hip against the counter next to him.

"I bet pretty boy problems are way different problems than my kind of problems," Dev said and lifted the peanut butter covered spoon to his mouth, sucking off the contents. He dropped the spoon back in the jar, scooping out a glob and offering it to Cash.

The range of expressions on Cash's face as he looked at the spoon, the jar of peanut butter, then over to the slice of bread... Dev busted out with a laugh. "I'm guessin' that look means you're not a double dipper?"

Dev dumped the rejected peanut butter on a piece of bread and spread.

"I can double dip," Cash started, shaking his head with a hard *no*. "But what you just did with the mouth first then into the jar, I'm out." The humor that welled up inside him brought forward a happy, easygoing place he didn't know was inside him.

Dev barked out another laugh and leaned into Cash, puckering his lips. Cash stared down at the offering then into Dev's eyes. Cash was slower to lean in and press his lips to Dev's. "You don't strike me as a guy who gives casual affection."

He lifted the spoon back between them, waving it in front of Cash as he reached for the jar of jelly. "You'd be right in that statement. Never kissed anyone but you like that. I've told you, there's somethin' different about you. You bring it out in me."

He interpreted this stare to mean he'd lost his mind.

Pretty boy was pretty damned astute.

"I guess I like to kiss bossy men," he said, waggling his brows. He dipped the same spoon inside the jelly, dumping a glob on the other slice of bread. His hunger required he lick that spoon before spreading the jelly on the bread. "Muscadine jelly. Bitter and sweet at the same time. Fuckin' good. Want a lick of this?"

He looked at Cash who only shook his head.

"That's what I figured. Is it the sugar this time or the one spoon for everything I've done, includin' my mouth?"

"Absolutely both," Cash answered. "You know, lots of people don't eat from a utensil and then put it back in the jar due to bacteria. But then spreading peanut butter into the jelly jar..."

Dev barked out a laugh and dropped the spoon in the sink. He put his sandwich together, looked in the cabinet for a plate. There wasn't one there and decided to just hold the sandwich. It wouldn't last long anyway. He quickly added the tops to the jars, and retied the bread, scooping it all up, dumping it on the top refrigerator shelf.

"Come tell me the problem you have with mouth bacteria on the sofa. I'm exhausted." Dev took the sandwich, grabbed a random bag of chips from the box, and plopped down on the sofa. "Some bossy pretty boy kept me up all night."

"I'm not pretty," Cash said, following behind him, sounding confused and flattered by the compliment at the same time.

Dev took a big bite of the peanut butter sandwich and cast a quick look over his shoulder. Scanned a fast eye up and down Cash's body for good measure. It wasn't a hardship. "You're pretty hot. Pretty fascinatin'. Pretty muscular. Pretty hair. Pretty voice. Pretty ass. Pretty cock…"

"Okay, I get it," Cash said, stopping a roll that could go on for hours.

Dev plopped his ass down on the sofa, spread his legs and placed the chips where his hips and thighs met. He hoped he enticed Cash as much as Cash enchanted him. Maybe he could get those lips wrapped around his cock one more time before he fell asleep which was coming on fast.

"The problem is, I didn't wrap up. I didn't even think about it. It felt so good, I lost my mind in there."

"Amazin', right?" Dev asked, grinning. It had been a while since he'd gone without a condom, and honestly, he hadn't forgot. He needed skin on skin with this guy. It felt so damn good.

Cash's eyes narrowed.

"Look. You ate my ass." Dev placed the sandwich on his thigh and reached for the chips, opening them. "Not only ate my ass, but you devoured the fuck out of me. Hands down, best I've ever had. You probably ruined me for anyone else. You've sucked my cock. You swallowed last night, and you came inside me. The chances I gave you anything are small. I had a bout with the clap a few years ago but nothin' since, and Tena gave me that shit. I cleared it up and wrapped up since. I think you're good. I love that shit. It feels better to me. I'd risk it with you."

Cash nodded. The crease in his brow didn't let up, probably considering the ramification of the clap. Dev answered as if he knew for sure.

"It's been years. I got tested by a doc the club uses. He came to the house, gave me antibiotics. I took them all and got tested again." Dev shrugged, took another bite of the sandwich and decided to add the shocking part to his explanation just to see how far that line between Cash's brows could crease. "I'm good. It was all Tena. I used to like to watch her fuck other people, especially after I bought her those fake tits. Sometimes I'd join in, sometimes not. It was a sick thing we shared. Hadn't been with her since then. What about you?"

He had to fight the laughter building inside him at the silence staring back at him.

One of those big palms covered Cash's eyes.

Any other time someone had given him a similar look, a fight or a parting of the ways came next. Neither of those options applied with Cash. He somehow knew Cash had the patience of… whatever was patient.

Dev took a bite of the chips in his hand, grabbed the rest of his uneaten sandwich and the bag, and got to his feet. Exhaustion barreled down on him.

"Change of subject," Dev said as he started for his bedroom. "Let's sleep for about an hour then you could wake me up with your tongue up my ass. Don't stretch me before you fuck me next time. I've seen that's hard for you…" He chuckled.

At the bedroom door, he stopped again, and shoved half the sandwich into his mouth as he spotted the unmade bed. He'd fucked Cash all over the blanket wadded in the middle. He bet the pretty boy liked clean beds. The chips were tossed on the dresser, and he grabbed the spread.

Cash wasn't in the bedroom with him.

From the door, Dev tossed the blanket toward the laundry room. His tired eyes landed on Cash who hadn't moved from his spot in front of the sofa. "I was tryin' to be funny, not assumin'. If you stay tonight, I'll make up the shower to you tomorrow. I'm not as perverted as I'm makin' it seem. Those days are long gone."

Dev hovered in the doorframe, staring at the handsome man who exuded clean-cut and good decisions. Which meant, Cash knew exactly what a bad decision Dev was. They stared at one another. Whether or not Cash wanted to stay, he had to feel the unseen bond they shared cinching tighter.

"Let's see if I can say it better. In the mornin', I'll wake you by gently stretchin' you open—you really seem to like that, so I'll give it to you. Besides, I don't like the idea of causin' you pain. It's a weird feelin' for me. I'll figure that out later. I'll wrap up and do my best to tenderly love you until all you see is me for the rest of your day."

Dev's shoulder hit the doorframe. He crossed his arms over his chest. His fatigue had him fighting back a yawn. "When I'm in you, I'll tell you how gorgeous you are to me. And you are. How much I've liked the last couple days. And I have. I also have a clean, thicker blanket ready for the bed. My sheets are pretty clean. I had a spill and had to change them a few days ago but I'll rewash 'em tomorrow if you'll agree to come back tomorrow night. Lots of condoms in the drawer because I'm responsible no matter how I present myself. I'll always use them with you, but you don't have to use them on me. Is that better?"

"I prefer condoms," Cash said. He tilted his head to the side and the muscles in his thick neck rolled, his shoulders followed as he started toward Dev. "I appreciate the words. I wasn't lying when I said I don't do this often."

Dev chuckled and nodded, pushing off the doorframe. "I don't know that I've ever spent three nights in a row with the same person. Not even when I was married. I've known Tena for twenty years. We met in elementary school. Got hitched three weeks after Mae was born. Marriage didn't suit us."

Cash nodded, watching him grab the blanket out of his closet. Cash stepped up to him and placed his palm over Dev's heart. The anxiety of Cash leaving evaporated under the touch. "No more talk of the past. It makes you edgy. Where do you want me?"

"Climb in the center of the bed," Dev said, relieved and excited Cash was staying. They locked gazes. Dev was a bulldozer that Cash managed to keep in check. "I'll follow. Want me in clothes?"

Cash shook his head, looking as if he were crazy. "Absolutely not."

The honesty they shared in the exchange silenced anything more Dev might have to say. What a rare occasion.

= ♥ =

Dev hadn't read Cash's mood properly.

He didn't care one whit about the mess...mostly.

He didn't care where they slept...mostly.

What bothered him was how Dev chose to be so careless with his body and his life.

He spoke of gonorrhea as if it were the common cold. Dev acted as if his life didn't matter. That his presence in this world didn't have meaning. Hell, take it a step further. Dev didn't seem to care if he lived or died.

Instead of saying any of that or doing what he really wanted to do and tell this man exactly how valuable he was, how Cash's own life only mattered because of the meaning Dev had placed in it twenty years ago, he did as Dev asked. He climbed to the center of the bed, after discarding his pants. "Here?"

"Look at you followin' directions. I wasn't sure you had it in you." Dev chuckled and whipped the blanket out in one sure move, letting it land across the mattress and much of Cash's legs. Dev turned off the overhead light, and followed him down, crawling across the bed, maneuvering until he was lying beside Cash, drawing the blanket up.

Dev lived with no pretense. He angled his body, nudging his knee between Cash's thighs, raising enough to position his cock comfortably. He drew the edge of a second pillow over with him. Another first in a string of firsts for Cash. He'd never slept with someone on top of him before. Even more weird, the position was perfect for him too.

"I won't always make you cuddle me," Dev said, moving his head and the edge of the pillow to the crook of Cash's neck. He yawned a deep yawn. "You could put your arms around me. Act like you're happy to be here with me."

Cash chuckled and lifted an arm.

"I'm not needy, but you could move your hand over me."

"I'm sure you're the exact definition of needy," Cash replied, bringing his palm up. He gently grazed his fingertips up and down Dev's back. "The choking thing was new to me."

He had no idea why he chose those words instead of taking the opportunity to get back to business and feel the guy out. Tired people always had loose lips.

"I know. You kept tightenin' your fingers then easin' off. It was sweet, but you're supposed to cut off air. It makes the whole thing better," Dev said, lifting his head to look at Cash.

"I don't know that I can do that," Cash said honestly, his fingers rose over Dev's shoulder until they touched his cheek. "You're too special to risk yourself like you do. Do you want to choke yourself during sex all the time?"

"No. Never before but I heard it's good. Some of the people I've fucked like it. I think it's risky too. I guess I trusted you.

But I've learned CPR on the off chance. Though that wouldn't have helped me earlier." Dev gave a puff of a chuckle and lifted his head again. The angle wasn't right for Cash to look at him, so he didn't try. "I get in the moment. They want to be strangled. I'm not really there for them. I have no idea how much time passes until I let go and their limp body falls to the floor."

*Hmm.*

Maybe that was added for shock value... Dev did that.

Silence blanketed them.

Why did he want to know if Dev was messing with him?

*Please don't let him be confessing a murder...*

"I'm fuckin' with you. She fell to the floor gaspin' for breath. She's good."

"Ha. Ha," Cash said, instantly relieved.

"What about fistin'?" Dev said, yawning again. His hard body relaxed against Cash. "I think I'd like your fist in my ass. It's supposed to help with the head issues. Am I sayin' too much? I'm freakin' you out, aren't I?"

"You know what else is good for your head? Going to a mental health care counselor," Cash suggested.

"You go to a mental health care physician," Dev shot back defensively. Cash chuckled, his chest rumbling underneath Dev's body. He tightened his arms around this crazy man.

"I have. Many times in my life," Cash answered honestly. "Still do when I need it." Any emotional distance Cash may have tried to place between them vanished.

He held Dev with a protective vise-like hold, drawing him closer. The reality of the limited number of times they would ever have this innocent, quiet time together, holding one another, began to tick away.

"Maybe I should make an appointment for myself tomorrow since I'm lying here with a man who wants me to choke him, while fucking him without any protection. Even going so far as to consider any future condom wearing."

"Sounds like a Tuesday night in my life." Dev lifted his head to defend himself. "I don't want you to choke me all the time. Just tonight. But doin' what you did in the shower. Takin' me off my feet. That shit turned me on. I've never had anyone do that to me."

An uncharacteristic move for Cash too, but he agreed, it felt good.

"Sleep for about an hour. Wake me up. Good?" Dev asked.

Cash nodded, his fingers mapping the hard planes and well-defined muscles of Dev's back for something to remember later.

"My buddy thinks I need a head doctor too," Dev murmured, his voice dragging. "No condom..."

Dev fell asleep as Cash stared at the ceiling. The close camaraderie they shared spoke of weeks and weeks, if not months and years, of closeness. Not the three or four days since they'd officially met.

Why had he ever followed Dev's directives and choked him? That kind of thing was so outside Cash's wheelhouse he couldn't even find a possibility of an answer. He liked making Dev happy though.

Damn, he was attached. So attached. Too attached. He should recuse himself from the operation. Then maybe beg Dev to leave with him. Let them have a chance at something more than Dev's complete downfall and destruction.

A lump formed in his throat.

He thought about the way he'd cleaned Dev when they were finished. Cash had soaped his hands, skimmed every inch of the biker reverently. Dev had let him, watching and relaxing into the touch. He had always dreamed of finding a connection like this. A give and take until they found what they liked, making it special for the both of them.

The double dipping peanut butter and jelly was going to be a problem though.

But why? Dev had a point. He ate the man's ass every chance he got.

Cash had to get out of his own head. It didn't matter how much he liked Dev. In the next day or two, it would all change.

He needed mental distance and pushed off his back, taking Dev to his. Dev was out and did little more than continue the turn, angling his body away from Cash.

The guy had a shit day.

Cash would make sure the agency took care of Dev financially.

First thing, Cash was cleaning this house. Maybe he should hire a grocery service. He could put that request in Dev's paperwork too, and a housekeeper. Cash rolled from the bed, gathering the drawings still littering the floor. He hoped the girls had stayed out of this room. Dev was excellent at recreating their intimate moments into sheet after sheet of beautiful, erotic porn. He loved Dev's drawings. He placed those on the dresser and quietly gathered the clothes off the floor before starting out of the room. He shut the door behind him.

The entire place was a mess. He kept going, picking up the dirty clothes until he opened the French doors to the laundry area. He could only laugh. Like everywhere else, he was knee deep in a mess.

His mother's voice came to his head, saying what she always said to get him to help with the chores: Cleanliness is godliness. A small concession, but he did like to clean.

He lifted the lid to the washing machine. Thankfully it was empty. He loaded it full and started the washer before going in search of trash bags. Of course, the box was empty.

Cash went back to his place for cleaning supplies. All the cleaning supplies.

He doubted there were many inside Dev's apartment.

# Chapter 20

"I'm home," Dev hollered before the back door to his mother's kitchen shut.

He listened for a response, hearing nothing more than silence from inside the house. He glanced around the darkened kitchen. The only light on was above the large kitchen sink.

The newly decorated Thanksgiving cookies and cupcakes placed on four covered cake plates in the center of the massive island snagged his attention. His stomach growled his approval as he went that direction first before seeking out the girls.

He looked over the selection, quickly identifying who'd decorated what. Abigail's designs sat to the right. They were all in different shades of black. Black icing, black sprinkles, a gothic vibe drawn on top. She had his love for art and the malevolent side of life. He snagged two of those, taking a large bite of one before shoving the rest of the cookie in his mouth.

To the left were Mae's decorations. She went with the colors of the season. All fall themed with no real design. He could see the effort she used in trying to make each one perfect. He took two from her plate too.

His mother had the most delicious sugar cookie recipe. One he had loved for his whole life. At least one plate of cookies was coming home with him tonight.

Laughter from the other side of the house drew his attention. He started down the long hall, holding the cookies in such a way that the icing job didn't get ruined. He'd learned that lesson the hard way last Thanksgiving. He'd stacked each one on top of the other in one hand. Both girls lost their minds at how easily he destroyed their creations.

It always amazed Dev how the women in his life tried to make him considerate and mindful. It never really worked until his daughters came along, and just like that, he tried to do better to please them.

Kids were a fucked-up mind game of devotion and love.

His mother had bought this house a few years back. It became her sanctuary. To Dev, the borderline mansion was big and sprawling while still feeling homey. She excelled in building a comfortable space. This home's theme was modern bohemian chic. One of the sofas cost more than he spent annually on groceries.

The place beat the hell out of the two-bedroom shanty Dev had grown up in in the middle of the worst part of South Dallas.

His father wasn't allowed there unless invited. His old man had tried to flex his muscles once. He came over, saying he owned this house and he'd be there when he wanted. His badass mother had come damn close to setting his beloved Harley on fire, flexing her own brand of control right back. Since then, he hadn't been back unless she approved.

Dev ate another entire cookie while walking the length of the hallway toward the farthest family room. Dev rounded the corner and found the three of them lounging on the couch. An animated movie played on the large television screen.

"How much Disney can two kids watch?" Dev asked loudly to gain their attention. "I get there's lots of death and destruction in those movies, but seriously, why do you two love 'em so much?"

Mae bounded from his mother's side, leaping toward Dev. All her love chimed in the single use of his name, "Daddy."

Man, he was a sucker for Abi and Mae.

She jumped up on the edge of the sofa and leaped toward him. But he had the cookies in that hand. He busted a move to catch her. Luckily, he did.

"We missed you." She wrapped her arms around his neck as he hoisted her up. She squeezed him as tight as her zero-muscled arms could. The movie paused. His mother untangled herself from Abigail. This was the first time he'd seen his mom since the boob job. He didn't mean to stare but they changed her smallish frame drastically.

"Mom…" he said, doubtfully.

She automatically knew what he referred to and began to shake her head. "I love them, so not another word."

Her arm came around him, giving a side hug. "I see you found the cookies."

"I made those," Mae said proudly to the ones in his hand. He instantly looked at Abigail.

"I ate yours comin' down the hall. They're good. I knew it was yours because they were the same color as your heart," he teased, trying for a compliment she'd appreciate and stuck his tongue out, knowing the dark dye in the icing left a streak there. It appeased her. She nodded. Her fingertip pressed on a word from the book in her lap, already halfway through the large novel.

"I feel like the Cullen's need to adopt me," Abi said in perhaps a teasing way. It was hard to know with her.

He nodded, raising his brows. She gave him a rare smile and began to read again.

"Are the Cullen's real? It didn't seem like they were," Dev asked his mom in a stage whisper meant to be heard by Abi. "She's not plannin' on gettin' adopted right? I like her. She's pretty okay to have around."

Abi gave a huff, never lifting her head from the book.

Mae's head went to his shoulder. Her lips turned to press against his T-shirt. She was so sweet.

"Daddy, I'm glad to see you, but we want to stay with Momo this week."

Mae couldn't have planned the timing better to draw him in then sucker punch him right in the gut.

"What? I drove all this way to get you. I can bring you back in the mornin'."

"Thank you for coming, but we'll just stay tonight. Can I watch TV?" she asked, moving to where her face was inches from his. He edged her down on the sofa where she bounded three jumps back to the remote.

"Girls, I'm going to feed your father. Y'all finish watching the movie," his mother said.

"That's code for stay in here," Abi explained to Mae.

"I know. You don't know everything," Mae shot back.

Dev started to intervene, hoping to stop an argument before it got started, but his mom ushered him from the room.

"No fighting," she said casually over her shoulder and got a *"Yes, ma'am"* back in unison.

All he could do was stare at her and her magical power, wanting to dissect exactly what she did to make them easily agree. She started down the hall where he was slower to follow. "How did you do that?"

"I'm forty-four years old. If I haven't learned how to talk to children, that's on me," she explained as if that answered anything. The logic was so iffy he slowed his steps even further, analyzing her Confucius says style of teaching. "I made you dinner. The girls helped. The mashed potatoes are a little salty. That's a Mae thing. She insisted you like a lot." Mashed potatoes generally meant homemade fried chicken. The rest was forgotten as he took long strides to catch up. "How was Keyes?"

Outside of the cookies, he hadn't eaten since Cash had brought him a vegan bowl of rice and vegetables last night that turned out to be pretty good.

*Cash.* The name bounced around his head like a happy little bouncy ball.

The guy hadn't been far from his thoughts all day.

He didn't understand it. Cash turned out to be an extreme source of happiness. His pretty boy had an ability to keep all the worries and discord at a distance. His head hadn't been screaming at him since the moment they met. He hadn't dialed Tena one time, let alone a thousand times, telling her what a cunt she was. He considered that a win. Life seemed easier to manage with Cash staying at his place at night.

Two mornings ago, when he'd awakened on his own and alone in bed, Dev had whipped off the blankets with force, ready to storm across the hall and demand another five-star fucking.

Then he'd entered the main part of his apartment. How the smell of disinfectant and cleaner hadn't assaulted his nose from the minute his eyes popped open spoke to how situationally unaware he was when it came to that generous man.

He swore his apartment sparkled like a Mr. Clean commercial.

Cash had washed every single surface in his house. Piles of clothing, towels, sheets, and blankets were folded neatly and left on the kitchen island. Cash had to have been up all night to manage all his mess. A handwritten note was tucked underneath Dev's wallet and keys. His cell phone was plugged into the charger next to the entry table.

Dev,

I let you sleep.

The only thing left to do is wash the sheets on your bed.

You were passed out. You didn't wake when I ran the vacuum.

I'll make good on your other requests this evening.

Text me when you get home. I've got an early morning meeting.

~ Cash

Cash left his phone number.

Dev read it again, noting the efficient script. No unnecessary words.

Why did it feel like a heartfelt love note?

Maybe because he couldn't remember anyone caring enough to clean for him then explain themselves in writing.

Dev used his phone that Cash had placed on the charger to snap pictures of the clean house then of the note.

He texted Cash, giving an oath to try to keep the apartment this clean forever.

He also tried his hand at sexting.

*"I'm fucking you so good tonight, pretty boy."*

He pushed send then sent another. *"Be ready. I'll do the stretching."* And another text. *"Fucking you right in the middle of my clean living room floor."* He had another thought, typing quickly. *"I'm sketching you the way you look when you come."* He pressed send again.

At this point, why stop? Fuck Cash's meeting. He grinned as he continued to type.

*"Maybe ink that picture on my belly. I've been searching for just the right tattoo for there."*

He pushed send and tossed the phone on the table to keep from sending any other messages. His depraved mind ran wild with ideas of inking the image of Cash in the throes of his orgasm for the world to see. He hadn't taken a step away before he picked up the phone and added.

*"With your tongue out, wanting to catch my come. My steel aiming at your mouth."* He pushed send as his cock proved how hard it could get.

He could get into sexting.

His body tingled and hummed any time he thought about the hours he and the pretty boy spent together, exploring each other's bodies. Sex was so much better when meaning and thoughtfulness were added. He'd never realized it could be so good.

Cash had such a strong sex drive. The guy's recovery time was insane.

He should get a stash of Viagra just in case he needed a lift to keep up with the guy.

He hadn't smoked weed in days. He'd been too obsessed with Cash to even think about it.

He gripped his cock and took a picture, sending it to Cash.

"Where did you just go?" his mom asked.

*Shit.* He'd completely tuned out. Only drawing back into the kitchen to find he was straddling a barstool, placing the cookies on top of the center island.

"Umm…" He rewound their conversation. Keyes had been their topic. He tried for a blind answer, hoping to hit somewhere in the range of her question.

"He's good. We started a new back tattoo on him today. It's massive. Gonna take time to fill in, but it's good. He's so fuckin' tough." Dev looked at his mom. "Never flinched once. We were there for most of the day."

"You're like that too," she said. "I remember when your friend set your back tattoo. You never moved a muscle. Did you invite Keyes to Thanksgiving?"

"I did but he says he's got plans. He's changin' in a good way. Real balanced." Dev tried for a succinct update.

"He was always oddly stable for what he grew up in." She placed the plate of mashed potatoes and green beans in the microwave. His heart sang at the fried chicken underneath the grease spotted paper towel on the stove. She pointed to the chicken. "What pieces do you want?"

"All of them." Obviously.

She laughed and nodded, bringing the plate to Dev with a napkin and utensils. She went for the refrigerator. "I invited your father to Thanksgiving only under duress."

"Why duress?" Dev asked about her terrible decision.

His mother's face contorted as she brought a cold bottle of water to him. "Your father's got something going on. He feels like he's being watched closer than normal. He's so reckless and full of ego. It could be anything. What do you know?"

"Let's see. I know he's a motherfucker," Dev answered, twisting off the top to his water bottle. "He's pretty sure I'm gonna grow a titty because I'm tryin' to be a mama to the girls."

Her jaw set and eyes narrowed as she brought the plate from the microwave to him. "He believes all parenting should be done by the mother. It was my role to do everything. He makes me crazy." She gripped the edge of the counter and bowed up like a boxer ready for their next fight. He grabbed a chicken leg and took a big bite. Flavor exploded over his tongue.

"Are you eating?" she asked, causing him to look down at the food. He resisted the urge to open his mouth to show her the chewed bite inside. "I mean regularly."

He shrugged. Maybe he'd send Millie on a grocery run tomorrow. When she dropped the haul off at his house, she'd see how clean the apartment was.

"Have you heard from Tena?"

His brows furrowed. Wasn't she just asking all the questions tonight. The lump of chicken he'd started to swallow lodged in his throat. He forced the food down, reaching for the bottle of water.

"Jesus, Mom. Why come at me that way?"

"Dev, she's their mother and they're hurting," his mother explained, drawing straight up confusion from him.

"She's a selfish cunt," he replied. Tena was trash to him.

"You know I don't like that word." Whatever played behind her eyes was probably better left unsaid. He'd only get angry and pop off, offering no real comfort.

"The difference is that she is one," he tried to appease her, and took a big bite of the mashed potatoes.

They didn't taste quite as good as they might have had they not been talking about Tena.

"Well, I've done some things you need to know about. I have an attorney ready to fight for sole primary custody. We don't want Tena dropping back into their lives and creating chaos again. She'll have to follow some structure. It'll help in the long run."

He hadn't thought about that and nodded. Except as far as he was concerned, Tena could walk off the edge of the world and die.

"I also have some fun things for the girls planned tomorrow and Tuesday. Then Abi wants to help me make Thanksgiving dinner. I'd like them to stay here this week and longer," she started. That drew his gaze to her. No one had ever had any faith in him being a father, no matter how hard he tried. His heart ached that his mother seemed on board that same train. "I know it's a long drive for you, but after your holiday rush, you could move in here too. We could tackle raising the girls together, the way you want them raised."

He let those words soothe the irritation building.

"I have money set aside…" she started.

He vehemently shook his head, cutting her off. "This is my deal. I'm payin' for my kids. So, you're sayin' I'd sell the Sunnyvale property and the girls would live here full-time? Go to school around here. What school district is it?"

As if he had any idea what school districts were any good in the first place.

"Honey, it's Carroll ISD. An excellent district. We could get a nanny for after school, when neither of us can be here. I'm not trying to take over. I only want to enhance what you've started. They're wonderful children. Abigail is so smart. Mae is equally creative. I was poor and young when you were born. I wanted the same things for y'all…" She shook her head. "I'm on board with what you're doing. I want them in a place where they can remain children."

Not only was she on his side, she just signed on to help.

Relief flooded him. He hadn't wanted to go against her too.

Dev put the fork down and reached for the napkin, wiping his mouth.

The instant emotion of finally having someone who wanted the best for his daughters had tears stinging his eyes. He reached for the water bottle, gulping several long drinks to hide his over-the-top reaction.

When he could hold it together enough to speak, he told her his plan. "I was thinkin' about sellin' the Sunnyvale house and expandin' onto my apartment, takin' the first and second floor. Maybe stick them back in the private school Abi was in... But it's my busiest time of the year. I'll make a ton of money over the next five weeks if I can put in the hours, and that's as far as I got."

"Babe, think about it," she said. "We have a week before school starts again. I wanted to take them to San Antonio for the weekend after Thanksgiving. It'll be fun for them."

Dev put his elbows on the edge of the granite, tucking his hands underneath his forearms, leaning toward her. The food was forgotten. "I think about you bein' so young, walkin' down the street and my old man bein' thirty years old, pullin' over on his sled to holler at you. That shit worries me about the girls growin' up where I live." The disgust of the reality of such a situation had Dev balling his fists. "You gave up your life for me and Shanna. You're supposed to be in the prime of your life now. Not saddlin' yourself with my kids."

She shook her head at him. "I'm not going to raise your children. You are. I'll be here to have your back like you've always had mine. Especially during the holidays when you make most of your money," she explained. "And I love this house. They will too. They already have rooms here. You can have the guest house. It's small but has its own entrance and bathroom."

He nodded, hearing Mae's footsteps running toward them. She bounded into the room, not hesitating to climb onto the stool next to his. "The movie's over. Do you like the fried chicken? Momo said it's your favorite."

"I can't believe I forgot to ask you about the man you kissed!" his mother exclaimed.

His scowl landed on his daughter. "What happens in Daddy's house stays in Daddy's house," he teased, and she grinned, giving a full-body shiver in her exuberance.

"Momo says sometimes boys marry each other, so you can marry him if you want." Her dreamy tone held hints of romance and fairytales.

"Thanks for the permission," he said to both the females in the room. "Where's your dog?"

"Abi took him outside. He's a lot of work." A long piece of Mae's hair fell forward, and she blew it out of her face.

Since they were going random, he decided to ask his mom about the younger boy Tena had mentioned. Hazy images and memories had started to trickle forward. "Do you remember the kid who got shanked…"

His mother finished his sentence. "When you were nine years old? You were stabbed too, several times. That was the bravest thing I think you've ever done. You saved that boy's life."

"Who was the boy?" he asked. He'd been in too many fights and had done too many drugs. He doubted he could remember anything correctly.

"Ryan Cashin James. I'll never forget him. I went to the court trials because they were prosecuting for you too. That little guy didn't leave the hospital for months and had many surgeries after his initial stay."

"I don't remember really," he said, honestly. "I wonder why I don't remember?"

"I saved a lot of the newspaper articles. I can pull them for you. I followed him for a few years during the parole hearings. When those boys were released, I lost track of Ryan. His parents moved around a lot. They had a traveling ministry if I remember correctly and lived a more basic lifestyle. The one time your father met them, he spouted an earful about their peace, love, and happiness attitude. He blamed them for you being hurt. You know how he is."

"Why did he meet 'em?" His father had never taken an active role in his younger life.

"They came to the shop to check on you. I wasn't there but the guys told me what he said. It's always funny how he becomes the opposite of whoever he's talking to. They were hippies so he went card carrying patriot."

Yeah, he'd witnessed that many times. His old man went off on both sides of the political spectrum just to be an asshole. As if his core belief system wasn't to be a disruptive anarchist.

"Why do you ask about him?"

"T," he said, not wanting to say Tena's name in front of Mae. He nodded to the little bit beside him who was all ears. "Brought him up. My neighbor has a similar scar, I guess."

"Is he blond and small?" she asked.

"Dark and tall," Dev answered and mouthed the words *hot as hell* before taking another bite.

"The last time I remembered getting information from the parole board, his parents were in…maybe the East Coast."

"This guy's from Southern California. Relocated here for work," Dev said.

"Invite him to Thanksgiving," his mom suggested.

"And have him meet my father? No thanks. I'm enough to handle on my own. Imagine if Dad started in on me nursin'. He's way too normal for all this family dysfunction. And it's not serious. He's just cool," Dev explained, reaching for the chicken leg and taking another bite.

"The offer stands," she said, smiling at Mae. "Are you ready for some ice cream?"

"I want the unicorn sprinkles." She bounced in the seat. "Daddy wants them too."

He lifted his brows and looked at his mother whose grin grew.

"Sounds good to me," he said, shrugging.

"She's got a good hold on you," his mother said, opening the freezer door.

"You got a good hold on me." Dev nodded and grinned at Mae, gently knocking her with his elbow. She beamed up at him.

"You got a good hold on me too, Daddy." She mimicked his move, trying to bump him with her elbow. He had to catch her as she almost fell off her stool trying to tap him.

He was such a goner with her.

# Chapter 21

The loud rap on the front door had both Joe and Cash jerking their heads in that direction. Joe mouthed the word, "*Fuck*," and grabbed his laptop and glass of water, darting as silently as possible to his bedroom. Cash closed the lid to his government-issued laptop and, as quickly as Joe, went the other direction to his bedroom. After stuffing it between the mattress and box springs, he looked around the apartment, using his long shirt sleeve to wipe the condensation ring from Joe's glass off the table.

He placed both palms on the front door, glancing through the peephole to see Dev lifting his hand to knock again. Cash centered himself, drawing in a deep breath as he opened the door.

"Hey," Cash said.

Dev said nothing as he walked inside. He glanced down the front of Cash's dress shirt and slacks to the Italian loafers on his feet.

"You clean up nice," he said with a single nod of approval. "I haven't seen you like this. Is this what you wear to work?"

Dev shook his head, not waiting on a reply. "No, it's Sunday night. You didn't go to church, did you?"

Dev could be disarming without even trying. The biker walked up to him. Stood about six inches from his chest, his handsome face closer, to have this conversation. Whatever was in the brown paper bag in Dev's hand was seemingly forgotten.

"If you go to church lookin' like this, I might go with you. You're awfully pretty to be so masculine."

Cash grinned at the compliment. Couldn't help it. "Still pretty?"

"My pretty boy." The words were said with a cocky twist. Not the endearment whispered into his ear during their sex.

"What's that?" Cash asked, nodding to the paper bag, the door still wide open.

In all the nights they'd spent together, they'd never stayed at his place. He got how that might look to Dev but there was no way they were hanging out here for any amount of time. They were too sexually energized. Every time they got together, sex happened in some impatiently rough kind of way. The anxiety-charged Joe would lose his shit if he had to stay hidden during all their grunts and moans.

"Homemade fried chicken dinner made by my mother and the best sugar cookies you'll ever eat, decorated by my girls," he said and pivoted around toward Cash's kitchen, looking around the apartment. "I promise, one bite of this chicken and you'll change your vegan ways. You do live super clean. There's literally nothin' out of place."

"I've told you normal people pick up after themselves," Cash said, keeping his foot at the base of the door to keep it open. He'd have thought that might be an obvious clue that they needed to leave, but Dev didn't seem to catch on. What he did do was give a shocked expression over his shoulder before he began opening and closing Cash's cabinets. "I already ate."

Dev took a plate out, shut the cabinet door and spun around, back to the bag. He glanced at Cash again, this time looking at Cash then the door.

"Why're you tryin' to get me to leave?" he asked and started digging the contents out of the bag.

"Because I only have one set of sheets here and we never even make it this long without landing on them," Cash explained.

He cringed, knowing everyone on his detail was secretly listening.

"All right then. I got a question for you," Dev said, leaving the food out on the counter, coming back into the living room. He went to stand about five feet away from Cash on the opposite side of the living room. Something was different about Dev tonight. Cash looked a little closer but couldn't quite put his finger on what. He wore the same style jeans, vintage with lots of wear and tear. A retro T-shirt, this one an Ozzy screen print, with all the straps and bangles lining his wrists and around his neck.

He was handsome in a rough but vibrant kind of way. Well, gorgeous in any kind of way actually.

Ahh. Dev's hair had been trimmed. It had an artsy vibe. Shorter on the sides and back, longer on top. He was also shaved. The need to get Dev out of his apartment explained why Cash had missed the new look.

"I like your hair."

"No," he said and pointed a finger at Cash. "Don't distract me until we're at my place, because if I stay, I'll have to wash sheets before I can hit the sack. Listen to me. I have a story to tell you. When I was nine years old, maybe ten, dependin' on when it was, I jumped into the middle of a street initiation. Some punks were in the middle of shankin' a kid. They planned to leave him to die. The kid was a quiet, skinny, goody-two-shoes kind of kid. He was walkin' home from school, and he should have never been in my neighborhood to begin with. He didn't fit there. He was small for his age, super clean-cut and clearly headed to bein' gay."

Everything inside of Cash stilled. Dev knew. Chills shot down his spine. Nausea swarmed him. His stomach churned with sudden anxiety. What could he say?

He let go of the breath he held and quietly shut the door.

"I don't remember a lot of my involvement, but I know I was able to take a couple of those kids down which scared the others off. I was better with a blade than any of those posers. The kid didn't deserve what he was gettin'."

Cash took careful steps toward Dev. His heart wasn't ready for this moment. Not like this. He'd truly thought they'd have a couple more days together before he eased Dev into his way of thinking. How wrong he'd been.

"What're you saying to me?"

"You're Ryan Cashin James, aren't you? My mother followed the court trials and then the parole because I was a victim too. The guys were convicted on my behalf as well as yours. At first, I didn't put it together but then on the way home…" Dev's hands moved between them. "Well, is it you?"

*Shit.* He couldn't tell how far down the rabbit hole Dev had gone. Clearly by his casual stance, he hadn't gotten as far as "undercover agent" but Dev was smart and crafty. It wouldn't take long.

It didn't matter. Job first. Silence deadened everything inside his head. His undercover alias was now compromised, leaving him with no choice but to take Dev down. He stared at Dev as he fought his heart's urge to wrap the biker in his arms and keep him all to himself.

Sadly, that wasn't an option. He had to diffuse the onslaught he knew was coming once Dev put all the pieces together.

Dev took a sudden step backward, triggering Cash into instinctive action. He grabbed Dev's wrist and arm with one hand, bending Dev's hand into an unnatural position. He wrenched Dev's arm around, twisting his body as the biker's chest pitched forward. Thankfully, the element of surprise was on his side.

He wrapped his free hand around Dev's bicep and spiraled the stunned biker to the ground. Dev sprawled across the faux wood floor. Cash's knee followed, landing between Dev's shoulder blades, pressing into his back. The whole maneuver took less than three seconds to execute. He reached for Dev's free hand, wrenching his wrists together.

"I would've just let you tie me up," Dev teased, looking back over his shoulder. Whatever he saw made Dev's body tense.

"Joe!" Cash boomed. "Bring the handcuffs."

Joe popped out from around the hall's corner, weapon drawn. Cash shook his head. Joe wasn't proficient enough for this kind of involvement. His hands shook as he aimed the pistol directly at Dev, which meant it was also too damn close to him.

"What the fuck?" Instantly, Dev bucked his body, fighting against Cash, trying his best to dislodge and break free.

"Turn the weapon away and give me the handcuffs," Cash yelled, adding a second knee to Dev's back to get him under better control. Cash's thumb added more pressure against Dev's bent hand. The action only sent Dev into a further rage.

"Goddammit. You sorry motherfucker. When I get free…" Dev tried to twist and turn. Luckily, Joe listened to Cash. The pounding up the stairs had to be David and the rest of the attorney general's surveillance team from across the street. It was all coming to a head. "I'm gonna kill every single one of you bitches when I get free."

Dev was a force to hold on to. The biker hadn't earned his reputation or his nickname by being accommodating. With the way Joe extended his shaking hand, his security detail needed to double time it up the staircase. Cash required their assistance. He couldn't remove his hands from the death grip he had on Dev's wrist. The biker knew what he was doing. They'd get into a wrestling match if Cash gave one wrong move.

"Open the door," Cash yelled to Joe who hesitated, the pistol in his hand now aimed at the entry. Joe had no idea of the other security team's presence. "Listen to me. Stand down, Joe. Those are my people coming through the door."

Seconds later, the door crashed in and David plus two other federal agents in semi-tactical gear with assault weapons raised poured into the small room with a practiced precision. Joe recovered from his confusion and holstered his weapon, finally able to help Cash apply the handcuffs to Dev.

Dev was like a bucking bronco. The cuffs were barely enough restraint.

The biker was strong. The way Dev wrenched his arms and kicked out at the agents had to cause the guy unnecessary pain. Every one of Dev's actions dared the agents to take a shot.

Clearly he didn't care if he lived or died.

"Goddammit, Devilman," Cash roared, keeping a distance as he leaned into Dev's line of vision. "You're making this so much harder than it has to be."

"Fuck you," Dev replied, kicking at Cash.

The countermove wasn't unexpected. He dodged out of the way.

"Flex-tie his legs," Cash commanded. He didn't like having to do this to Dev, but his rage was out of control. Dev was going to seriously hurt himself if they didn't restrain him.

David continued to stand with his weapon aimed at Dev, his finger close to the trigger. He watched the others forcibly work to contain Dev's legs and tie them together. It took several minutes.

Dev's rap sheet was chocked full of resisting arrest charges. It had seemed excessive. Not anymore.

Cash stood, crossing his arms over his chest, not liking any of this one single bit. All his protective juices flowed, needing an outlet. They manhandled the ties around Dev's ankles. The verbal threats never stopped pouring from Dev's lips. The agents added a second set of Flex-ties right below Dev's knees, making it impossible for Dev to move his legs.

"Sit him up," Cash demanded, his tone hard and unyielding. He had to hide all of the hurting he was doing on the inside.

Somewhere in the back of his mind, Cash now understood this was never going to turn out any differently. No amount of effort at forging a bond with Dev was going to change this outcome. Those were Cash's fairy tales at play.

His heart hurt as he watched Dev fight his team to force him to sit upright. Every move they made, Dev countered. The biker had to be in great physical pain with the way he contorted his body to keep from doing anything they wanted.

Eventually, they got Dev to a sitting position. His chest heaved under the exertion. Hate radiated from every pore on his body. His hair hung in his eyes. Cash had to fist his fingers to keep from reaching out to sweep it off Dev's forehead, allowing him to see better.

Cash walked over to Dev, tugged at the fabric of his slacks to make room as he bent at the knee. Cash balanced on the balls of his feet, getting on Dev's eye level. The man refused to glance his way.

"You need to look at me," Cash said with a steely tone.

He waited several long moments before Dev's hard, hate-filled glare landed on him. Rage, fueled by betrayal, danced like the devil behind Dev's beautiful blue eyes. The very thing Cash had dreaded most was happening. Dev would never think of him the same again.

Cash pulled himself together enough to hold Dev's stare. He tried to make his voice stern yet encouraging. "This is going to go one of two ways. You can work with me, and I'll protect you. Or you can fight me and be put away for a very long time. It's your choice."

"I know my rights," Dev growled. "And not one of you sorry motherfuckers have read 'em to me."

"Oh no. You have no rights. I'm with the Attorney General Exempt Operations. Your rights ended the minute I stepped into this building. So which way is it going to be, Devin?"

"I should've left you to die on the street." Dev spit at him again. This time, the gross wad landed on his dress shirt.

Cash let go of the breath he held and closed his eyes as he got to his feet.

"These guys know you got railed with a big, fat one up your ass?" Dev yelled.

Here they went. Hoping to curb the diatribe about the sex he and Dev had shared, Cash looked pointedly at Joe. "Gag him."

"He sucked on my asshole like it was a fuckin' Blow Pop. You sure drank my come every chance you got…"

The hurt building inside Cash made him lash out. "They know everything, Fox. You've been under constant surveillance since I moved in here. I hope the memories can keep you company as you sit in that cell all by yourself for the next thirty years." Cash started toward his bedroom, unbuttoning his shirt as he went. He heard a yelp and a slap and assumed Dev had gotten a chance to bite at one of the agents.

"Cash," Joe said and started toward him. The confusion on the young agent's face needed to be addressed, but not right now. He lifted a hand to Joe, stopping him from saying anything more. He'd explain when the time was right.

"This operation's now under the control of the US Attorney General's office. Under his authority, there's no further communication with the local DEA office until I say so. Call Agent Fox. Get her over here. Tell her it's time."

He let the bedroom door fly shut behind him.

His heart hurt so damned badly.

Compartmentalize the pain. Think with a clear head.

It was hard to think at all with Dev handcuffed and sitting on the floor in the other room.

He scolded himself. *You have to stop this. Dev was never going to be yours. You knew the consequences when you accepted this position. Pull it together. You have a job to do.*

Cash continued to remove his shirt, folding it inside out.

If he were going to get through the next twenty-four hours, he was going to need all the help he could get.

# Chapter 22

Dev's blood boiled.

The rage consumed him and burned like acid through his veins.

What the fuck had he let happen?

How had Cash snuck so completely under his radar and made him fall hook, line, and sinker?

His stupid plan for the night was to walk into this apartment, carefully tell the man from his past that it was okay to be himself. He no longer had to hide or be afraid. Then he was going to ask that man for something more permanent. Whatever Cash needed, whatever rules he played by, Dev had decided to play by them too.

It had all been fairy tales and unicorns prancing around his head as he dreamed about his magnanimous idea to let Cash off the hook for his secrets, give him a safe space to be himself. He'd envisioned intimate meals, a clean house, and fantastic sexual quests in their future. He saw he and Keyes hanging out with their two normal guys, living a made-for-TV life. In the dream, Mae and Abi grew up well-adjusted and happy.

Less than thirty minutes ago, he'd been planting daisies in the front yard of his and Cash's Southlake, Texas, home. Dev wanted to give Cash a beautiful life, making up for the cruelty and pain of his past. He'd been so lost in the concept of him and Cash and their coupling he hadn't even fought Cash when he took him to the damn floor.

He'd thought it was their style of foreplay more than anything else.

He sure didn't have Cash down as an undercover on his bingo card.

What a goddamn idiot.

His old man was right, he was nothing more than a giant fucking pussy. He'd tossed away his long-standing values and obligations to his brotherhood because someone in the world was finally fucking nice to him.

All under a fake pretense.

A strategic federal plot to take him down. Make him feel good and wanted... And it worked. His jaw clamped shut, letting that pain take over his soul. He hurt so bad.

"Motherfucker!" he seethed.

He had violently fought the restraints binding his wrists and his legs, heedless of drawing blood in order to get away.

A fucking gag in his mouth? Even he knew that shit was illegal.

If he could get any part of his body free, he vowed to kick every one of these motherfuckers' asses.

Reasonable thought trickled around the edges of his rage. Instinct had him turning his head, looking at each agent inside this room, committing their images to memory. They'd regret this day, guaranteed. There were now five men in this small living room behind him.

A living room he fucking owned.

"Goddammit," he roared, struggling to get free.

The one agent who he hadn't sought was the same man who had deceived the hell out of him. That agent sat relaxed to the right of him as if he didn't have a single care in the world. Stupid jerk.

As much as he tried to ignore Cash in his peripheral, he couldn't. His heart pumped wildly. How the fuck could he have been so damn oblivious?

Dev stared down at the designs in the rug underneath his booted feet. His chest heaved in and out with every breath. He had to get control of himself.

How could that full of joy, scrawny kid be the same man sitting emotionlessly beside him?

Memories of taking that gorgeous ass over and over again refused to be squelched. How sick was he to still want that motherfucker?

He'd never gotten his fill. He craved Cash's touch.

Now he'd never know that feeling again.

The bitterness inside his soul mocked him where he sat. He struggled to contain his emotions. The passion Cash stirred within him sheltered a part of him that absolutely refused to believe this was the end.

Stupid fucking feelings.

The strong fingers squeezing the breath from him in short intervals. Cash wanting to please him, but also worrying about his safety… He'd believed Cash when he said he didn't normally do those things. The way Cash fucked him repeatedly, especially in the beginning, spoke of long droughts in the bedroom. Only extreme desire had someone recovering that quickly…

Dev settled back into the strong metal chair they'd wrangled him into. He hadn't made it easy on them. He dropped his head, chin to chest, closing his eyes. Why was he thinking about these things right now?

Maybe because he loathed himself. He'd fallen hard and fast for his pretty boy. Cash had held him in his arms, listening as Dev spoke about nothing of consequence. His life was falling down around him, and he'd felt ten feet tall with Cash. No mountain too high to conquer. The pretty boy had given him strength and courage to continue to fight another day.

If right this minute Cash put his arms around Dev and told him it was all going to be okay, he'd believe him.

What a needy pussy he'd become. His lip tucked between his teeth as his head fumed. He forced his brain to think of a way out of this. They had to know he'd let them kill him before he ever gave away a club secret.

But what the fuck did he even know any more about the club dealings?

*Think.*

"Goddammit."

If he could roll back time, he'd go all the way back to his youth and leave Cash lying gutted on the street.

That fucking demented good side of his personality rang across his mind, *No…*

What the fuck?

The devil inside him dominated his thought. Without question, it was a hard *yes*, that if given the chance, he'd leave that weird, naïve, happy little kid bleeding out on that dirty South Dallas street.

You'd think after all the years of trouble and every damned time he tried to do something right, it fucked up, that that heavenly angel on his shoulder would have tumbled off to its death by now. Dying the same death he'd just envisioned for Cash.

But it hadn't. The good refused to ever give up hope, no matter how much destruction it ultimately caused. This time, that winged celestial bastard got him tied the fuck up with a gag in his mouth, knowing this party had only just gotten started.

His true strength in life was pissing people off. His incessant flow of biting words made people crazy mad. The gag had taken that from him.

Why had tonight gone so wrong? What did he say to cause Cash to play all his cards?

His whole fucking plan was to tease Cash about being the kid he once knew.

*You still can tease him. He's into you.*

He growled, the sound eerie from behind the gag. That goddamn voice of honesty and truth needed to shut the fuck up. Cash was so into him that he was tied up with a gag in his mouth. Fuck you.

Cash Ryan was living his last days on earth.

For fucking sure.

*No. Not him. You need him.*

Fortunately, before he found a way to fist fight his brain, he heard the front door open and tilted his chin that way. His glare turned menacing. His jaw clamped shut so tightly his teeth ground into the cloth of the gag.

*His sister.*

She didn't look surprised to see him nor was she a stranger to these agents.

His world darkened another degree. What the fuck was she doing there? His thoughts were spinning. It couldn't be what he was thinking. Shanna working for the feds? Was she behind all the club's recent problems? Had Shanna turned on her family in the worst possible way?

She couldn't come back from this.

When his old man found out his perfect girl sold him out...

*Shit.*

Rage was back. He couldn't take overt betrayal. His heart pounded, no rammed, against his rib cage. His fucking head hurt. His vision darkened under the violence he wanted to cause.

*Motherfucker.*

How the fuck was he going to keep his sister breathing once his brothers found out what she had done? Nothing was off limits for those sick freaks. Their disgusting ideas of retribution played in the backdrop of his demented mind. The way they'd teach Shanna a lesson before her death caused fury like he never experienced before to explode out of him.

He fought to free his arms and legs and banged his forehead against the hard wood of the table. The growl resonating inside him lasted longer on the release. How could he protect her?

"Why's he gagged?" Shanna asked, her feet coming into his peripherals. He beat his head hard on the wood tabletop and bounced the chair up and down, wanting one of the legs to land on her shoe-covered foot. She needed to suffer for the position she had put him in.

A strong arm circled his neck. With an unbridled force, his head wrenched backward, the chair teetered precariously on two legs. He was dragged several feet away from the table. The dark voice in his ear sounded very much like his soul felt.

"Stop messing around. Nobody here believes you're crazy. We'll all be right here until you listen no matter how long it takes."

Even under the brawny arm biting firmly into his neck and the deadly voice against his ear, he didn't believe for a second he was in any real danger. Hints of compassion laced Cash's threatening words. The cologne he'd once praised on his lover swirled subtly around them. The scent held the exotic promise of something more. If Cash had wanted to hurt him, he easily could have. Instead, the tight hold had tenderness.

*Fuck that.* The man needed to get that goddamn stirring breath off his face.

He started to tell Cash exactly that, knowing the words were coming out jumbled and mumbled at best.

"Dev, stop," Shanna commanded. His head jerked in his sister's direction.

How fucking dare she talk to him in such a reasonable manner? Fuck her. He said about those same words to her, unleashing a rant while manifesting laser beams to shoot from his eyes and singe her very being.

Shanna acted as if he were nothing more than an annoying gnat as she reached for an unused chair and started to pull it out from the table to position herself in front of him.

"Be careful. He's turned himself over several times. Lunged forward to head butt an agent. He's angry," Cash said, putting him back down on all four of the chair's legs. His palms came to rest casually on Dev's shoulder. Dev moved, trying to shrug Cash away until he lifted his hands.

Shanna laughed with her teasing, singsong tone. "He's being tame then. I'm surprised you got him in the restraints. Most usually don't."

"Only because I caught him off guard," Cash confessed.

Damn fucking straight that was the only goddamn reason he was tied up right now.

She stared Dev directly in the eyes and placed the chair about three feet from him. Her patient smile showed she had no fear of him. Just because she was right didn't mean she needed to gloat.

"Can we ungag him?" she asked.

He decided to answer for everyone in the room with a resounding *yes* that sounded very much like a woof.

"He won't let you speak if you do. I tried," Cash said. Of course, he wasn't going to let Cash speak to him for any reason. Who could know if he felt that same way about Shanna. They'd have to remove the gag to see. Dev cut his gaze toward Cash who took his seat to the right of him again.

Based on the firm set of her jaw, Shanna didn't like Cash's answer but didn't buck him.

*Interesting.*

The master liar and sexual deviant wannabe must be the superior here. *Great.*

"No matter what you may think, you're not under arrest," Shanna started. Cash burst out with a harsh bark of laughter. The mean glint Shanna showed moments ago was again pointed at Cash before she turned back toward him, lessening the severity of her look. "Dev, I'm an undercover special agent for the FBI. I'm on a special task force led by the DEA here in Dallas."

"Fuck you," he said through the gag. Fairly sure that was clear enough. What the fuck was she even talking about? She worked for the FBI? He'd assumed she'd flipped on the club, but working for the FBI? What the actual fuck?

She only shook her head, brushing him off. "Can't you ever be more imaginative with your insults?"

"Fuck you, you stupid fuckin' bitch," Dev replied.

"It wasn't an invitation to insult her further," Cash said, steel infusing his tone.

The narc could use whatever voice he wanted. He didn't care. "Fuck you, you goddamn son of a balls lickin' bitch. I'm gonna kill you when I get free of this chair, you asshole." It was hard to breathe through the tirade, but he managed to let go of another growl to cement his promise.

"Dev, stop. Let me finish then you can put on your show of defiance if you still want to. You guessed right about Cash. Well done. He's from our childhood, and he's also part of the DEA." Shanna lifted a hand, giving him a so-so motion.

Cash took over the explanation, making everything crystal clear. "I'm in Dallas under the orders of the US Attorney General's Exempt Operations division. We're called AGEOs. It's the reason you haven't been read your rights. It's the same reason you'll go missing if you don't agree to do as we ask," Cash explained.

"Fuck you," Dev snarled and bounced his feet and chair around to go kick that stupid motherfucker's ass just for the tone he used.

"You're what?" Shanna barked. Her utter surprise yanked Dev's undivided attention to her but not his movement. It may take him ten minutes to get to Cash, but when he did, he was going to fuck the guy up. They thought he'd tried to head butt before. Wait until his forehead smashed that pretty boy's nose.

Cash gave his sister a distracted wrinkle of the brow as if her question was nothing more than an annoyance. "Settle down,

Dev," Cash commanded. "Agent Fox, under the authority of the US Attorney General, from this point forward, you and Joe work for me. Any communication with your current superiors must go through me first. It's the way it has to be for now."

Cash got to his feet with those catlike reflexes that had driven Dev wild. Now they only pissed him off at how much he missed. All the signs were there. Of course this guy was too good to be real. He reached across the far side of the table, handing Shanna an iPad.

"Forgo reasoning with him and show him what's been done to him. We have to calm him down before we can hope for any rational dialogue."

She looked disgruntled as hell but took the offering.

"So Cash isn't DEA?" Dev watched from the corner of his eye as she asked the nerdier one with the shaky hands. The guy shrugged.

The gravity of a situation Dev didn't fully understand landed in Shanna's troubled stare that was pointed back on him. She got to her feet, letting go of a deep sigh. Tension filled the small room. "This just got way more serious, brother. You need to listen to me very carefully." She went around her chair, pushing it back toward the table. "Can we move him closer to the table so he can better see what I'm talking about?"

He could no longer see Cash. Those stealthy wildcat ways had slipped somewhere behind him. He heard a deep sigh and the gag at his mouth loosened. "If you make one more move to hurt yourself with the table or the pad, I'll tie your chest to the chair. Got it?"

The gag came out of his mouth. Every bit of saliva went with it. He had to work his jaw with his lips completely closed to make everything inside his mouth work properly again.

"Let my hands and feet go. I won't do anything," Dev countered, hoping he sounded truthful. Cash tilted him back on the two legs and pushed his chair forward again. The defiance embedded in his soul couldn't help but try to actively make his body heavier to complicate the movement.

"We'll take it in steps," Cash said once Dev was settled. The frustrating man casually took his seat again as if he hadn't made all the tension in the room palpable.

Dev held his tongue mainly to see what intel Shanna had that caused her to turn. His club, his brothers, and Keyes needed to know.

Nothing had changed for him. By doing this, they may have pushed him back into the underbelly of the club he'd been trying so hard to break free from.

*Fuck the DEA.*

*Fuck the attorney general.*

*Fuck the AG whatever unit.*

But he'd need his brothers' help to exact the retribution he planned. They thought he was the devil before. They didn't understand the meaning of fires of hell raining down on them. But they would…

# Chapter 23

Cash watched silently as Shanna spoke in meticulous detail about what the DEA knew of Dev's outlaw bike club activities. She didn't reveal everything, only enough to make Dev understand the government was fully aware of the Disciples' illicit drug dealings.

What Shanna didn't know, what most people in this room didn't understand, was how far reaching the drug operation really was and how much had been stolen from both the enormous drug loads as well as the actual money from the sale of those drugs. The theft of money was currently the hardest part to pinpoint.

The layers involved in moving those drugs were deep. The longer the questions went unanswered, the graver the danger for every member of the club, their families, and all the innocent undercover operatives involved in running those operations.

Cash had already risked too much by allowing Shanna to reveal so many truths to Dev, but he saw no other way to shift Dev's allegiances. If they could somehow manage to gain Dev's cooperation then prove his worth in the field, perhaps they could better determine the source of all the thievery before the cartel, or worse, the rogue agents, put their boots in the Disciples of Havoc brothers' asses.

Havoc was too big. Tens of thousands of members worldwide. The potential bloodbath on American streets would rival any war zone.

If Dev didn't cooperate, then Cash had played his cards all wrong and risked every person's life inside this room as well as the lives of many innocent agents on the streets.

Dev would become collateral damage in keeping his operatives safe.

Cash's stomach knotted. The stress of his actions had bile rising in his throat. He cared too deeply for Dev.

All the Dev-infused emotion had grown into something more… Cash couldn't lose Dev, but he also knew there was no way this hardcore rebel could sit on the sidelines for any length of time. He'd have to incarcerate Dev. The image of Dev being completely alone in a federal jail cell with no access to anyone while Cash continued this investigation made his heart hurt.

*Be positive*, he lectured himself. So far so good. Cash had been able to unfasten the handcuffs at Dev's wrists. The biker's arms and hands were free now. The ones at his legs and feet were still tightly bound to the chair. Only because he didn't trust anyone else with Dev's security and they hadn't gotten to the hardest part yet.

Cash wore nonchalance like a cloak. The one-two punch they were poised to give ate at his soul.

He had to give Shanna kudos. She'd put a lot of effort into preparing her approach to Dev. She had systematically skimmed over the details of the theft, making it clear that Dev had the ability to protect his club. Showing that at any point in the street transactions—from receiving the illegal goods to distribution—something could have easily gone awry. Never pointing fingers at the actual members of the club. The reins in the hierarchy needed to be tightened. Their father had become lazy, allowing too many opportunities for things to go wrong.

She explained how the local Dallas district attorney and their raid earlier in the year on the club and its holdings was unexpected on the federal level. Shanna described how she was responsible for finding the information on the relationship between the club brother, Ray-Ray, and the new Dallas district attorney.

She was damned good at presenting her case as if the Disciples were ultimately being used while still playing on Dev's deep dislike for his father. Though they'd been at this explanation for a couple of hours, Dev finally started to engage, asking questions.

The last load of information that Shanna dumped was detailing different areas of Dev's personal life. They hoped this intel held a strategic advantage.

Cash's true hope was that Dev might redirect his vengeance and retribution to something that didn't involve Cash's head on a platter—if he'd interpreted Dev's gagged threats correctly.

Maybe if Cash had had a few more days, he might have found another way.

It took effort to hold on to the sigh wanting to release as Shanna started with Dev's younger years. The iPad rested in front of Dev on the table. With a swipe of her fingertip, she turned pages as she reminded him of their father's physical and mental abuse. How he had taken the trouble a young Dev caused out on their mother. She flipped through the Child Protective Service reports, pages and pages outlining mistreatment.

Then came Keyes Dixon.

"Keep him out of this," Dev threatened. Keyes's lifelong protector raced forward, his tone dark and deadly. Dev's scowl deepened as his gaze jumped from Shanna to Cash.

Shanna had missed her calling as an FBI strategist with how well she had played her brother.

"Keyes's rap sheet's too long and varied, like yours," Shanna said, giving a small but seemingly approving chuckle, most likely designed to keep Dev comfortable with the direction of her information. "I decided your rap sheet's a how-to-become-a-criminal guide."

She managed to gain a fraction of amusement from her brother if the bow of his chest said anything.

"I want to show you what Keyes has been up to." Shanna held Dev's intense scowl until he finally looked down at the iPad. "See this man?" She tapped the screen with her fingernail, indicating a handsome blond guy dressed the way Cash wished he could. "His name is Alec Pierce. An attorney who works for the Dallas district attorney's office." She used the pad of her index finger to flip through various photos of Alec. Of course Cash had seen these pictures. Each was strategically selected to show a young, happy, wealthy man enjoying life. "Alec is also the son of the United States Speaker of the House. Speaker Pierce is from Ellis County."

Dev's jaw set then the questions tumbled from his lips. He answered many on his own. "Are they fuckin' with Key? Are they blackmailin' him? Nah, he's an open book. Everybody knows his shit. He wouldn't turn without tellin' me. Whatever the fuck you're thinkin's wrong."

Shanna's hand came forward to wave in Dev's face. "I'm not finished. Give me a second. What Keyes is doing is voluntary. Keyes has been seeing Alec for about the last ten months now. They're serious about one another." She showed pictures of Keyes with Alec all around Alec's residential property. They were in various states of dress, holding hands, holding one another. In those photos, the warmth and love the two men shared couldn't be denied.

Dev was too expressive. For the briefest of moments, Cash saw the approval. Perhaps he even appreciated what his friend had found.

"What do you want me to do to keep this information from the club?" Dev asked, looking straight at Shanna then over to Cash. The hostility ebbed, leaving genuine concern behind. "My brothers will kill him and not think twice. You need intel? Is that it? What do you want to know exactly? The drug runs are secret. Most of the brothers don't know about 'em. I've only seen various drugs. I don't know about weapons, but they could be in there. We're tradin' lots of shit and none of it's legal. I'll get you the information on the next drop."

"I know all about those," Cash said. "And the lumberyard on Red Bird Lane in Duncanville. We're more interested in the larger theft and—"

Dev cut him off in midsentence. "That's me, man. I got three boxes of fentanyl patches at my place right now. Go get 'em. I take off the top of every run. That ecstasy you took." Dev nodded. "From a run. It's all yours. I'll get you more if you guys wanna just keep it and call it done. Or I'll stop takin' off the top. No problem." Dev glanced over his shoulder to look around the room to make the offer to everyone. Dev's abrupt change in attitude and his honesty was refreshing. The way he took responsibility was admirable, but not near the sizable theft Cash was referring to.

"Dev there's more," Shanna said. Dev's brief moment of I-can-solve-this faded. His dark brows dropped into a hard V.

She worked the screen, pressing buttons until she was back on the Child Protective Service report. The screen detailed a time their father was coming off a high and turned into a fire-breathing dragon, finding fault with everyone. He took his frustrations out on his family like a punching bag. In his fit of rage, their father had kicked Dev. His booted heel slammed down on Dev's genitals. The injury was a purposeful and intentional act.

Cash waited, not knowing how much Dev had been told about this time when he was barely old enough to walk. His gaze riveted on the man who did in fact look like the devil himself. All those ominous features morphed into hate. The story held Dev captive as he read down the page.

Time stood still.

Cash could sense Shanna's sorrow in a tangible way. His own heart stung as he stared at Dev, the one person who had penetrated the carefully constructed walls Cash had placed over his heart too many years ago.

His gut did a quick march, instructing, no demanding, he keep the next bit of evidence from Dev. They already had his help by only revealing Keyes's information.

And if they didn't, Cash could find another way to enlist Dev's help.

*Money.*

The guy needed money. It was in Cash's authority to offer it up.

He lifted a hand to stop Shanna, but she refused him. Her unyielding stare challenged his command. "He deserves to know what he's dealing with."

Shanna's fingers slid over the page, drawing forward the damning evidence. "These are your medical records from that time." Shanna pointed to several words she had highlighted on the page.

*Testicular trauma.*

*Sterile.*

*DNA testing.*

Shanna bravely turned the next page.

Dev's facial expression shifted from shocked to nonbelief to great pain to rage in seconds flat. His chest rose and fell in labored breaths. "This can't be fuckin' true."

Cash read fear and uncertainty in Dev's focused attention. He grabbed the pad, reducing the size of the document to look at the entire page. Cash swore he could feel Dev's heart thumping inside his own.

They'd executed the perfect breaking point where Dev's emotions were concerned. Keyes's welfare and his beloved children who weren't truly his biological kids. The girls belonged to Dev's father.

Cash's rush of deep, unabated sorrow wasn't unexpected. He cared deeply for Dev.

More than in any other time in his life, Cash wished he could reach out and offer comfort in whatever way Dev needed.

"Give me my phone," Dev hissed between clenched teeth. If destruction had a tone, Dev's voice spoke it well.

"Absolutely not," Shanna said, but Cash reached into his breast pocket where Dev's cell phone rested.

"You're not planning to call your father, correct?" Cash asked and held the cell phone at a distance until he felt reasonably sure that Dev wasn't going to blow them out of the water before they ever truly got started.

"Fuck you. Give me my goddamn phone," Dev demanded, showing he may cooperate, but it wasn't going to come easy. A positive Cash guessed.

"Say you aren't calling your father, and I'll believe you," Cash hedged, moving the phone closer to Dev but still out of reach. Dev had to learn Cash wasn't a lap dog either.

"I'm callin' Tena…" Dev's hard stare laser beamed on him. Cash sat back in his seat, obviously preparing for another crass round of details about their private time spent together. It never came. "Narc."

Intuitively he understood they had crossed another line together. What it lacked was the sizzling chemistry they'd shared. In its place was a tentative, fragile all-business truce.

They were where they needed to be, but at the cost of something very dear and meaningful to Cash.

Cash nodded and felt a shuddering of breath inside him. He started to hand over the phone and stopped, pulling back. Dev was nothing if not smart and cunning. He needed more than his own head guaranteeing their future. "If I give you this phone and she confirms the truth, two very big *ifs*, I want your agreement to work with us."

# Chapter 21

"Give me the fuckin' phone and you don't die at the end of this," Dev countered with all the piss and vinegar of someone not tied to a chair. Cash found it intriguing how Dev exuded so much confidence when he held none of the cards.

"Okay," Cash started again, listing Dev's negotiated point into the mix of his own. "I give you the phone, Tena confirms the truth, I keep my life, and you join the operation."

Dev stared at him, a vein in his neck pumping to a tempo Cash could practically hear in the silent room. His breath was measured and steady like a feral animal presenting a faux sense of calm.

"I have room to continue the negotiations," Cash explained, making sure Dev knew all his options. He swiped a finger over the phone's screen and entered Dev's passcode to show they had the information. He kept going, opening the contacts, navigating down the list to find Tena's number under the name Raging Cunt. He let his finger hover above the call button. "If you blow this cover, the entire club will be taken down by midnight tonight and you won't get your retribution."

Dev barely glanced over at the clock on the wall, seeing they were just past one o'clock in the morning.

"You aren't givin' the Disciples near the respect they deserve. I blow the whistle, and they'll be gone by the time you get there."

Cash doubted that very seriously but let Dev bluster. The intel showed the Disciple brothers were an underfunded band of misfits lost to a world of anarchy, alcoholism, and addiction.

Instead of challenging Dev, he placed the phone on the table in front of him, and pressed call then the speaker option. Cash's hand circled the outer edge of the phone, ready to pull it away if necessary.

On the fourth ring, Tena answered. Techno music blared loudly in the background. "I'm surprised it took you so long to call," she yelled.

"I got one question for you," Dev started.

"No, I'm not coming home. Figure it out."

His jaw clamped shut as he stared at the phone's screen for several long seconds. "Is my old man Abi's and Mae's real father?"

Silence held between them before she broke out into a hysterical cackle of laughter. Whatever tickled her really had a grip in both the length and loudness of her voice. When the laughter turned mocking in tone, Cash's heart hardened against her.

"I wondered how long it was gonna take you to figure it out. I decided you weren't going to. It's so obvious."

Dev's deep tanned complexion drained to pale as he absorbed her words.

"How do you know for sure that my old man's their father?" he asked. This time his voice was quiet. His eyes and mouth took a downward curve.

"Grow up, Dev," she started. "And I've already talked to a lawyer who says you've raised the kids as your own, there's nothing you can do except maybe give them to your old man. He'd fuckin' die. If you decide to do it, take video. I wanna see his face."

Dev's fist suddenly slammed down on the table, rattling everything on top.

"How do you know they're his?" His voice was so commanding Cash found he wanted to try and answer the question. David positioned his rifle toward Dev. Cash lifted out a hand, motioning him to stand down.

"You're sterile and you wanted kids. Fox is one of my best customers. He's been fuckin' me since I was fifteen years old. He took the condom off a couple of times so you could have the babies you wanted. He thought it would calm you down. Fat fuckin' chance."

The silence in the room was tangible. The vein in Dev's neck double timed its beat. Dev closed his eyes. The cords and muscles in his arms, shoulders, and neck tensed and bulged. He didn't breathe.

The uncontrollable rage built so fast Dev's fist came down on the phone as he burst up, sending the heavy table crashing over. Cash launched himself forward in a reactionary measure, hands splayed to the guards, keeping them at a distance. There were too many guns in the room. He used his body to protect Dev as the biker balled his fist and repeatedly punched the now broken tabletop.

"Don't shoot!" Cash yelled at David, catching the rifle lifting toward what they perceived as a clear threat. Shanna reared back.

The chair impeded Dev's advancement as he swung around, encircling his heavy arms around Cash's waist, those strong fists digging into his back, trying to wrestle him to the ground. Cash managed to hang on, wrapping his arms around Dev's body, using all his force to take Dev to the ground without hurting him. The chair came with them.

"Lower your weapons. I've got this."

"Dev. Devin. Listen to me. Hear me out. I have an out plan for both of us and the girls." Shanna started yelling, racing around Dev as Cash executed a move to lay Dev's body face down on the rug, barely keeping him there and only by gripping and angling the chair to where Dev's knees and ankles might break if he continued to fight.

Cash lifted his hand to the agents, motioning them to follow his order and lower their weapons. He moved to where he angled his knee between Dev's shoulder blades. One hand on Dev's back and the other on the chair, keeping Dev locked in this position.

Thankfully the chair was interrogation worthy with a strong, heavy bottom designed to stay together at all costs.

Otherwise, he wasn't sure they could have contained Devil-man.

The agent in Shanna vanished. She became the sister, dropping down on his level, her body splayed out like his, with her face mashed into the rug, facing Dev's.

"The girls are yours. I've already ensured they'll stay with you. They're your children, Dev, no matter what anyone says. You've raised them so much better than we were raised," Shanna started.

"They're our fuckin' sisters," Dev hissed.

Cash felt Dev's body quake underneath his palm. A violent, angry scream came from Dev, as if he were challenging the universe. Dev fought for control. He knew the man wasn't one to cry but the cruel world had finally bested him. Cash eased his knee off Dev's heaving body.

He didn't like the idea of breaking this strong man any more than he liked to see Dev suffer. And he had done both.

If he had the full power of the United States government backing him, then they owed Dev a giant debt. The government would pay.

"Give us a minute," Cash said to David.

"Not a good idea." David, his equal and someone Cash had worked with before, gave no room for negotiations.

"Then you stay. The others need to leave. He needs space." Dev buried his face into the rug.

His own heart was lanced open with pain. From where Cash stood, he vowed he'd do whatever it took to find a healthy way out for this man.

His hand, still on Dev's back, caressed over the strong muscles as he lifted all the way to his feet. When the front door closed, he pulled out his pocketknife and ran it over the ties binding Dev to the chair and put it aside.

Cash lowered the blade, pushing it against his thigh, and took a breath. He began to right the table that was mangled and beaten beyond repair. The cell phone was destroyed. Several moments later, Dev pushed back on all fours until he sat on his heels, drawing Cash's attention there. Shanna came up too, mimicking Dev's stance.

"Our lives aren't good, Dev. They were never good. While you're watching out for everyone else around you, you don't see what's being done to you. You were smart to get Abi and Mae out of here. That club doesn't value you. Dad has never valued you. They use you. And if something didn't change, if I hadn't taken this job, I'm certain we'd all be going to prison right now."

Cash couldn't see Dev's face, but he watched the shiver his big body gave from behind.

From over Dev's shoulder, Shanna's direct gaze pinned Cash, willing him to stay in place. Dev cast a glance over too. His red-rimmed eyes morphed. All the hate in the world replaced the sorrow the longer their stare held.

A lump of dread formed in his chest. Cash hoped his own pain stayed off his expression and out of his eyes. He'd hoped that Dev would remember their time together and not sweep him under the same rug with everyone else.

Their stare spoke of how thoroughly Dev intended to cast Cash aside.

It didn't matter. His heart required him to do everything in his power to help Dev.

Cash looked away, no longer wanting to see the hate Dev carried for him. He picked up the iPad and glanced at David who appeared untouched by the emotional downpour playing out in front of him.

In every case he and David had worked together, David had carried that same detached expression. It made him good at his job. Normally, Cash felt the same way. David had to assume Cash had lost his mind and he probably had.

"We have a cover planned for you. Something hastily thought through. If you think of anything better, we'll consider your ideas." The iPad had a giant crack down the center of the screen. He powered it up, glad to see it still worked, and went through the files, searching for the one they had prepared for Dev. "What's said in this room, stays in this room."

Whether Dev understood or not, he held more power than he recognized. Days ago, Cash had started the document of considerations for Dev to become a contracted informant with the government. Cash knew what he wanted to add to the list of stipulations Dev required and began to fill them in.

"You'll have a substantial salary for helping us. You'll have to reduce the time you spend in the tattoo parlor, probably by half. We'll need your focus elsewhere." Cash walked toward Dev who rose to his full height. He wrote one hundred thousand dollars in the blank space and turned the screen to Dev.

Dev stood motionless, staring at the screen. "More."

"It's a couple of months of work. Max," Cash explained.

"More," Dev demanded, crossing his arms over his chest. His voice was strong. He stood with his shoulders back. His guarded gaze spoke of many possibilities. Cash guessed his daughters were his biggest concern. It could be the vengeance he planned to enact on his father. They'd have to wait and see. "If I'm about to piss off a bunch of clients who've been on my schedule for months and take the hit on all those badass reviews about to come, you need to double that total with an option to re-up if this goes longer than sixty days."

Cash gave in with a nod. It seemed reasonable to him. Or not, who cared.

If the theft on this case did in fact reach substantial totals, they'd owe Dev a gratitude.

"Once I have your signature, if things get dicey, we take you and your daughters into witness protection. It's also an option for you at the end of the operation. You good with that?"

Dev stared at him. One brow lowered the other raised.

"What?" Shanna's hand came to Dev's shoulder, encouraging him to voice his concerns. Dev shrugged it off with a disgusted roll.

"I want all evidence of my children belongin' to anyone but me destroyed. All of it. Gone. Never to be seen again. Of course, my old man doesn't want the girls, but the risk is too great and he's a fuckin' pedo. Tena was fifteen. My mom was about that age when he met her. Abi and Mae will never be anywhere near that club." Dev's arms tightened over his chest, his fists tucking underneath each bicep. "If I can make any changes to their DNA records, I want it permanently made. If not, I'll be takin' measures into my own hands. Just so everyone's clear."

"Of course. That's not a problem." Cash nodded to Shanna, pretending he knew those conditions were easily executed. "Go see if Joe can take care of that for us." When she went out the door to find Joe, he turned back to Dev. "What else do you want?" he asked.

"I want full custody of the girls. Tena's out without drug testin', parentin' classes, and wearin' more clothes around them. The classes are a thing, right?"

Cash nodded as he wrote, but again, he wasn't certain. He'd make it happen. "What about Keyes?"

"I want Keyes solid. Whatever's goin' on, him and that dude are out of the crossfire. Keyes is the best person any of us will ever know. I guarantee he's not involved in whatever you're lookin' for."

"Done. What else?" Cash had already added that condition, plus adding professional security for the girls. No more prospects lurking around a backyard. He glanced over at Dev, their gazes held.

The deep connection they had shared had truly severed.

What he wished for more than anything was that Dev used his snarky attitude to ask for their relationship to continue. He'd grant that request in a second. Let Dev use his body to take his frustrations out on.

=♥=

Maybe for the first time in his life, Dev's ability to think was in massive overload. Nothing computed properly inside his head.

Had he covered all the bases for Abi and Mae?

He needed to be clear-headed to figure this shit out.

One thing he was for fucking sure about was the clarity he had in wanting to wrap his hands around Cash's neck and squeeze the life out of him. He envisioned blocking the airflow so completely that those motherfucking sorry eyes bulged out of their sockets.

At least he wished he felt that way and that pissed him off too.

Before anything more than meaningful hate came to his mouth, he cut his gaze away from Cash. The hurt ran too deep to think of anything more.

His jaw clamped shut as he realized exactly how badly he'd been played. Cash knew it all and had worked him like a textbook, using his loneliness against him.

*Goddammit.* How could such a pitiful life still shatter into a million painful pieces?

He could barely hold himself together.

"You're being short-sighted," Cash encouraged. "Wipe your police record. Add a get out of jail free card."

"Yeah, all that, and wipe Keyes's record too, and I hold the right to add to the list once I can fuckin' think straight again." Dev let go of his arms, shaking them out, trying to release the tension. He turned around, looking about the living room, then went in the direction of the only armchair in the room. He dropped down in the seat as if he hadn't sat once in the last week.

He had to find a way to gain back control of his life then this situation. Be open to the pivot when the chance came. It was the only way to survive through this massive, bullshit nightmare he'd landed in. Fucking Tena. Fucking Keyes. What the fuck was he up to?

"What am I gonna have to do?"

He wouldn't make eye contact with Cash. If he hung on to his hate, this went a million times easier.

"I need access to your club and to your father."

"Fuck that," Dev countered. *No.* He never agreed to get Cash on the inside. He didn't remember exactly what he promised, but he felt like he agreed to provide the intel himself. It seemed reasonable enough to assume he could teeter a line until some out presented itself. And he sure as hell had to find a way to make his father pay for what he had done. A tricky retribution but one guaranteed to happen... If he bought some time, found what the feds were looking for, and framed his old man, well, life got better for everyone. "Tell me what you want to know. I'll get you the information."

Cash's expensive loafers came into view. Dev looked up, refusing to make eye contact, staring at the first buttoned button of his fancy dress shirt. Cash shook his head as if Dev's suggestion was nothing more than pomp.

"From this point forward, I'm your boyfriend..."

Dev burst out with a loud harsh laugh, cutting Cash off. "Fuck no. Absolutely not." He shook his head to drive the objection home and buried his face in his palm again.

"And you're taking me to Thanksgiving with your family then to the club BBQ over the weekend. I need access to everyone, from brothers to the female club members. And all parts of the clubhouse and your father's bike shop."

"The women aren't members. They're club whores. It's a prestigious title they earn. Don't belittle them," Dev stated haughtily as if Cash implied differently. "Why the fuck do you need access to everyone? I told you ninety percent of the club knows shit about what's actually goin' on." Dev gave a zero percent chance of him spending another minute more with Cash than necessary.

Frustration wafted off the pretty boy, *Good, Deserved*. Cash took a deep breath as if trying to steady his building aggravation if the purposeful pace across the room and the flush creeping up his neck meant anything. So, better than good. Dev made a promise to himself to embed himself under Cash's skin any chance he got. *Fuck Cash.*

"I'm trying my best to stay patient," Cash said as if that mattered at all.

"I don't give a single fuck what you do," Dev countered, swiping a hand through the air like Cash was nothing more than an irritating gnat.

Luckily for one of them, Shanna came back through the front door. Joe, the nerd, in tow.

"He can do it," Shanna pronounced boldly. Dev cast a careless glance Joe's way.

If he could help with his girls, he might forgive him for pointing a shaking gun in his direction.

"We're going to hold off, Joe," Cash directed, his steely eyed stare focused only on Dev. "I'm sorry you weren't clear on how this works, but you don't have the option to choose how this plays out. Your job is to get me on the inside and keep me there. Then it's all other duties as assigned."

The vein in his temple throbbed. If he didn't settle the fuck down, he'd have a stroke right there in the seat. He'd focus on the one obvious issue with Cash's plan, the one universal truth of a one-percenter bike club like the Disciples. "Dude, I'm glad you're so open and out, but my brothers don't do gay."

"But you don't care what anyone thinks," Cash shot back. "I don't either. Get me comfortable with your parents and inside the BBQ. I'll handle the rest." Cash's fingers snapped as if he just thought of something. "I need inside church."

"Yeah right." Dev chuckled at the absurdity. Who did this guy think he was? Church was only accessible to the brothers. Cash going inside... Never gonna happen. Off the table of possibilities. Dev held his side. He'd hurt his ribs in one of the fits he'd thrown tonight. The laughter had them stinging. "You aren't gettin' inside."

"No, but you'll get me in there," Cash said as if Dev had magical fairy powers.

"This isn't gonna work," Dev said, cocking a look over his shoulder to Shanna. "How many times have you seen church in your life?"

"It was this," she started to explain. "Or I'll have to go undercover on the inside."

"Fuck that," Dev said, shooting up to his feet. Every member of that club wanted a chance at Shanna. They didn't have the allegiance they used to have. Many of his brothers were unethical pervs. One too many drinks and they'd corner her alone, take it from her, damn the consequences. This wasn't a fucking game.

"Is there any other curse word you're willing to use besides fuck?" Cash asked, his anger finally getting the best of him. Dev counted it a win with many more pushes in that direction coming soon. "This is a plan in motion, Dev. Your job is to sell me as your guy. If not that, make me a friend or prospect."

Dev burst out with a hilarious, yet painful, laugh and dramatically rolled his eyes. "You a prospect? Pfft. I have a better chance sellin' you as my boyfriend."

Cash only splayed his hands out in front of him as if Dev had finally caught up. That pissed him off too.

"This the best idea you got? You're the fuckin' feds. Are you fuckin' serious?"

Cash's brow dropped, the heave in his big chest increased. Dev instantly knew what caused the look.

"Fuckin', fuck, fucker, fucked. Fuck you."

"Shanna, then we go back to you," Cash said, leaving the group standing there. "I'll be your boyfriend. We can keep you safe. Dev can sit this one out."

Dev pointed a finger at Cash's retreating back, instantly seething. "Shanna's not goin' inside that goddamned club. I've listened to the most disgustin' talk about my sister. Those sick bastards don't listen to the word *no*. She's not goin' in." He flipped around to Shanna. "Our old man boasts about your rack. You aren't goin' in there."

"It's not your decision," Cash said dismissively, going for the refrigerator. "Have David and his team follow Dev to pack a bag. He's out of here."

"Fuck you all." Dev looked between the three people, Joe actively getting smaller. "I know what you're doin' and it worked. And if you can create the paperwork that gives me full custody and cuts Tena out until she's well, make that shit happen right now." Dev twirled around, letting go of a long, exhausted yawn. "I'm hittin' the sack. You ruinin' my life exhausts me."

"Hang on. I'll go with you," Cash said, grabbing a bottle of water and shutting the refrigerator door.

"You aren't goin' with me. I fuckin' hate you," Dev said, never slowing his roll toward the door. "I'd rather take the risk of my old man gettin' the girls then spend another second more than I have to with you."

When Dev started to open the front door, Cash lost his shit from the kitchen. "Dammit, Dev. David, arrest him."

"Oh fuck you," Dev said and tossed his hands in the air. "Come with me if you have such a hard-on. I got you. I'll suck it. Five hundred dollars." He went through the doorway, past the agents loitering in his hall. "I'm chargin' you all rent for standin' here. This is bullshit."

"Shanna," Cash instructed from somewhere behind him. "Can you go with him until I can get there?"

"Sure thing."

Dev shoved his key inside his apartment door, walking through without a backward glance. He didn't bother to shut the door. His privacy was fucked for life.

How the fuck was this ever going to be okay?

# Chapter 25

"When are we gonna talk about what you revealed last night?" Shanna asked, barreling into Dev's apartment. She used all the piss and vinegar Cash had come to expect from a Fox family member. He centered himself, anticipating this exchange, and shut the lid to his laptop, not wanting anyone to see his current viewing choices.

He raked a hand over his tired face. Tension-filled exhaustion was a bitch. In lieu of having this conversation last night, Shanna had chosen to go home for a few hours to get some rest. Hopefully, she'd gotten some.

Cash on the other hand had personally outfitted Dev's apartment and bedroom with cameras and listening devices. Then opted to be the one who stayed in Dev's living room for the night in hopes that the biker felt more comfortable with him being there than he would David.

He spent the rest of the early morning hours completing reports, updating his superiors on the change in circumstances. Both his superiors inside the local DEA office who he lied to, saying he'd worked his way into becoming Dev's boyfriend.

Then to the superiors who mattered, telling the AG's office the truth.

Luckily, without too much difficulty last night, Shanna and Joe had agreed to hold his secrets until he had time to explain. As much as Shanna wanted those few minutes to be right now, they had to get Dev wired and out of the house to see if the biker truly planned to cooperate. They'd follow Dev's every move, both by the visual and audio equipment he'd wear, as well as the GPS tracking devices on all his vehicles.

The next seventy-hours were crucial in showing whether Dev was going to cut it as an informant. The biker was so damned volatile, making it hard as hell to predict what might happen from here. Regardless of the reassurance he had given his superiors about the role Dev committed to play.

He'd gotten kudos for taming the famous Devilman, a celebrity in the world of law enforcement. If they only knew Dev's current activity inside his bedroom.

"Can't you make him stop?" Joe asked, following Shanna into the apartment with all the same frustration. His own eyes red-rimmed from exhaustion, Joe held handfuls of surveillance equipment. He dumped the contents on the small kitchen table Cash worked from. "He's insane. He has no sense of dignity."

"What?" Shanna asked. Her full focus landed on Dev's shut bedroom door.

"At least he's finally kept the door closed," Cash muttered, understanding exactly what Joe was talking about. His attention going to the equipment Joe had dropped there. The days of a wire and recorder strapped to someone's chest were long gone. Cash fingered the necklace that had a hidden camera and listening device in its design.

"What's he doing?" Shanna asked again.

"You haven't seen? Thank goodness. I wondered what you thought," Joe said, looking at the closed door with Shanna. "He's been naked since the minute he hit the apartment. He dances with his junk on full display in front of the cameras then jacks off to a bunch of drawings. He's done it three times now. He's crazy."

Cash appreciated Joe leaving out Dev's preferred place to rub one off had been the living room close to where Cash sat. What Joe and Shanna didn't seem to understand and Cash knew as the truth was that Dev was putting the show on for

Cash. Determined to toy with him. Get embedded under his skin, and it worked. He'd been riveted to the show.

Shanna gave a disgusted huff and stomped toward his bedroom door, banging hard with her fist.

"What?" Dev asked in that fire-breathing tone he used so well. The door flew open. Of course he was still nude. No other person on the planet was as free with their body as Dev.

When he saw Shanna, his bravado changed in a second. He dropped his hands to cover his junk. It didn't work. Dev was a hanger as well as a grower. Cash's lip twitched, but he held back any other expression.

"Put some fucking clothes on. You're embarrassing me," she demanded. Her hands flew in the air in a disgusted lift. "Why's every member of my family so weird?"

Shanna covered her eyes and turned her back on Dev. When she did, Dev dropped his cock, and flipped Cash the bird. "You need to make yourself known, little sis. I gotta make sure they see I'm not hidin' anything."

"You're being an ass," Shanna shot back over her shoulder.

"Right, I'm the ass." Dev stepped back, still facing Cash and reached for the door, sending it slamming shut. Again while flipping Cash off. Based on the creaks in the floor, Dev headed toward the bathroom. Cash could only mash his palms in his eyes, willing himself to think clearly. This was too much. Seriously one of the longest nights of his life.

Shanna let go of a deep, years in the making, frustrated sigh, and started back toward Cash. "So explain this Attorney General Exempt Operations unit and why I now work for them."

Since Cash had left lots of information out of his explanation last night and didn't plan to fill in those holes until he had to, he had to be thoughtful on the best way to proceed. His silence brought Joe's attention back to him too.

"The AGEOs is a revenue generating department inside the Department of Justice. There's little known about them except they deal with some shady shit. Laws don't apply to them. They fly safely under the radar until something significant happens then they swoop in, correct the situation, and leave. They're stealthy like that," Joe explained, giving away more than Cash had planned to say. "Something must really be wrong if Cash is here, working undercover."

The worry on Joe's face showed as Cash turned toward the coffee maker. He had kept a steady stream of fresh coffee brewing through the night. He'd had about six cups of strong black brew over the last few hours.

Cash poured himself a cup as Joe continued, "The main responsibility of the AGEOs is to run trafficking operations all over the country to gain access to the bigger suppliers. They deal directly with the cartel and the mafia. Most agencies never know they're involved. They trade everything. And have large revenue quotas that make billions of dollars for the DOJ every year. Their operations run for years, decades even. If Cash is here, then others are too. This is big." Joe spoke as if Cash wasn't standing between him and Shanna. "Right?"

"Who else is AGEOs?" Shanna asked, not allowing Cash an opportunity to answer Joe's question.

Cash glanced over his shoulder to Joe, who apparently had a decent working knowledge of his unit. He wondered what else Joe knew.

"I don't know," Cash finally answered when Joe only lifted his shoulders. "And it's done that way on purpose."

"Oh hell no," Shanna said, waving her hand in her face, trying to absorb it all. "I'm keeping things from my girlfriend who is also my handler, and my superiors. I need to know what you know."

"Joe's covered it well enough for now," Cash said, refusing to be backed in a corner. How did he tell these two very talented agents how out of control this operation really was? Dev was too big a loose cannon. Their focus had to remain on getting Dev under control before they took the next step. "I can say there's something much bigger at play here. It's our job to identify what that is."

"What do you think it is?" Shanna asked, her brows knitted together.

"What happened to get you assigned to this case?" Joe had been with the DEA for six years and was asking the better questions.

"I don't want to speculate." Cash placed the coffee mug on the table and glanced up. "I need you both on my team, and I need you to trust me."

"Why all the secrecy though? We're being recorded right now," Shanna said, clearly confused. "Who sees this?"

"From this point forward, only my team in the attorney general's office. The AG's office has reconfigured the intelligence we send and receive. They'll route whatever information they want the Dallas DEA to know. We have to keep our story straight and keep the truth hidden. I wouldn't have included you this far, but he's so damned difficult," Cash pointed a finger toward the bedroom door. "No one in the Dallas DEA field office needs to know about Dev's involvement with us until we learn more. They only need to know that I've worked my way in as his most current boyfriend."

Shanna stared at him. Joe did too. Their uncertainty showed. Cash got it. He'd been at this long enough to understand what he was asking of these two agents.

"Okay," Joe finally said and hooked a thumb toward Dev's bedroom door. "That's why you've made everyone believe you're so into him. I get it. Now you're dating. It looks like a legit undercover strategy. I get that too."

Dev's bedroom door opened, leaving Cash momentarily caught off guard. He was too tired. Between the literal porn show he'd watched all night and the way the biker pulled off swagger, Cash's body had been tense and turned on for the majority of the last few hours.

The differences between good and evil solidified inside Cash's head.

The devil was, undeniably, here on the earth. Just as gorgeous and intriguing as Cash had always been taught. This morning, he wore aged black boots, vintage torn, faded jeans, a dark Linkin Park T-shirt, and chains and straps on both his arms and around the neck.

Then came the tattoos. All the sexy ink. Dev also wore his cut. A new piece added to his normal apparel. He was honestly too attractive to turn away from. He embodied the very definition of sin. Too enticing for his own good.

"Dude," Dev started with attitude. "Ain't nobody gonna believe you're my boyfriend lookin' like that."

Cash was having a stunned silent moment while Dev was having the exact opposite reaction.

*Cool.* He glanced down the length of his body. Besides the exhaustion that had to be on his face, he was still very well put together. "What's wrong with the way I look?"

Dev rolled his eyes dramatically. With full-on swagger, he came to the kitchen table, spreading his arms out wide. He nodded to the surveillance equipment on the table. "Dress me up."

"First, why can't I pull off your boyfriend," Cash challenged, unwilling to let it go. "I'm a professional. I make money based on my position, clothes, and choice of vehicle. I fit my assigned persona. We met when I moved into the building. We're solid."

"Pfft." Dev refused to look at him while effortlessly brushing off his reasoning. "They'll see cop a mile away."

"You didn't," Cash shot back at the ridiculous notion. No officer wore clothes as expensively made as his. Dev's foreboding single brow arched, his jaw set. His gaze cut to Cash.

"I was preoccupied," he replied harshly. "But I was figurin' you out. I'd've gotten there."

"Dev's right. You can't go in like that," Shanna said. "We've got to tweak your wardrobe and possibly your story. You and Dev don't make sense. We're used to people trying to slum it. Dev would be up for that. The club understands that mentality. Even revels in it. When Dev brought Holly around, the brothers lost their shit. It's a notch on the bedpost thing. But they know a relationship is never going to work out."

She made sense.

"How do you know about Holly?" Dev asked Shanna. His eyes narrowed as he glanced over at Cash, figuring it out on his own.

Shanna gave that signature Fox eye roll. The one that said her brother was the stupidest guy in the room. Cash found immense pleasure out of all these little truth bombs of knowledge erupting on top of Dev and his awful attitude. "You can't believe someone like her would just fall for a guy who refuses to make a commitment and lives their life on the streets," Shanna countered. "Of course, she was DEA."

"What the fuck? She was a speed freak," Dev shouted as if saying it louder made it more believable. "You want to know where your product went? Up her nose. I couldn't keep up."

Cash nodded, knowing everything the biker said was true. Holly currently sat in a mandatory inpatient rehab for the addiction she'd developed while on the job. "Right. She's off the team. So what do I need to change about my clothing?"

"Everything," Dev started, disgusted over Holly. "And if you could grow a vagina, that would help."

"You need to grunge it up," Shanna answered, ignoring her brother, eyeing Cash closely. "Not wealthy grunge but don't try to look like a brother. Normal people streetwear."

"Okay. I'll go shopping..." Cash started and Dev cut him off.

"No, you'll never figure it out on your own." He spoke as if Cash were the dumbest person on the planet. Another irritating family trait. "We'll go shoppin' this afternoon. Pick me up at two o'clock at the ink parlor, drive that fancy car. We need to be seen together and my old man is usually in the bike shop in the afternoon. Another brother'll probably be lurkin' around. I gotta go and start cancelin' appointments. I should just start writin' the negative reviews myself. Goddamn that shit pisses me off. I want to up my payment from the government. No, I want to add a condition to my terms. I want the government to delete all my negative reviews on every platform and keep 'em off for five years. It's only fair."

Cash laughed at the perfect comedic swerve. Dev had all the confidence in the world for someone looking at decades behind bars if he didn't do what was requested of him.

"Joe, show him what he's wearing," Cash said, pointing to the surveillance equipment on the table. He tuned Joe out as he reached for Dev's new cell phone. In the wee hours of the morning, all of Dev's vehicles had been outfitted with the best tracking equipment available. They would hear every word the biker said and those of the people around him. They'd also be able to ride along on every trip he took.

Cash waited until Joe stopped speaking to hand over the cell phone. "You need to find an excuse that people will believe as to why you're backing off the ink parlor. Whatever you say, make it believable. I think the girls' situation is a valid reason, but you decide what's best. We'll touch base with you about midday. I'll be in the parking lot at two o'clock sharp."

"Gotcha, bacon," Dev said, pocketing his cell phone. He grabbed the keys to his bike off the entryway table and left the three of them staring after him. Cash eyed Dev closely. The insults were expected, but Dev cooperating so easily left suspicions.

"I want all his movements, every word captured. If anything is off, I don't care what it is, I want to know," Cash said.

Cash left the apartment. David was on Dev detail today. They'd watch from the street and take action if needed. At least for the next few hours, he had to trust the plan, but first, he needed sleep if he was going to be on his toes when he met Dev at two.

=♥=

*Motherfucker.*
Dev's pissed off levels were getting the best of him. He had to focus on something other than all this raging anger clouding his best judgment.

What the fuck was he going to do?

Of course he couldn't rat out his brothers. If they ever found out, they'd kill him and every person he found dear to his life. And they always found out.

Every patched member of the club lived under that very fear.

Ray-Ray dating that bitch DA was still vibrating through their circles, the idea of retribution building. If Ray-Ray turned up dead tomorrow, no one would be surprised.

If the club found out Dev even pretended to walk this informant tightrope? *Shit.* He'd beg for death with how badly they'd torture his ass.

The only calming force in his life at the moment was the Harley between his thighs. He needed to ride more. A crucial decision if he planned to navigate the next few weeks.

Was there a chance he could find his way through all the chaos?

A better question. When was his old man's last day on this planet?

The vengeance within him was so strong Dev had to push the thought away. The fear and hurt for Abi and Mae made his thought processes too unsteady. He'd deal with the problem of his old man next.

Dev took the turn into the ink shop's parking lot, taking note of the different vehicles in the lot. He glanced in the mirror, watching his tail pass. The club prepared for these situations. It wouldn't be easy for them to watch him, but he was certain the four pieces of surveillance equipment on his body, including his new cell phone, had him covered.

He'd have to be sneaky, and thoughtful, which was technically his specialty.

If he could keep the fucking pretty boy out of his goddamn traitorous head for more than fifteen seconds at a time, he'd be better off.

His body tightened, not in an angry, fuming kind of way. The accompanying sentimental emotion hit next. He pulled his bike into his designated parking spot, popped the kickstand in place with more force than necessary, and lifted off the bike. All the while, thinking about how he'd purposefully taunted Cash last night.

It did bother him for a fraction of a second that the others could see him too. Teasing Cash with what he'd never have again was worth his lack of privacy. If the others were turned on too, or even grossed out, it was an added bonus.

His cell phone vibrated in his back pocket. He almost didn't answer for fear it was Cash. Outside of making Cash's life a living hell, he refused to speak a single word to the man.

Curiosity got the best of him, and he pulled his phone out to see a San Diego number. He slid his finger across the screen.

"Yo." Seemed greeting enough.

"Devilman? Parker." He figured he should know the gravelly voice but didn't.

"Yup."

"We're clutch, man." Dev had no idea what the guy was talking about and couldn't question it with all the surveillance. Cash and his boys were certain to be listening to the call.

"Bangin'," he answered vaguely. Maybe that would cover whatever Parker was referring to.

"Yup." The phone connection went dead. He'd have to reexamine what all that meant at a later date. See if he owed the guy anything.

"You sure are nice lookin'," Millie said from the front door, holding it open for him. "I always like to watch you walk. You have a great strut."

He grabbed the door and swiped a hand forward, urging her inside. She earned her way in first with that sweet compliment. "Quit butterin' me up. You're never takin' another day off again. I hope you enjoyed it."

She laughed, a hearty sound. "We have a full day ahead of us. You're here early, we shouldn't get behind."

"About that…" He went around her to the pad at the desk. "Can you call Ollie Pecker and see if he knows someone of quality that can take some of these new clients for me? I gotta trim my schedule pretty quick."

"What? Why? The girls?" Millie asked, rapid-fire.

The way she said it made it seem a good enough excuse for now. "Yeah. Sure. The girls. Tena's a cunt."

"She sure is." She turned away to make that call.

He entered his passcode for access to the scheduling program, seeing the bookings, one right after another, for the next three days then again on Friday, Saturday, and Sunday after Thanksgiving. Jesus, all the money he'd be losing. Anger filled his soul again, thinking about all those bad reviews. He was gonna have to come up with a giant fucking lie to help pacify these customers.

"Ollie wants to talk to you," Millie said, handing him her cell phone.

"Ollie, man. What's good?" Dev said by way of a greeting. He swiped a finger over to the next week's schedule and wanted to fist punch the screen. He was stacked with customers.

"Devilman…" He made the word into four syllables longer than necessary. "You need some help?"

"Yeah, what time you got available?" he asked and began mentally ticking off the names on the list, trying to remember each one. Maybe he could keep his regulars, pawn off the newbies…

"I got some time. My son's got some time. Someone's got our business," Oliver said. That someone was probably Dev.

"I'm going through the list now. Most of these I'm lookin' at, I've finished the design and it's been approved. So what's my cut for handin' them over?" he asked, highlighting the ones to be called.

"Ten percent," Ollie said. Dev furrowed his brows hardcore. Ollie didn't sound like he was joking.

"Twenty-five," Dev countered, his bottom line.

"Fifteen."

"Twenty-five," Dev said, infusing a hard edge to his tone. He wasn't budging.

"Twenty."

Dev squinted, trying to remember if he'd ever thought of Ollie as dumb. "Twenty-five," Dev barked. He couldn't be clearer.

"That's not how this works," Ollie chimed. "You come down. I go up."

"Say twenty-five. I've done the art. You just have to ink it. And you better be on your A-game. The first complaint I get's comin' off your ass."

"All right. Send me what you got, and we'll go through it. Tell Millie I'm single again," Ollie said the last part a little louder, as if Millie was listening.

Dev grinned, his first real smile of the day. "You tell her. You'll be workin' with her. She's part of the deal. She needs to keep an eye on you. Be my quality assurance."

"Tight. Way to sweeten the offer," Ollie said, sounding genuinely happy.

Dev handed the cell phone back to Millie who took it but didn't bring it to her ear. She stared at him. "It's more than the girls. Is it a club thing? You're wearing your cut. You never do anymore."

She wasn't wrong. But he had to distance himself from their casual, friendly relationship. She'd figure it out otherwise. Girl was smart. "Ollie wants to fuck you, so watch out. At least make him take you to dinner first. He's about to make a lot of money."

Ollie's bark of laughter sounded through the phone, drawing her attention there. Perfect way to throw her a curveball. She wrinkled her brow. Who could blame her? Ollie wasn't much to look at and his personality was worse.

Another smile crossed his face as she shook her head, staring at the phone, then holding it with two fingers as if she might catch something, refusing to continue the call. He chuckled as he took the phone from her outstretched hand and brought it to his ear. "She'll call you back in a little while."

He pushed end and dropped the cell phone back in her hand. "I don't want to sleep with him."

"Then don't," he said, the humor still in his voice. "But I need you to keep a good eye on everything. Watch their shit. Watch my shit. I'm guessin' Ollie's son will probably use this place if I can even get these people to consider a change. If anything isn't right, you stop the work and call me immediately."

"Of course, I will," she replied as if that were a given. "But you're giving me anxiety."

"It's about to be so much worse," he mumbled. Then grabbed his cell phone to begin rerouting his customers. Before connecting the first call, he met Millie's troubled gaze. "But I got this. Trust me?"

She nodded and thankfully let that be enough. He appreciated her faith in his lies.

# Chapter 26

Cash pulled his sport's car into the South Dallas Walmart parking lot, taking his foot off the gas pedal, letting the car coast to a stop in the parking lot just off the main entrance. "Why are we here?"

"You said, take me to the place I buy my clothes." Dev waved his hand toward the store in an exaggerated gesture. "There you go."

Cash stared at the front of the store. He looked up and down Dev's clothes. He didn't see a clothing brand and honestly hadn't been inside a Walmart in ten plus years, maybe longer. Only then when his mother made him go grocery shopping. As a kid, Walmart had meant new clothes, and he usually didn't get those.

Even with those memories flashing through his mind, this couldn't be right. Dev was yanking his chain. Walmart didn't sell hot guy biker clothes.

"I don't believe you."

"I don't give a good goddamn what you believe. You wanna look like this." The man was always so full of over-the-top brashness. Dev swept a hand down the length of his body then toward the Walmart ahead of them.

Rationally, Cash understood the clothing inside Walmart was fine. He was on assignment. If Dev bought his clothes in Walmart, then Cash needed to too.

Any purchase he made didn't have to leave with him when he took his next assignment.

Hell, he only had to wear the clothes when he went out with Dev. No other time.

The car idled through his indecision. He couldn't make himself pull forward.

Oh man, Dev was so screwing with him. Apparently still very pissed off at what Cash had done. He'd picked Dev up over twenty minutes ago after Dev had made him wait out front for so long he'd sent a text threatening to come inside.

Just when he thought Dev was calling his bluff and he'd have to go into the ink parlor, for nothing other than to remind Dev who ran this show, the biker had sauntered out with the cut on his back. He dropped down in the car as if it were the most common thing in the world to do.

Dev hadn't uttered a single syllable until seconds ago. Only pointed Cash in the direction of the store while keeping his attention plastered to his phone.

"I don't believe your boots came from this store," Cash countered.

Dev didn't reply to that statement. Whatever he was watching had him enthralled.

"Where else can we go?" Cash asked.

"You're a fuckin' snob," Dev muttered, his eyes focused on the small screen.

That made Cash laugh out loud. He'd grown up in a travel trailer. Didn't currently have a place to live. Everything he owned fit in a suitcase and a garment bag. Becoming a civil servant meant he'd never made that much money, and what he did earn was split between a savings account and his parents' ministry. He was the exact opposite of a snob. When he opened his mouth to say that very thing, Dev turned the phone for him to see the screen.

He didn't care about whatever video Dev was watching. They were on a timetable. Today was Monday. Cash was meeting Dev's parents on Thursday. If karma worked in his favor, maybe he could find the information they needed by Sunday and be free one week from today.

If it happened that way, maybe by next Tuesday he could persuade Dev to date him. The idea of pulling this case together in a week was the only way his heart participated in any of this plan. Of course it was a longshot. But a two-hour nap after being awake the previous twenty-nine hours, and that nap happening while he was alone in his bed, sent this whole situation into the next level of panic.

His desperate heart wanted Dev.

Why? Who knew. The two of them couldn't be more opposite.

More importantly, the dangers of this case were off the charts. He needed to worry about his own safety more than protecting a man who refused to make eye contact.

"Where do I go?" Cash responded.

"To the front parkin' space. It just came open." Dev pointed to the front of the store where a car currently backed out of a space. "See? Floor it. You can get there before that Civic pulls in."

Defeated, Cash dropped his head on the head rest, staring up at the cloth-covered ceiling. "Is there a Harley store around?"

Dev chuckled. Not a funny *haha* sound but a laugh intended to make fun of Cash. "They'd see you as the poser you are."

"Then tell me where?" His head rolled Dev's direction.

Dev rolled his eyes, his face buried in his phone again. "Head back to my shop. There's a thrift store nearby. I buy most of my shit there."

Like a Goodwill? He spent too many years wearing their clothes. He held in a sigh and cast a glance back at Walmart, wondering if it might be a better option.

"You're a snob," Dev said.

Maybe he was.

"Guide the way."

=♥=

Dev literally did everything he could think of rather than pay Cash one bit of attention. But if something didn't give, he was going to have to hop over the sales counter and begin ringing these people's purchases up himself. Anything to have something to do other than molest the secret agent he refused to ever acknowledge in any sort of meaningful way again.

He currently stood hunched over the service counter, elbows on the worn Formica, watching the chick behind the counter ring people up as he flirted shamelessly with every customer in the building. Well, except that one customer.

The one who held him captive, both body and soul. The fucker. The same one who had charmed his way into a makeshift fitting room in the back of the building, tucked away inside the employee storage area.

Watching Cash turn on the charm to sweet-talk his way into a dressing room helped Dev better understand why he hadn't stood a chance against the undercover agent. Had the pretty boy talked to him with that same genuine smile and deep, sexy drawl? Oh fuck yeah, he had. At least it made him less angry with himself for being in this position. Not one person in this place could resist Cash. He was polished, all shiny and shit, but also had a way of being relatable. His rocking body with all those handsome good looks... *Mmm.*

The thrift store had rolled out the refurbished red carpet for Cash.

"There he comes," the cashier said quietly to Dev, onto his pretense of ignoring Cash. He steeled his heart and stiffened his spine as he glanced across the room. The employee-only door was a straight shot from where he stood.

Cash used the lane like a catwalk, sauntering down the aisle. He turned this way and that, grinning at the customers, mapping the area as he came forward. Fucker was good at mesmerizing his prey. He'd give him that. The tension Dev had carried since last night had eased. He couldn't keep his eyes off the man. Cash's genuine alluring grin was in place as he used his fingers to sweep the lock of hair back off his forehead. His always perfectly styled hair was messy from all the changes of clothing.

Dev liked those strands being disheveled, falling into Cash's face. He was truly a beautiful man. His heart wanted the dream he'd been so swept away by almost twenty-four hours ago. He envisioned Mae grinning up at Cash.

The image he'd created of having someone normal and nice in the girls' life now put a frown on his face. His girls. Pain slashed across his heart again as he thought about them. It had been stupid of him to entertain any thought or dream of normalcy. Nothing could ever change his existence. He knew his place in life. The reality of never being allowed out and always having to walk the club walk turned his stomach.

He didn't have the luxury of such foolish fairy tales.

The shackles tightened around him like the zip ties last night.

"You got yourself a hot one," the cashier murmured, her voice in awe. The older woman currently being checked out cut her gaze to Dev then over to Cash.

"Shameful," she muttered and buried her face in her wallet.

"Fuck you, lady," Dev sneered, standing to his full height. His guard instantly raised. "No one asked your goddamn opinion. Did they?"

Cash walked straight up to him. The smile was still in place even though it didn't reach his eyes. "What's going on?"

"She's a fuckin' bitch," Dev stated, nodding to the lady who gathered her things while giving him a hateful look.

Cash cut his gaze to her. The range of emotion on Cash's face tickled Dev. Those manners probably didn't allow him to call anyone a bitch, for any reason. The confusion caused a well of laughter to bubble inside Dev that may have come out a bit hysterical. And that was one hundred percent Cash's fault.

"What'd I miss?" Cash asked, brow furrowed.

"The chick behind the counter said my boyfriend was hot," Dev said loud enough for everyone in the store to hear. "Which isn't a fuckin' lie, but that bitch old lady said we were shameful." Dev had no way to know for sure, because he refused to ever look at that bitch again, but he felt her gaze fixed on them as she started to leave the building. He was nothing if not a showman. Dev cupped Cash's neck and stepped into the man, drawing him closer. He leaned in to tenderly press his lips to Cash's.

The anxiety within eased the second their lips touched. His heart gave a happy flutter.

Cash applied the smallest hints of pressure to the kiss before he opened. The tiniest parting of the lips in invitation for Dev to deepen the kiss. Dev lifted his gaze to Cash staring down at him. Cash's hands came to Dev's hips, tentatively testing the touch then the hold.

He should pull away. If he knew what was good for him, he needed to pull the fuck away.

At any other moment in his life, this kiss would have turned pornographic just to get under the old lady's skin, and any other homophobe in the building, but shit had changed for Dev. All those deep feelings that had developed at such a rapid pace were now ripped open and raw. At the same time, they lit his body on fire by just having Cash's touch again.

His body took the decision away. The tip of Dev's tongue slipped into Cash's mouth, met with a similar hesitation from Cash. Dev closed his eyes. All the frantic feelings that had taken root from the second he'd looked up to see that kid, Joe, holding a pistol on him, evaporated. The mounting worry for the future. The insurmountable grief of his precious children not being his. Ties to the club cinching tighter around him again. The pain of betrayal by someone he cared deeply for. They all vanished as Cash's velvety tongue moved against his.

From the first moment he and Cash had clasped hands with one another, they belonged.

Fuck no, he didn't believe in destiny or fate. That would mean he didn't have a choice where Cash was concerned. By God, he had made his own decisions. Out of every person he'd ever met, his mind, no, his heart had chosen Cash and given itself freely with no expectation in return.

Last night, when he first found himself completely alone inside his bedroom, the grief of losing Cash was too intense. It took a couple of hours to examine the unstopping pain. It wasn't for Keyes or his sweet little girls. He'd take care of all three of them. What hurt Dev the most, what made him show his ass in front of the camera, run naked around his room, jack off to the sketches he'd drawn of Cash was the knowledge he'd lost the man he wanted most in his life.

A tide of needy warmth overtook Dev. He kept the kiss slow and soft. He let the kiss show Cash's apology, at least his soul took Cash's sweetness that way.

How easily he forgave this man when he had never offered another human being the same consideration. Dev wrapped his free arm around Cash, circling his back, keeping the man flush against him. Cash followed the hold, wrapping his arms around Dev in return. The hand at Cash's neck trailed to his cheek and jaw, caressing the light stubble. He let himself just be inside Cash's strong arms.

Cash was the first to break the kiss, but not the moment. He reared back, drawing a deep breath. His hooded gaze locked on

Dev's face. Dev didn't move. Instead, he memorized the tight hold Cash held him in and the hard as steel cock pressing near his own. Cash's massive chest heaved in another shuddering breath. A blank canvas of flesh he'd love to decorate. The word *Taken* would be the first thing he tattooed right across Cash's heart.

The faint buzz of the fluorescent lights penetrated his bubble. The tap of fingernails hitting the cash register buttons came in next. Reality slammed back in place. As with everything, Dev's dark side pushed the desperate sense of love—he refused to even think the word—aside. He furrowed his brows and stepped away, giving a critical stare down the length of Cash's beautiful body. His gaze lingered on the outline of the hard cock.

"Happy to see me?"

*No.* His heart begged him to ask Cash to give them another chance. To let them figure out the club problems together. To open to the idea of Dev being the man by his side.

A defiance he'd been born with wouldn't allow his mouth to utter those words.

"About as much as you," Cash muttered after several long moments. "How do I look?"

No matter how many buttons Dev tried to push, Cash acted like he knew exactly what Dev was doing. After several seconds, Cash dismissed Dev, turning toward the cashier, having to know Dev wouldn't be honest.

"You look good," she said with a giant grin and a nod. The customer being checked out nodded her approval too.

After he had their answer, Cash turned back to him and tried him again. "What do you think? Do I fit?"

"No," Dev answered honestly, shaking his head. The clothes were fine, but Cash was never going to shake the good off. "No, you're not gonna fit. You'll see. Change and buy your shit." Dev patted the stack of clothes on the counter. "It's probably about twenty-five bucks. Could you hurry? I gotta go get my sled."

Something close to a crestfallen look crossed Cash's face. Those strong shoulders dropped a degree or two. He had no idea what the disappointment meant. What did the pretty boy even have to be disappointed about? He'd fucking won in every way. Even now, Dev had to fight the urge to drop to his knees and blow the guy with as sexy as he looked in those tight-fitting jeans.

That pissed Dev off too. He dismissed Cash, pulling his wallet from his back pocket. "Take off the tags before you change, I'll pay."

"No, I'll pay," Cash said as haughty as the King of England, then pivoted around, taking long strides back to the dressing room.

Fuck it, if it wasn't just as nice to watch Cash leave as it was to watch him come. Come. Coming. Dev shook his head, trying to clear the image of Cash's orgasm painting his belly as he unloaded in Cash's ass. His cock hardened so fast it physically hurt.

Dev rolled his eyes then his shoulders, deciding to give this one to Cash. He left the store, going out to the sidewalk and pacing the length of the parking lot while he waited. He had to snuff out these feelings. Unload them.

He reached for his phone and palmed the device. Only then did he remember it was the new cell, the one given to him by the feds. Hate and anger seeped out of every pore in his body. He wanted to do nothing more than lash out in some violent way. His hand squeezed around the cell phone. He couldn't even check on his kids without the entire federal government knowing what he was saying.

*Fuck it.* He had to get used to it. He missed Abi and Mae.

Desolation replaced the anger as he pulled his mother's contact number up and pushed *call.*

# Chapter 27

Still reeling from the sweet, tender kiss, Cash tucked his wallet back into his slacks pocket and grabbed the large sack of new-to-him clothes. He reached for the supposedly used Doc Martens that he swore looked brand new. Dev hadn't been far off on the price of all these clothes. After wearing nothing but thrift store goods for his young life, Cash had sworn he'd never buy another piece of used clothing. What a bad decision that had been.

He'd spent forty dollars and some change and had a week's worth of outfits. Even better, this bag had caused Dev to kiss him as if he were the most irresistible man alive. He might not ever wear anything else again.

His heart searched for Dev before his gaze did. Between the overhead fluorescent lighting in the store and the darkness of night, Cash couldn't see out the windows. He pushed through the front door and scanned the parking lot. He didn't see Dev there either.

With a jiggle of the wrist, he turned his wristwatch so that he could see the time. It was half-past eight which meant they'd spent many hours inside the store, finding and trying on his new wardrobe.

His forward stride slowed as he spotted the outline of Dev's body in the distance, just beyond his car. He paced back and forth, away from prying ears and eyes. He spoke quietly into the phone, seemingly unaware of Cash's approach. Though Cash doubted that Dev was truly unaware, which meant they were back to Dev's disdain and distance. Great.

It didn't stop Cash from staring. *Dev. Devilman.* The handsome biker had worn his cut for the entirety of their day, having turned it right side out once he'd left the car. He gave off the air of his well-chosen nickname. Nothing had changed in the man's beauty except Cash might add the word *smooth* to the many adjectives used to describe Dev.

He wasn't sure how a man who barked the word *fuck* in every conceivable way could be considered effortlessly charming, but Dev pulled it off.

At the trunk, Cash put the boots down on the pavement and fished out his key fob. His gaze locked on Dev's as he walked. Just that small stare caused him to fumble with the buttons on the fob.

Dev, with his long gait, took maybe ten steps one direction before he turned and returned on the same course. His natural strut, so full of fire, oozed swagger. Dev was comfortable in his own skin. What a fascinating trait.

*And he voluntarily kissed me again.*
Whether or not Dev wanted to believe it, that tender kiss was more than show for an irritable old lady's comment. Their connection was undeniable.

How had they come together again? What space-time continuum mishap kept putting the two of them together?

He knew that answer before he spoke the question. Dev had saved his life. Now it was his turn to save Dev's.

Why hadn't Cash left college and come to Dallas to find Dev then? He always wanted to know more about the guy. Dev had stayed in his heart since he lay injured on the street, looking up into those compelling blue eyes, Dev begging him to hold on.

Fear, pain, and uncertainty had kept him away. Dev's bigger than life persona was just as shiny back then as it was today.

Fate had tied them together. That was the only viable explanation to describe him being right there, right then.

He mashed the open-hatch button, drawing Dev's gaze in his direction. His footsteps halted. They stared at one another. More than anything else, he found he wanted to bare both his head and his heart to this man. Make Dev understand why Cash was doing what he was doing.

If they worked this case carefully, Cash had the ability to save the entire family from the hurt headed their way.

If he and Dev could find a way to forge this path together...

If Dev stopped fighting and took a chance at trusting Cash, they could end this swiftly and go on with their lives.

"What?" Dev shouted defensively, louder than required for the fifteen steps separating them.

Cash didn't respond. He dropped the clothes in the trunk then picked up the boots, placing them inside too. He had to get a grip on all these wayward thoughts. Dev's volatility always rested on the side of anger. Cash shut the trunk as the sounds of gravel crunching on the parking lot came toward him.

Dev didn't say a single word, only opened the passenger side door to drop down into the seat. The door slammed shut harder than necessary.

If he really did own this car, he'd be mad with how hard the door had been closed.

No, he wouldn't. Dev could do whatever he wanted. Cash would still be held spellbound by the man. Be proud to have him by his side.

= ♥ =

Since all the patience in the world was currently sitting in the seat next to his, driving this bad ass sport's car at the posted speed limit, Dev decided to taunt a reaction out of Cash. Using their sex tape as a trigger was a total dick move, he knew it, but that was nothing new. He was full of dick moves.

What bothered him the most was all the romanticizing he'd done. Days ago, Dev had developed a genius plan to give Cash this video as a Christmas present. The perfect gift. They were hot as fuck together. In his head, he'd seen them adding multiple recordings to their sex tape inventory, all for their personal viewing pleasure. Maybe even hire a trained porn videographer to record future videos to add to their private collection.

That was until he landed face first on Cash's rug.

His need for vengeance returned in double time after that fucking kiss in the goddamn thrift store. He needed to bury Cash, not give the guy tender kisses in the middle of packed stores.

Rapid-fire bolts of anger shot down his spine, riling him just enough to keep provoking the undercover agent.

Since Cash was dead set on letting him have his privacy, meaning the guy hadn't questioned what he'd watched earlier in the afternoon. And after the pretty boy kissed him as if he were the finest treasure on the planet, Dev cranked the volume up on his phone and started the recording from close to the beginning.

In this video, Dev was the one doing the fucking. The secret recording of the very first time he and Cash had come together. The extraordinary sex that started a chain reaction, ultimately landing him in this seat next to Cash, right then.

With his fingertip, Dev pushed the play button. Seconds later, he heard Cash whisper, *"All night."*

*"Right on but come for me now."* They couldn't have scripted it better. He turned the phone toward Cash, but kept it tilted enough to watch the screen. To see his hips pounding against Cash's ass.

"What's that?" Cash asked, his gaze jumping to the phone.

*Good.* The car swerved in the same direction Cash had looked.

Dev decided that probably wasn't the question it seemed to be. "You're fuckin' hot. No wonder I lost my shit over you. But I'm hotter. Look at my stomach, man. I can fuckin' move. No wonder you fucked the shit out of me. I'd fuck me too. I wish I could fuck myself…"

"Dev, what is that?" The car continued to swerve off the road.

The slamming brakes jerked Dev forward as Cash quickly stopped at the curb. They were maybe five hundred feet from his ink parlor. With precision, Cash worked the gearshift into neutral to let the engine idle. He grabbed for the phone, but Dev quickly yanked it out of his reach.

"Did you video us?"

"Fuck yeah. That's what happens when you crawl in bed with the devil," Dev taunted. It was a giant fucking lie. The whole thing happened on a happy accident. "Your body's out of control. Your moves are film worthy. Do they teach you to milk cock so good to help suck me into doin' what you want?" Dev laughed out loud at the innuendo. "Suck me. You suck cock like a professional. Milked me dry. You had me beggin' for it."

Even as Dev said the disparaging words, everything inside him begged to find a different way to torture Cash. Not trivialize their time together. Even if their sex had been based on a lie, it still meant everything to him. He had understood what cherished and loved felt like in those hours they'd spent together.

"Hand me the phone," Cash demanded, his voice harsh and angry as he reached for Dev's arm.

"No, look. Here it goes. That look right there…" From the corner of the dash, Dev tilted the phone so Cash could watch himself come. Even now the look on Cash's face did it for him. His cock hardened so fast he had to angle the phone away from Cash while sticking his hand inside the waistband of his jeans to straighten his cock to grow at a better angle.

Cash stopped trying to fight for the phone. Instead, he pushed back in the seat next to him, horrified. "Everything you look at on that phone is recorded by us. The video you just watched goes to Joe and David…and beyond. What're you doing? How could you record us without telling me?"

All really good questions Dev didn't give a shit to answer.

Well, except he didn't like the idea of anyone else getting to see Cash come in the same way he did. A strong, weird possessiveness overtook Dev. Cash reached for his arm again, a formidable strength dragged his upper body across the car for better access to the phone.

Dev registered how badly he'd fucked up but fought the hold, mainly due to his aversion to Cash ever touching him again.

He spotted the hookers at the street corner ahead. Before he could hatch a proper plan, his free hand reached for the door handle, shoving the door open. Cash grabbed his shirt sleeve, barely keeping him from leaving the car. "Give me the phone before you get out."

Dev twisted and darted, pulling Cash's upper body with his until the struggle became real. He busted a move. The same one he might have used had he realized he was being taken down inside Cash's apartment last night. He executed the perfect karate chop, driving his hand into the back of Cash's elbow. Either the tactical special agent was going to allow his arm to be broken or he'd let go.

"Goddamn it, Dev." Cash let go.

He darted several feet from the car's opening as the driver's side door opened. They'd drawn all the attention from the women and one guy still standing on the corner.

"Hey, Devilman." Since this was his corner, and he'd been with all of them at one time or another, he had no idea which one had chirped the words. They all drew Cash's very focused attention.

The idea came together in a split second. One of the women started toward Dev with that come hither walk perfectly executed, but Dev shot a finger toward the guy lingering on the corner. His name was Ted, went by Rocket. He looked youngish in his barely there clothes and teasing attitude, but he was actually older than Dev.

Dev pushed the button to power off the cell phone before shoving it in his front pocket. He'd deal with the repercussions of his actions later, or never. Whatever. He glanced back at Cash then reached for his wallet, making a show of pulling it free so Cash could see he planned to pay for Rocket's time. He used his own saunter as he started forward.

"What's it gonna cost me, Rocket-man?"

The guy's pretty pout perked up, becoming everything Dev needed him to be. The hooker pranced forward. He wore black assless chaps, a black cowboy hat, and heavily applied black eyeliner.

The perfect wardrobe to tease and tantalize. As if Rocket had called Dev before coming out tonight and asked him what to wear to help drive Cash mad.

"What're we doin' tonight, daddy?" Rocket asked. Dev opened his wallet, stretching it wide just in case Cash didn't have twenty-twenty vision. "Is it both of you?"

Dev cast a quick glance over his shoulder, making sure Cash had stayed on that side of the vehicle. He was standing between the open car door and the driver's side, staring at him and Rocket. Anger had pushed his brows down. That crease between them was formidable.

"Just me tonight, Rocket," Dev said, turning back to the hooker. "He's waitin'. I'll fuck you fast."

"With or without a rubber?" Rocket asked. Oh man, he wanted to laugh straight out loud at all these perfect questions.

"Pfft. Without, of course." As if there were no other option. "You know me."

"Two hundred dollars."

Dev lowered his gaze to his wallet and shifted swiftly up in surprise. Their dual spontaneous showmanship came to a sudden end at the price point, especially for a hooker who worked a twenty-dollar corner. More like ten bucks for Dev. A fast fuck in broad daylight and an appreciative slap on the ass when done.

"Cash, I'm short twenty bucks. Can you spot me?" Dev asked, again glancing over his shoulder.

Cash only glared at him. The crease between his brows grew two times the size of the Grand Canyon.

"You'll get the rest when I see you next time," Dev said, taking out all his money, consisting of forty-seven dollars, most of that in single dollar bills—his cash tips from this morning. He tucked his wallet away, started for Rocket, handing the money over as he draped an arm around his shoulders. A small alcove in the building was right off the intersection.

"Want a third, Devilman?" Dollie, one of the women at the corner, called out. "I'll come tickle that pretty ass for a fifty." She was messing with him, clearly assessing the situation properly. Dollie wore a big blond wig and had big fake titties that she showed off about as much as Tena did. To prove his point, she flipped one out.

"Next time, Dollie," he said, walking with all the brashness something like this required. More than anything, he wished he could see Cash's reaction. But if he looked, he'd give his ruse away. Almost to the corner, Dev whispered against Rocket's ear, hoping his litany of recording equipment didn't pick up his words. "Casually look over your shoulder and look at the guy I came with. Tell me how he looks."

"What?" Rocket said, looking up at him. The guy was cute as shit but lacking in the brains department.

"Dude. I just paid you twenty-seven dollars more than I've ever paid you. You gotta pay attention and do what I tell you to do." Right as they started around the corner and out of Cash's line of sight, Rocket did what he asked, looking back at Cash.

"He looks pissed off and hurt," Rocket said, his hands coming to Dev's belt buckle.

"What the fuck are you doin'?" Dev hissed, batting the guy's hands away. If he wasn't so focused on fucking with Cash's head, he would have laughed at Rocket's confused expression. Dev dismissed Rocket, reaching to tuck the necklace into his T-shirt to hopefully hide the visual and mute the sound. "I'm not fuckin' you. Stand there for a few minutes and make some loud grunts like you're gettin' the best fuck of your life."

His needy dick, the one that had aggravatingly stayed in various stages of arousal for the entirety of the afternoon and all of the evening had flatlined on him. Which made no fucking sense with as hard as he'd been when he left the car not two minutes ago.

"You aren't gonna fuck me?" Rocket asked, a little loudly.

What was wrong with this guy?

Dev's brows dropped as his hand went to Rocket's lips, shutting him up. "Make the goddamn noises. Tell me I'm a god. The best fuck you ever had. But build on it. Make him believe I'm fuckin' you and you're lovin' it."

When he got a nod, he lowered his head, thinking about Cash and the video. Even being regretful for his actions, his cock built when he considered Cash. He dropped his arms to his sides, not even caring about the sex tape anymore. Fucking Cash had ruined him. This was the worst possible revelation. What was he going to do?

His eyes lifted to the faux marble exterior of the building. Every part of his life had taken a skidding nosedive into implosion and his cock chose now not to work for anyone but the narc special agent.

Rocket's grunted cow moans drew Dev's focus. "That's not what a sex moan sounds like, and you know it." Dev gave a grunt and used his hand to encourage the professional sex worker to try harder to sound like he was actually having sex.

The hooker finally caught on, making Dev lift a finger up, instructing him to wait a few seconds and motioned with his other hand for Rocket to do it again. He nodded his encouragement.

His dick's functionality shouldn't take precedence over making his father pay for what he had done. It sure shouldn't be more important than working every minute of the next however long it required to secure his children's future, but goddamn, he needed to hate Cash to survive. His vengeance needed the outlet.

He motioned again. This time Rocket sounded genuine.

"I wanna keep the money," Rocket whispered.

"Did I say I wanted it back?" Dev whispered. "Slap some skin together. He knows I like it hard."

Rocket slapped his hand against his stomach. "How long does this need to last?"

"A few more minutes. Groan again. Sell it."

This time Rocket nailed it. "Fuck me, Devil…man."

After a couple more minutes, Dev encouraged Rocket to staged completion. When Rocket went silent, they stared at one another. Dev spoke very softly. "Say somethin' about needin' to go clean up."

Dev did the same. He unfastened his jeans to better look the part of a guy sated from sex. He decided to walk the block or so to his shop. He couldn't look Cash in the eyes, not right now. The agent was too observant, he'd figure out the scam.

The sport's car roared to life, following slowly beside him. Cash didn't push him any further, only tagged alongside him, pulling into the parking lot until he pointed to his bike. Cash got the unspoken message and did a U-turn to aim toward the exit.

His life was just too fucked for words.

# Chapter 28

"Who the fuck is that?" his old man called. His voice grated on Dev's very last nerve.

Dev dropped his chin to his chest, staring down at the concrete pavement of the parking lot, or as Dev liked to refer to the building he shared with his old man, the actual portal to hell.

Was it too much to ask for thirty fucking seconds alone to regroup, to pull together his scattered thoughts before anyone, let alone his father, spoke to him?

Tension raced over his body. His fists tightened. Restraint and secrecy weren't something he did well at all. He had to remember Abi and Mae. He'd made a damn good deal. He could secure their lives if he dug deep enough to find a way to follow through.

"What the fuck's your problem?" his old man asked. Closer now based on the proximity of the gravelly voice.

He tossed a thumb over his shoulder toward Cash's exiting car, pulling out onto the street, and said the words he'd practiced over and again. They tasted like sawdust on his tongue.

"He's a dude I'm fuckin'. I guess I'm technically seein' him. Regular people like their relationship statuses identified."

The words sounded stupid, like he was some sort of adolescent. He had to sound more convincing if he wanted anyone to believe him.

"Huh." His old man made a squeaky noise with his teeth. "I figured you and Keyes were shacked up together somewhere with how protective you are over him."

Instantly, Dev's back went ramrod straight, his chest expanding. He cut a violent gaze toward his father. The old man hadn't seen how protective Dev's protective side could be. He was going to show him a trick or two soon enough. "We're brothers. We're supposed to have each other's backs. The way you had Smoke's back over Keyes every goddamn time."

Fuck, he pivoted away, taking several steps closer to his sled, his fists flying out, fist-fighting the air in hopes of releasing any of the anger building inside him. He could kill that old man where he stood and be better for it.

"Only an observation," his old man's hand came up, trying to show something. Dev had no idea what. "I like some ass every once and again. Somethin' about a hard body is appealing from time to time. Not somethin' I'd bring to Thanksgivin' dinner though."

Dev got a wink after the last statement. A fucking wink. Did his father have facial tics he didn't remember? What did that mean?

His fists fell to his sides. His breath panted in short bursts. If Dev could figure out how to close his ears and not actively hear another word that rolled from those lips, he would. His old man completely misread Dev's seething and threw out a fist to bump in commiseration. Dev let it hang there between them.

There was literally no way he could bring himself to tap it back.

After his obstinance turned awkward, his father dropped his hand and tucked it into his pocket. The outside motion-detecting overhead light affixed to the building dimmed. He stared at his father in the dark. All feeling for the man was gone, nothing left behind. All he could think was how much he wished he could walk away.

"Your mother's not gonna let me come to Thanksgivin' unless I apologize to you. You know that's not my way," his old man said, staring him straight in the eyes. He kicked at the gravel on the lot. "But I should've held my temper. I got shit goin' on…"

"Like what?" Dev pressed, completely out of character.

Maybe if he could get whatever information the feds wanted, he might never have to look at Cash or his sister again. He and the girls, maybe his mom, could hit the road. Start new somewhere else.

"Boy, you just don't know. I need an active second," his father said in a rare moment of honesty. "I'm gonna be true with you. Not to piss you off, just the facts. I like Diesel a lot better than I like you. He's like the son I've never had. He holds himself together better than you do, but that second spot is rightfully yours. I want you, no I need you, to step up and take it."

And there was the *in* Cash needed. He felt the shackles of the ruse tightening around his ankles, binding him into an unwanted life. He should say he'd do whatever his old man needed, be what the club needed him to be, and he would say it, just not right now. Too much bad had hit him at one time. He had to have a minute to settle in.

"So is this your apology?" Dev asked, digging his hands inside his jeans pockets to hide the fists.

"Yeah, I guess," his old man said, looking dejected, maybe even crestfallen. "Your mom said Tena took off. How's that gonna work? Your mother shouldn't have to raise your kids. Nobody raised my kids but me and your mama."

Of course, he came with the bullshit.

Instead of explaining what a shitty life he'd had to live because his old man refused to ever be a true parent, Dev stalked toward his bike. "My kids are none of your damned business." Right before Dev reached for his handlebars, he stopped and poked a finger into his own chest, surprised he didn't break the digit with the force he used.

"Tena ain't been any help to me in years. Mom wanted to spend time with the girls and asked me if she could, so back the fuck off." His father's hands lifted in the air in surrender again. "And from this point forward, you make another wisecrack about how I parent, and you'll be eatin' the pavement, I guarantee. Got it?"

Based on his father's grin, he didn't lay the threat down properly. The old man would learn soon enough. "Fair enough. That guy you're datin'... He gonna be their new mama?"

The hate radiating over every pour in Dev's body wanted him to execute one of his perfect right hooks, knock his old man's lights out. He'd love to drop his father to his knees.

Instead, he began his undercover operation. Fuck everybody. He didn't give a shit who was responsible for whatever theft Cash was there to investigate. He promised himself his old man would take the fall. Spend the rest of his shitty life in prison. The idea brought immense demented joy to his heart. "Remember that kid that got beat up by the street gang when I was younger?"

His father looked confused at the sudden change in topic as he thought over Dev's question. The silence spoke to a memory that should have been etched in his parental heart. Any other father would surely remember the day his only son was left bruised and bleeding while trying to save another person's life.

"His parents were hippies that stopped by, and you ran 'em off?"

"Was the dude tall with a long beard?" his old man asked, smiling. Clearly, he remembered.

"How the fuck would I know that? Anyway, that kid's him." He again tossed his thumb over his shoulder to where Cash had driven out of the parking lot.

Dev sealed the credibility for Cash's presence. They had a long-standing connection that meant more than the high-class slumming it with the low-class. It should keep his old man from sniffing around Cash's background until Dev had something more concrete to say.

He caught his father's surprised expression. Dev might have been married but he'd never had a relationship with anyone before. He didn't know how it worked or how to imply a committed coupling. He and Tena could barely stand one another in the best of times.

Dev finally finished the thought when nothing else to say came to mind. "We reconnected, I guess."

"Okay," his father said and shook his head. "Don't really care. Think about what I said. It's time for you to take on your responsibilities. Let me know what you decide at the barbeque this weekend."

His father nodded and left Dev standing there, going back inside through the open warehouse doors. The overhead light flashed back on as he drew the cargo doors closed from the inside.

At least he had until Sunday to get his head straight.

He mounted the bike, grilling himself. He had to do better with the explanations.

=♥=

"What the hell are you doing, Ryan?" David met Cash in the front foyer of the apartment building.

They'd been busy on the interior of the building today. The apartment directly below Dev's had its door propped open. David and team had left the unit across the street and moved in. Their new apartment was already outfitted for their use. Which meant several card tables filled with monitors and computer equipment were set up in the middle of the living room. Nothing else was there.

Cash had been so consumed with exactly how fucked he was he barely noticed the newly installed window coverings in the front windows of the building, all closed tightly. Nothing could be seen from the street. There were two large cameras installed on both the ceiling and the base of the stairwell.

They were no longer hiding while inside this building.

Cash rolled his shoulders, wishing for a home gym where he could go for the next few hours and beat his body up. Since the mind couldn't think of two things at once, the pain of such a workout might give him some coveted peace inside his head. A pretend sense of calm until his termination papers came through. "I'm assuming you've seen the video?"

"Everybody's seen the video," David bit out with disgust. "We all know every sordid detail." David's hand shot forward as he pointed a finger in Cash's face. "So, I repeat… what the fuck are you doing, Ryan? You're jeopardizing my life, and the life of every agent in this building. We all deserve better."

He took a settling breath, absorbing David's anger. He disagreed that the reveal of the video put anyone in any more danger than they were already in. What he had to keep in mind was his position in this case. He was the lead. He owed no one in this building an explanation.

His spine steeled as his hands went to his hips. His thoughts turned professional, if not superior, moving past the condemnation David was determined to dish out.

First things first. "Who's seen the video?"

"I didn't squash it if that's what you're asking," David said self-righteously. "Everything you've been doing, I let pass because I didn't technically know what was going on behind closed doors. But his phone has incriminating pictures of you. That video of you two is straight porn. I made the decision to turn it in. Either you didn't know it was there, which shows me doubt in your investigating abilities or you determined the video was fine, which means you've put yourself in a position to be blackmailed. My safety is at risk with you."

"That's ridiculous and dramatic." Cash pivoted around, starting for the staircase. He stopped from taking the first step up with his hand gripping the banister. "Blackmailing's not a credible concern. Maybe revenge porn. Maybe compromising my undercover position with the video getting out. But I don't believe either will happen. Your safety as well as everyone else's on this case is still intact. If he were going to risk this team, it would have happened at any point today. We all know the dangers involved with every case we're assigned to."

"I've worked multiple operations with you. This is so off brand. I think you need to remove yourself. Get someone in here that can do the job we were sent to do. Not you protecting that gang member at every turn."

Cash had to stop himself from arguing Dev's value. Instead, he understood his very argument proved David's point. Maybe David was right, but everything inside him vehemently denied what David said. Yes, the video was a game changer. He certainly may be removed for misconduct, but he'd moved this case along faster than David or anyone in the attorney general's office thought was possible. He stood by his decisions.

It was a shame that the video would cost so much. He and Dev had had a breakthrough this afternoon. The tension between them had eased away. It would happen again. He was certain they were stronger with Dev on their side.

Then Dev had jumped out of the car to fuck another guy. That stung.

*Fuck.* Cash scratched the back of his head.

"Collins is waiting for your call," David said as if Cash hadn't spoken. "You've got a flight to DC in the morning.

Everything I've said to you, I've said to them. You should pack as if you're not coming back."

Cash revealed no outward emotion while rejecting everything David implied. Even if it were only for the next twelve hours, Cash was the lead on this assignment. It was all he kept thinking as David sneered at him. The disgust was so evident that, even if Cash found a way to stay, David had lost respect for him. Their working relationship was done.

He cleared his throat and squared his shoulders, starting up the stairs. "I need the transcript from Dev's phone today. He's angry and acting out, but I believe we have him."

The sounds of Dev's heavy pipes rumbling out back drew their attention that way. Moments later, the back door opened. Dev strolled through as if he didn't have a single care in the world. Their gazes met and held as he walked forward.

Just the way he moved tied Cash in knots.

The awful day just got harder and harder.

Dev had fucked another man virtually in front of him. Cash might not ever fuck anyone else for the rest of his life.

And this preoccupation Cash had for Dev gave David's concerns merit.

Thankfully, Dev started talking to him, meaning nothing else mattered and he could shut down those random thoughts.

"My old man questioned me about you. I told him a partial truth. You were that kid from before. I figured that was the best cover to keep him from snoopin'."

Cash's eyes were drawn to Dev's body like a magnet as he turned the corner to go up the stairs, passing him as he went.

"He's still alive so I'm showing restraint. I need a raise." The biker never stopped walking up the stairs.

"I've been called to DC in the morning. David's in charge while I'm gone. He's not as lenient as I am."

Dev ignored him as he went through his apartment door, sending it slamming shut behind him.

"Don't shoot him while I'm gone," Cash instructed David and started for his apartment. "I'll take his sofa after I check in with Collins."

His heavy steps went up the stairs, while digging into his pockets for his key. As he started to push the key inside the deadbolt, the door opened on its own.

Joe stood in the foyer, looking far more anxious and worried than normal.

Right. He hadn't taken the proper time to deal with Joe, one on one, since everything went down last night. He let go of a breath, scooted past Joe into the apartment and shut the door behind him.

Joe had only moved a couple of steps out of the way before he began to whisper ninety miles an hour. "Earlier in the day, I tried to stop the video Dev was watching from being logged, but David said we had to have it for evidence. I thought that was a bad decision and I clouded the view. It's hard to make out what anyone is seeing."

Cash nodded as Joe's gaze searched his.

More words tumbled from his lips. "I couldn't talk to you because y'all were together and David would hear, so I made the decision myself. I put Dev's cell phone on a fifteen-minute delay to give me time to go through it before David and his team could hear or see anything. I blocked David completely from seeing the last interaction you and Dev had that made you pull over. David also didn't see Dev speaking to his father tonight. I don't know if you even know about it yet. I pulled the conversation and saved it until I could speak with you. Am I in trouble? David said he suspects you'll be fired and he's gonna be the new lead which is a terrible idea. Dev won't work with him."

Joe was jittery as hell, anxious as always, but continuously proved his worth. He put the team and the case over the man. Both personally and professionally, Cash greatly appreciated the effort. He wasn't sure he deserved this much loyalty and respect.

Cash clamped a reassuring hand on Joe's shoulder, squeezing. "Thank you. My superiors know what's happening. I've been honest. It'll only be embarrassing to look them in the eyes after the video. Apparently, I'm being called to DC tomorrow."

"Okay then. Should I make contact with the AG's office on your behalf?" Joe started again, still edgy. He kept his voice to a soft whisper. "I know everything on Dev's phone is considered evidence. But David's a huge jerk. For as long as I've been on this case, it's been chocked full of those domineering kinds of guys who can't see past their own opinions."

Joe paused, wringing his hands, then met Cash's gaze.

"I altered quite a bit out of the video. I couldn't get away with deleting the whole thing. The parts I left in, I darkened.

It's hard to see. The sounds are muted. I overrode the original file and replaced it with the new one before sending it on. So I tampered with evidence."

Relief flooded Cash so fast his knees felt weak. "Thank you," he mouthed quietly.

The emotions on Joe's face changed again. He stepped closer, speaking even quieter than before. "Dev didn't have sex with Rocket."

"What?" Cash wasn't sure he'd heard right.

Joe nodded. "I've been the one tracking Dev's phone all day. They didn't catch that I took it off-line when he started to play the video a second time. I searched through his entire phone. He has more pictures and videos of you and him. I left the tame ones. I believe Dev thinks the phone stops recording when he turns it off."

Cash nodded, full of appreciation for his privacy in matters that really didn't belong in evidence, but his heart wanted other details. "What happened with the prostitute? I felt like Dev and I were making ground."

"Come on. I'll show you what happened." Joe started toward the spare bedroom. "I think you have Dev where you want him. Especially after hearing what he said to his father. It wasn't the words but the way he talks about you."

The place where his aching heart hadn't given him a second's rest eased. "What makes you say that?"

"Lots of things. Like he said your name randomly nineteen times today before you two ever got together at two o'clock. Your name just bursts out of his mouth. The guy needs serious ADHD medication. Then he was talking to his father and sold you as his boyfriend. Even I totally bought it. Not only that, he brought you up twice with his father. It all sounded very reasonable and emotion driven. Another thing..." Joe paused and made eye contact. "His father's still alive. Dev didn't end him. That has to mean he's in, or at least he's getting there. His father asked him to ride second, and he agreed to think about it."

Cash nodded. It did sound promising. He'd have to think about the offer of being second... Yet, he was being called to DC tomorrow. A very rare and foreboding happening during the middle of a case.

# Chapter 29

Every decision Cash had made since arriving in Dallas played in a mocking loop through his head. By getting away, coming to DC, he was finally able to catch his breath from the Dev-induced haze. He saw the errors of his ways.

How had he let things get so far out of control? The brief images of the video Joe had showed him, of him and Dev making vigorous love, kept popping into his head. The humiliation of knowing his superiors had access to those videos, even distorted, sent waves of anxiety and tingles of dread rippling over his body.

He ground his teeth. His jaw clamped tight. Rationally, he understood Dev had no idea of the far-reaching consequences of what he had done, but it didn't matter. That was who Dev was. Act first, deal with the aftermath later, or never.

Now that he was on the verge of being fired, because there was no other viable explanation as to why he was being called to DC except his termination, he worried the government wouldn't honor the deals he made with Dev. Even now, on the cusp of losing his job, Dev was still the only person who mattered.

Cash glanced around the small, secure sitting room of the Washington DC Department of Justice headquarters. The door was shut, no windows, or even pictures on the walls, and he was completely alone. He'd been there for quite some time. The attorney general wanted to meet with him personally.

There was a time when all this quiet wouldn't have bothered him. He'd been comfortable in solitude. Now, a sense of panic welled inside him.

He couldn't keep his thoughts off Dev. He wondered what the biker was doing right at that moment. How was Dev reacting to David's controlling ways? Did Dev use the same chaotic unreasonableness that he did with Cash?

Would Dev try to kiss David like he had kissed him yesterday? His heart sank, knowing the odds were fifty-fifty.

The Deputy Assistant to the AG came through the closed door. "Hi. I'm Lily. Good to see you face to face." She came forward with her hand out. He got to his feet, taking in her sedate smile and utter professionalism, just like in every call he'd had with her. She met his grip with an efficient, quick shake. That persona used to be him. "The attorney general will see you now. Follow me."

Cash nodded, taking a pause to pull his inner self together. He squared his shoulders, standing to his full height, looking down at his slacks. He brushed at the wrinkles before drawing the lapels of his suit coat together to button them.

Why was all this so melodramatic to him?

Because no matter how Joe altered the video, it was still clear what he and Dev had done. He was into Dev. The idea of having the entire department watching his sex tape, then watching him walk through this building to his termination, meant very little compared to the sorrow he felt for being forced to leave Dev.

Cash tuned it all out as he walked through a secure area of the AG's office. In all the years he'd worked for the organization, he'd never been this far inside the building. Instead of going to the elevators, leading to the top floors where the AG's offices were, they went to the furthest corner of the space to an office with a closed door.

Collins knocked on a thick hardwood door, built for privacy. They waited until a masculine voice beckoned them inside.

He wasn't sure if his face flushed, but his body heated as he entered the room where his actions would come to a reckoning. He did his best to stand tall and rack his brain for any excuse to make this all right. Just like every time he tried to find a lie to explain his choices, nothing came to mind. His actions were inexcusable.

"Take a seat," Collins said quietly, motioning him into the leather-bound chair directly across the desk from the AG. "Give the attorney general a minute longer."

Cash nodded, forgoing the "yes, ma'am" he'd normally give. He didn't trust his voice not to waver. He took the seat. The AG had a cordless phone at his ear. While he was listening intently to whomever was on the other end, his unreadable gaze remained riveted on Cash.

He held the stare, keeping his face blank. Not giving Cash any clue as to what thoughts were going through his head.

The AG was a no-nonsense man. He handed the phone to Lily without saying a word. She took it, brought it to her ear, and left the room.

"How are you doing?" the AG asked. His voice sounded genuinely concerned.

Cash had no idea how to answer such a loaded question. He opened his mouth, but no words came then he closed it again.

"I understand. I'm sorry to keep you waiting. Let me begin," he said and reached for his eyeglasses, putting them on as he sifted through the paperwork in the folder in front of him. "Of course I want to issue a formal apology on behalf of the entire United States Department of Justice. As far as I know, Deputy Assistant Collins was able to quash the video as soon as we were made aware." The man looked over his glasses at Cash. "I'm told very few eyes have witnessed any part of its contents. We've placed a warning over the file and marked it highly classified. As soon as legal confirms, it will be destroyed. By gaining Devin Fox's cooperation, you've accomplished more in Dallas than we ever thought possible. We can't have your cover jeopardized now."

*Okay.* Cash blinked. The AG nodded and looked down at his papers again.

"Thank you. I'm confused. Why am I here?" Cash finally asked.

"Always getting to the bottom line." The AG chuckled. "Your personal file reflects as much. Agent David Durham had a significant lapse in judgment by allowing that video out. As your lead security detail, he should've had your back at every turn. That's a red flag. Your partnership is now of critical concern to us. You're putting yourself on the line, moving faster than any of us believed possible. You don't need to wonder about the loyalty of the agent at your back."

The uncertainty had to show on Cash's face as the AG continued his explanation. "We've removed David and his team. I believe that consists of two additional agents." He looked down at his wristwatch. "The phone call I was on confirmed his removal. It's the reason for your wait."

Cash nodded. His eyes narrowed as his brain tried to catch up with the shifting events. "Additionally, it's time to bring you in for a formal face-to-face briefing on the Disciples of Havoc operation. I wasn't sold on your value here. Deputy Assistant Collins advocated for your assignment to this case. My hesitancy was due to the pure chaos in the structure of this operation. I wasn't sure anyone could gain any clarity, but it appears you'll get deeper inside than even she believed you could. I'm going to give you an overview, the deputy assistant will field the questions she's at liberty to answer later. First, I want to ask you what you think of Shanna Fox?"

Cash sucked in all that data for analysis later and tried his best to answer the questions put to him. "I initially had questions, but she's been supportive since day one. I've grown to trust her," he answered honestly. "I was pleased she agreed to work with us." Not that he'd given her an option, but she also hadn't asked for an out either.

"Good. I believe she can be a valuable resource who's been underutilized. I haven't filled David Durham's position. I'm looking for the right person. Someone outside of our organization. For the next few days, we want agent Shanna Fox to assist you in security. Can you handle Devin Fox's protection until I find the right person to put in the field with you?"

"I believe so, with Agent Fox's help." Cash gave a single nod of confirmation.

"Good. She's being briefed right now. Give me a few days. I don't want anything to jeopardize how far you've gotten, which also means you need to watch yourself closely."

The AG gathered his hands together on top of the file, staring Cash straight in the eyes. He looked as if he wanted to say more but held back.

"We needed a different perspective on this operation," he finally said. "A field view, if you will. That's the reason we've been purposefully vague with you and will continue to be, but the stakes have raised. Last evening, we intercepted Russian chatter that hasn't been fully dissected. We believe the outer ring to the Disciples trafficking operation is beginning to recognize the extent of the loss."

Cash nodded. He had a limited opportunity to ask questions and several raced through his mind. He decided on, "It would help to know what kind of loss."

"Four hundred and fifty million dollars has gone missing over the last four years. Although the sum seems large, to the overall operation, it's a drop in the bucket. At first, the loss appeared to be tied to mere negligence. Now, we see something more systematic. We need to know who is involved, and where that money is, before the Russians begin searching."

The emotions of the day and the abrupt shift of events from when he'd walked through this office door had left his body in need of a long, punishing run to loosen all the twitching and tight muscles. At this point, the video meant nothing. His career wasn't in jeopardy. Cash had been called to DC to finally gain an understanding of the assignment, which had only become more convoluted with each revelation the AG revealed.

So it was the Russians who were involved, not South America as Joe had indicated.

How was that much money lost, and not a larger concern? The Russians had never been big players in the drug trafficking game, but they were mighty in tactical brutality.

Cash nodded again, only out of sheer professionalism. Up to this point, he'd dealt with small-time rogue agents. Four hundred million dollars had vanished, and no one could find the reason why?

"Also, about Joe Wiscaver. Deputy Assistant Collins is bringing him fully into Exempt Operations. He's become an asset to you, and us. He's gone above and beyond. We'll continue his cover as your official handler with the Dallas DEA field office. Do you agree?"

"Yes, sir." Cash nodded. He hadn't known Joe long, but he'd come to trust him completely.

"Our indirect communication will go through Agent Wiscaver. Good?"

"Yes, sir," Cash nodded again. He had so many questions, but the answers would come from his field work. He couldn't imagine what was in those files if they refused to share the data with him for fear it would risk the veracity of his investigation or it didn't matter.

The AG pushed out of his seat and gathered the file before walking around the corner of the desk. He shook his head as he met Cash's gaze. "I truly apologize. I thought better of David. If you receive any grief over the contents of the video, please let me know directly. I'll take care of it."

Cash got to his feet, still reeling at the turn of the events. He wasn't fired. Instead, he'd been complimented on a job well done. "Sir, can I ask what you believed happened with the money?"

"I'd rather not speculate but I'm counting on you to find out."

At the door, with his hand on the doorknob but the door unopened, he looked back. "I need you to do your job to the best of your ability. Only…don't linger. At the very least, the bleeding has to stop before it turns into an international incident."

Cash gave a single nod in understanding.

"Please keep in mind, if you find any connection to Speaker Pierce, you contact me directly."

Cash nodded his acknowledgment again. "Thank you, sir."

As the AG left the office, Cash took his seat, bringing his hand to his face. Almost half a billion dollars missing with a foreign entity now beginning to understand the loss? Not to be overly crass, there was no way those dumbass bikers had the capacity to steal on that level. At the very least, they'd flaunt what they had accomplished.

He reached for his phone. No member of the Fox family was safe. But who did he call for help?

They were alone in this deal. The heavy weight on his shoulders felt like a ton, maybe even the weight of four hundred million dollars, resting there.

=♥=

Dev sat on the edge of the patio, on one of the most relaxing pieces of outside furniture he'd ever sat on, at his mother's house. A lot had changed in the forty-eight hours since he'd been there last. His mom had snapped her magic fingers and had a mini playground installed. A pretty and functional playhouse and sandbox in which Mae currently played and a hammock Abi lazily read from. His old soul daughter angled a foot on the ground, gently pushing to set the hammock gently swinging.

Much like he'd done since first arriving, he had to fight the tears. Tena hadn't been wrong. His heart wanted a house full of kids, with a cock-addicted partner, who loved him and their kids, and also loved to cook. In return, he'd be a loving, functional dad and badass husband.

A dumb life goal made by a prepubescent mind. It still hurt to know it was never going to fully materialize, no matter how hard he tried.

He had wanted six kids. One for every day of the week except Sunday, that was the day to do the devil's work. He gave a small smile, looking down at his ankles, one crossed over the other. He crossed his arms over his chest and closed his eyes. He was doing his best to hold himself together.

These plans were made with Tena. By the time they were fifteen years old, they had their first of many chases by the police. Dev had sped through the city's streets on his sled at the time. At some point, Tena decided to fuck it all. Her shirt went flying toward the cop car. Her bra came off next. Her tits were smaller then. He still remembered the feel of them pressed against his back. They rode together until he ran out of gas.

During that chase, they'd made their future plans. His smile grew at the memory.

He'd spent several days in local lockup over that stunt. He hadn't meant anything by it. Back then, he never saw the trouble he caused as anything more than rebellious mischief.

Shortly after, Tena had started working that twenty-dollar corner like the pro she was, determined to get her hooking business started. She hadn't had to rely on anyone but herself. He and his scary reputation was all the implied muscle she needed to keep herself safe. It had never occurred to him to object. Instead, he did quite literally the opposite. He'd liked having an independent businesswoman on his arm and had really liked to watch her work.

He'd rather cut off his own hand than watch Cash fuck or be fucked by anyone else.

He recognized how insane that sounded. He suffered quite a bit of guilt over his and Cash's sex tape being put out into the world. The goody-goody special agent didn't strike Dev as someone to get off by knowing people were watching him get pounded. Besides, Dev didn't want others to know how good Cash was in the bedroom. The pretty boy was a pleasure giving machine. The way he ate ass alone...

Dev saw himself beating every motherfucker in town who came sniffing after Cash.

Cash had fucked him like he wanted to own him.

Pretty boy fucked him so good he couldn't get it out of his head. Cash had ruined him. He'd planned to swing by Double Ds on the way to his mother's house tonight. Find some willing body to wreak havoc on, fuck for so long and hard that he forgot about the pretty boy. He'd driven straight there instead.

The security detail following him were better at their jobs than most. He actually never spotted them. *Whatever.* He got to spend more time with his girls.

What had Cash's superiors said about the video? Who knew what the government thought about such things. Unexpected, consuming rage sent his blood boiling. He absolutely refused to work with any other agent.

He was dick-whipped and somehow innately understood his pathetic plight.

"The girls got their hair cut. You need to make it a big deal," his mother said, placing a tray of drinks on the patio table.

"I did. Mae showed me when I first got here." He didn't reach for a glass. Instead, he turned back to the girls. "She showed me hers and Abi's nails too. Aren't they too young for that?"

His mother didn't reply. After a second more, Dev looked over at her. She beamed at him. "Those are children's press-on nails. What's got you so down today?"

What didn't have him down?

"Nothin'," he finally said. Honestly, except for the tears trying to well in his eyes, nothing had changed for him. Maybe when given the choice to be Abi and Mae's father, these feelings had cinched tighter, but he wasn't certain of that. He'd already been so crazy in love with them.

"Why're you crying?" his mother asked quietly. He could hear the concern in her voice. How did he say his dreams had died without giving anything away?

"I want to add Shanna and Keyes as custodian if somethin' happens to me," he said and lifted a hand, brushing away a tear that built enough steam to slide to his cheek. "I get you're always here for them, but Dad's right, you don't need to be strapped down with them if shit goes bad for me."

"Are you planning something to happen to you?" she asked.

A fair question that quirked the corners of his mouth. "No. But you never know. Dad hit me up about becomin' second. Let me know Diesel's the son he never had, but the second position is my birthright. He also thinks you're goin' through somethin'."

Switching the topic to her might be the perfect diversion to distract his mom. "The things we do when we're young..."

"Second that," he teased and threw out a fist for a knuckle touch. She leaned in, obliging him.

"What do you think about riding second?" she asked.

Oh lord, what did he think about having to go back into a world where he had to idolize his old man, lick his ass with compliments, shower the narcissist in adoring adulation? He couldn't get the idea of just killing him out of his mind. It would solve all his problems. He didn't say any of that, though. Only stared at her and shook his head.

"Then let Diesel have it. You're too independent to ever be a second. You're a first, Devin. I've only stayed with your father to help you navigate all those ridiculous rules. Let's make a break," she said pleadingly.

It didn't work that way, and she knew it. He'd given his vow to be a Disciple's brother for life. To leave before his official retirement was the ultimate betrayal. They'd fuck his shit up. She knew that.

And honestly, if it were only that easy. He'd take the ass whooping to the inches of death to get the girls out of there. With the government, and the shit they knew, he wasn't sure there was a place far enough to run away.

*Take Cash with you.*

"Fuckin' hell," Dev muttered and slapped the side of his temple to dislodge the awful thought.

"Language, son. Mae says they have over thirteen hundred dollars in a swear jar at your house. That's shameful." She used her mom voice as she scolded him. The kitchen door opened, drawing his attention. Shanna came through. She looked more like the sister he used to know in her jeans, a vintage T-shirt, light jacket, and running shoes. Her hair was left long and loose.

The windbreaker probably hid her weapons. He furrowed his brows.

"There's a timer going off," she said, shutting the door behind her.

"Oh no." Her mom darted up. "That's the cornbread. I need to get the pecan pies in the oven too." She scooted the heavy chair out, motioning for Shanna to take her seat. "I'm baking like we'll have twenty-five people here on Thanksgiving."

Shanna didn't take a seat, nodding her head to the yard. He guessed that was his instruction. He removed his necklace and bracelet, leaving those and his phone on the table before following after her. He figured he wasn't breaking too many rules if he was with Shanna.

"Have you heard from Cash?" he found himself asking, hating that was his first thought. Infuriated with himself that he'd let the thought out in words.

"No, have you?" she asked, her eyes lifting to his. He shook his head. "David and his guys are off the case. Completely removed."

"What? Why?" Dev asked, surprised.

Shanna shrugged. "Joe says the high, high powers weren't happy he let the video circulate."

Dev's brows dropped. "Circulate how?"

"Don't know."

"Who's tailin' me then?"

She gave a laugh. "That's why I'm here. Can't let my big brother get hurt." However she interpreted his look made her say, "Afraid I'll shoot you?"

"Afraid you can't shoot," he shot back, his mind reeling. "What about Cash? Is he still on the case?"

"I'm assuming yes, but I don't know."

They both crossed their arms over their chests and stared at the girls. Maybe as long as a minute passed before he confessed, "I didn't know the video wasn't secure. I was only tryin' to jack with him. He hurt me."

"By secretly recording a sex tape?" Shanna looked up at him accusingly.

"It was an accident. I didn't know the phone was recordin'." He waved a hand, dismissing Shanna. She wasn't the one he needed to apologize to. Her opinion didn't matter. "There's no guarantee I can find any answers y'all want. Maybe it's better for me just to drop off the planet."

"What about them?" Her thumb hooked toward the girls. "They'd be destroyed."

"You take care of 'em. You're a better person than me anyway." When Shanna glanced up alarmed, like that was the worst idea she'd ever heard, he added with a snicker, "At least you got a good job with benefits. Tell me you have benefits. Otherwise why would you ever take that job?"

"How did he hurt you?"

The vulnerability of the ache in his chest had his lips clamping closed. His heart hurt so damned bad. With his life in tatters, seriously riding on a dangerous edge, the only thing he knew for sure was he wanted the outcome that made this soul-deep pain subside.

"Something keeps pulling you and him together in the worst possible situations. It's hard not to question Cash's tactics. I heard David recommended his immediate termination after the video went out. When they reassigned me, it was made abundantly clear that it's a secret operation and Cash is the lead. He's responsible for all our safety. They respect him. Say we're lucky he's here."

Dev didn't say anything more about Cash. He couldn't trust his voice.

"Don't give up on us, Dev. We need you. Can you imagine living a life free of the backward ways the club runs. It's dictated our whole lives. The Disciples before everything. Women have no value. I know the way they talk about me because they say it to me."

Dev's jaw set, his teeth grinding together at the thought. "I'll hand 'em their fuckin' teeth."

"Not the point. Let's do this, Dev." She placed a hand on his arm. "That club is supposed to be a family with loyalty and trust, but the only one you actually trust, or even like, is Keyes. That says something, don't you think? Let's make our lives better from this point forward."

"Where is he?" Dev asked, ignoring the truth of her statement for the moment and redirecting the conversation back to Cash.

"On his way back now."

Dev nodded. The relief was so strong it made him unsteady.

"You think you know the club. You don't," Dev started to explain. "We're a vile, rotten, scumbag bunch of men. You're gonna get dirty if you press this."

"Then let's get dirty for the last time," Shanna said, looking up at him. Her gaze was the sincerest he might have ever seen.

"Y'all, come in! Pizza's here," his mother called out, drawing their attention. Mae finally spotted Shanna and started jumping, skipping toward her.

"See what I learned," Mae called out. "It's a skip. Can you skip?"

"Everybody but you can skip," Abi said, holding the dog in her arms as she came to Shanna's side, giving a side hug. "I'm almost finished with *New Moon*."

"Daddy, can everyone but me skip?" She stretched her arms out, and he reached down to lift Mae, giving Abi a raised eyebrow about being mean to her sister.

"I feel like there's got to be someone else that doesn't know how to skip. Just makes sense," he said, resting her on his hip. She put her arms around his neck, squeezing. Exactly the hug he needed. "You'd think with all the food we're gonna eat on Thanksgiving, we should save room."

Mae stuck out her tongue. "It's turkey and dressing. Yuck."

"Hey now, that's my favorite meal of the year." He tickled her side until she was in a fit of giggles. The best sound in the world.

# Chapter 30

Dev woke to the ding of his text messages. He reached for the phone, only opening his eyes so the facial recognition would open the screen. He read Abi's text message, letting him know they were awake and starting Thanksgiving dinner. He had to get over there and help them carry heavy things in preparation for the special lunch.

He glanced at his bedroom door as if he could stare his way through it to see the room on the other side. He had no proof Cash was just beyond the threshold of his bedroom door, but somehow, he knew that a closed door and about fifteen feet separated the two of them. He could feel it.

The guy was as quiet as a church mouse. Dev felt like a caged lion.

The thin wood was such an inadequate barrier that kept them apart.

Was he really ready to see Cash again? No.

*Yes, you are. Go be reasonable and figure this out.*
If he could punch his brain right now, he would.

His flair for the dramatic took over. More than anything, his hands itched to fling the door open and demand Cash pay attention to him.

There'd been no "I'm home, honey."

Or "how'd you fair without me?"

No "I know we're in a fucked-up place but I'm glad to be here with you again."

No "thank you for being so good while I was gone. I didn't deserve it."

Cash had just ignored him. Continued to ignore him. Dev hated being ignored. His very being was the opposite of ignorable.

He had all this hell going on with his life, and he'd been fucking worried about that disappearing asshole.

Maybe Dev's Spidey senses had it wrong. Cash wasn't the one out there.

Honestly, his intuition had never been overly accurate or helpful. Why start now?

Maybe he suffered from Stockholm Syndrome where he'd developed an unhealthy fixation on his captor.

Did that happen in like three days of being held hostage emotionally, if not physically?

Seemed the best explanation. All this crazy emotion was Cash's fault anyway. Yeah. He, and his response, were all on Cash.

Dev stalked across his bedroom for the door to say that very thing to that domineering motherfucker. Seconds before his hand touched the doorknob, he reared back to cup his palm to his mouth, checking his breath.

It was fine, but the fact that he checked made his shoulders slump in defeat. He had a big thing for Cash. He couldn't let it go and apparently didn't want to.

With less attitude and feeling like a fucking pussy, he opened the door and listened. The only sounds came from deep, even breaths. His heart lurched forward so violently he looked down to see if it had in fact flown from his chest. His feet followed the direction of his heart's command, purposefully, yet quietly, to the sofa.

At the edge, he spotted the big guy, way too large in both height and circumference for his couch, crashed, sound asleep. Cash slept in his fitted athletic wear. The man was beautiful.

Way too handsome to have to sleep half on and half off anything.

Too nice-looking to have to live such an honorable life. Cash missed his calling as a porn star or an escort. After Dev got a taste of what the guy had to offer, he'd pay a shit ton to be with Cash again.

His cock stirred under the appraisal.

Dev suspected Cash's exhaustion was at least partially his fault. He lowered to one knee, his gaze riveted to Cash's sleeping face. Maybe he could see hints of the young boy he used to be. The wayward strands fell forward. Dev thought about the last couple of times they had slept together. He'd encouraged Cash to sleep, gently caressing his fingertips over Cash's shoulders and back. Once asleep, Dev fingered the sweep of hair before rubbing the softness against his fingertips. It humanized Cash. Made his perfection seem closer to normal.

Dev lifted a hand to brush the strands off Cash's face the way he used to.

He barely touched Cash when the slight movement startled him awake. His eyes flew open, widening to the size of half dollars. Less than a second later he bolted upright, his hand jerking toward his hip where a weapon might be holstered. Cash came up empty handed. His pretty boy's entire body moved in that fluid way Dev found so sexy.

Cash hopped on the cushion in a crouching position, wedging in an awkward position against the arm of the couch. The man's speed and strength were astounding and a complete turn-on.

Dev remained absolutely still, not moving a single muscle. A grin split his lips at the position they were in. "Down, boy. It's just me."

Cash stared hard at Dev then glanced around the room, turning this way and that, his muscles tense. After a few breaths, Cash finally relaxed. He eased back and dropped down on his ass. The man was limber, Dev knew from experience. Cash rubbed one eye. "You startled me."

"Sleepin' like the dead doesn't seem very undercovery," Dev said, teasingly.

Cash looked over at him. "Undercovery? That's not even... Never mind. It probably isn't," Cash finally responded, his hand dropping from his face. "What time is it?"

Dev watched the boyish charm fade. The pretty boy transformed into the man he'd gotten to know. Dev slowly dropped his other knee to the floor, rested back on his heels as Cash placed both his feet on the floor in front of Dev.

"I'm sorry," Dev found himself murmuring. The words encapsulated a host of deeds he'd done wrong, but he couldn't finish the sentence. Apologies were so foreign to his lips he wasn't sure he'd uttered it correctly.

"No, I'm sorry. I appointed myself as the security personnel watching over you. I felt like you'd be more comfortable with me, but I've been burning it at both ends. I should've left Joe here last night." Cash started to rise, and Dev reached out, cupping the man's calf, stopping him from doing anything more than taking notice of Dev and his intention. Cash dropped back on the seat, eyeing Dev.

"Not what I meant," Dev started and the position he'd kept them in finally registered. He was on his knees between Cash's parted legs. Everything right in Dev's body had him zeroing in on the stretched fabric between Cash's lower stomach to his ass. The air between them sizzled to life. Cash's dick hardened under his appraisal, his nipples tightened into small pebbles.

Dev's boldness had him reaching out without even considering the action. He cupped the growing cock. Cash let him, not moving a single muscle. His gaze tracked every one of Dev's movements. Those light green eyes transformed from confused to darkening with lust in seconds.

Now Dev understood exactly why he'd made the decisions he had. Why he had desperately wanted Cash to be in his life long term. How he hadn't even questioned such a fine man's sudden existence in his life, or why that man was so willing to spend time with a guy like him.

Dev squeezed his fingers around Cash's thick cock, committing the size and length to memory. Sex was going to happen between them again. He promised himself that. But not while his new, confused feelings were still so raw. Once he was able to put Cash in the same category as everyone else he'd ever fucked, then he'd fuck the shit out of the guy at every given opportunity.

And that wasn't today.

Even with those thoughts crashing around inside him, his hand refused to let go. His palm gently pressed then coasted up Cash's length. Only then could he manage to remove his trembling hand, fisting his fingers as he pushed to his feet and finished his apology. "I should've realized the video was being seen by everyone and I didn't. I'm… My bad."

As Dev started to turn away, Cash reached for his wrist, halting him. Those eyes that spoke to his soul, penetrated, keeping him in place. "It's not just you. I've crossed lines I've never crossed with anyone else, but I did it willingly. I wanted to. I still want to, Dev."

The tone Cash used drove his truth home. Dev's entire body did an inner shudder that he was relatively sure he'd kept hidden. At least he hoped he had. The tactical chess game they were now playing didn't allow for any give, only taking. At least where Dev was concerned.

He had to fight to keep himself from caving, moving forward, taking what was so clearly being offered. He wanted Cash's body so bad it hurt, but instead, he twisted his wrist out of the hold.

"Coffee?" Even though everything inside him absorbed his pretty boy's words, letting them heal some of the residual pain of being badly used, he wasn't ready. "My girls have already texted to tell me to get on my way. We should probably hit the road soon."

"What time is it?" Cash asked again, still sitting exactly in the same position. Dev shouldn't like the easy comfort between them, but he did.

"Eight thirty."

Cash's eyes nearly bugged out of his head. He rolled to his feet.

"What time did you get in last night?"

"I guess I got to your place about two this morning. Where's my phone…" Cash searched the sofa, pushing his hands between the cushions until he found the cell and started working the screen. "Shit. I missed a meeting check-in."

"It's a holiday," he said, dropping a pod inside the coffee maker.

"Not for the bad guys," Cash replied, his attention focused on his phone. Dev couldn't help how his gaze traveled to Cash's cock. Work, time, and cell phones had destroyed the hard-on. Dev shook his head in disappointment.

"I'm a pretty bad dude and I took the day off," he murmured, pushing a coffee cup under the drip.

"You aren't that bad, Dev," Cash said.

He let Cash's assessment go as the memory of calling the club Prez in San Diego to do that slimeball in... He snapped his fingers as it hit him. That was what Parker's call had meant. He'd taken care of Stink. All the dots connected inside his head in a moment of rushed clarity.

"What?" Cash asked.

"Nothin'. If you're ridin' with me, I'm headin' out in about thirty minutes. It's a haul from here," he explained, wishing he had the details of how Parker had handled the end of Stink's life. Dammit, all the surveillance ruined a good story.

"Don't leave without me," Cash said as he left Dev's apartment. He hadn't needed the sounds of Cash's solid tread or the door opening and closing. Dev felt the loss the farther Cash went.

# Chapter 31

Whatever Cash expected, it wasn't this. He surveyed the room where he sat. Dev's mother's dining room reflected the overall house in that it was both spacious and yet somehow homey. It was a beautifully decorated room full of chic, modern furnishings, sprinkled with photographs and mementos, showing the love and history between her and her children.

A complete spread of holiday themed food, probably enough to feed the entire bike club, was both artfully arranged on the table and overflowing in the kitchen.

Including Dev's two children and himself, six people were at the table. One spot left open, not at the head of the table, for Dev's father who hadn't yet arrived. Fox wasn't necessarily late. They started Thanksgiving dinner early, without him. The food was ready. That simple.

The weirdest part for Cash wasn't the absence of the bikers he had hoped to begin indoctrinating himself with, but instead the inclusion of children. He had never really been around kids. He had no brothers or sisters, and as a child, he hadn't attracted those sorts of friendships. He'd been home-schooled since his accident. His church family consisted of the stragglers his parents connected with. His work in law enforcement required a cloak of secrecy.

Having a five-year-old girl plastered to his side required him to think differently. To concentrate on her constant engagement. To listen to her words and try to understand the speak of a small child. Yes, she was adorable. Sweet and overly attentive. A very pretty little girl who had the makings of being a beauty when she grew up. Petite compared to her equally impressive older sister.

Mae may be more outgoing than Abi since Mae chatted nonstop, open with her love of life and family, while Abi was solidly marked with the Fox blood. Anytime she looked at you, you felt like she was making fun of you inside her head.

Both girls were crazy about their father therefore curious about Cash. Abi made Dev work a little harder to gain her attention than Mae did, but she seemed to do it on purpose. Probably a trait she learned from her dad.

"He's the one Daddy kissed when we were at the apartment," Mae burst out, giddy with joy. Her hands rushed to her lips, covering her mouth as if she'd dropped the biggest secret of them all.

"I knew she couldn't hold it," Abi said, using her fork to pick at the cornbread dressing on her plate. She had proclaimed to the table she didn't like onions and picked every one out of each bite. "You owe me five dollars."

"I do not. I didn't make that bet, you did," Mae shot back. Since each girl sat on either side of Cash, Mae was almost in his lap when she spouted off at her sister.

"Not at the dinner table," Dev said. He sat to the left of his mother, directly across from Mae and reached over, tapping the side of the plate with his fork. "Mae, eat."

"I wondered if you were the one," Carly, Dev's mother, said. "She's been talking about you more than she's talked about her new puppy. She's taken with you."

Cash glanced down as Mae wiggled her hips to scoot closer to him in her seat. Her big eyes stared at him. She wore a bigger smile now and a happy shiver encased her whole body.

"Momo says boys can marry each other. Do you have tattoos?" she asked, not waiting for his response, she continued, "I didn't see any the other morning." She turned back to her grandmother as if they were having the conversation. "He wasn't wearing his shirt when he was in Daddy's apartment.

That's why I think they're gonna get married. Wait." Her finger came up as if she had a great idea. She looked at him again. "Was that line going up your chest a tattoo?" Again, she didn't wait for his answer when her curious gaze shifted to her father, not missing a beat. "You can fix that tattoo, right, Daddy? It wasn't very good."

"Mae," Dev warned, looking at her then her plate.

"I'm all done," she answered, pushing the plate away. "Daddy can give you tattoos." She moved her hand over her body then down each arm. "He's gonna give me tattoos when I'm fifteen." She looked back at her father for confirmation.

"Eighteen," Dev said and extended a hand to push the plate back closer to her. "Eat more green beans. They're good for you."

"Eighteen," she confirmed proudly. "I'm gonna do a sleeve of all the princesses. Daddy can draw them. He drew them once when I couldn't sleep." As she spoke, her eyes grew bigger. He could practically see another lightbulb moment gaining momentum. "You can have all the superheroes. You look like one. You can draw them, can't you, Daddy?"

"Told you. We have a bet on when the ADHD, emphasis on the H, is diagnosed," Dev said to Cash, referring to their earlier brief crash course on Dev's children's habits he'd gotten on the drive over this morning. Dev had barely stopped shoveling the food in his mouth since they'd sat down, and added another bite, nodded, then covered his mouth and looked pointedly at Mae. An instruction of silence she seemed to understand. Mae covered her mouth too.

Another interesting thing Cash had noticed was that Dev's mom had an influence on him. Dev was different inside this house. More relaxed, more civilized, less edgy. The curse words he used in every sentence he spoke were barely uttered since they'd been there.

"He has the biggest muscles out of all Daddy's club brothers," Mae burst out. Again, those adoring eyes lifted to Cash.

"He's not club…" Abi said to Mae before stopping and asking, "Does he look like the rest of Dad's brothers?"

The sounds of motorcycle pipes rumbling loudly stopped everyone from saying anything more. A tension infiltrated the room, infecting every person sitting at the table. Cash glanced at Shanna who sat directly across the table from him. She squared her shoulders, her spine stiffening. Even the chatterbox beside him stopped talking and moving.

As if the room was held suspended, they all waited for the source of the pipes to arrive. Dev's fork had slowed its path to his mouth. Cash found himself pausing too.

"Where's everybody at?" A loud, deep voice boomed from the kitchen. Anger laced each syllable. Seconds later, a door slammed shut with too much force.

He'd heard the voice through surveillance but nothing like the hard edge or booming sounds.

"We were almost done," his mother whispered with a sigh to the table, reaching for her glass of chardonnay. "We're in here, Edgar."

Cash lifted his brows at the use of Fox's given name. He looked at Dev who gave a noiseless laugh and shrugged. "She refuses to call him what everyone else does. It drives him crazy."

"What the fuck?" Fox pronounced, coming inside the dining room. "You fuckin' said be here at two. It's one thirty."

Nothing prepared Cash for the underwhelming visual. Fox. The man who made grown men cower was intimidating as hell, but Cash wasn't sure why. He looked like a standard run-of-the-mill older man. A mechanic. His face was weathered and worn. His head shaved almost bald with long hairs popping out of places they shouldn't.

His swollen pot belly indicated too much beer and not enough physical activity. He had aged tattoos on both exposed arms, and also on his neck, based on the cut of the faded T-shirt he wore. There were also assorted mismatched tattoos on his face. His biceps were large, and his hands showed a strength the rest of his body lacked. An unkempt beard and mustache shot wildly in every direction from underneath his nose down his chin.

He wore a belt holster, decorated with a one-percenter design. A Glock was secured inside. There were other notable weapon accessories attached to the belt—a couple of knife holsters, one housing a horizontal knife, the other holding something close to a bowie knife.

Generally, those weapons were worn for show, not force.

Probably at some point in his life, Fox had been considered attractive but not anymore. He didn't fit this family. Dev had started eating again, reaching for a bowl of mashed potatoes.

He wasn't as completely unaffected as he tried to appear to be. Cash noticed the tension flexing in his neck and shoulders.

"Sit down. Stop trying to intimidate the room. We aren't having it today," Carly said as if he were Mae's age and needed redirection.

Fox had a crazy-eyed stare as he went to the foot of the table. "You're fuckin' almost done. Goddamn. I fuckin' put this food on the table and you start without me?"

"Edgar, the food was ready early and who knew if you were actually going to show." Carly pointed toward Cash. "Dev's brought a guest. Could you show some manners and respect? We left you a place." She then pointed to the open place setting next to Shanna, close to where he stood.

Cash had to resist the urge to square his shoulders as not only Fox, but every eye in the room turned to him. If he picked up the swell of Dev's chest, it didn't speak of pride at his supposed boyfriend, more a show to suggest he wasn't putting up with anything derogatory that might tumble from his father's mouth.

"Cash, this is Edgar. Edgar, meet Cash."

Cash nodded to Fox.

"I'm Fox," Dev's father said and poked a finger in his chest as if Cash might not get it. He took the seat next to Shanna but looked disgruntled as hell. "What're you starin' at?" Fox barked at Mae, grabbing a spoon from the cornbread dressing.

"You," Mae answered with a little less happy in her tone. Fox's gaze swept to Abi.

"You ain't got nothin' to say?"

Abi continued to stare at her plate, not making eye contact with her grandfather as she spoke. "He always says that to me. You'd think he'd figure it out."

"I'd've beat your ass in front of everybody if you ever said anything like that to your grandparents," Fox said to Shanna. The spoon clinked hard against the china plate. A lump of food plopped down.

"Since I've never met my grandparents, we really don't know that," Shanna started but Dev cut her off.

"If I ever find out you laid a hand on my kids, I'll fuckin' kill you that day, old man." An underlying promise rang in the oath. Cash believed every word.

"Well, goddamn. I'm gettin' attacked by everyone at this fuckin' table. Happy fuckin' Thanksgiving. Give me some of that cold turkey I paid for." His hand extended to the platter of cut turkey placed closer to his wife. "And where's my fuckin' beer?"

Dev's mother let go of an impatient sigh, but got up from her seat, throwing the napkin in the chair. "I'll be back."

When she left, his father rose, picking up his plate. He went around the table and took Carly's seat at the head, replacing his plate with hers. Cash half expected the plate to be slung across the room, but instead, Fox put the plate on top of Mae's. "Get to your place at the end of the table."

Instant tears sprang to her eyes as she scurried out of the seat.

"Goddammit," Dev roared and took his freshly buttered yeast roll and threw it at his father like a pitcher at a baseball game. "Don't talk to them that way. I've fuckin' told you. It's comin' for you. Guaranteed."

As Dev spoke, he rose, rounding the table, using all his strength to knock the back of his father's chair forward. He met Mae who'd changed course to head to her dad. He gently scooped her up then went for Abi, taking her hand and carefully moving her out of her seat. The move was impressive with as angry as he was.

Cash's gaze followed them. Three sets of eyes were focused on him. He guessed that was his cue. He lifted the napkin from his lap, setting it on the table.

"Grab your plate and mine. My old man's a pig. Nobody wants to watch him eat anyway."

Cash cast a quick glance at Shanna who shrugged and reached for her plate and Dev's, getting up from her seat.

"Good. More fuckin' food for me," Fox growled, seemingly unimpressed by their show of disdain.

The silence lasted until Cash reached the kitchen then an all-out brawl began between Dev's father and his mother in the dining room. Dev put Mae down on a barstool and grabbed new plates, handing one to each of his daughters.

"Remember, you're the one who wanted to come." Dev glanced pointedly at Cash.

"Momo and Fox fight a lot. More than Daddy and Momma. Momo doesn't like Fox. Nobody really does except his brothers at the club and that one woman and her daughter." Mae explained as Cash took his seat next to her. The entire experience became way more biker-oriented than he'd originally thought it was. Dev's big hand came to Mae's head, drawing both hers and Abi's attention.

"Fightin' isn't normal. Your prince needs to not yell at you like that," Dev explained in a "do as I say, not as I do" type of remark.

"Or you'll beat him up?" Mae asked happily. Abi nodded as if it was a given.

"Oh, one hundred percent *yes*." The certainty rang true. Cash didn't doubt it in the least. Dev was sweet with his girls. All the while, ignoring the crash of broken glass coming from the other room.

=♥=

"I need a fuckin' bump," Dev murmured, coming to stand at the edge of the back porch where Cash and Shanna quietly talked. He was edgy now, wanting to crawl out of his skin. His father's bad attitude left a lasting mark on his mood.

"No, you need some ADHD medication," Cash answered as if he were an expert head doctor.

"I don't have ADHD. I think I'm fuckin' bi-polar. My head never stops." Not exactly the truth but sounded disagreeable so he stuck with the argument.

Abi swung lazily in a hammock with his mother's cell phone in hand. Mae played with her Barbies, or whatever they were, finally giving Cash a moment's peace. Maybe his shiny newness was finally wearing off. The pretty boy had stood up well to their obsession.

"You've been diagnosed with ADHD since you were nine years old," Cash said, nonplussed, while staring out into the darkening sky.

"What the fuck?" Dev burst out and crossed his arms over his chest, feeling disgruntled as hell until Abi glanced at him. She was on high alert since Fox's arrival, keeping an eye on things. He lifted a hand, letting her know it was all okay. When he spoke again, his voice was softer and calmer. "Y'all know more about me than I know about myself."

As Dev stood there, he let the quiet and Cash's presence ease some of the tension that had formed from his parents' latest epic battle. The quiet was bliss.

"I'm officially moving into your building in the apartment below yours," Shanna said.

"You're payin' rent," Dev spouted, not caring about the rest of it. His backup security protector was a slip of a girl who had spent most of her life wanting to end him. For sure, the feds were paying for her stay. "Price went up twenty-five percent. Extenuatin' circumstances. I believe it's in the contract."

Shanna laughed as if he were ridiculous. When he started to explain just how serious he was, his mother came through the patio door, like a housewife from the 1950s, carrying a tray of coffee cups on saucers. "Cash, I let it go for this long, but now I need to understand how you two connected with each other after all these years. Come have some coffee."

His mother's doe-eyed look directed at the pretty boy completed the multiverse dimension he felt he shifted to. His two little girls were dressed like a Gap commercial, sister and boyfriend were by his side, and his mother acted like a reincarnated June Cleaver.

What had happened to his life?

And why the fuck did this look so damned appealing.

# Chapter 32

"You wear the necklace like this," Joe corrected, reaching for the weighted skull at the base, turning it forward as if Dev were a complete moron. It wasn't his fault the camera shifted when he moved. Dev scowled down at the agent, fiddling with the piece of clearly faulty surveillance equipment.

"If I move and it turns, what's good about that?" he asked, envisioning a million different ways this could go wrong.

"Yeah. Be careful then. We added this patch," Joe said, reaching for the cut and handing it to Dev, nodding for him to put it on. Right when he was about to blast the kid for touching his cut, much less daring to suggest he'd alter the once sacred garment, he looked down at the patch. His eyes narrowed at the intricately styled insignia patch with the numbers 666 embroidered on top in thick red yarn. The patch represented the beast inside him. A perfect representation.

"Why've I never thought of it?" Dev asked, rubbing his fingertips over the raised design.

"Be careful touching it," Joe said, then used his shirt sleeve to wipe over the patch. "The circle in the middle of the six is a recording device. Cash had it made for you. We tried to make it look weathered. It still looks new to me, but it represents your devilman."

The mark of his beast. Who'd turned informant. Gotcha. Great.

His stomach twisted. Until tonight, he could mentally pretend to only be playing along with Cash, waiting for his out. That time had passed. Now he was planning to take an undercover agent into sacred territory.

If he ever found out one of his brother's had turned this way, he'd have no problem ending his life.

His own father would lead the pack to end Dev's.

"Why am I recordin' anything if Cash is with me?" Dev asked, searching for a way out.

"Anytime you're out in the world, you're required to have surveillance equipment on you. It's part of the agreement you made," Cash said in a professional tone, strolling through the front door of Dev's apartment.

"You need to fuckin' knock. It's still my private space to live," Dev shot out angrily. Cash lifted a fist to knock on the open door. "You're a dick."

Cash rolled his eyes.

"Is he ready?" Cash asked, ignoring Dev's comment.

"Yup," Joe answered, turning in such a way to include Cash. "Wear the vest..." Dev gave him a brutal look. "The cut," Joe corrected, hands held up in apology. "Wear the cut the entire time. It's our best vantage point. I'll be monitoring and recording everything."

He allowed himself the slow perusal up and down Cash's body, hoping to make the agent as uncomfortable as Dev's cock was now inside his fitted jeans.

In an ever-changing world of different looks, Cash had shifted again. The clean and shiny was still there, but now it was masked underneath a layer of darkness. Tight black jeans, a fitted black button-down left open a couple of buttons on the top and the bottom. He wore black chains around his neck and wrists. Black boots on his feet. Dev bet the slight heel on the bottom lifted Cash's already tight ass. He vowed to find that answer out for himself.

Dev slid his gaze up to Cash's hair. Today, it wasn't styled. Instead, he wore silky waves pushed off his face. That had to be his natural hair. Cash was a gorgeous man.

Further pissed off and now even more disagreeable, he swept his gaze down in an overt inspection. Two hardened nipples poked against the material of his shirt. Then he went lower, to the outline of Cash's cock in those snug jeans, positioned perfectly for anyone who was willing to look. Which Dev certainly was.

No doubt that was the reason the shirttails were left untucked and unbuttoned.

Cash represented Dev's boy toy. The kind of guy that compels a one-percenter biker to take a beautiful, hulk of a man to a club BBQ.

"You look gay."

*Like hot gay.*

Gay put together like a fucking mythological god. Gay in the way every man on the planet wished he looked.

Like gay in a come fuck me cuz I'm so goddamn sexy way. Dev's exact kind of gay.

"Which I am." Cash's hands splayed out as if it were obvious. "I tried to look like I fit in…"

Dev burst out with a laugh. "You don't fit in." Levity was good.

Cash's brow furrowed to somewhere between worried and crestfallen. "Do I at least look like something you'd break the rules to bring to the party?"

"Goal achieved." He made sure that hadn't sounded like a compliment.

"You have the surveillance equipment you're planting?" Joe asked Cash.

Dev left them there to do whatever it was secret agents did. He couldn't stay another second in all that nice-smelling cologne and handsome good looks. He had to regroup. Cash regularly stunned him, but man.

Even harder than keeping himself together was the glaring reminder that he had to guard his words. He sucked at not saying exactly what was on his mind the second it landed there. It made him obsessive to have to hang on to his thoughts and keep his trap shut.

The blessed feeling of anger built fast. He sneered, a growl settling in his chest. He grabbed the helmet he generally used and clomped back for the entry. He shoved the brain bucket into Cash's chest, pissed at himself for being such a fucking pussy.

This wasn't a game. His life depended on his ability to outmaneuver every motherfucker he encountered. Sure, he was smarter than all those fuckers, but he was used to using brute force to relay a point in any given moment. This bide-your-time bullshit rankled.

He grabbed a thicker jacket and his sunglasses before heading out the door. He didn't stop until he was hiking a leg over his sled. He glanced over his shoulder, glad to see Cash there. Otherwise, given the option, he'd have left him at the apartment. It'd be safer for everyone.

"Get on," Dev grumbled.

"I'm not going to fit back there," Cash said, shutting the back door behind him.

"You'll fit." Fifty-fifty chance actually. Dev hoisted the bike between his thighs. "If those tight ass jeans stretch."

"Why don't we take your car?" Cash asked, coming to stand right beside him.

Dev sighed. "You want to sell this, right? Not let anyone suspect nothin'?" He waited for Cash's nod. "My guy would be huggin' that fat cock against my ass. It's how we roll. Knowin' a hot pussy's back there means somethin' to that relationship. Get on."

He didn't leave room for more discussion by starting the Harley with a roar.

Cash straddling his bike when they arrived wasn't the requirement he stressed it to be. He wanted to continue to make Cash as uncomfortable with him as he was with Cash.

Cash's hesitancy made Dev scoot forward on the seat.

The indecision lasted so long he wasn't sure Cash was going to take his directive. Then the pretty boy hiked a leg over, scooting far back on the pillion. Cash sat down carefully. When the bike didn't waver, he put his helmet on and positioned his feet.

"You can't sit that far back. You're gonna fall off."

Cash moved slightly closer to Dev's back.

Oh hell. He immediately recognized the chaos this was going to wreak on his system once they started the ride.

Why was every decision he made a bad one?

"Have you fuckin' done this before?" Dev shot his chin over his shoulder, glaring at Cash.

"No," Cash yelled over the rumble.

"Your thighs need to hug my hips and legs," Dev barked. "You control this ride. You gotta hold on to me. We move together. Scoot as close to me as you can. So close, I could be ridin' in your lap. Wrap at least one arm around my waist. Otherwise, we're gonna drop this bitch."

Cash moved forward, doing exactly as Dev asked.

*Motherfucker.* This was going to be a long-ass night.

= ♥ =

Cash had seen a lot in his days as an undercover agent. He thought nothing could surprise him, but tonight proved him wrong. Many hours into the club BBQ, the scenes playing out in front of him spoke of a bad biker flick. Everything was present. Debauchery, orgies, loads of drugs, and loud, angry rock 'n' roll music. The only thing not there was the local law enforcement that should have shut this party down a long time ago.

An intricate stereo system dated back to the 1990s played every rage and emo song he'd ever heard recorded and many he hadn't. Dev partied hard, easily shifting from group to group. He got along well with everyone, both men and women alike.

Of note, especially after his and Dev's first night together, was that Dev bypassed all the weed and pills on offer.

Cash sat on the outskirts of the party in a lawn chair Dev had provided for him. He wasn't necessarily with the women. Or club whores as the group referred to the women who were present. There were very few wives or girlfriends at the party. Nor did he sit with the men, who were all either prospects or patched brothers. He sat on the periphery of the good time, pretty much alone.

An enormous bonfire blazed on the side of the property.

The coveted Disciples of Havoc clubhouse sat on the other side. A place Cash was biding his time to explore thoroughly. The party carried over inside. By the way the bikers and their female partners came out, he assumed it was the designated place for sex. Well, the raunchy group had no problem throwing down wherever they stood.

Where Dev hadn't completely abandoned Cash, he ignored him nonetheless. Dev's old man on the other hand had made sure Cash was introduced to everyone. Of course, he picked up the subtle digs when Fox explained his and Dev's relationship status.

The brothers nicknamed him Mr. Clean. He'd been teased about his clean clothes, clean skin, clean hair. Of course, he went along with it, encouraging the humor, marking and memorizing each person he ran across.

About every fifteen minutes, Dev brought a new can of beer to Cash, taking his old one. The biker made a show of opening the new beer can for Cash who never drank a sip. Then Dev would lean over to fondle Cash in a way the entire group could see. Each time, a button came undone. Then he got a massage to the chest or pinch to a nipple. Eventually, Dev's palm ventured to stroke over his cock, squeezing and molding through the denim.

Each time the subtlety of the action dissipated. Cash's shirt was completely unbuttoned. His jacket and each lapel pushed to his side. His belt had come off and now hung around his neck like a scarf. The button of his jeans was undone. The zipper lowered marginally. Dev should give a masterclass in teasing seduction. Even in these dire circumstances, Cash's body responded, seeking out more of Dev's touch.

The last time Dev came to him, Cash brazenly reached for his biker's longer pieces of hair, tugging him down for a porn-worthy kiss. When Cash let Dev's hair and mouth go, Dev's defiant gaze connected with his. Cash mouthed the word "clubhouse" hoping he'd catch the hint.

Dev had sauntered away as if he hadn't spoken. He got that they needed to take their time. The more intoxicated the members of the club were, the easier it would be for him to case the entire place. Maybe, whatever sexual act was currently happening in the distance might occupy more of the group gravitating that direction. If so, he wouldn't even need Dev with him as he checked out the clubhouse.

"Come on." Dev came into his line of sight.

Cash shoved to his feet, placing the beer can next to the leg of the chair. Dev leaned in close, removing the belt from around his neck then pushed his jacket off his shoulders and carelessly tossed it over the back of the chair.

Dev reached out, drawing their bodies tightly together with one arm.

"Come spend time with me in the clubhouse." Dev's palm tenderly caressed down Cash's back, trailing with purpose over the curve of his ass until his fingers gripped a globe. Their stare held. "I got somethin' special for you. You're gonna like it."

The way Dev tried to seduce him felt very much like an emotional trap. A bad, bad idea. He was too raw to play this game with this man. Cash tried to force reason to the forefront. He glanced over his shoulder to the partygoers. If Dev was putting this performance on for his brothers, it worked. Every eye in the vicinity was on them. But the way Dev handled him felt very real. Reality versus pretend was merging together.

"Open your mouth, baby."

The way the word *baby* sounded, caressed Cash's very soul.

"Someone's gotta get us home," Cash murmured. A tiny sliver of rational fear worried he could be drugged right now. He'd let Dev fuck him and love every minute, but he had to stay coherent. Dev's overwhelming presence was all the misjudgment he could allow himself tonight.

"Open your mouth," Dev commanded before leaning in to press his lips against Cash's. The biker stayed right there in Cash's face as he said, "I got a room here for us. These fuckers better start gettin' used to you being around. I like you here with me."

His penetrating gaze urged Cash to comply. "Open because it's me askin', my pretty boy."

Problem solved. The endearing pet name and sweetly muttered request was always going to be his downfall. He complied, opening his mouth. He no longer had a choice. If this was his end, he'd die remembering the allure in Dev's blue stare.

Dev placed a small tablet on his tongue. Cash didn't want to close his mouth. Dev's hypnotic mouth opened, angling his head as he lifted to sweep his tongue forward. He drove deep inside Cash's mouth.

The pill easily dissolved with the unique taste of baby aspirin. His biker wasn't trying to drug him. The staggering relief allowed him to see the honesty in Dev's seduction techniques. As Cash's hands came to Dev's hips, a strong palm cupped the back of his head. Dev's fingers threaded into his hair, holding Cash in place as he devoured him.

The kiss intensified until Dev was fucking his mouth by way of his tongue. That strong, sexy body ground against his, rutting there for the entire club to see.

Cash's restraint broke. This was all Cash had wanted for days. He closed his eyes and let himself just feel every inch of Dev's desire. The deep tangle of their tongues and clicking of their teeth, a show of dominance and tempting promise of more to come. With both of his palms, he gripped Dev's ass, driving his hard-as-stone cock against Dev's.

As quickly as the kiss started, Dev wrenched away. His mouth tried to follow Dev's, wanting more as the biker gripped his hand tightly again. A dazed Cash found himself being dragged behind Dev, taking long strides toward the clubhouse.

"About fuckin' time," Daphne, the only woman there who'd introduced herself and spent time talking to Cash, yelled after them, humor lacing every word. "Dev's been eye fuckin' you since y'all got here. Ride, cowboy, ride." She was loud and brash, certain to have turned the heads of anyone not paying attention.

Cash did his best to commit the interior of the clubhouse to his lust-filled brain. An enormous wooden bar with every type of liquor bottle on top took up most of the room along the back wall. The surface was old, scratched, and dated. Apparently, tonight was a serve yourself free-for-all. No bartender in sight.

The rest of the large space had black leather sofas, loveseats, and sturdy chairs that had all seen better days. The various stages of undress and sexual activity currently taking place on the furniture and even the floor were a shock to his senses. Not quite an orgy, but it wouldn't take much to get there.

Dev stepped over the legs of a brother lying on top of a woman. Cash just couldn't bring himself to call her a club whore. They were going at it hard if the groans and grunts meant anything.

"Get up," Dev said and grabbed the jeans gathered around the ankles of another club member, tossing the lower half of his body to the side so they could walk past.

Dev used leverage to swing Cash forward, busting a quick move. Cash twisted, Dev's strong palm pushed him down to the sofa. Dev was so captivating. He didn't give Cash a second to adjust his body before straddling his thighs, coming down directly on top of him. A mischievous grin lit Dev's face as he smiled down at him. Dev reached for his nipple, giving it a hard squeeze. The sensation sprinted through his balls, straight to his cock.

"You ready to become my bitch?" The words were said loudly for all to hear as if this was some sort of rite of passage in their relationship. "That means I'm gonna fuck that perfect ass right here until I've had enough. Put my claim on you in front of my brothers. I'll own you. You ready for that, pretty boy?"

*Oh hell yes.* He liked those words more than he should. Cash splayed his hands across Dev's thighs, squeezing the muscles to tug Dev down hard on top of him. At the same time, he thrust his hips forward, grinding his cock into Dev's jean-covered ass. It seemed to be answer enough.

The devilish grin held Cash mesmerized as Dev tantalized him in his slow descent, pulling a grin from him seconds before their mouths came together again. This time, Dev wasn't demanding. He was sensual and sexy. That velvety tongue lapped across his. Cash's eyelids closed, and he settled back on the sofa.

Dev's body weight fully relaxed on top of him. He wrapped his arms around Dev, pushing his hands underneath the T-shirt's hem. Dev shrugged out of the cut, carelessly letting it fall away. He reached around to the clasp of his surveillance necklace, easily breaking it free then tossing it on top of the cut. The kiss continued. Dev ate at Cash's mouth as if he were a special treat. His biker acted as if he couldn't get enough. Cash pushed the T-shirt up, needing skin on skin contact. Regretfully, he had to break from the sweet kiss as he brought the T-shirt over Dev's head.

Dreams did come true. Cash moved his hands eagerly over Dev's strong back, mapping each dip and curve of muscle as his gaze locked with Dev's.

Dev let him have this moment. The biker's body was suspended above Cash's as he massaged and caressed his palms forward. After their first couple of times together, their sex had become this. Holding one another, learning everything about the other's body, being what the other needed.

With his fingers, he traced the intricate lines of Dev's tattoos then moved on to tease Dev's hard, beaded nipples. They were too tempting tonight, tight and sensitive based on the way Dev bowed his back but didn't back away from the touch. Cash lifted to lick over the firm bud.

He missed them this way. The hours they'd spent alone, only the two of them, trying everything possible to bring the other pleasure. Dev swept a calloused palm across his cheek, cradling his jaw. Dev held his face as he suckled Dev's nipple into his mouth. He lifted his eyes to look directly into Dev's. The rawness reflected back at him was almost too much for his heart to bear.

"I can't get you out of my fuckin' head. Help me forget everything but this?" Dev whispered huskily. Cash removed his mouth, drawing Dev closer to him.

"I would go back to the way we were in a second," Cash whispered so quietly he wasn't sure Dev could hear him. "Only me and you."

Dev's penetrating stare held Cash captive. His expressive eyes spoke directly to Cash's soul. The world faded away. The noises in the room disappeared. He'd found his one, his heart's true desire. He loved Dev with everything he had to give.

=♥=

"You and me," Dev said and slanted his mouth over Cash's, driving his tongue forward, giving Cash his heart in the kiss. Their mouths melded and molded together perfectly, Cash's tongue searching and seeking so eagerly. They were so damned good together.

The needling in the back of Dev's head tried to remind him of his current objective. Get Cash into the clubhouse and the sacred space where church was held. But he hadn't lied when he'd made his bold claim. He didn't want to leave until they'd fucked. He wanted his brothers to see that someone worthy had found value in him. He truly enjoyed Cash being there with him tonight. That was the only reason he had taken so long to bring Cash into the clubhouse. His undercover captor had fit well with his club.

Dev's inner primal beast longed to, no demanded, he follow the long-standing club tradition and fuck Cash right where they sat. His body hummed and tingled with the need to dominate Cash, force his submission. Make Cash stop this bullshit investigation and be his bitch whether he wanted to or not.

Based on this fucking kiss, Cash wanted it as bad as Dev.

Dev lapped at Cash's tongue, sucking it deeper into his mouth as his hips started to roll. With clumsy fingers, he unzipped the zipper. Dev shoved his hand at the binding material as he continued to eat at Cash's hot mouth.

The obstacle that kept him from getting completely inside Cash's jeans was all his doing. His hips kept a steady grind, rolling against Cash's hard groin. He refused to budge a single inch to fully free Cash's cock.

Only the need to breathe had Dev tearing his mouth from the hot as fuck kiss. He extended his neck, leaning forward, urging Cash's wicked lips there. His undercover agent didn't disappoint. Teeth lightly sank into his skin, biting him, before those lips latched on with purpose.

Cash's heavy cock finally sprang free, filling Dev's palm. He nearly groaned at the sensation.

Shit, his life was fucking perfect in that moment.

# Chapter 33

"Leave a mark," Dev instructed. His desires shifted as Cash turned on the pressure at his neck. He wanted Cash inside him. His fat cock hitting all the right places. His palm came to Cash's head, his fingers threading through his thick hair. The suction so intense his balls churned, eager for release. "Remind me where I fuckin' belong."

A deep sense of regret slammed into him when Cash let go to take a breath. Dev circled Cash's shaft and squeezed the exact second Cash's tongue swiped roughly over the skin he'd made raw. Cash's teeth nibbled a stinging trail to his ear. The warm tip of his tongue teasing and tracing the outer shell before plunging deep inside.

Holy hell, that felt good.

The gentle rocking of his hips, back and forth, made his knees weak.

Cash was his brand of turn-on.

Pretty boy whispered into his wet ear, "Make love with me. Let me make what I've done right."

Those sexy hands worked frantically to free him of his jeans, coasting on the promise infused in every one of Cash's words.

He'd barely noticed Cash's efforts until his palm slid down Dev's naked ass, searching for his rim.

"Oh fuck yeah!" They were exactly on the same page. Cash's fingers at his hole were the only thing that could have made him move so quickly.

He pushed off the back of the sofa. His unsteady legs resisted his effort to stand between Cash's parted thighs. Dev glanced around the room, then smirked. As suspected, no one had stuck around to watch him fuck Cash. Better for him.

The visual of Cash on that couch below him might be the best pornography he'd ever seen. Damn, he wished he could capture this shot of Cash to draw later. Those tight fucking jeans spread open wide. The waistband of his underwear had been caught beneath his balls, shoving his sac forward. That thick cock stood hard and erect, so full it leaked for him. The cock of his dreams. He moved his inspection higher to the shirt he'd methodically opened one button at a time throughout the night. The splayed sides now showcased that muscular chest, rising and falling under Dev's perusal. The hard tight buds of his nipples protruded toward Dev, begging for his touch. Cash's lips parted, his gaze searching. Desire and untamed lust surged off the man.

They needed to be alone for this. No peeping eyes to witness Dev's utter annihilation to everything he once held dear. Once he allowed himself to be with Cash again, to soar to the heights he only experienced with this man, he'd never be the same again.

Their relationship shifted again. The invisible bindings tightened around him. Dev was shit to do anything more than let it happen. Fuck the consequences. He reached out and Cash met him halfway as he got to his feet. They were steps away from the meeting room. Church. Whether that was Cash's ultimate goal or not didn't matter. It was all the distance Dev was willing to cover before he offered his heart and his soul.

Three steps. Dev grabbed the always available pump bottle of lube from the clubhouse counter and gave it to Cash. He took the three strides to a place he knew was off limits, inviting Cash into the club's inner sanctum. Knowing the consequences of his actions if they were caught made the moment all that much sweeter. Dev had to pull his pants up to dig the key from his pocket. He couldn't get the key in the lock quick enough. The door opened and he strode into the private room willingly with Cash's hand firmly in his. Fuck the rules.

"There're no recordin' devices in here," he explained, unwilling to take the chance of getting Cash removed from the case again. At least that was what he told himself. Honestly, he didn't like the idea of anyone peeping and leering at the beauty following behind him. "I guarantee you're safe in here. No one in this club wants what's discussed in here put on record."

The door shut. Dev twisted the lock. Cash's strong arm swept around his waist, drawing him against the wall. He shoved the bottle of lube haphazardly on the shelf beside them. In quick, efficient movements, Dev's jeans were pushed down his hips again. Cash's finger prodded against his hole as their bodies met groin to groin. Cash was so close the warmth of his breath danced along his jaw.

Pretty boy's chest rose and fell in heavy breaths, bated with anticipation. Spellbound, he let himself tumble deeper into those beautiful eyes that spoke of honesty and truth and all the things he shouldn't trust.

"I'm into you. So into you," Cash whispered and shook his head, his brows furrowing slightly as if he were frustrated with himself.

Dev gripped Cash's hips, smoothing his palms up Cash's sides. He traced the long deep scar with his fingertips.

"No, it's more than that. It's been more than that for more years than I can say." Cash's palm landed flat and heavy on Dev's chest, over his heart. "I know who you are. I've always known who you are. You're my hero. My life's love. It all came together for me the first day I moved into your building, the minute you pulled your bike onto the front porch with such a show of dominance. Everything my imagination conjured of you snapped into place as reality. You're my real-life hero. I love you. I loved you back then for trying to protect me, and I love you now for the same reasons, and many, many more."

Time stood still. Emotions flooded Dev's entire body on hearing those words. Love, acceptance, hope, doubt, fear, shame slammed through him like a tsunami.

Cash didn't make sense.

He'd had to battle his way through life, kicking at the edges of a world he never fully understood. Hate and destruction followed his every move.

His life didn't consist of happily ever afters.

"Nobody loves me," Dev whispered, the sound filled with the hoarse, harsh chords of disbelief. As much as he may have wanted someone—*this man*—to want to be with him, to love him, the years of emotional abuse at the hands of almost every person he knew had the defensive walls building around his heart.

Cash had the ability to destroy him, and none of it had to do with the case, the club, or his children. Cash could tear his fragile heart apart, creating irrevocable damage.

The man almost had a week ago.

"I do." Cash held Dev's chin, angling his head where he had no choice but to stare Cash in the eyes. The fingertips at his heart began a gentle caress. "When I heard this operation involved you, I lied. I never lie." Cash shook his head as if to emphasize his point. "But I did that day, swearing I could handle our history and continue to make the decisions I needed to make. That you or our history wouldn't be able to sway me. That was the lie I gave in order to come here and do whatever I had to do to protect you. I know now, eventually, I would've come back to Dallas anyway. I've always wanted to know you. I'm connected to you in such a way I didn't fully understand until I saw you again."

*Oh fuck.* Seriously? Knowing all this changed everything. His life couldn't go back to what it was before. He was a dead man.

Dev lifted his palm to cover Cash's hand over his heart.

=♥=

Cash understood this clubhouse was the last place he'd wanted to have this conversation. Now wasn't the right time, but the sweeping emotion coursing through every fiber of his body had driven his words.

Dev's brow wrinkled, something akin to anger crossed his biker's handsome face.

*Rejection.* Cash's body went numb, fear washed over him, stealing his breath. He cast his gaze to the ground.

Cash reached for his jeans gathered around his ankles. He'd played this all wrong. He needed to have paused, not pushed. Allowed Dev to come to him.

Dev's strong hand on his arm caught him off guard. He looked up the length of Dev's gorgeous body. Their gazes met, but he had no idea what was going on behind those soft blue eyes.

"Make me forget," Dev finally murmured. No sooner had the words filled his ears than his body was drawn back up against Dev's. "Make me believe you. I don't understand what's going on with me, but goddammit, I wanted the relationship you just described. Make me believe again."

Cash's heart fluttered back to life, violently lurching from his chest, landing in Dev's unsure hands.

Dev had thrown down the gauntlet, a challenge Cash was determined to conquer. Something bold inside him made him say, "You still want me. I can feel it in you."

Cash used his strength to roughly tug Dev's tight jeans further down until they dropped to his ankles. His other hand covered Dev's lips, keeping him from saying a single word to ruin this moment. He'd gladly give Dev whatever time he needed to show him how badly he was wanted.

"I'll protect you. I won't let anything happen to you or the people you love. It's me and you against the government, this club, or anyone else that gets in the way of our happiness."

He gripped Dev's hard cock and stroked from tip to base. "Say it. Me and you against it all, and I'll believe you."

Seconds passed, Cash gripping Dev's cock tighter, his hand pumping back and forth, just the way he knew Dev liked it, increasing the rhythm with every pass.

He crushed his lips against Dev's, his tongue swiping brazenly through Dev's mouth, swirling with Dev's in a passionate dance until he pulled back again, inches from Dev's handsome face. "Say it. You and me against it all."

"Fuck me raw," Dev whispered.

How many times could Cash's heart seize while blazing with out-of-control emotion strumming through him? By falling in love with this man, Cash was certain the answer was an infinite number. He continued to drive his hand back and forth. He narrowed his gaze on the movement, his mouth watering for the cock that had a small bead of pre-come gathering at the tip.

Even in such a dangerous location, with time against them, Cash had no choice but to drop to one knee and greedily take the rigid length into his mouth. He swallowed Dev whole, taking the cock to the back of his throat.

"Fuck, how do you do that?" Dev hissed, his hand dropping to Cash's hair, fingers threading and sifting through the wavy strands.

Cash was happy. Dev's cock in his mouth made him happy.

He'd never experienced such inner peace before. Yet here it was. He'd be a fool not to do whatever it took to stay by this man's side. He was home. Dev was his safe haven.

As he bobbed his head, sliding the wet cock in and out of his mouth, Dev pistoned his hips. They were so in sync with their need. Cash licked and lapped around Dev's broad head, dragging more of his salty essence across his tongue, sending Cash's desire skyrocketing.

He angled his hand at the base of Dev's cock to grip his sac, massaging the balls. He reached around with his other hand to finger Dev's hole. He was met with Dev's hand already at work, stretching himself open for what was to come. Cash lifted his gaze as he bobbed his head back and forth.

"As much as I hate to say it, we don't have a lot of time," Dev hissed, his eyes like laser beams, tracking each thrust of Cash's mouth.

The fingers in his hair tightened. Cash didn't want to stop either. Dev's taste, that unique flavor that was all his biker, goaded him to milk Dev dry. He knew with all certainty that this man was good for multiple orgasms.

Dev tugged Cash's head back by the hair. The strength and force he used gave Cash no choice but to let Dev's cock pop free. "We don't have time for this right now."

The haze of lust he was lost in wanted him to argue, to go back to devouring the delicious cock still in his hand, but he let go, and removed his hand from Dev's ass. He stood while reaching for the bottle of lube.

"Turn around," he ordered, squirting a generous amount of the lubricant on his fingers. He carelessly tossed the lube back on the shelf.

"Make me feel it," Dev said. The good-natured grin Cash had grown to love spread across Dev's handsome face as he leaned in and pecked him on the lips before turning and offering him his ass.

What a beautiful sight.

Cash gripped his cock, coating the length with the lube. He traced Dev's rim with his fingers pressing against Dev's hole, easily slipping two fingers inside. "I'm making love to you," Cash whispered, stretching and widening Dev as he spoke. "Do you hear me?"

"Yeah." Dev glanced over his shoulder and reached back, taking Cash's cock in his hand. He brought it to his hole, positioning it before he pushed back against the tip.

*Jesus.* The man took almost all of him on the first go. Cash's world blipped, short circuiting his brain. The sensation of being so deep so fast was heady. An unsteadiness swamped him for a second before reality swooped back in at hyper speed. The air conditioning tickled his heated skin. The erotic moan from Dev sent Cash's senses into overdrive. He tucked his hips to keep himself lodged in Dev's exquisite channel.

"Fuck me, baby. Hard." Dev bucked against him, sending Cash's cock out only to push forward again. Every nerve ending in his body was set alight as Dev dropped his forehead against the concrete wall. "Yeah, baby. You got it. Keep goin'."

*Baby.* He loved that word.

It was all the encouragement he needed. Cash gripped onto Dev's hips, thrusting, and driving in and out of that delicious heat. He prayed this moment never ended while fighting an orgasm building at warp speed. He thrust his hips, pushing in and out of Dev's hot ass.

"You feel good," Cash murmured as Dev started pushing back against him.

"It feels better than that," Dev mumbled, his moans building in steady rhythm with Cash's moving hips. "Oh jeez...fuck." Dev's entire body reared back, his head landing on Cash's shoulder, his hands reaching behind him to grip Cash's ass. He thrust his hips, pounding against Cash, taking all of him in quick, short bursts.

Cash lost his shit, forcing Dev's body forward, against the wall. He fucked Dev hard and fast, pistoning his hips wildly. "I'm gonna come."

Clumsily, he reached around Dev's body, taking Dev's cock in his hand.

"No, don't touch..." Dev pitched forward, his body tensing and locking, breath coming in low and shallow pants. He gripped Cash's palm at his cock, turning his awkward hand job into a deep stroke with determination. Dev's ass constricted and pulsed around him, scrambling his brain with pleasure.

Liquid heat coated his palm and fingers. The proof of Dev's desire was all he could bear. His own release burned a path from the back of his neck to the bottom of his spine and ripped from his balls, slamming through him with such a force he barely had time to withdraw his cock before painting Dev's perfect ass with his seed.

The earth shifted under his feet. Cash used Dev's body and the wall to stay upright. His forehead landed on Dev's inked shoulder blade.

"There's a roll of paper towels on the shelf by the lube. I need those," Dev groaned. His voice sounded very much like Cash's body felt, haggard yet sated.

He forced himself to take a closer look at the coveted, secret room, the heart of the club. How had the importance of his surroundings taken such a backseat to the man in front of him?

*Shit.* The reality of where they stood and how long they'd been inside this sacred space motivated him into action. He looked down at his come dripping off the curve of Dev's ass.

"Hang on." He reached for the jeans gathered at his boots, pulling them up as he grabbed the blue disposable shop towels. He handed a wad to Dev before unrolling another bunch, swiping away the dripping evidence of his release on Dev's back and ass.

He had no idea why he was so damned content, but he was. He had no fear. His heart connected with Dev, which meant everything else was bound to work in their favor. It had too. Life wasn't that cruel.

Cash wadded the towels and placed them aside before digging a hand in his jeans pocket for the small surveillance screw he needed to plant inside this room.

"You good?" he asked Dev, turning away to scan all the electrical outlets.

"I got fuckin' come all over me," Dev said, bending over to wipe the towels over his jeans. "I guess it means I had a good time."

"Hmm," Cash answered, fishing around his jeans for his pocketknife. The outlet on the far side of the room appeared to offer the best visual as well as audio positioning. The contentment in his head continued as he unscrewed the outlet's cover and carefully replaced it with the tiny camera screw, twisting the plate back in place. If it worked, they were set.

Balancing on his heels, he stayed low as he palmed his cell phone to dial Joe. When the call connected, he pushed the speaker button and turned the volume down low. He didn't wait for a greeting, simply said, "I'm here. We good?"

Dev came to him. His biker's rough, calloused palm caressed his cheek, his fingertips moving along the light stubble on Cash's jaw. It didn't freak him out in the least with how taken he was with Dev.

"You're really easy on the eyes," Dev said in a hushed voice. The sweet grin he gave spoke of appreciation as Cash rose to his full height.

"That's the way I feel about you," Cash murmured. He leaned in until his cheek came to Dev's. He breathed in the man's scent. The cell phone was between them.

"I can see you two. Are y'all kissing?" Joe asked. "Please don't do things I can't scrub from my head."

Dev reared back, looking Cash in the eyes, ignoring Joe. "Take me home?"

*Gladly.* He looked around the room for a back exit. "How do we leave here?"

Dev rolled his neck then his shoulders, scrubbing a hand down the length of his face. "I promise there ain't no one in the clubhouse until I come out. As much as they like to watch each other fuck, that doesn't apply to us."

Something in Dev's gaze looked calculating. Not of a man who had taken the same leap into love as Cash. His soaring heart dipped as he played back their verbal exchange. Dev hadn't responded to Cash's confessions. His biker wasn't in his same mindset.

*No.* His heart crashed as he realized what he had done.

Of course, the case, the job. Dev had agreed to get Cash into this room. Their sexual chemistry was over the top. They had put on a show for his brothers. *No.*

A short pant of breath escaped. Rejection made him unsteady.

Dev gave his shoulder a light shove. "Stop lookin' at me like that. I heard what you said. We can see how it goes. But when you walk out of here, don't look all sad. Walk with a limp. Make them believe I tapped your ass hard and rough. I'll handle the rest."

Hurt blanketed Cash, descending with remarkable speed and accuracy. His heart broke. He nodded, trying to find some inner pride in order to have this breakdown in private later.

The pain must have reached his eyes. Dev was on him, pushing him back several feet until his ass hit the large wood table in the center of the room.

"Stop lookin' all hurt. I don't like it. You got in my fuckin' head, is that what you need to hear? You fuck me so good you make me crave you. When those fuckin' green eyes land on me, it makes all this okay, and it's not okay, but you make it feel okay."

When Cash held his tongue, trying to pretend those words were anything close to the sincerity of the love he offered, Dev's brows drew together, his palms encasing Cash's cheeks, forcing their faces closer.

"I can see how we fit. I can't tell how all this is gonna work, but I can see we fit together like missin' puzzle pieces. It's all I have to say right now. It needs to be enough because *I heard you*, I got it. But you hurt me real bad. I'm not givin' it all back to you right now."

The stare held until Dev used his palms to nod Cash's head.

"Say it's enough for now."

"I don't know if I should hang up or say goodbye. It seemed rude to just end the call, but inappropriate to hear all this. I suggest whatever is happening should probably leave that room and happen inside this building," Joe suggested with a bit of urgency lacing his tone. "Shanna's up here. She says Dev doesn't have his phone on him."

"Where's your phone?" Cash asked.

Dev smirked, still all in Cash's personal space. "I protected you. I told you there were no recordin' devices in here. I knew what we were gonna do. My necklace and phone's with my cut. I got you."

"I'm ending the call," Cash said to Joe. After everything he'd been through, how had he not considered Dev's recording devices?

Dev went for the lube and paper towels as Cash's indignation with himself reached an all-time high. He pushed off the table in complete internal meltdown mode. "What the hell am I doing? I'm in the middle of Satan's den, confessing my love for the first time in my life. What the fuck are you doing to me?"

# Chapter 34

"Fuck is my word," Dev said, chuckling under his breath.

Cash had no idea how Dev found any of this funny. It wasn't. Far from it. In a not too distant past, Cash's peers viewed him as the utmost professional. His presence on a case was sought after for how he handled himself in the field.

He pressed his palms into his eyes, hoping to mash some sense into his brain.

Dev went for the door leading to the clubhouse, pressing an ear against the thick wood. After several seconds, he cracked open the door to peek into the clubhouse. With an attitude full of confidence—technically just normal Dev—he widened the opening, sweeping his hand out to encourage Cash to precede him. "Told you. Nobody's comin' in the clubhouse until we leave."

His biker locked the door and tossed the paper towels in a trash bucket by the sofa in the clubhouse. The lube was placed back on the end table in easy reach of anyone else in need. They both finished dressing. Dev shoved his necklace in the pocket with his cell phone. Neither spoke as Dev reached to clasp his hand. Taking the offering was instinctual for Cash, even after several long minutes where he'd utterly berated himself.

Dev took the lead, guiding him out of the building. Just barely past the threshold, the multifaceted biker became the showman, the over-the-top bad boy, whooping loudly toward the partygoers.

"It's official. You missed your shot. He's off the market, boys. He's mine." Dev kept their pace steady, his hand tightening around Cash's as he headed back to the chair where Cash's jacket lay over the back. Dev put on the performance of his life by grabbing Cash's cock through his jeans for the club to see.

To the club's credit, some did give a halfhearted whoop along with Dev's blustering, as if Cash were a prime grade selection of beef. He reached for his things from the lawn chair.

"Give me the keys to your bike, smooth talker," Cash said when Dev took over the zipping of Cash's heavier jacket. "You're a lot to handle."

"Know how to ride a bike?" Dev asked, his tone doubtful as hell as he decided the zipper only needed to rise about halfway and brought it back down to the center.

"Yeah." Cash wiggled his fingers for the keys.

Dev's gaze lifted to his, one brow arching, the other lowering. His eyes narrowed. "You said you'd never…"

Cash cut him off, "ridden on the back of a bike. I haven't. I do ride."

"Did you just call me a dumbass?" Dev declared.

Cash's fingers wiggled again. "Only a small one."

Just like that, the doubt changed. Dev dug his hand in his pocket, producing the keys, and dropped them in Cash's hand.

"You're a showman, aren't you?" Cash said quietly. Dev answered by dramatically pulling Cash into his arms, drawing him roughly against his body for the entire club to see. He kissed Cash in the same manner, hot and heavy, rough, mouthy, and full of invasive tongue. One hand went to Cash's cock, the other grabbed his ass. Dev gyrated his hips while stroking Cash front to back.

He couldn't help growing hard under the ridiculous assault.

Dev's head reared back and the shift in weight took Cash by surprise. Dev leaned against him. Cash helped hold the biker upright as he howled at the moon. "My bitch is gonna fuck me on the back of my bike tonight."

Dev winked his way. "Bareback with multiple come-loads. Fuck the devil right out of me." Then he gave another whooping holler.

= ♥ =

Dev's motivation for his actions was to be bold—his normal state, to be brave—something he tried to be every minute of every day—and to put on such a show for his brothers that no one questioned why he and Cash had stayed alone inside the building for so long.

The other reason for his exiting performance was that he got to pretend to his brothers that someone normal, so wonderfully, beautifully normal, wanted to spend time with him. So much so it appeared Cash had left his good values back home, putting them aside to come hang out with Dev in his natural environment, full of sin and debauchery.

The sweet words Cash muttered earlier, the love and devotion stated so clearly, were now etched on his heart forever. Fuck whatever happened tomorrow. Tonight, he had the man of his dreams in his arms, and he wanted to be there.

Dev hadn't spoken a single lie tonight. He planned to fuck the shit out of both pretty boy's mouth and ass and have it all returned on him. But their sex was private from here on out. The place he wanted to make love to Cash was inside his bedroom. Private. No one watching. He still had to figure out how to record them without anyone else knowing... Because fuck if he was giving up having a replay of their adventures.

He had fallen hard for a guy with a cock so addicting that he actually considered turning on his brothers. Hell, he had turned on his brothers. Cash being there with him tonight was the proof. The sick motherfuckers needed a good old fashion wake-up call.

= ♥ =

So many times in this operation, Cash found himself just enjoying his unguarded moments with Dev. The ride home with Dev hugging his body, holding on for what he claimed was dear life, had become one of those precious times.

The chilly night air had them both bundled the best they could. Well, Dev had his leathers in his saddlebag. He was fine, but Cash was too. They rode up and down the streets of downtown Dallas. Dev guided him on a scenic route, twisting and turning as they went. They were fluid together, like always. A trait he'd never experienced with another living soul before.

What Cash loved the most about the ride was Dev's roaming hands. He'd happily brave the chill as long as Dev's hands continued to touch his skin as they did. Up and under the hem of his jacket and shirt, tweaking his nipples then caressing down to massage his cock.

His biker lifted his helmet, the one Cash had insisted he wear, to place a kiss between his shoulder blades or yell a comment about how Cash's cock felt in his ass tonight. Dev was feeling good, but not drunk or even tipsy. He was engaged in every single minute they shared together, just like Cash.

"Turn right here," Dev instructed. He did, taking them down a darkened road. With a twist of the throttle, he opened up the bike, riding full speed until Dev tapped his leg, indicating he take a turn again. He slowed them down, leaning into the curve before coming to the end of a residential street.

They weren't in the best neighborhood. Actually, worse than a bad neighborhood based on the condition of the homes around them. Any other time, Cash's senses would be on heightened alert, wondering where he was being taken, but not tonight, not with Dev at his back.

Dev motioned him onto the edge of a vacant lot at the end of the road. As he popped the curb, he saw a highway right below them. The further he went on the property, the more he saw the buildings in downtown Dallas in the distance. The colorful lights of the skyscrapers were on full display.

He cut the engine, balancing the bike between his parted thighs. Dev took his helmet off and dismounted the bike. Cash lowered the kickstand, carefully letting the bike lean.

"Come see." Dev motioned him toward the edge of the property.

Cash rested back on the seat, slower to move as Dev walked ten or so paces ahead of him. He recognized how completely fucked he was. Everything Dev did turned him on. He loved watching Dev move. Coming or going. Didn't matter which way, Dev oozed sexy. The most alluring man he'd ever known.

His slightly bowed legs as he walked… Cash had to wipe the drool off his lip. He wondered if Dev was made that way or was it something he developed as an adult? Did anyone really have that much natural swagger?

Dev cast a glance to his side then stopped. He did a full-body turn as if searching for him. Once he spotted him still on the bike, the grin he got matched the very attitude he'd just been questioning. Dev pivoted around, giving Cash the pleasure of watching him walk back toward him.

"You look hot on my bike. You just guaranteed you'll be fucked on it when its warmer outside."

"Will it hold us?" Cash asked, hopeful.

"We're gonna test it and see," Dev answered with certainty in his tone.

Dev came straight up to him, his hand going to Cash's jaw, tilting his head back for an open-mouth kiss. All the feels were there. Dev kissed him hard and fast. Dare Cash hope with hints of possessiveness? His lower lip was sucked into Dev's mouth, the gentle sting of teeth biting into him sent a zing of pleasure straight to his cock.

The dominance continued as Dev reached for his hand then tugged him off the bike. Once Cash lifted off, Dev linked their fingers together as he followed after Dev to the edge of the property.

"Is it safe here?"

"It is for me," Dev said. "Don't be a pussy. It's a clutch vantage point to see the city."

Cash lost his train of thought as he stood at the highest point of the property, looking down over the colorful lights of the highways mixmaster interchange below. The traffic zoomed up and down the streets and bridges. The white and red of headlamps and taillights mixed with the blue overhead highway lights. In the distance, the Omni Hotel and Reunion Tower ball sparkled brightly in the sky. Behind those, many other buildings, in all different bright colors, added to the gorgeous skyline.

"Dallas is beautiful," Cash said, taking it all in.

"Like this it is. It makes you forget people like me are crawlin' all around the city."

Cash glanced over at Dev. Saying something like that was probably the only thing that could have pulled him from the view. He slid an arm around Dev's waist, turning them until he drew Dev's back against his chest. He added his other arm too, tightening his hold to keep Dev there against him. He went back to watching all the moving and mesmerizing parts of the scenes playing out in front of him.

When Dev's body relaxed into his, Cash received the true gift. The warmth and feel of Dev cuddling back against him reminded him of their nights together before he'd ruined it all.

Dev placed his hand over Cash's, holding them close together.

"I wish you had come back earlier," Dev murmured. "Like ten years ago. Maybe I wouldn't've had the problems I have today had you come back."

"You wouldn't have noticed me back then," Cash said, placing a kiss against Dev's ear.

"I'd've noticed." Dev glanced over his shoulder, looking as if Cash were crazy. It was a sweet gesture. Cash lifted their joined hands to Dev's face as he started to turn away, drawing his face back. Cash met Dev's lips with a sweet lingering kiss.

Dev stared into his eyes. He wished he knew what was happening inside the biker's head. Instinctually, he locked his arms tighter around Dev's body, keeping him close.

"I might've been on a course of destruction, but I wasn't a fool. I'd've seen you. My girls like you, and they're my girls. I feel it here." Dev's free hand landed on his own chest, covering his heart. "I wish I had ten more just like 'em. It hurts me that I can't. When I started tryin' to pull my shit together, I had this dream of ownin' land, like a lot of it. I put a shadowy figure in as my partner. I couldn't figure that part out. We'd have lots of kids. I liked the family picture inside my head. I've always wanted lots of kids."

Cash nodded, still close to Dev's face, listening to what felt very much like a dream. When Dev spoke of his family, of the beautiful love and devotion he had for his children, Cash could see how such a family could complete this man. It didn't seem too much to ask.

Maybe someday, Cash may have a place of priority in Dev's life. What a gift that might be. "I like your children too. You've done a good job raising them. Mae's obvious in her devotion to you, but I watched Abi watch you then try to ignore you when you pay attention to her. She mimics you."

"You caught that?" Dev asked with a chuckle. "She got that 'not givin' a shit' from me. She throws it back to me pretty well."

"Maybe because she knows you're solid for her." A brilliant lightbulb moment presented itself and he had to grin. "She knows what makes you pay attention. I should take notes."

Dev turned in his arms, coming chest to chest with Cash. He was lost to the handsome, upturned face. Cash murmured, "You have me on a short leash. That's not safe for any of us. For me to be so focused on us."

Cash touched Dev's cheek, gently stroking until his fingers tangled in the strands of his hair.

"I got you," Dev murmured. leaning into the caress of his hand. "I control more than I let on. Nobody's gonna lay a finger on you unless it's me. I guarantee."

"And how's that looking?" Cash smiled at Dev's words. "You laying a finger on me?"

"You got a hundred percent chance of that." Dev grinned. "Take me home? Sleep in my bed?" Dev gave him that sly grin that made his knees weak and started to pull away.

"Or you in mine." Cash's bedroom didn't have the cameras watching every move they made.

Dev pulled from his arms. Cash trailed close behind Dev, heading back to the bike as Dev spoke the sweet words. "Wherever we both are is where I wanna be."

# Chapter 35

Getting in and out of the car to open the gate was pissing him the fuck off. All the unnecessary steps were dumb. He had to have the securest building on the damn block as far as he was concerned. Three federal agents lived on the property. All the cameras… Goddamn the government being so close was hard to stomach. The thought had shooting stars sprinkling his vision.

Ask him a month ago, or any other time in his life, if he'd ever straddle the narc line between the club and the government, and he'd have laughed in your face then pummeled the shit out of you for being so damn stupid.

Justifications spun through his head. Sniffing around Cash's fantastic ass didn't mean he'd turned. He was playing both sides against the middle. He did that shit all the time. Besides, the feds knew everything going on. He hadn't told them a damn thing they didn't already know.

Inviting Cash into the room where they held church, then watching him set up surveillance after getting fucked so good inside the room…

Dev winced at the thought. He'd crossed the line. No way around it.

He let the gate hang open as his phone began vibrating in the passenger seat as he continued driving to his parking spot. He'd had a hell of a day. Every minute had been spent on getting the girls settled into their new lives. The public school system sucked. Way too much unnecessary paperwork. To unenroll them in one school and enroll them into another had taken two-thirds of his day. The girls hadn't helped with all the hugging, tears, and sadness they gave to their friends as they cleaned out their desks and cubbies.

Meeting the real estate agent to sell the Sunnydale house took the rest of the day. Tena's tacky furnishings were gonna be a problem if he wanted to get top dollar. He needed to get the prospects over there to clean up the place and toss her shit out. Then he'd have to spend a pretty penny renting some fancy staging furniture. So much bullshit. He better get that extra fifty grand out of the deal that the real estate agent had promised.

The day came with a surprising amount of emotion for Dev. When he'd originally bought the house, his vision was clear. He saw the house as one of those super-functional sitcom family homes. Fresh paint, pretty blooming flowers, a white picket fence for his kids. He never suspected their past would follow them. He should have known better. Life always found a way to kick you in the balls.

The property became a "pushing up daisies" kind of place. Whoever got the home needed to concentrate on putting some happy back in its walls.

Honestly, he hadn't wanted to let the house go. He struggled to sign the contract with the real estate agent. As fucked as his life had gotten, he still wanted all the things that house represented. Instead of Tena being his partner, he easily envisioned Cash in her place and that scared the hell out of him. The changing visions were crystal clear in his head though. An obtainable reality.

*Right.* If Dev lived through the end of this case, his prize was Cash leaving for the next assignment. The most likely result of all this was Dev coming to the end of his life. It could be the other way around. Cash could die and Dev would live on, but it hurt too badly to think of it that way, so he didn't.

He had to get the girls' lives settled before too much longer. He needed to set up a will. His mom needed to have a hand in helping to raise them... Maybe Keyes. Lock it down tight so Tena didn't fuck with them too much by coming and going. Keyes wasn't a half bad idea. He'd take the job seriously. Let his mom be the grandmother she was so good at being. Those thoughts hurt too. More than anything, he wanted to be there as Abi and Mae grew into young women.

If Keyes was their new father figure, he was going to have to learn how to properly spell Mae's name... His heart lightened at how Keyes remembered their birthdays and Christmas, never late with the gifts, yet always misspelled Mae's name, all the cards addressed to May.

He parked the car at the back of his building and picked up the cell phone. Ironically, he saw a message from Keyes. Shit, maybe that was why he had Keyes so much on the mind. Keyes was going after someone. A prospect... Fuck. He hadn't thought twice about their conversation earlier that evening. He opened the text with his thumb as he cut the engine off.

*"I fucked up. He's beat down. I have his patch."*
Dev's mind raced. Thankfully that was a fast process.
*"Cummings?"* Dev typed. The prospect who had been unexpectedly released from prison today. Keyes was good and pissed off about it.

*"Yeah. With witnesses."*
Dev knocked himself in the head with the butt of his palm. He should have ditched the real estate agent and gone with Keyes. The one thing they didn't need right now was witnesses.

*"Fuck, Bro, what were you thinking?"* Dev asked.
In today's world, witnesses came with cell phone cameras. If that shit got recorded, Keyes was in trouble.

*"I got his patch. Whatever happens, he ain't gettin' this one back."*
Anger hit him from another direction. This was where the club's bullshit came back to mind. Members being voted in, prospects moving up, all without proper protocol and the blessing of every brother. It was horseshit. Since he was back in the second position, his muscle was flexing further, and he could face the problem head on. Anybody voted in without everyone's approval was gone.

The other thing he was going to do was make sure all those motherfuckers treated Keyes with respect every time they crossed paths. Keyes could be a fire-breathing dragon, and they still needed to walk up and dap the guy.

Anger made him jab his finger down on the call button, done with texting.

"Yeah?" Keyes answered.

"Lay low," Dev instructed in no uncertain terms. "If you need somewhere to go, come to…" Well fuck, where did he say? "Holly's."

He decided to keep it simple. Keyes wouldn't need a place to stay anyway.

Keyes stayed silent. They both had secrets from one another. That needed to end soon, too.

"Tell your old man for me?" Keyes asked.

"Fuck, man, I should've gone," Dev said. His head hit back against his headrest.

A harsh bark of laughter came from the other end of the phone. "He'd be dead right now if you went. My old man was spewin' out of his goddamn mouth. Pissed me the fuck off."

Yeah, he needed to hear that the late Smoke Dixon had left a litany of hate alive and well within the club prospects to shift the self-regret back to anger. "I knew I hated that motherfucker." A growl resonated, understanding how he'd have absofuckinglutely made the whole situation worse.

"Yeah, I'm out," Keyes said. The call went dead.

Fuck. There was no way Keyes wasn't going to be arrested with that bitch DA still in office. She'd milk the arrest for everything she had. Dev grabbed his car key and shoved the door open, searching for the club lawyer's name in his contacts.

Keyes had that lawyer boyfriend. He might know best how to proceed, but their attorney had the soul of a cage fighter. She needed to be aware of what happened.

Dev made it just inside the building when a hand shot out, grabbing the front of his T-shirt. He bristled as Cash hauled him forward, the back door slamming shut behind him. His body was pushed backward, banging against the wall beside the door. Not an easy shove, but not hard either, just the perfect amount of manhandling. Cash's mouth captured his, that sinful tongue executing the perfect deep dive.

He'd give the move a ten out of ten.

Everything else was forgotten as Dev dropped his keys and his phone to the floor. His hands itched to touch Cash, and he wrapped his arms around the big body.

Welcome the fuck home.

=♥=

The kiss hadn't been planned. He'd only meant to greet Dev at the back door. Cash had moved on pure emotion. He'd waited all day to have Dev in his arms again.

The air around them zinged with electricity and sizzled as they kissed. Their chemistry was way off the charts. He was lost to the feel of Dev melting in his arms. A long deep meaningful melding of mouths. Dev kissed him with desperation.

His Dev.

His Devilman.

His partner.

His foxy Fox.

He caressed Dev's cheek. He cherished this complicated man. Dev's hardened nipples brushed against Cash's chest, telling him everything he needed to know about Dev's desire. Last night, until this morning when they were forced apart, he and his biker had stayed glued to one another. Dev had slept in Cash's bed. They'd eaten breakfast together, worked out their schedules for the day together, showered and dressed together, never more than a few feet apart until Dev had to leave to take care of the girls.

Tonight, the way he caged Dev with his back against the wall, had to make it clear what he wanted. They needed to be upstairs well ensconced in one of their aggressive, sexual all-night quests. A multiple orgasm event. Dev had making up to do for the drought he'd caused last week and the last ten hours.

Today, Cash decided to be Dev's personal bodyguard. Allowing himself all the time he wanted to spend with Dev during their workdays, stakeouts, dinners, family obligations, quiet evenings just between the two of them alone and naked. His hips rolled into Dev's, driving the thought home.

"Get a room," Shanna said disgustedly as she walked in through the back door. She'd been Dev's tail today. "You guys have two of them, like fifty steps away from where you're making out right now."

The reminder had Cash slowly breaking from the kiss, but Dev didn't let him go. He kept him pressed head to toe against his love. His body tingled with unbridled desire. Feelings he'd never experienced before fluttered throughout his body.

Honestly, his concentration had been shit all day. He secretly stalked Dev's GPS. Not to track his whereabouts but to have a sense of being closer and connected with the man.

He'd lost his mind.

"Mom called me today while you were with the girls. She's worried and asked about you. You aren't doing a good enough job at selling your happiness. If she picked it up, others will too." Her no-nonsense tone sounded more in the range of a challenging sister than of professional agent. This time she spoke to Cash. "We've also got an emergency call with the Dallas DEA field office for an immediate update. Something happened today we need to know about."

"Probably about that Cummings dick who got released from prison tonight," Dev said with attitude, bucking against Cash to put some space between them. "I don't remember a lot about him, but I think he got released years early. He's a prospect. One of your people had to get to him. He had to have negotiated out."

"What reason was given for his release?" Cash asked, alternating his gaze between Shanna and Dev, hoping one of them might have the answer.

"Don't know but Keyes had a hard-on for him. He went over tonight and fucked the dickweed up. There was somethin' about Cummings's kid, I think. I had to lie about where I was. I don't fuckin' like lyin' to Keyes." Dev's frustration edged up a notch with each sentence he spoke. He paced the length of the small back entry, five steps one way then five steps back. Finally, he bent and snagged his keys and phone off the floor and kept going down the hall toward the front of the building. "You got my phone call recorded. When you hear the name Holly, it's code for Cash. I haven't told him anything. Not even me bein' into dick. I don't like to fuckin' lie to him, for fuckin' sure."

Dev clomped up the staircase in his heavy boots. Cash and Shanna followed at a slower pace.

Dev's voice traveled back down to them. "I didn't even know how bad I was at impromptu lyin' until y'all came along.

I'm a pretty fuckin' honest guy. What the fuck? I gotta eat somethin'." Dev's apartment door slammed shut behind him.

Cash looked down at Shanna who stared up at Dev's angry retreat with her hands on her hips. "He can sure switch gears really fast."

"He's just in a bad spot," Cash defended Dev and started for his apartment. Shanna followed, her chuckle had a bit of ridicule in it.

"Right."

Dev's words did concern him. They needed to spend more time prepping. Bringing Holly back into the narrative wasn't the best diversion tactic Dev could have used. He needed to have a long list of ready answers for any situation.

Cash had to do better, focus on what was important if he truly wanted Dev safe.

"What's the deal with the Cummings release?"

"Don't know anything about it," Shanna said. "We should know though, right?"

"Yes." Cash nodded at what the implication of being left out of such an important finding meant. "We should've been one of the first units notified."

Dev's door opened, pushed wide. Dev was nowhere to be seen. That had to be some sort of invitation without Dev having to actually ask Cash in.

"I've got a meeting and an update," Cash called out, assuming that was meant as an invitation.

Shanna went ahead of Cash, to his apartment.

"Well fuckin' hurry it up then," Dev shouted back. Still no sign of the man.

Cash gave a small smile, dropping his chin to his chest, trying to understand where the breakdown in communication came from within the DEA. Whoever that person was, they needed to be investigated closely.

# Chapter 36

Cash had to be good and pissed off by now. Dev saw no other way around it. A deep self-reflection may have caused him to rethink his actions of the day, but he'd never been any good at inner discipline or the regrets that generally followed.

What he had done instead was intentionally set fire to all of Cash's rules today. The dark inner place inside his heart gave a wicked gleam of approval and added that he had not only set them ablaze but burned those bitches to the ground. He had crossed every line. Done it on purpose.

Hell, it wasn't even his fault. The course of the day was set in motion the second Keyes was put in custody for his crimes against Cummings.

By Dev's best estimation, it hadn't taken twelve hours for Keyes to wind up in lockup. Any question about Cummings turning on the club was erased with how fast Keyes had been detained. Meaning his best friend needed every bit of help Dev had to offer. Fuck the rest of the bullshit.

So, no matter what anyone had to say about the reasoning behind Dev's actions today, at least he fully understood the consequences and still made the decision to go off grid. He considered that maturity on his part.

And the fucker, Cummings, was still alive, albeit in a county hospital bed, but the turncoat would survive his beating. The easiest option would have been to go to Parkland Hospital and end the weasel's life. Be done with the loser prospect and whoever paid such a price for whatever intel they thought he had, but Dev didn't choose that really good idea. He'd get there, but not today. Again, adding massive maturity points to his decision-making skills.

Where things got iffy for Dev was the full-scale, apeshit, toddler-style tantrum he had impromptued inside the entry of the jailhouse where Keyes was being held. Had he had time to think, he might have come up with something better to get Mack and his old man out of the waiting area, where Alec Pierce, Keyes's boyfriend, was already there waiting.

In the end, Dev's best efforts were in vain. An employee of the correctional institution, a Disciples paid informant, had alerted his old man of Alec's presence, efficiently tying Alec to his job as a Dallas assistant district attorney. That was ultimately what made Dev throw his promises to Cash and the operation to the wind.

His old man's guard had gone up immediately, wanting the who, and what on Alec Pierce and why the fuck he was there for Keyes. Vengeance had been clear in every syllable spoken. Dev had instantly volunteered to sneak back and figure out why Alec was there. He'd also made his intentions known by stating it was the club's second's responsibility to see this through. When he stripped both his sled and his body of all the tracking and listening devices, even the ones placed there months ago, before Cash had shown up on the scene, that was the moment he sent the double flying birds to the contract he had negotiated with the federal government.

He'd left his cell phone at the ink parlor, next to his speaker, playing "Fuck Tha Police" by NWA on a loop. He figured his choice of song added a bit of dramatic flair to his insolence.

Maybe he wasn't as grown up as he pretended to be. Fucking okay with him.

With a burner phone in hand, he grabbed a helmet and left through a side door exit where he'd strategically parked earlier. That location blocked him from any visual of the main road where Cash was parked, keeping an eye on him.

He only had two people to stay in touch with. One was his fucking loser old man. And the second was Officer Grisby, who he'd connected with to stay up to date on the pending charges against Keyes.

The secret ride back to the jailhouse had been slow as he stayed off the main roads. Adrenaline pulsed through his veins in shockwaves. The stakes were damn fucking high, coming at him from many different directions.

His hiding place was behind a large pillar on the third floor of a high-rise parking garage catty-corner to where Keyes was locked up. He'd been there now for hours, tensed up and scoping out everything and everyone associated with Keyes. He had to make sure no one else from the club showed up unannounced. It wouldn't be good for Keyes if they did.

With a badass pair of binoculars in hand, Dev easily identified Clyde, Keyes's uncle—unrelated to the club. It took a minute to figure out who the hot older guy was, but with Grisby's help, he learned he was Keyes fancy new attorney, Marc Manners. By the familiar shake of hands and pat of the shoulder, Alec must be on friendly terms with the attorney.

All the fucking lying and half-truths were hard on Dev. It gave him an extra edge of anxiety. It took him half the morning to remember the kid Keyes had mentioned last night. Then another couple of hours to trust Grisby enough to ask him what Alec did for the DA's office. Everything came together moments ago when he saw Keyes pop out the door by himself, his big body tensed up tight. His buddy scanned every direction, making Dev edge behind the pillar to stay completely hidden.

Keyes was nervous. He should be.

Dev continued to watch, certain that his freaked out best friend, all puffed up to his full size, was expecting to have to defend his man. His head went silent in the lightbulb moment as Alec finally left the building, several moments later.

The super nice-looking Alec only had eyes for Keyes even though Clyde and Manners followed Alec out, standing with him in a small circle just beyond the now closed doors. Keyes was generally fierce when angered, which based on the way his fists kept tightening and his brawny biceps flexed, he clearly was, and with good cause. His gentle giant friend looked ready to fist fight the world if need be.

Another startling find was that Keyes didn't look as out of place with Alec as he thought he might. Dev swallowed the lump of envy clogging his throat and put the binoculars down. He still watched the overall scene. Keyes had found the life Dev coveted the most.

Whether Keyes or Alec knew, they wore their devotion to each other for the world to see. It was right there, even at this distance. Dev could feel their love from his hiding spot. How Keyes must have struggled to learn how to deal with the genuine affection for someone so polar opposite.

Dev could say the same thing about him and Cash. Except Keyes was a far more likable person than Dev could ever hope to be.

How brave was Alec to willingly put himself out there with such a risk from his club looming over them. Damn.

Someone above their station in life wanted Keyes, and Keyes was smart enough not to turn away from it.

Dev's heart stuttered violently at the impact of that thought. He looked down to make sure the useless organ hadn't fallen out of his chest with the way it bumped around like it did.

Images of the handsome Cash staring at Dev with the same devotion pouring through his gaze that Alec used with Keyes... All the dangers Cash was taking to be with him. Same as Alec. They'd both completely disregarded appearances, employment, and personal safety to help in whatever way they could.

Cash had put everything he held dear on the line to be with Dev. Everything. Shanna had stressed as much.

The scene playing out in front of him could easily have been between him and Cash. Except for the badass Ferrari they were walking up to. Dev didn't expect Cash had that kind of money. Dev was probably closer to being able to buy that kind of cage.

Well, goddamn. Dev's brows furrowed. He might have had that kind of dough if he hadn't had to cancel his fucking ink appointments...

He shook his head at the sudden violence inside him. *Stay in the moment, dumbass.*

It was fucking hard to do, knowing he'd lost tens of thousands of dollars at the government's demand. More than that even. There were potential long-term effects to canceling all these appointments.

*Breathe.*

Remember Cash's special way of speaking directly to his soul. The sweet way he made love, the perfect amount of gentle persuasion and hot as fuck thrusts while rubbing against his prostate. Cash was the kind of man who stuck around, even when things went south. No question in Dev's mind. If the table were turned, Cash would risk everything, exactly as Alec was doing right now. He'd use every connection he had to free Dev of the jail cell.

*Love.*

Such a simple four-letter word for such a complex, scary as hell connection. Not even an emotion. A state of being so into another's soul you lost yourself in the best possible way. Dev had tumbled off into the abyss, headfirst, eyes wide open. When he did finally reemerge back into the world, he hoped he'd be someone he liked a whole lot better.

Not that he was ready to commit his undying love to Cash.

He wanted to. Someday.

Cash was hotter than Alec. His agent was the most beautiful man on the planet.

He wanted the dream of him and Cash as a couple. Them being the ones who raised the girls. If they survived this mission Cash had dragged them into, maybe they might have another couple of kids. Chestnut-haired babies with green eyes and big lips. Since he was fantasizing, he tossed three babies in the mix. All boys. They had the two girls. Those little guys didn't need any of his DNA messing up their genetic tree, but he'd raise them like his own. Love them for his whole life. Make them proud that he'd been their old man. Just like he wanted to do with the girls.

He'd never be out carousing when he could be at home with his family. They'd have drive-in movie night, birthday parties, baseball and softball games. He'd go to all that shit.

Drive-in movies probably meant a daddys' night out. He laughed to himself. A porn drive-in movie. Did they make such things? He'd fuck Cash on his sled, see if that bitch held, then parade his mister around on a leash, making sure everyone knew to whom Cash belonged.

His fierce sweet bear of a protector.

A gentle breeze blew across his heated skin, sending a shiver of anticipation racing up and down his spine. He wasn't sure he could ever truly tame the devil inside, but he bet Cash could handle anything thrown his way.

The world around him snapped back into place like a slingshot. What the fuck was he doing daydreaming like that?

He'd missed Keyes and Alec getting into the car as his depraved images replaced reality. The brake lights were on, but the car remained in the parking spot.

Keyes's big back tattoo came to mind. An ode to Alec.

Dev wanted Keyes's happiness and knew this most recent event jeopardized everything for his friend. After a few long moments, the car backed up. Alec and Keyes left the parking lot, breaking Dev of the trance that held him spellbound.

Dev took a cleansing, centering breath. First things first. He needed to get back to the ink parlor ASAP. He'd be hearing from Keyes soon based on the note he'd left on Keyes's bike on the way to the jailhouse. He needed to be a reassuring friend. Try to calm and be available for Keyes as best he could. He'd have to remember to guard his words since the entire fucking government listened to every word he said.

*Fuckers.*

Dev placed the binoculars in his saddlebag and took time to send his father a quick text message. "*Keyes went to Cummings's house to protect an abused kid. Dude at the jail was a CPS worker. Keyes was never interviewed by him.*"

Sounded convincing, especially since it was at least a partial truth. He pressed send.

He gathered the rest of his shit then mounted his Harley. He was off, twisting down the ramp, following the exit out of the garage.

Surely, Cash had to have figured out by now that Dev wasn't at the ink parlor. He'd assigned himself to be Dev's tail today.

Bet the agent was having a fucking cow over his whereabouts right now. That'd be painful to birth.

It didn't matter. Dev had needed time to reconcile all this foreign emotion and uncertainty inside him. He was focused now, ready to get this operation behind him so he could move on to a better life.

# Chapter 37

Unbridled fury wasn't in the top ten words to describe Cash's anger level when he finally heard Dev's Harley pipes sounding off in the distance. His dangerous gaze snapped toward Joe who looked relieved, yet worried as hell.

"Tell Shanna he's here."

Cash took long, purposeful strides from his apartment toward the back door. Rage, resentment, and pain pumped through his veins. More than even those emotions, he was concerned as hell. Every member of his team had been working in overdrive, trying to find what had happened to Dev. Cash had feared for Dev's life.

He pushed through the back door, the cool early evening air did nothing to appease his heated frustration.

For the first time, Cash wasn't taken by the look of the biker on his bike. He seethed on the inside. Tension tightened the cords and muscles throughout his entire body.

Dev had made a grave mistake by confusing Cash's generosity as a manipulatable cowardice. He was done. His hands went to his hips, his chest pumping up and down with heavy breaths. Dev pulled through the gate and parked his bike within inches of Cash's feet. He didn't budge a single muscle.

The dark sunglasses made it hard to know for sure, but he suspected that fuck-you glare that Dev always wore in his eyes was there and aimed at Cash. He'd show the biker *fuck you*.

At the exact moment when they had exhausted every measure to find Dev, when Cash had decided to push the nuke button on the entire operation, sending the calvary in to locate Dev and blow the case apart, Dev's text messages to Keyes transmitted in real time over Joe's computer screen. Once Joe verified the text messages did in fact come from Dev's phone, texted by Dev himself, overwhelming relief flooded Cash. Dev was safe. That lasted about two minutes flat before rage consumed him.

Cash had crafted an email to his superiors to explain Dev was out of the investigation. He and his children were to be placed in a forced witness protection as far away from Dallas as they could get them.

The email sat waiting for Cash to push send. He hadn't yet, only because his frustration level was so high that he needed to cool down. Level-headed people didn't react based on anger. Once Cash went back upstairs, the draft was as good as sent.

As he started to say that very thing to Dev, then tell him to spend the next few minutes packing his belongings, Dev yanked his perfectly fitted sunglasses off his face. Their gazes connected. The *fuck you* wasn't there.

"I'm sorry," Dev said as he booted the kickstand into place and dismounted the bike. "I know I freaked everyone out and the blame's all on me." The biker was full of remorse as he came straight toward Cash.

Cash threw out his arm, not allowing Dev to pass. They were having this conversation right there, whether Dev liked it or not. Instead of bypassing Cash, Dev walked straight into him, cupping a hand around his neck, drawing Cash forward. It startled him as Dev pressed his lips against Cash's closed mouth. It wasn't a chaste simple kiss, nor a deep passion-filled kiss. It was a sampling of something sweet and possessive that Cash didn't participate in but allowed to happen.

He refused to be led by his dick for another second.

But the crazy organ inside his chest disavowed that declaration.

His cock did too. *Treasonous bastard.*

They double-teamed him. His rational brain against his heart and that hardening appendage that he was about to cut off for life. The steady growing organ behind his fly slowed at the thought of never being satisfied again. *Good.*

"Don't be too mad at me," Dev whispered against his cheek. Cinnamon on Dev's breath caught him by surprise. Maybe the biker had prepared to talk so closely to him. "I was at the jailhouse with Keyes."

His cock completely deflated at the lie Dev tried to use. His resolve built faster than any other time before. Dev was going into witness protection. "No, you weren't. We had people there, watching for you. You can't lie to me like that anymore. I'm done."

Dev chuckled as if Cash's threat level was nothing more than a tremor registering as a one on the Richter scale. He stayed in Cash's personal space. "I promise you, baby, that's where I was. You aren't ever gonna find me unless I wanna be found, and I wanna be found by you. I have a new deal to make. Come upstairs with me. Let's talk about it in private. Just me and you." Dev's eyes slid to Cash's lips where he bent and placed another lighter kiss.

Dev threaded their fingers together as Cash shook his head *no* and refused the handhold. "I'm tired of the games."

"Me too." This time, Dev did walk around Cash, keeping an eye on him to make sure he followed.

Shanna and Joe waited in the inside hallway, each holding up a wall as they hung back. Their frustration at Dev's disappearance was apparent in their glaring gazes. Dev did something remarkable, shocking Cash. He apologized to each of them as he passed by, promising to do better in the future.

The pieces of their lives were shifting again.

Shanna raised her brow at Cash, who shrugged, "Stay here, be ready. He's not going to like the next few minutes. Shoot him if he tries to run." He followed Dev up the stairs, speaking loud enough for Dev to hear.

Every member of the team deserved an explanation. Something more than Cash falling at Dev's feet, begging for whatever crumbs Dev was willing to give him.

Dev didn't stop his forward momentum until he came to his bedroom. Cash stood in the doorway, watching as Dev went for each of the cameras inside the room. There were two. He gathered them then dropped both to the floor and stomped on each one with his heavy work boot. They crushed easily under the weight.

"Goddammit," Cash swore, knowing several thousands of dollars had just been destroyed. He threw his hands in the air. He loved a crazy man who he was going to have to send away. Honestly, he wasn't sure there was a place far enough away to hide Dev, to keep him safe. He was a menace to himself.

"You're too volatile. Witness pro—"

Dev cut him off, talking louder than Cash. "We don't need those cameras anymore. You take care of Keyes for me. Get him out of this and out of the club for that matter. And when this ends, I keep my kids and everything else we talked about before with their birth records, then I'll give my oath to find your problems in the club. I'll be all in for your operation. No more games. I'll handle it."

A flush rose over his skin, an angry heat spread through his body, swallowing him whole. "You've already said you were all in."

"Did I?" Dev answered, tilting his head as if assessing the situation. "That assumption was on you. Truthfully? I never agreed, no matter what I implied. Not fully. I was ridin' the line, tryin' to find a way out."

Cash's stomach turned. If he'd had anything to eat today, he might actually have thrown up. Realization crashed against the frustration, leaving a blessed numbness behind. From this point forward, he refused to hold back a single word.

"I've given you everything you've asked for, and everything I am as a man, and you've been *fucking* with me? Are you serious?"

Dev nodded, coming toward Cash. If it wasn't a coward's move, he'd have stepped back to make sure Dev kept his distance. Instead, he flung out his arm, his hand shoving against Dev's chest. The biker did what he asked and stopped, only slightly crowding him.

"I know you've given me everything. I was there with you until the night you took me down. I wanted to commit that evenin'. That's what I was tryin' to do before it all went to hell. Shit, I'm still there with you right now. I can't shake you from my head. You're always there, helpin' me keep my shit together. I just don't like bein' fucked with. And you fuckin' fucked with me more than anything or anyone else in my life, and that says a lot because people really like to shit on me. In those first few days we were together, I liked the world you pretended to create with me." Dev paused then narrowed his eyes and added, "Honestly, my behavior's as much on you as it is on me."

It took several seconds to decipher what Dev was saying. Cash's mouth opened then closed. He shook his head. "I didn't pretend. I never pretended. I broke all the rules for you. I continue to break the rules for you. I told you…"

Dev's strong palm covered Cash's hand still keeping Dev at bay. He curled his fingers around Cash's hand, using force to bring his hand to Dev's lips. He placed a tender kiss on Cash's palm.

"Today, while I was watchin' Keyes, I saw a version of you and me. I don't know if we can get there. I'm not as docile as Keyes, and I don't think you're as patient as Alec. We have real danger headed our way. But we can try if you still want to. I'm all in. I'm a narc. There's my oath."

The heavy weight of sudden defeat blanketed Cash. A small part of him wanted to throw Dev's words in the garbage where they belonged, but every other fiber in his body had him closing his eyes, letting Dev's explanation matter.

Dev still didn't crowd or talk over him. He only waited. Cash's heart ached, wanting him to accept the simple declaration that truly made sense.

How could he?

He'd welcomed Dev inside his body last night, making love with him until his thighs and legs quivered, barely able to walk from the bed. The entire time, Cash gave his undying devotion. Every second had apparently been a game to Dev.

"Whatever you're thinkin', stop," Dev said and took the step separating them. "Give me a chance to prove what I'm sayin' is the truth."

"Where were you today?" Cash asked, his voice raw and husky. He started to move away, to get distance, but Dev's arm shot out, circling his waist, yanking him forward. Rather than release his hand, Dev threaded their fingers together.

"Third floor of the parkin' garage catty-corner to the Dallas jail. My old man found out about Keyes's dude through a contact at the jailhouse. I volunteered to stake it out, to see what was what then report back to him with a big fat lie. It wasn't even hard for me to lie to my old man. Then when I was there, watchin' everywhere, I began to see you and me in

Keyes and Alec. I saw how it could work between us. I saw a future, one I liked a whole lot. I don't know how to get there, if we can even get there…" Dev took a breath but his gaze never wavered from Cash's. "If any of my brothers find out what I've done, I'll die that very day. But we can try."

Cash closed his fingers around Dev's. His oath meant everything. "No one's going to find out. Only limited people know about your involvement. I'll protect you. But you can't go without me. I can't be your shield if I don't know what you're doing or where you are. I should've been there with you today."

"Understood. At the time, my old self was questionin' shit. I decided I could sneak around better by myself because you're so big and pretty. People see you. I probably won't make that decision again, but if I do, I'll give you the heads-up." Dev kissed Cash's lips. "I sure kiss on you a lot. I haven't ever done that before. So do we have a deal? You got Keyes for me? I don't need the dough. Just Keyes and Abi and Mae."

Cash paused, staring at Dev before he said, "Yeah." Nodding once. "We have a deal if you agree we're a team from this moment forward, no matter what. You move one step and I know."

"Vice versa," Dev easily promised, nodding. "Tell me I haven't ruined any chance of those three words you said to me losin' their meanin'. That wasn't my intention. I just get this tunnel vision sometimes…"

What held Cash's tongue was the rawness of his feelings. He'd broken through his own natural reserves, uttering words of love and forever devotion that shouldn't have been muttered so soon. He'd put himself out there, over and over again. He'd thought Dev had been there with him too then… He released a pent-up sigh as he bent his forehead to Dev's, changing the course of his words.

"…It's all right. I've fucked it up, but I'll be workin' to hear them again. And it seems like I need to add the condition of you in there. I want you with me like we've been. It's nonnegotiable for me." Dev's brow furrowed as if he were contemplating an alternative and didn't like the options.

"You didn't mess anything up. Those feelings are all still here," Cash whispered. A comfortable silence held between them before he said, "I love you. I always have, and I'm afraid

I always will. Tell me the truth, and I'll believe you, for better or worse... are you fully in?"

"All the way in." Dev answered in a hushed breath. The sincerity pushed into every syllable made Cash wonder if maybe Dev was answering all the meanings of his question. Before he could give more thought to that, Dev tilted his chin up to press another kiss to Cash's lips, sealing their deal. Chaos might be barreling down on them but at least, for right this minute, they were in this together.

The Tattoos and Ties story continues in Justice. Coming soon.

Sign up for release day emails at www.kindlealexander.com

# Note from the Author

Send a quick email and let us know what you think of Chaos at kindle@kindlealexander.com.
For more information on future works, sign-up for our new release newsletter from our website: www.kindlealexander.com or come friend us on all the major social networking sites.

# Books By Kindle Alexander

If you enjoyed Chaos then you won't want to miss 's bestselling
novels:
Breakaway
Reservations
It's Complicated
Painted On My Heart
The Current Between Us (with Bonus Material)
Closet Confession
Secret
Texas Pride
Full Disclosure
Double Full
Full Domain
Always
Forever
Havoc
Order

## A Wilder Inc. Series
Secret
Breakaway
Level Up

## A Reservations Night Club Story
Reservations Book 1
It's Complicated Book 2

Made in the USA
Coppell, TX
31 July 2024

35401250R00197